PASSION BURNS

She felt his warm, rough fingers slide from her hair to her throat, over her shoulders, and downward to tease beneath the restricting lace-covered bodice. With what seemed like infinite slowness, he unbuttoned each tiny black pearl stud. When all were free he parted the garment and drew a ragged breath.

"Christ, you're a bittersweet woman, Delilah. So damn beautiful. So bad." His eyes lingered on her milk-white flesh. "I think you need taming. Am I right?"

"Yes," she whispered breathlessly. Her pulse pounded in her ears, drowning out logic and thought. "Yes. . . ."

Delilah's Flame

Delilah's Flame

by
Andrea Parnell

AN ONYX BOOK

NEW AMERICAN LIBRARY

With love to Genia,
my sister, my friend

NAL BOOKS ARE AVAILABLE AT QUANTITY DISCOUNTS WHEN
USED TO PROMOTE PRODUCTS OR SERVICES. FOR INFORMA-
TION PLEASE WRITE TO PREMIUM MARKETING DIVISION, NEW
AMERICAN LIBRARY, 1633 BROADWAY, NEW YORK, NEW YORK
10019.

Copyright © 1988 by Andrea Parnell

 Onyx is a trademark of New American Library.

SIGNET, SIGNET CLASSIC, MENTOR, ONYX, PLUME, MERIDIAN
and NAL BOOKS are published by NAL PENGUIN INC.,
1633 Broadway, New York, New York 10019

First Printing, December, 1988

1 2 3 4 5 6 7 8 9

PRINTED IN THE UNITED STATES OF AMERICA

Prologue

California, 1859

"Dang it, gal! Yer a-cheatin' ol Sulley." Sulley Jones's grizzled black beard swayed with the motion of his shaking head. "Blast it! I never shoulda taught you all o' my tricks." His coal-black eyes drilled an accusing look at his pint-size poker opponent. "If yer pa . . ."

Lilah Damon cut Sulley off with a merry laugh as she scooped a stack of wooden matches, her winnings, from his hand.

"Papa doesn't know. He thinks you're teachin' me solitaire." She carefully added her latest winnings to the growing pile of matches beside her on the bunk.

"Don't you tell him no different," Sulley growled.

Lilah laughed at Sulley's threatening tone. Once or twice a week the old prospector stopped by her father's camp for a hot meal and a little conversation. Usually he spent the evenings playing cards with Lilah, finding his friend Clement Damon's young daughter the most refreshing person in the valley.

"I won't," Lilah said sweetly. "Poker is lots more fun than solitaire."

"Well, then, you better stop yer cheatin' or nobody's gonna set down with you. Why, if we was playin' fer nuggets I'd be busted." Sulley slapped his knee. Grinning, he got up from the second bunk in the Damon tent, gathered up the deck of cards, and slid them into the pocket of his flannel shirt.

"Sulley, you ol' sidewinder." The more time she spent with Sulley, the more Lilah sounded like him. "How can I practice if you take the cards?" Hands on her hips, she stood on the bunk to talk eye to eye with her friend.

"You don't need no more practice. Them little fingers is slippery as a snake's hide already." Sulley rested a callused palm on Lilah's curly hair and planted a quick kiss on her forehead. Not ready to go to bed, Lilah frowned and pleaded for one more game. Sulley shook his head decisively. "Nigh on yer bedtime now," he said, neglecting to mention that his dried-out throat craved a long drink of whiskey from the bottle stashed at his camp. "Tomorrow," he said. "Now, git yerself to bed before yer pa comes back and skins us both."

Lilah bounced down on the bunk. "Papa says I've gotten wild as an Indian out here in Californy."

"That ain't fer from the truth, gal." Sulley scratched beneath his hat. "The way you scat around here whoopin' and hollerin'. I heared you say a word the other day oughta have got yer mouth soaped out fer. Hope yer pa don't ever hear sech talk."

Lilah giggled. Not worried about her papa ever giving her more than a gentle scolding, she yawned and stretched her arms. "Good night, Sulley," she said softly as he trimmed the lamp and eased himself past the tent flaps.

Lilah sighed. Papa would be working late across the compound in the smaller tent he used as an office for the Damon Star Mine. Tomorrow was payday for the thirty Chinese workers he employed to dig out ore. His choice of employees hadn't made him a popular man in California, particularly since he paid his Chinese miners the same wages he paid the few whites who also worked with him. But little Lilah Damon wasn't aware her father had enemies. She only knew she had the best papa in the world and that there was no better place to live and play than in the Damon Star camp in the California hills.

After Sulley left, Lilah brushed her hair, counting the strokes the way Mama had taught her. It was one of her favorite things to do. The brushing always made her think of Mama. She closed her eyes as she pulled the bristles through her hair, almost seeing Marie Damon's soft smile and hearing her musical voice. Three years earlier Lilah's mother had died giving birth to a second daughter. Lilah's little sister stayed the weekdays in town with a nurse Papa had hired.

Lilah wanted her sister in the camp and frequently tried to convince Papa she was old enough to care for Sissy. Papa had pointed out that Lilah herself still had Loo, the half-Chinese girl who lived with her grandfather, attending to her. Undaunted, Lilah kept pestering him to bring Sissy to the camp. Papa hadn't yet agreed to that; he had promised to take her into town tomorrow for a visit.

Smiling and deciding she would take her doll to see Sissy too, Lilah began braiding her shiny tresses. Poker wasn't the only thing old Sulley had taught her. As she worked, she softly hummed the tune of a song he often sang. Sulley claimed hearing his young friend's sweet rendition of "Oh! Susanna" brought tears to his eyes. Lilah liked singing almost as much as she liked playing cards and often entertained Sulley or Papa with a song she had made up herself.

Just as she finished one braid and started on the other, a loud clap like thunder sounded close to the compound. Lilah shrieked and lost her hold on the sections of hair. Another clap sounded and the tent walls shook. Lilah, terrified of storms and the occasional earth tremors that came in the camp, shrieked louder and snatched a blanket over her head.

Her trembling increased with the clamor. She wished Sulley hadn't left so soon. She wished Loo was with her or that Papa had already come to bed. She wished she wasn't alone. Finally she gave a choked cry, grabbed her rag doll, and dashed out of the tent in her night-clothes, dashed blindly into the blackness of a nearly moonless night. All around rose scared screams, those of the Chinese workers also emptying out of tents.

A few coherent voices warned of an attack, and Lilah realized the sound she had heard came from neither storm nor tremor, but instead from the beat of hooves on hard earth. Crying out in terror, she bolted across the grounds with the others. Maybe renegades were riding into camp. Maybe Indians were coming to kill them all. Sulley had warned her that a band of renegades roamed the nearby hills and that a little girl should never go out alone. Papa had said it too, so it must be true.

Outside the camp, swirls of dust soared up like thunderclouds as forty or more stampeding horses bore down on the compound. Like bolts of lightning, hooves flashed and struck the earth. The shrill screams of the frightened animals pierced Lilah's heart. Whimpering for her papa, Lilah clutched her doll to her chest and kept running.

But when the stampeding herd flattened the make-shift fence bordering the compound, she stopped, face ghostly pale. Lilah screamed. Even a child of ten could see the horses would destroy all in their path. Her young mind searched for a reason this devastation had come to her father's camp. Was it her fault? Was it happening because she had once told Papa she wished Sissy had never been born? She had wished it for a while because having the baby made Mama die. But didn't God know she didn't wish it anymore? Didn't God know she loved Sissy more than anyone, anyone except Papa?

Where was Papa? She needed him. At any sign of trouble she wanted her father, and now, feeling the full measure of panic and confusion in the Damon Star camp, she sought him frantically. Around her the shouts of alarm rang louder and stronger. People scrambled in every direction, looking for cover on the flat ground around the creek.

"Papa! Papa!" her voice, too soft and too full of terror to be heard, called desperately. She was glad Sissy wasn't in the camp, so very glad Papa had left her in town. At least Sissy wouldn't be killed because Lilah had wished something bad.

Bewildered by it all, Lilah dropped her doll and followed the horror-ridden few racing along the creek bed, her only thought to find Papa. She tried to spot him among the frightened, running men but saw him nowhere. Hands clenched into tight fists and pressed against her cheeks, Lilah stopped again, thinking she might have a better chance of seeing him if she stood still. Crying, her feet cut by sharp stones, Lilah stood alone on the bank, but only seconds, before being knocked to her knees by someone running past. Lilah quickly clambered to her feet, but now stood almost petrified except for her sobs.

She could see six riders driving the horses that had been corralled above the creek. Lilah wondered why those men had freed the horses and why they drove them through her father's mining camp. Didn't they know people would be hurt?

"Stop! Stop them!" Lilah shouted, and waved her arms wildly at the advancing herd.

"Lilah!" From far away she heard a shout and whirled to see her father racing toward her. Screaming his name, she broke into a run, only to be halted after a few steps by his yell to turn back. Lilah obeyed as she always obeyed her father, but now stood even more perilously close to the path of the oncoming horses.

Clement Damon ran as he had never run. With his precious Marie gone, he had only his two daughters left to him in the world. He would never stop blaming himself that Marie had died. His precious Marie. If he had stayed in the East where she could have had a doctor, she might have survived. But here . . .

He ran harder, his lungs burning and near to bursting with the effort. It was his fault too that Lilah was in danger. Befriending and hiring Chinese workers was dangerous in this valley. Still, he hadn't taken the threats seriously. He wished he had.

God! The horses were almost on her. Why hadn't he listened to Marie and stayed in Pennsylvania? Why had he let himself be lured to the goldfields? God forgive him. He had spent her life to have his adventure. If it cost him his own, he could not let Lilah double the price.

Hearing the horses almost on his heels, he added the last of his wind and strength to his strides. He would have been at her side in another instant, except that the stampeding horses raced faster than Clement Damon.

Lilah, small hands clamped bloodlessly tight, held her breath as her father twisted and spun, dodging one horse and then another. Before he could clear those last few feet, a dozen more crazed horses bore down on him. He leapt away from a big bay, only to land in the path of a roan mare whose foam-flecked shoulder struck him in the back and drove him to the ground.

Years later Lilah would still remember the deadly thunder of horses' hooves crashing into dry earth, crashing over tents and housing sheds, crushing the life from her father's legs. His scream, one of agony, one of unbearable pain, set the memory forever in her mind.

Lilah watched in horrified fascination as the horses trampled her father. She felt every blow on her own small frame, and through silent lips screamed each scream with him, her mouth woolly dry, her jaw slack. Her eyes were frozen on the spot in the dust cloud where her father had been a moment before.

The horses thundered on. She watched them come, knowing she would be trampled like her father and yet unable to move so much as an inch to save herself. Lilah covered her eyes with her small hands and waited for the crush of death. She thought it had taken her when two strong arms gripped her waist and jerked her from her feet with such violence that the air gushed from her lungs.

When her breath returned, she found herself inside the opening of the mine. She could see no one but could feel the press of bodies crowded in beside her, smell the acrid scent of fear in the small enclosure. Her own fear churned wildly in her stomach and threatened to erupt. All around, Chinese voices murmured words she could not understand. From outside, as the sound of the stampede died away, came her father's moans.

Ching, the one who held her, whispered a Chinese prayer. She had heard him say it before, but never with such intensity as now. Hearing the strange chanted words restored life to her numb limbs. Her father wasn't dead. She heard him calling.

"Let me loose, Ching," she cried as she twisted and pulled to wrench herself free. "Papa . . ."

"No, child. You cannot go."

"I will!" Lilah screamed, clawing and kicking at Ching. "I will! Papa needs me!" She gave a push, one of great strength for a small girl. As Ching stumbled and fell back over a barrel, Lilah flung herself away and dashed out.

Clement still lay in the dirt, his legs bloodied and twisted, his face battered and bleeding. Sobbing, Lilah knelt beside her father and with the hem of her torn nightgown wiped the blood and dust from his face. No longer knowing fear or terror for herself, she only glanced up as she heard again the sound of running horses.

"Lilah, go back," her father whispered, seeing the approach of the six riders who had driven the herd. "Go back."

"No, Papa," she cried. "I'll stay with you."

Tears streamed jaggedly down her cheeks. Her small frame quaked with sobs as the riders circled the pair on the ground and reined their horses to a halt.

"Good God! It's Damon!" A lean rider on a pinto horse started to dismount. "I'd better see . . ."

"Stanton," her father whispered.

A second man, heavyset and with a rumbling voice, drew his Colt six-shooter and waved it at the first. "Leave him, Stan. It's no more than he deserves for coddling these damned Chinese."

Lilah looked up slowly. Her blood ran like dry sand in her veins. She shook as if her bones were a dangling stick toy tied at the end of a string. Six faces, obscured by dust and sweat, but with eyes that blazed, loomed out of the darkness. She couldn't bear the sight. Her eyes fell, lingering on the stirrup of the man Stanton. On the leather foot cover, a silver medallion reflected the glow of the torch flame. The image on it, a winged S, scorched into her mind.

Clement Damon tried to rise. Failing, he cried out, then slumped back and remained motionless.

"Papa!" Lilah screamed. "Papa!" Heart pounding like a great stone against the walls of her small chest, Lilah sprang to her feet. She lunged at the nearest rider, the one who still held a gun in his hand. Her tiny fists beat at the man's boot. "You've killed my papa! You've killed my papa!" Lilah's small fingers clutched the boot as she tried futilely to pull the man from his horse. "You'll pay," she screamed with tears flooding her face. "You'll pay!"

"Goddamn Damon brat!" The man kicked out both boot and stirrup, catching Lilah squarely on the forehead, toppling her to the ground beside her father. Blood trickled from the wound on her head.

"Damn, Newell! You didn't have to do that," the man called Stanton said.

Newell spat on the ground and shot another look of warning at Stanton. "Forget the brat, she loves the Chinese as much as her father did. Now, fan out, let's see how many of those yellow bastards are dead."

14 Andrea Parnell

Sobbing, Lilah crawled nearer her father and buried her face against his chest. A long while later she awoke from a faint in the arms of Ching. Flames raged all through the compound. Someone had taken her papa away.

1

California, 1872

Too late. Lines of disappointment creased Tabor Stanton's brow as he entered the Broken Spur Saloon in Crescent City. Delilah's sultry voice, hot and seductive as a torch's glow on a dark night, rang out the words of her last number.

> *Listen to me, stranger, whatever your game,*
> *I've come here to warn you of Delilah's flames.*

Stripes of silver sparkled in her black costume as she spun slowly across the stage. The usually rowdy saloon crowd sat and listened as quietly as a passel of mice waiting for the cat to get past.

Flames. He could almost feel them in the room. He could almost see them in Delilah's fiery red hair. She was the most-talked-about entertainer around. Remarkably so, since no one knew much about her. Last year he'd caught her act when he'd made a trip north, seeing her perform once in Yuba City, once in Chico. He had tried to catch up with her again, but learned her short tour had ended.

Propped against the back wall, Tabor eased a leather pouch and a pack of papers from his shirt pocket. He could have used a drink, but the barkeep had quit pouring until Delilah finished her song.

She's no redheaded angel, don't you fall for her smiles. 'Cause the devil taught Delilah how to use her wiles.

The black plume pinned in the red curls fluttered as Delilah pranced her way to the front of the stage.

Jake, barkeep and manager of the Broken Spur, used the corner of the once-white apron covering his ample belly to wipe large beads of sweat from his brow. He contemplated asking Delilah to stay on a few more days. It sure would be nice if she did. Normally he'd be worried about the lapse in drinking. This one, though, wouldn't hurt his business any. Delilah had a way of building up a powerful thirst in a man. Ten minutes after she left the stage, his customers would pour down the liquor like it was the last day any of them would get a drink.

While Delilah rolled her hips and winked at her audience, Tabor rolled a smoke and struck a match against the rough surface of the wall. A tiny flame flared up in the darkened room. Onstage Delilah momentarily diverted her eyes to the source of that light. Her smile deepened. Not for him personally, he was sure. After all, for Delilah he was just another cowboy in a sea of faces. He had to hand it to her, though. The lady knew how to hold a crowd. He couldn't help wondering why she wasted her talent in mining and cattle towns when she could play any hall in San Francisco.

Nobody knew Delilah's real name, nor any more about her than was told by the handbills advertising her act. Rumor was that she was British and spent only a few months each year performing in the States. He'd heard men speculating she was a baroness or duchess keeping up one of those large British estates gone penniless. He could believe that. Delilah was as fine a woman as he'd ever seen, certainly not the usual dance-hall doxy. Everything about her bespoke class, and that custom-made costume she wore would cost six months of a cowboy's pay.

Tabor's eyes surveyed every curve of Delilah and every detail of the costume. The rows of black satin ruffles on the sleeves made the mass of red hair tumbling over one shoulder look like a cascade of fire. Silver shoes drew his eyes to black stockings and lace garters. Delilah showed more leg in her dance numbers than most men ever saw on their wives.

As she propped her foot on a chair and swung her skirt up over one knee, Tabor exhaled a breath and threw his half-smoked cigarette to the sawdust floor. He crushed the smoldering butt with his boot heel, never taking his eyes off Delilah. Certainly no performer since Lola Montez had taken California with such intensity. Miners and cattle hands rode as much as fifty miles to see Delilah's fire act and hear her sing. Not one ever complained the trip wasn't worthwhile.

Delilah, hands on her hips, bent over the footlights and sang to a man at the table nearest the stage:

She'll tempt you, she'll tease you, she'll raise all your hopes.
Then leave you standing with your arms full of smoke.

She bent lower, tickling the man's nose with a feather-trimmed fan. A unified gasp rose up in the room as the rough crowd waited in hopeful expectation for Delilah's bosom to fall free of the daring neckline of her costume. She shimmied provocatively, heightening the anticipation, then reached into her bodice and drew out a lacy black hanky.

With languid movements, Delilah trailed the scrap of cloth over the curves of her breasts. With absolute silence reigning in the room, she tossed the handkerchief toward a dusty cowpoke, who surged to his feet and caught it. A cheer boomed out from the crowd as the lucky man pressed the perfumed handkerchief to his lips and gave a whoop.

Tabor smiled a knowing smile. That fellow wasn't the lucky one. He knew the way Delilah played her game. In a minute, as part of the finale, she would produce a small silver mirror from her pocket and reflect a beam of light into the room. The man that light settled on would be the one who received an invitation to join Delilah for the evening. Sometimes the invitation led to the privacy of Delilah's hotel room—if the man was lucky. He'd planned on being that man and being lucky. As women went he had a weakness for redheads.

You think that if you hold her it would be paradise,
But if you love Delilah there's a terrible price.
So listen to me, stranger, whatever your name.
You can get burned in Delilah's flames.

The melodic strains of her voice floated through the saloon and gave every man listening the feeling of having a sweet, burning fire licking over his skin.

If she takes a shining to you and takes you to tame,
You'll find you've been burned in Delilah's flames.

On the last line Delilah pirouetted slowly, slipping the small mirror from her pocket as she turned. The light flashed on a portly man dressed in a blue serge suit.

"Hell," Tabor mumbled beneath his breath. She usually went for the fat prosperous types. She had again. Damm it! His disappointment was enough to choke on. If ever he needed to lose himself in a woman, it was tonight. Scowling still, he glanced hastily around. The saloon girls standing back in the shadows looked like wilted roses with Delilah in the room. Several eyed the lean, handsome cowboy hopefully. Tabor gave them no encouragement. His gray eyes went back to Delilah. He'd settle for a soft bed alone.

Delilah smiled, made her bows, blew kisses during a couple of curtain calls as the Indiana girl and a pair of dandies who rounded out the troupe joined her. A short while after she left the stage, one of the male performers delivered a note to the man in the blue suit. Grinning, the fellow fished a few coins out of his pocket and tossed them on the table, then hurriedly left the saloon.

"Pour me one, Jake," Tabor called, having made his way to the bar ahead of the crowd. As he sent a shot of whiskey down his throat, Tabor Stanton told himself there would be another time. He'd have been lousy company anyway. Settling up his father's affairs wouldn't be a pleasant business. Frowning, Tabor flipped Jake two bits for the drink and headed next door to the Holman Hotel.

"Loo, help me with this screen," Delilah, smelling freshly of expensive perfume, said in her soft but aristocratic voice.

Loo, Delilah's half-Chinese companion, a woman ten years her senior, placed a decanter of whiskey and two crystal glasses on a small game table. That done, she helped Delilah adjust the dressing screen so that it concealed the door that opened into the adjoining room.

Meanwhile Delilah spread a white linen tablecloth over a larger table and hurriedly opened a traveling case. From it she took two English bone-china dinner plates, two silver goblets, and place settings of sterling flatware. Last she removed a silver candelabrum and four scented candles wrapped in blue paper. When all was as she wanted it, Delilah stepped back to the dressing table to splash a bit more scent on her throat and in the cleavage between her breasts.

"You'll suffocate the man if you use any more of that," Loo said.

"I wouldn't want to do anything that kind to Hoke Newell. I want the old cuss to writhe and squirm with the agony of having what he wants most snatched away from him." Delilah's tightly clenched hands reddened. The muscles in her face tensed. All trace of the aristocratic British accent deserted her. "I remember my poor papa lyin' in the dust, hurt and bleeding. And Hoke Newell sittin' on his horse glaring and cursing. I remember it all." Her fingers went to a point just inside the hairline on her temple. "I still carry a scar—"

"Hush," Loo said. "You'll spoil your looks if you get any angrier. I lost my grandfather that night. Remember?"

"I know, Loo," Delilah's voice softened and regained the cultured tone. "This is for all of us." She filled her lungs with a deep breath. "Have Seth and Todd got the girl ready?"

"They're ready. Calm yourself. You weren't this nervous before."

"I know. But according to the detective I hired to investigate those six, Newell was the leader. In a way, he's more guilty than any of them." She took another look in the mirror at her pink satin gown trimmed with yard upon yard of frothy white lace. The bodice, fitted with long loose sleeves, dipped as shockingly low as that of the black stage costume. To make her appearance even more tempting, she unfastened the top two of a row of tiny silver buttons. "How's Dinah?"

Loo handed her a pair of pink slippers. "Fussing because she always has to go to bed early."

Delilah stepped into the shoes. "Stay with her. I don't want Newell to see her." She glanced anxiously at the door. "I'm ready."

Loo looked her over. "You're very unsettling in that color."

"I know." Delilah smiled.

Normally pink was forbidden to redheads. Delilah, however, liked the clash of color with her fiery hair and the interesting effect pink displayed on her fair skin. Fortunately she lacked the florid complexion and freckles common to many with her hair color. Her younger sister, Dinah, hadn't been as fortunate and bore a sprinkling of pale freckles from head to foot.

Delilah fought back a twinge of guilt as she thought of Dinah. Maybe she had been wrong getting Dinah involved in this. She hadn't seen any other way, though, and she really couldn't take the time to worry about it now. She wanted to satisfy herself that all the preparations were complete and were flawless.

"You've forgotten the diamonds," Loo said, and went quickly to the dressing table, where she opened Delilah's embossed leather jewel case. Loo lifted out a necklace containing a central tear-shaped diamond centered in a setting of twenty smaller stones. With deft hands Loo fastened the gold chain of the necklace around Delilah's neck. "Now you're ready," she said, smoothing a tier of fire-red curls back in place.

A knock sounded from the door. "And not a minute too soon. Newell's here. I can't wait to have the old coot squirming." Delilah again squeezed her hands into fists. "I keep picturing Papa that night—"

"Hush," Loo said, placing a finger to her mouth. "Watch your temper. Don't lose it before the job is done."

Delilah laughed lightly and pressed Loo's hand. "You're right. Now you'd better go." Quietly she opened the door behind the screen. "And don't forget to turn the light out in there."

Loo smiled. "I know what to do."

Giving her cheeks a pinch and taking a deep full breath, Delilah moved quickly to the door, where another soft knock sounded.

"Come in," she said to the man in the blue suit, at the same time giving a nod to the two tall young men who accompanied him.

They nodded back in understanding. A handsome pair, blond, brown-eyed, with attractive regular features and full, luxuriant mustaches, they made a marked contrast to the older, much shorter Newell.

"Todd, you and Seth stay by the door and see that we're not interrupted," Delilah instructed. Almost soundlessly the pair left. Delilah turned her eyes on Newell and gifted him a look full of promise. "I've ordered supper for us, Mr. Newell." The words rolled out slowly, like honey pouring. "I hope I haven't been presumptuous."

Taking Newell's hand, she drew him toward the settee. No doubt he had been a handsome man a decade or more ago, but now his too-strong jaw had softened to jowls. A decided paunch hung at his middle; his dark hair remained as little more than a circle at ear level. Newell's deep-set eyes, however, still bore a hint of the ruthless vitality of earlier days.

"Not at all, Miss Delilah. Nothing would please me more than having supper with the most beautiful woman in California."

Newell smiled at his good luck. Not many conquests were left for a man who had carved an empire out of this rugged land. Not much challenge at all. Running for governor offered a little excitement. But hell. He was a shoo-in. What popularity couldn't get, money could buy. He'd already put his money where the votes were—in the right pockets. Yes, by God, he would be the next governor. But in the meantime, Delilah would be a mighty fancy pastime.

"You flatter me, Mr. Newell," Delilah said, and followed with a light little laugh. "I hope you won't stop."

"Call me Hoke." Newell settled his large frame onto the velvet-covered settee and leaned his head against the crocheted antimacassar. "And don't you worry, madam, I won't stop until you tell me to."

"Why, Hoke, honey." Her voice smoldered and Hoke Newel felt the heat of it stirring his passions in the hot, quick way of his youth. She went on, "I believe we are beginning what will prove to be a long and delightful evening."

Hoke Newell agreed. It had been too long since he had felt arousal such as this Delilah made him feel. Years had passed too since women had offered him any challenge. He found most of them all too willing to tumble with a man of his means. For him things that came too easy were hardly worth having.

His eyes dropped to the necklace that dangled a diamond pendant on Delilah's porcelain skin. She'd done well for herself. Not a simple woman like most. She had an amazing way of making him feel he was in the presence of a great lady. He was certain morning would find him in Delilah's bed. He was just as certain nothing would be usual or dull about the preliminaries.

When Todd served their supper of roast partridge, venison, boiled potatoes and carrots, and fresh-baked bread, Hoke had already consumed nearly a full bottle of wine. Delilah fussed over her guest, tucking the linen napkin into his collar, adding a second serving of venison to his plate, and keeping his wineglass full whenever he drank it down. For dessert she served him fresh strawberries and insisted on feeding him each plump berry with her fingers.

"Delicious, madam," he said as she offered him the last of the berries. He bit into the red morsel, letting the juice dribble onto his lips and chin. "But not the tastiest delicacy here, I daresay."

"Perhaps not," she answered, dabbing his chin lightly with a napkin. "I'll call Todd to take these dishes away and then we can get on to more stimulating activities."

"About these boys you travel with—is there any . . . ?"

"Todd and Seth?" Delilah smiled seductively. She knew what Newell thought, what anyone might think, having seen the two men who, along with Loo and Dinah, traveled with her. If only he knew how wrong he was, he wouldn't be giving her that hopelessly lecherous smile. "Now, aren't they handsome young men?" she went on. "They're brothers, you know. I must have interviewed a hundred performers before I found the perfect two. Don't you think Seth and Todd add a distinction to my acts?"

Hoke snorted. "I don't think they're part of the attraction at all. When you're onstage, nobody's eyes are on anything else. Don't see why you use them."

Delilah thought she detected a note of jealousy in his voice, and it pleased her. To have Newell feel possessive would make it much easier to do what she intended.

She thanked Todd as he loaded the soiled dishes onto a tray while Seth stood guard at the door. Todd's face betrayed no emotion. He was well-coached. Both were, not only for the acts in which they portrayed Indians or other characters, but also as bodyguards.

Slowly sipping her wine, Delilah thought more about Newell's comment. The acts, to be sure, were not Todd's and Seth's most important function. Delilah needed her privacy to carry out her plans. And on such occasions, she preferred not having even the hotel staff in her room.

Todd and Seth, handsome, muscular, and strong, were handy with guns if necessary. Best of all, both were loyal, and even if they didn't know just what went on in Delilah's rooms after performances, understood it was in their best interest to do as instructed and make sure she was not disturbed. Neither brother actually aspired to gracing the stage, but had been persuaded by Delilah's promise that the pay they received after three seasons of performing would be enough to pay for the ranch they wanted.

For that promise the brothers agreed to do whatever she asked. For her own protection she told them as little as possible. Seth and Todd asked no unnecessary questions of Delilah. Even the brothers didn't know her other identity. After months of travel together, however, the pair regarded Delilah and her female companions with brotherly affection that went beyond the bonds of the working agreement.

The lock clicked shut as Todd closed the door behind him. Delilah turned her gaze fully upon Newell.

"You really must tell me about yourself, Hoke. I particularly want to know what your passions are."

She offered Newell an imported cigar from a wooden box and struck a match.

Hoke laughed and leaned forward for a light. He was right. Nothing usual about Delilah. Briefly he told her how he started in California with little more than a pick and a tin pan and built one of the largest mining and cattle empires in the state.

"Of course some figure I don't have a legitimate claim to my land. Some say I got most of it claim-jumping and running off squatters. Back in those days a man owned what he could hold on to. If somebody stronger came along and took it, a fellow got what he deserved for not being man enough to keep what he had. I keep what's mine."

"A remarkable story," she said when he finished. "But you haven't told me about your passions."

"I believe, madam, I have only one passion left. That is to be governor of California."

Delilah poured two brandies from the crystal decanter. "Surely, Hoke, for a man of your experience and with the ambition it must have taken for your accomplishments, there must be more you want than simply to be called governor."

Newell drank deeply and puffed smoke from the cigar. "You are perceptive, madam. Truly perceptive."

Delilah smiled and insisted he have more brandy. As she turned to pour it, she cautiously opened a tiny snuffbox and sprinkled a white powder in his glass. "I hope you'll tell me what it is you're after as governor." She handed him the brandy, waited until he downed a swallow, then patted his hand and smiled. "I can be very discreet."

"Of course you can," Hoke agreed, slurring his words slightly. "It won't be a secret much longer anyway. There's quiet talk of a new rail line in this territory. I want it run by my ranch. Got a big stake in beef cattle. A rail line would triple my profits."

"And as governor you would have the means of assuring the line goes where you want it."

"As governor I would have the means of assuring everything in California goes where I want it." Newell took hold of Delilah's hands and tried to look her in the eye. He found it difficult to focus. "I'm a man who gets what he wants," he said thickly.

"I'm sure you are," Delilah remarked sweetly, slipping her hands free. Her voice turned chill. "And I haven't a doubt you'll get everything you deserve."

Tabor Stanton heard the door of the room next to his close for the third time. She must be having a parade march through, he thought irritably. What lousy luck he was having today. After missing his chance at spending an evening with Delilah, he had had the misfortune to occupy the room next door. He could just visualize what was going on with that bald bastard she had singled out in the saloon. Through the wall he heard muffled laughter and even detected an occasional word, neither of which painted as clear a picture as his imagination.

Stretching out on the bed, he cursed Delilah and cursed himself for lacking the foresight to bring up a bottle. When laughter rang out anew after a few moments of silence, Tabor angrily arose and headed back to the saloon. Apparently he wasn't going to get any sleep for a long while. That being the case, he needed something more than his thoughts to occupy him for the night.

Hoke rubbed his eyes, embarrassed a little that the lady held her liquor better than he did. He lit a second cigar, hoping a few draws of the pungent tobacco would revive him.

"I believe I'd enjoy it, madam"—Newell paused and cleared his throat—"if you would tell me your passions."

"Unlimited," Delilah responded. "I love song and dance, the applause of the audience, handsome men— but my greatest passion is for cards. I love a game of poker above all else." Her lids dropped slyly over her blue eyes. "You can't imagine the things I have lost." She sighed. "Would you care to play a game?"

Newell nodded. "After that enticement, how could I say no?"

"I expect I should," she said as she opened a fresh deck of playing cards, running the smooth, cool surfaces slowly through her hands. She never broke a new deck without thinking of old Sulley. Over the years she had continued practicing the tricks Sulley taught her, had even added a few of her own. Her lids fluttered flirtatiously. "I'm sure I'm no match for an experienced player." With deliberate awkwardness, her delicate hands shuffled the cards.

An hour later Hoke laid another winning hand on the table. Delilah spread her cards across from them and let her shoulders slump a little. Another losing hand. Hoke Newell looked as pumped up and pleased as a new rooster in the hen yard.

"I tell you, honey," he said as he made a second stack of gold pieces on the table, "I don't feel right winning all this money from a woman. Kind of grates on my honor to take it."

"Now, Hoke, you won it fair and I insist you keep it. It's only the night's receipts, and I don't suppose I'll miss that too much," Delilah said, stretching back in her chair so that the little silver buttons strained on her snug bodice. The diamond around her neck bobbled on the chain and caught the lamplight so that it briefly reflected muted rainbow colors on Hoke's starched shirtfront. After a moment Delilah got up and refilled the brandy glasses. "Here," she said lifting her glass for a toast. "Let's drink one to luck."

"And to ladies," Hoke added.

"Why, thank you, Hoke," Delilah whispered as she eased open the third button on her bodice. "My, I'm getting warm." She fanned her bosom with a card. "I just know you're going to give me a chance to win back my money."

Hoke followed her movements as best he could, his mind filling with thoughts of unfastening the remaining buttons. He took a swallow of brandy and nodded. "Why, madam, I believe you told me you've already lost all the money you have with you."

"But, Hoke, dear," Delilah leaned close and whispered to him, "I have other things of value."

"The diamonds?"

"No." Delilah shook her head slowly and cast her eyes at the double bed across the room. "I will wager a few hours of my personal attention against all the money you've won. Oh, and, say, all you have in your pockets."

Hoke's eyes opened wide. "Why, I'm carrying more than five thousand dollars."

That would just about cover the payroll he'd stolen from her father. Delilah opened a fourth button and leaned forward. A trace of perfume wafted up from the warm flesh uncovered.

"Such high stakes ought to make this an exciting hand. You aren't afraid to play one more, are you, Hoke?"

Newell breathed in the exotic scent. "Afraid? Hoke Newell?" He could hardly hold back his laughter. Delilah must be drunker than he was after all. A bet like that, and she hadn't won a hand all night.

"My deal, I believe." Delilah dealt out the cards

with a new expertise Hoke was too dazed to notice. A wide but false smile covered her hatred for the pompous man across from her. She'd endured just about as much as she could stand of Hoke Newell. Cards fanned out, Hoke discarded two and took the replacements. Delilah did the same. "I believe my luck has changed, Hoke. Look at this."

Hoke dropped his cards to the table. He held a pair of nines and a pair of fives. Florid color rushed into his face when he saw Delilah's hand.

"Straight flush? How the hell did you do that?"

Delilah didn't respond. By her estimate, the powder she'd dropped in his last two brandies should take effect in a few more seconds. She gave a genuine smile. Precisely as expected, Hoke Newell, still stuttering, collapsed on the card table.

Delilah slipped the hidden cards from her sleeves, then pulled the roll of bills from Newell's coat pocket and stuffed it in a silk purse along with the gold coins from the table.

"I cheat," she told the unconscious man.

Grumbling with the effort, Seth and Todd carried Hoke Newell's weighty body through the door hidden behind the dressing screen, depositing him in the bed of the adjoining room.

"Is everything packed, Loo?" Delilah, dressed in sedate gray traveling clothes, paced and watched as the men stripped Newell of his drawers. Seth crammed the drawers into a valise with Newell's blue serge suit, shoes, and hat. The man's gold watch and cufflinks he left on the dressing table.

Loo's soft voice reassured: "Packed and on the way to the coach."

"Is that reporter on the way too?" Locating a newsman who favored Hoke Newell's opposition hadn't been too hard. She simply sent him a tip that a shocking story of importance awaited at the Holman Hotel.

"He'll be here in an hour."

"The girl?"

"Seth's slipping her in the back way in half an hour. She's perfect. Older than you are, but she could pass for child."

"Dinah?" The twinge of guilt made itself known again. Delilah found it harder and harder to justify introducing Dinah to a life of dance halls and saloons. Since the younger girl had blossomed with maturity the past year, she collected her share of catcalls and solicitations from audiences. Too often she looked as if she enjoyed it.

"Dinah's in the coach and asleep," Loo told her. "Stop worrying. Todd has sent word to the other papers too. Everything is going as planned."

"I wish I could be here in the morning to see Newell's face when he wakes up." She felt no guilt at all about ruining Hoke Newell. Her father wasn't the only one who'd suffered because of him. The latest had been a prospector named Reed who after years of scouring the hills for gold found his luck in copper ore instead. His luck had held only until he met Newell. Reed's story had made it possible for her to exact her revenge.

"Too risky," Loo reminded. "He'll be in a rage. And you need to be as far away as the coach can get you."

An hour after dawn Hoke Newell awakened dull-witted, head pounding. He felt the heat of another body beside him in the bed and for a time a slow, satisfied smile spread across his face. Delilah. Somehow he'd wound up in her bed after all. Too damn bad he couldn't remember the details.

Feeling a chilling draft, Newell rolled his bulky body over and lifted up on his elbows. How the hell had that hall door gotten open? Groaning, Newell pushed himself up a little higher. The effect sent a wave of dizziness through his head. How much liquor had he put down last night?

"Door's open," he mumbled. "Better close it. Wouldn't want any . . ." It seemed his head cleared with a flash. Only the glare stayed with him a few seconds afterward. "Jesus!" He bolted up in the bed. "Goddamn flash pan! Who the hell . . . ?"

Hoke Newell's head spun around. His eyes landed on a face he'd never seen before, that of a dark-haired girl who didn't look a day over twelve.

Naked beneath the sheet, she answered with an innocent smile. " 'Mornin', Hoke."

The bewildered Newell's head jerked back toward the door, only to be met by another sudden flash. He knew that voice. Perkins. That reporter from the *Chronicle*. The one who thought Spiers ought to be governor. It came to him at the same moment that he'd been set up. Growling another curse, Newell charged out of the bed, bent on destroying camera and reporter. Finding himself without a scrap of clothing, he thought better of it and hastily grabbed the bedspread to cover himself.

"You're finished, Perkins!" Newell snarled. "Just as soon as I get out of this hotel, you're finished!"

Perkins stood his ground. "No, Newell. You're finished. When my story goes to press with this picture, you won't be able to stay in the territory. Seems some new evidence has come to light about that copper mine you made a claim on last year. Turns out the original owner didn't sell it to you like you said. Reed got himself shot and left for dead. Didn't die, though. Just been scared to come out of hiding—until now.

Made his statement to the marshal yesterday. Reckon they'll be looking you up anytime."

The issue of the *Chronicle* with Hoke Newell's story reached Delilah three days later. The young girl found with him told a tearful story of being dragged into his room. Shortly after giving her account of the incident, the girl disappeared from town.

"You got him," Loo said quietly. "Newell's disgraced, ruined. He hasn't a ghost of a chance of acquittal." She went on solemnly. "Showing him as a molester of young girls has cost him all public sentiment."

Delilah nodded, pleased with the execution of her plan. Arranging the arrest of Newell naked in a hotel room precluded his holing up on his ranch under the protection of his men. Like his old partners, Frank Ackley and William Hoage, convicted of fraud last year, Newell faced a long prison term. She wondered if any of the three realized the part she had played in bringing them to justice.

Her smile fading into seriousness, Delilah reread the account of Newell's arrest, then struck his name from her list. The next name, the fourth one, was Stanton. The detective had not uncovered much information on Stanton, not even a good description. He had apparently been in Mexico a number of years and only returned to California in the past few. Consequently she had no firm plan for Stanton's demise.

According to the report, he was in Yuba City. Tomorrow she would be on the way there too.

2

Goddamn rattling! What did she have, a band playing in there at dawn? Furiously Tabor flung the covers aside, then cursed at the pounding the quick move set off in his head. Hell! Hard drinking had its drawbacks, all right. Groaning, he slid his long, well-muscled legs over the side of the bed and anchored his feet on the floor. He got his pants from the bedpost on the second grab and slipped them on, bent on stepping next door and demanding quiet. Hell, he'd paid for a room and he expected to be able to sleep in it.

What he saw when he opened the door was a flurry of activity one room down. The next room, Delilah's, was empty except for a cleaning woman sweeping the carpet. The songstress, it seemed, wasn't responsible for this disturbance. A man carrying a camera rushed past Tabor and down the stairs. Laughter erupted from the dozen or so men milling around the second doorway, followed by what sounded like bellowing and threats from inside. Another man left in a hurry, accompanying a blanket-clad young girl.

Tabor slammed his door, giving up on peace and quiet. From the floor near the bed he scooped up a rumpled handbill he'd picked up when he bought the bottle. Delilah. Flame of the West. Next performance, Yuba City in three days, his destination too. This time he'd be there early enough. Maybe he'd meet her. The chance of that would be the only pleasant thing to anticipate in Yuba City.

"Why can't I have a solo number?" Delilah's younger sister, a pout marring her otherwise pretty face, tucked a brilliant red curl under her black wig. "And I don't see why I have to wear a wig all the time. It's hot. And you don't wear one."

"Sissy, please," Delilah said, worry clouding her voice.

The pout grew more pronounced. "I've asked you not to call me by that baby name," she said curtly.

"Dinah," Delilah corrected. Her sister didn't seem to be happy with anything lately. Her interest in performing particularly alarmed Delilah; she didn't want her little sister getting too enthusiastic about a segment of their lives that would be brief and temporary. "Can't you be satisfied that another of those men is going to jail? You have to remember we're making this tour for the same reason we made the last one, for revenge against the men who hurt our father."

Dinah looked away, miffed. Delilah bemoaned this one small hitch in her plans. The operation leading to Newell's arrest had run as smoothly as the one last year setting up Ackley and Hoage. But this one gave her much more pleasure. Her fingers slipped unintentionally to the small scar in her hairline, her memory to the night thirteen years ago when she'd gotten that scar. Newell deserved having his life destroyed. No amount of time cleansed him of his crime against her father and those unfortunate Chinese miners.

"I am glad he's going to jail." Dinah relinquished her pout and sighed. She loved her older sister but she was getting tired of being told what to do and even how to think about everything. "I know what he did to Papa," she said. "You know I care just as much about Papa as you do."

Dinah sighed again. She did love her papa, only it was hard for her to get as determined as her sister about avenging him. Papa didn't seem unhappy, not even at the times he was in pain. He didn't even know what his daughters were doing. If avenging him was so important, why did Delilah go to such lengths to keep it secret from their father?

Delilah wouldn't even tell her the names of the six men. Keeping their identities secret was another decision Delilah forced on her. Still, it was fun traveling around and seeing people and places she'd never have had a chance to see otherwise. At least it had been fun last season. This time she'd much rather have stayed home. The corners of Dinah's mouth drooped as her mood swung lower. It probably wouldn't have made any difference if she had stayed home.

"Then try to remember what counts." Delilah saw her sister's attention lapse and her gaze shift to the coach window. "Dinah? Are you listening? The performing isn't important."

"Well"—Dinah's green eyes flashed back to her sister—"if it isn't important, I don't see why it should make any difference if I have a solo number."

"Dinah . . ." Delilah dropped her voice to a soft and indulgent level. "I'm not even sure you ought to be out here with us. You're only sixteen. I don't like drawing attention to you in dance halls."

"Don't talk to me like I'm two." Dinah hated it

when her sister used that maternal, all-knowing voice. "I'll be seventeen in a few months and I'm certainly not a child. I can fit into all your costumes."

"That isn't the point." Delilah wondered if she'd ever been as impossible as Dinah. She had to admit she had been, four years earlier when she had demanded that her father allow Dinah and her to leave Aunt Emily's household and make their home with him. Acknowledging that stubbornness was a family trait, she smiled sweetly at Dinah. "I'm responsible for you. I don't want anything happening that you—"

"Oh, fiddle! I'm old enough to be responsible for myself. You just want everyone looking at the famous Delilah."

"Dinah, that's not true!" One annoying thing about Dinah was that she knew her sister too well and sometimes saw her true feelings even before Delilah knew them herself. This time Dinah was wrong. Delilah hastened to convince her. "I enjoy singing, but I despise being onstage and having those men look at me and reach for me and yell at me. You remember how last month that cowboy in Chico pulled out a knife and cut one of the garters off my leg before Todd and Seth could get to him. I wish we could finish with the other three men on this tour and never have to do this again."

"Humph," Dinah said. "You may wish that, but you don't despise being onstage. You even winked at that cowboy who cut your garter off." Dinah thrust her chin out. "I see the way you smile and strut and come alive when the music starts."

"Dinah, don't be petty. I have to act that way." What was bothering Dinah? Until a few months ago she'd always had a golden disposition. Now nothing suited her. It seemed whatever Delilah's opinion was,

Dinah's was opposite. "I could almost think you're jealous."

"Jealous?" The big green eyes widened. "Jealous. Because my sister is the beautiful Delilah every man dreams about. Because she does a daring fire act and wears breathtaking costumes and is onstage the whole show while I get to be an Indian maiden in one act." Dinah tapped her foot. "And those hot buckskin costumes cover me from head to foot."

"Dinah, what is the matter with you? You've been irritable since before we left home. I know you miss Papa. I do too. But we'll soon be back home and you can forget all this. After Yuba City we'll pay off Todd and Seth and everything will be finished for this year."

"I'm not irritable." Dinah settled back against the leather-covered seat in the coach. What was the use? She could never explain why she was out of sorts. It wasn't Delilah's fault she was older and prettier and more desirable. Nevertheless, always being second was tedious. "At least not just because I miss Papa," she added. "And I still don't see why you get to do everything and I get to sit back and watch."

Delilah breathed another sigh. Her weakness had always been giving in to Dinah. Since their mother died she'd felt responsible for her younger sister. Time hadn't dimmed the feeling. With only one more show to do, she could afford to compromise. Next season, though, they'd have an understanding or Dinah wouldn't come along.

Delilah laced her fingers together, still uneasy with her decision. "All right, Dinah. We have a couple of days before the show. We'll try to work out a number for you to do alone."

"Promise?" Dinah, face beaming, leaned across the coach and kissed her sister on the cheek. "And the costume?"

"One of the costumes you have will do."

Dinah bit back the retort dancing on her tongue. Instead she smiled and nodded. She had a few ideas about the costume.

The black stallion snorted and tossed his head. He didn't like being tied in the sun any more than his master liked the task that awaited him inside the tumbledown shack outside of Yuba City. Tabor Stanton rose from his knees and brushed the dust away from his trousers. *Stanton*. That one word burned into rough wood was all that remained of his father, that and the few belongings in the old shack. He almost regretted having made the trip up to see his father last year, preferring the memories of his boyhood to those of the sick and rarely sober man he'd visited.

His father had been dead a couple of months when word reached him. Tabor Randall Stanton. The man who'd given him his life, his name. He'd been a strong, vital man once, before the bottle got him. Tabor had been a lad of sixteen when his father packed him and his mother off to a ranch owned by his mother's sister and her husband. The older Stanton had promised it wouldn't be long before he joined them. He'd wanted to work a claim a little longer.

His father had never come, not even when Tabor's mother died. Stan had never gone back to his claim either. He'd wandered around from town to town, doing enough work to buy his whiskey. Later he had gone down to Mexico and stayed a long spell. By that time Tabor no longer wanted to see his father. He'd seen too much hurt in his mother's eyes all those years of waiting. Eventually Tabor had left the ranch and gone into the navy.

After resigning his naval commission he'd returned to the ranch and his Aunt Sarah had told him his father was ill. She insisted Tabor go and see him. He'd resisted, but given in when Aunt Sarah said it was what his mother would want. He knew that was true. She'd loved his father until the day she died.

Tabor led the stallion behind the shack and tied him in a shady spot. While the horse pawed impatiently, he filled a bucket from the water barrel.

"Easy, Admiral," he said. "I don't like it here either. Steady, boy. We won't stay long." Placing the wooden bucket within the horse's reach, he gave the animal a pat beneath the mane. What his father had in that shack could hardly have been worth the ride. A man named Cleve Wilkins had written that his father left some things for his son, with instructions not to give them to anyone else. He'd been tempted not to come, but Aunt Sarah, who was as good as his conscience, had sent him off again. Well, here he was, and anxious to be done with it.

"Howdy." The greeting came from a face with so many wrinkles it was hard to tell which one was the mouth. "Name's Wilkins. I buried your pa."

Tabor extended a hand and shook the weathered one offered by Wilkins. "Thanks," he said.

"Ain't no need. Stan weren't much, but he was my friend. Known him since he came up outta Mexico. Me and him did some prospectin' together. This here's my shack," he said, ambling past Tabor and inside. Tabor followed.

The shack looked the same as before, sparsely furnished with a table, two straight-back chairs, a single bunk, and many empty whiskey bottles. "I didn't see you when I was here before," Tabor remarked.

"Naw. I was in the hills. Jest came back here ever' month or so. Last time I found your pa dyin'. He was down by Fetter's Creek. Stan never got strong again after that bout of fever last year. Musta fell and broke his neck. Weren't no time to send fer a doc. Wouldn'ta done no good no way. He only choked out a few words 'fore he died, bubblin' blood out with them. Think he wanted to go anyhow." Wilkins sat in one chair and offered the other to Tabor. With his teeth the prospector pulled the cork from a half-empty bottle. He wiped the neck on his sleeve. "Want a drink?" Tabor declined. Wilkins upended the bottle and guzzled down most of the contents. "Best thing fer cuttin' dust outta a man's whistle. You stayin' the night?"

"No. I'll be going on into town, heading out tomorrow." Tabor pulled the leather tobacco pouch from his shirt pocket and started rolling a cigarette. Seeing Wilkins eye him covetously, he offered the pouch to the old man. "Keep it," he said.

Looking pleased, Wilkins rolled a cigarette for himself and lit it. "Been outta tobaccy awhile," he said. "Don't git into town much. That's what took so long gittin' a letter off. Had to git somebody to write it fer me."

Tabor frowned. It was hard to think the man his mother had talked about with such pride had ended up like Wilkins. Why did a man who had a loving family let go of everything to become an aimless prospector and a drunk? His mother had never stopped hoping her husband would come back to her. Over those years she waited, she let herself believe he was trying to save enough money to make a down payment on the ranch bordering Jeb and Sarah Cooke's property. Even back then Tabor could see his mother held on to an empty dream, one that eventually broke her heart.

Tabor finished his cigarette and, hoping to cut short what was an unpleasant deed, reminded Wilkins of the reason for his trip. "In your letter you said my father left some things."

"Ain't much. But it was real important to Stan. His

dyin words was; 'Give them letters to my son.' Made me promise I wouldn't give 'em to nobody else, then shut his eyes and died. Reckon he had a notion he might go. Musta got everything ready a while back." Still talking, Wilkins rose from his chair, shuffled across the room to the bunk, and dragged it aside. With a knife blade he lifted up a loose floorboard. Underneath rested a rusted tin box. Wilkins lifted the box out. When it was open, he tossed two sealed letters and a tarnished metal disk on the table in front of Tabor. "That there's silver," he drawled. "Needs cleanin' up."

While Tabor examined the envelopes, Wilkins poured whiskey on the blackened metal and used his bandanna to polish it.

Tabor picked up the shined disk and looked at the finely etched symbol. "The flying S," he said. He'd helped his father decide on that symbol for the Stanton brand. There had been a pair of those silver medallions, one on each stirrup of his father's saddle.

"Your pa was hard put for money sometimes—most times. He never would part with that piece. Some nights he'd sit here drinkin' and twirlin' that medallion in his hands. Said it was all he had left of what he started out to be. He didn't have nothin' else to leave you but that. He wanted you to have it."

Tabor closed the medallion in his hand. His throat tightened up, surprising him that he had any emotion left for his father. He'd tossed his hat on the table when he'd come in. Now he retrieved it and fastened the medallion on the band. He cleared his throat and glanced down at the letters Wilkins had given him. One was addressed to him; the other, with a request that he deliver it, was addressed to a name he didn't recognize. Tabor tore open his letter and read it.

Dear Son,

I know there's nothing to make amends for what I did to you and your mother. I reckon you won't ever forgive me, and I won't ask. I made my own place in hell and I'll lie there. I hope you'll take that letter to Clement Damon in San Francisco. He's a man I owed a debt I never could pay. Sometimes a man does things he regrets the rest of his life. I know I took all her dreams but I loved your mother, son. I loved you too.

Your father,
T. R. Stanton

Tabor shrugged and put the note back in the envelope. A few words that had taken less than five minutes to write. That was all his father had left to explain the lost thirteen years. He guessed he'd never know the answers to all the questions he had about his father. Whatever had brought him to ruin was a secret buried in that grave out back. Stan had wandered up to Yuba City only about a year ago. Most of the townspeople didn't even know he was around. Wilkins didn't know much about his past either. He said Stan didn't talk much. That was one of the reasons they got along well.

"Anything else I need to take care of?"

Wilkins didn't seem to hear the question. His weathered face crinkled up and he rambled on with talk about Stan. "Was another fella named Chapman your pa did some prospectin' with down south of here 'fore they had a fallin'-out. He come up to see Stan once. Ain't seen him since before Stan died, though. Reckon he left these parts. Anyhow, Stan said they was square."

Tabor reached into his pocket. "I owe you for the burying."

"Naw," Wilkins insisted. "Stan was my friend. We

was even. I reckon all his business is done now." He scratched his brow beneath the grease-stained hat he'd never taken off. " 'Cept one thing. Stan had claim to that piece of ground he'd been working down south. Never yielded up more'n a few small nuggets in two years. Jest kept him in whiskey and tobaccy." Again Wilkins scratched beneath his hat. "Stan left thinkin' he'd never make a good strike there. Don't know what become of that claim. Reckon it'll show up around here and I'll send it to you."

"You do that, Wilkins." Tabor got to his feet, ready to leave the stale air and dingy interior of Wilkins' shack, more anxious to leave the rush of memories trying to jell in his mind. He shook his head, wanting to break the image of him and his mother and father together years ago, happy, hopeful, seeing the future his father talked about. He remembered life fading out of his mother afterward when the letters stopped and the years passed without word from her husband. He remembered the broken man he'd seen in this shack, a man reeking of whiskey and half out of his head from years of its poison. "Thanks for taking care of . . . my father."

Wilkins finished off the whiskey. "Weren't nothin'," he said.

Wearing a pink lace dress and ostrich feathers in her hat, Delilah sat in the small dining room of the Murray Hotel in Yuba City. The burly marshal, Walsh Peregrine, sat across from her, a teacup lost in a meaty hand more accustomed to a beer mug.

"Yes, ma'am," Peregrine said. "Sure is a pleasure having tea with Miss Delilah."

"It's a pleasure for me, Marshal." Delilah fixed her sparkling eyes on Peregrine and briefly placed a delicate hand over his. A flush sped to Peregrine's face.

"I've heard what a strong and upstanding man you are. I've been real anxious to meet Marshal Peregrine since."

Peregrine straightened his shoulders and smiled. "Well," he drawled, "I reckon I've got a little reputation as a lawman."

"You are too modest, Marshal." Delilah sipped her tea and offered Peregrine another cookie. "Of course, a lady likes that in a man."

"And you are some lady, Miss Delilah. Talk about how purty you are don't tell half the truth."

"Thank you, Marshal. That's a lovely compliment. I'll bet an important man like you hears all the talk around here. I'll bet you know about everything."

· "Sure. I know most everything. Wouldn't be much of a marshal if I didn't."

Delilah fluttered her lashes. "An acquaintance told me she had an old friend here, a fellow named Stanton. She asked me to give him a message. Do you know the man?"

"Stanton." Peregrine rubbed his chin. "Don't think I do. 'Course, he could be one of the prospectors near here. Don't know all their names. Some of them don't remember themselves."

"Maybe so," Delilah said, disappointed. She'd hoped to at least get a line on Stanton while in Yuba City and, if it proved feasible, to stay long enough to deal with him. Now it looked as if this stop was in vain. She wished she'd canceled out and closed the tour early. Already she was having second thoughts about letting Dinah perform alone.

The marshal stiffened in his chair. That busybody Abigail Fisk had just entered the dining room and was asking for a table all by herself. That could only mean she'd spotted him through the windows from the sidewalk and had come in to collect some new gossip. How was he going to explain to his wife why he had time to take tea with an entertainer? He reached for his watch chain and pulled a gold-plated timepiece from a vest pocket and made a show of flipping open the cover.

"I sure hate to leave, Miss Delilah, but I got to be relieving my deputy. If I hear anything about that Stanton fellow, I'll let you know."

"Thank you, Marshal. I appreciate that," she said softly, happy to be rid of him since he had no useful information for her. "It's time for me to leave too. I always try to have a little nap before a performance, but I just couldn't stop in Yuba City without meeting Marshal Walsh Peregrine."

Peregrine blushed again. A detail not missed by Abigail Fisk, he noted. Damned nosy spinster. He tipped his hat and smiled as he passed her table on the way out.

The Nugget Saloon filled early. Word had gotten around that this was Delilah's last performance until next year. Men rode in all afternoon, started drinking early, some occupying themselves with poker playing until the show started. Nobody was happier about the turnout than Fat Jack, the saloon owner.

At ten bucks a head for a seat, he counted money all afternoon.

Dinah, alone in her room, practiced the steps to her solo number. When satisfied, she got out her costume and a pair of scissors and made a few alterations to the buckskin garment. She would have to wear the wig with the braids. A redheaded Indian would be laughed right off the stage. Costume on, wig in place, Dinah looked herself over in the mirror. She didn't look sixteen. Anybody in the audience would think she was eighteen or older, especially if she didn't wear that sack of a dress onstage.

Turning to check the fit of her costume from every angle, Dinah thought about what her sister had said. Delilah had suggested she was jealous. Well, why shouldn't she be? Her older sister had everything, including the face and voice of an angel. She didn't have freckles either. Every man in California desired Delilah. No one even noticed another woman when Delilah was around. Well, only one man did, the only man in the world who made Dinah's heart leap with happiness. Barrett Fenton was the man she loved, the only man she'd ever love. The painful thing about it was, he would soon be Delilah's fiancé.

Dinah sniffed. Delilah got everything first. How could Dinah be expected to be satisfied always being a shadow of her sister? Still sniffing, Dinah went to work with her scissors again. Tonight they'd see which one of them everyone was talking about after the performance.

"Dinah, are you dressed?" Loo called from the hallway.

"Almost." Dinah hastily got out of the buckskin dress and folded it into a bag. She slipped on a wrapper. "Come in," she said, smiling innocently as she opened her door to Loo.

"I've come to take you over to the saloon." Loo helped Dinah out of the wrapper and into a street dress. The only part of the costume Dinah wore was her wig. While Dinah adjusted the fit of it, Loo picked up her bag from the bed. "I'll take this," she said.

"No." Dinah quickly took the bag from Loo. "I'll carry it. You have to get Delilah's things."

Loo smiled. She usually carried both. Having been with both Delilah and Dinah since they were small children, she knew it wasn't like Dinah to volunteer to do anything resembling work. Not that she was normally unpleasant, it was just that Dinah was accustomed to being waited on hand and foot. Delilah indulged her. But maybe growing up was changing the spoiled little girl into a gracious young woman.

"Dinah, hurry." Delilah drew in her breath as Loo tightened the laces on the bodice of a pink-and-silver costume. "We don't want those cowboys getting any wilder because we kept them waiting." Loo pinned the black feathers in Delilah's hair and handed her a new black lace handkerchief to tuck into her bosom. "Ready?" she asked, turning to look at Dinah.

Dinah spun around and smiled. "Not Dinah. Bright Moon, Indian princess," she said, leaning forward for Loo to blacken her brows with charcoal and stain her cheeks with rouge. Green eyes glowing, she blew a kiss at Delilah. "Thanks for letting me have my solo number."

"Just remember not to get too close to the tables," Delilah warned. "I'm sorry I'll miss half your number, making my last costume change."

"I know," Dinah said, her face going expressionless for a moment. "But that's all right."

Five minutes later found them waiting on a set of rickety steps behind the curtains as Fat Jack stepped to the stage and shouted the house quiet.

"Gentlemen," he bellowed. "And the rest of you. Fat Jack and the Nugget Saloon present the brightest flame in the West." Applause, shouts, and whistles shook the room. "Delilah!"

To a thunderous greeting, Delilah hastened onstage, bowing and blowing kisses to the crowd. After a moment the noise died down and the piano player struck the chords for "Beautiful Dreamer," Delilah's first number. She liked starting off with a gentle song and a genteel manner. Looking for all the world like a delicate southern belle, Delilah sang her song, bringing tears to a few crusty faces, ending the number with a curtsy.

One dark and handsome face at a front table remained unmoved by Delilah's first song. It was the closest Tabor Stanton had ever gotten to Delilah. He was amazed to see she owed none of her beauty to powder or paint. If anything, the vivid color on cheeks and lips dimmed her beauty. The skin on her shoulders was milk-white and looked soft as spun silk. He wasn't surprised her eyes were blue or that they were clear and deep as a summer sky.

She moved like a lady. She spoke like a lady as she introduced the other members of her troupe, two tin cowboys and a girl billed as Bright Moon, probably the world's only Indian princess with freckles and green eyes, he imagined.

Delilah narrated softly while the girl and the two men performed a dramatic enactment of an Indian girl who hurled herself off a cliff rather than be captured. The girl was good but the crowd grew restless toward the end, ready for another song by Delilah. She obliged with a high-stepping number and a medley of popular tunes.

Tabor felt heat rising in him as Delilah swirled in front of him and swished her skirts only inches out of his reach. At the point in the show where there was generally an intermission and Delilah changed to the costume for her fire dance, Fat Jack announced a new act. Bright Moon would give her first solo performance, a dance called "The Maiden and the Butterfly."

The Indian girl marched onstage wrapped in a bright-colored blanket, the butterfly with folded wings. Gracefully Bright Moon floated across the stage, alternately folding and unfolding her arms as if she were a butterfly fluttering her wings. Finally she stood with her back to the audience, arms out, the blanket flowing from them. Slowly Bright Moon folded to the floor, like a butterfly alighting, then suddenly sprang to her feet minus the blanket. Her arms were bare, the fringed buckskin dress barely capping her thighs.

Several men lunged toward the stage and had to be shoved back by Fat Jack's men. Even for a saloon the costume was daringly short. Bright Moon, though, was hardly still long enough for eyes to linger on her shapely limbs. She whirled and leapt and spun, a maiden chasing a butterfly, ending her dance with a leap that culminated in an amazing split. Slowly Bright Moon wrapped herself in the blanket—the maiden again became the butterfly.

Shouts rattled the glasses at the bar. The men whooped and yelled things polite ears shouldn't hear. For the first time Bright Moon seemed aware of the ruckus she'd started. Looking a bit pale and confused, she made a quick bow. Before she could exit, one man who'd had more than his share of whiskey actually made it onto the stage and snatched Bright Moon's blanket from her shoulders.

"Got me a squaw," he shouted, seizing Bright Moon's arm before Todd could get at him. The man jerked Bright Moon into his arms, whacked her on the butt, then kissed her sloppily on the mouth. She shrieked in horror. Todd flung an arm around the drunken cowboy's neck and threw him roughly from the stage.

Delilah, returning just as Dinah's number ended, called to Loo before reaching the stage. "Drat!" she said. "I missed the whole thing. I couldn't find the black garters anywhere. Dinah said she put them in my bag. I had to keep the pink ones on." She stopped short, seeing what was taking place onstage. "Oh!" she cried. "Sweet Jesus! Loo! What is she doing? That costume!"

Delilah was one step away from rushing onstage to

rescue Dinah, but Seth beat her to it. Holding Dinah's shoulders, he led the trembling girl down the steps while Todd hauled an angry and disappointed patron out of the saloon.

"Dinah! Dinah! Are you all right?" Dinah sobbed that she was. "Oh, Dinah! How could you do this?" Delilah cried, getting an even more shocking look at Dinah's shortened costume. "You're nearly naked!"

"Don't say anything else. Not now," Dinah whimpered, shivering beneath the blanket Loo put around her. "I want Seth to take me to my room."

"Go with her, Loo. Stay with her," Delilah pleaded.

"I will. Do your number," Loo said coolly, putting her arms around Dinah. "I'll take care of her."

Shaken, Delilah made her way to the stage while Fat Jack introduced the fire dance she'd made famous. She was still dazed when Todd lit the ends of the two batons she used and as Fat Jack gave an order for the lights to be dimmed. She went through her dance without being aware her feet moved to the fast tempo of the piano music. Fortunately the act was so familiar it came automatically. Without a missed move, Delilah twirled the flaming batons, the silver in her costume reflecting the fire.

Unlike Bright Moon's dance, Delilah's brought awe and silence. She moved with such speed, tossing the batons, catching them, spinning around the stage, that nothing seemed visible but the flashing flames. When her pace showed and she tossed the batons to someone in the wings, only a murmur sounded from the crowd. Several seconds passed before the hypnotic spell of the fire dance was broken and the men shouted for Delilah's song.

She'll wrap her arms around you and whisper some things,

You'll think sweet Delilah has made you her king.
She'll hold you, she'll kiss you, she'll drive you insane,
You'll want to get burned in Delilah's flames.

No more genteel lady, Tabor thought. She'd become the naughty, bawdy woman every man in the saloon wanted for at least one night. What was the real woman like? he wondered. The British accent was real, he was sure of that. Where did a woman like Delilah come from? And where did she go when her tour was over? He'd sure like to find out. He hoped he got the chance.

When it's all over and she's left you alone,
You'll find sweet Delilah has all that you own.
So if you choose to love her you've no right to complain,
You've had your warning, stranger, of Delilah's flames.

A heavyset man wearing a star on his chest edged his way through the tables and passed a slip of paper to Delilah's man before the song was over.

You'll want to get burned in Delilah's flames.

Easing a black handkerchief from her bosom, Delilah sang the last words of the chorus and gave the handkerchief a toss. When the owner of the local dry goods store caught it and yelled his sentiments to her, Delilah eased her hand toward her pocket and the handle of the silver mirror. The white metal felt cold as a chunk of ice. She let it go. For once, for the only time ever, she ended her performance without reflecting the mirror's light on a man in the audience. But tonight, worried as she was about Dinah, she knew she couldn't manage the phony smiles and gay banter expected of her. Instead of singling out a man for company, she waved and blew kisses. The crowd roared and she thanked them with bows and more kisses then said a goodnight.

"Damm it!" Tabor Stanton swore softly. More bad luck. No mirror. No chances. Maybe this time he would settle for one of the saloon girls. He headed for the bar with half the other men in the place and found a spot where he could rest his elbows and drink.

Just behind the curtains Delilah read the note from Peregrine, then hurriedly sent Todd to find the marshal.

When he joined her backstage, Delilah placed her hands on his forearm. "You have something to tell me, Marshal?"

Peregrine wagged his head but just stood staring dumbfounded for a few seconds at Delilah in her silver-and-black costume. When she pressed his arm, he remembered what he had to say.

"That fellow Stanton you asked about. That's him at the end of the bar. Tall fellow in the black shirt. Registered at the hotel this afternoon. Been staying with an old prospector at a shack out in the hills. Reckon that's why I didn't know nothing about him."

Delilah's heart lurched like it always did when she saw one of those men. *Stanton*. The only one who had shown a trace of regret that night. Only it hadn't been enough to make him defy his friends and help her father. No. Stanton was no better than the others. He'd ridden away too, and never looked back.

"Thank you, Marshal," she said, forcing her voice to be calm. "I'm sure my friend will appreciate having her message delivered to Mr. Stanton."

"Always at your service, Miss Delilah." Peregrine smiled. He could afford to. Abigail Fisk had made her report to his wife, but Martha had been too interested in hearing all about the famous Delilah to give him a tongue-lashing.

Delilah paused in thought for a moment, glad she'd foregone the mirror stunt and hadn't tied herself up to chat with a stranger all night. Still there was the fact she had devised no plan for Stanton. She knew almost nothing about him. Acting without every detail planned was unlike her. Maybe she felt a little reckless because of what Dinah had done and wanted to speed things along. Maybe she was angry and it seemed to her at that moment that Stanton represented all the bad things that haunted her dreams. She made a hasty if regrettable decision. Threading her way through the room, she approached the bar.

Tabor saw her coming and marveled that the raucous crowd of men turned suddenly gentlemanly as Delilah walked by. Hats were tipped, niceties were uttered, paths were made for Delilah to pass through. Like every other man, he watched her, as elegant a woman as he'd ever seen. She had her mind set on something. He wondered what. When she singled him out at the bar and extended a hand, he was amazed.

"Mr. Stanton," Delilah said in a sugar-coated voice. "I've looked forward to meeting you."

3

"Delilah." The deep voice held strength and confidence and just a hint of self-satisfaction. He raised her hand to his lips, an act that seemed totally unnatural in a California saloon and from a man wearing two Colt revolvers strapped to his sides.

Her heart thumped queerly when his lips touched her skin. Under other circumstances she would have been pleased by his chivalry. Not since she'd been in Europe had a man kissed her hand. Stanton did it with the proper savoir faire. Though she had never felt anything but hatred and disgust for the men on her list, Stanton wasn't at all what she'd expected. Tall, lean, and passably handsome, he was a good twenty years younger than Newell and the others. She placed him at about thirty.

For a moment she was taken aback. At the time of the attack he could only have been about sixteen. Of course he might be a few years older than he looked. In any event, he would have been nearly grown at the time in question. Younger men had taken up guns and turned to killing.

His having been only a boy at the time might explain why tracing him had proved difficult. She had remembered the names Newell and Stanton. Since Hoke Newell later became well-known, he had been easy to find; so had Ackley and Hoage, and even the Penn brothers. Those four had remained friends of Newell's, Stanton was the exception. Apparently he hadn't kept in contact with the others over the years. She was glad; otherwise he might have heard of their troubles and become suspicious.

Smiling, Delilah invited Tabor to a table and asked Fat Jack to send over the bottle of French wine she'd had delivered to the bar. One thing she had never been able to master was drinking the horrible whiskey these places served. While she waited, she gave Tabor, seated beside her, an analytical look. Rugged, he had a trace of arrogance only half-hidden in the gray eyes. That at least didn't surprise her. His hair was black, a bit too long. Did that mean he couldn't afford the price of a haircut? At least he was clean and smelled . . . rather nice.

The barkeep came and poured her wine. She eyed her companion more discreetly now: worn boots, gray cord pants, a black shirt and leather vest. The gunbelt and ivory-handled guns were probably the most expensive items of his attire. He didn't look as if he'd fared as well financially as his former companions. She saw a ray of hope. If Stanton had become just a drifter or cowhand, concocting a quick plan would be easy. She could be done with Tabor Stanton before she left Yuba City.

Her eyes narrowed slightly. "Won't you join me?" she asked, signaling the barkeep to wait a moment.

"No, thank you. I'll stay with whiskey." Reluctantly the barkeep left, his gaze so intent on Delilah he backed into a customer and got splashed with beer.

Tabor's eyes hovered on her too. With the grace and refinement of a duchess she sipped her wine. He could easily believe the talk that she was from down-in-the-pocket British aristocracy. As a naval officer he had spent time in England. Only the years of training genteel British girls received in the social arts could account for her elegant manners.

He couldn't figure Delilah out. That diamond around her throat would keep a good-size estate running a couple of years. That she had so much tied up in the diamonds dispelled the theory she was in need. She was a riddle, all right, a beautiful, tempting one. A grin manifested itself on his lips as he recalled he had always liked a good riddle.

He contemplated her even more inquisitively. That red hair glowed like hot coals against her pale skin. The deep color did battle with the brilliant blue eyes. A woman with looks like that needed nothing more to have what she wanted in life. Again he came to why. Why was Delilah playing a saloon in Yuba City and a dozen towns like it?

Delilah demurely diverted her eyes from Tabor for a moment, then glanced back at him. "It occurs to me, Mr. Stanton, that you may be wondering how I happen to know your name."

She was a fine actress. He could almost swear she had managed a blush. "You are correct, ma'am," he said, even more convinced he would enjoy solving this puzzle.

"I pride myself on being a forthright woman," she said softly. "You caught my eye during the show. I had someone ask questions to satisfy my curiosity. I hope you don't mind."

"Not at all," he replied, feeling a touch of amusement. To his knowledge the only one around who knew his name was the hotel desk clerk. He had told the bespectacled clerk he was in town on business. If Delilah's game was casing for the wealthiest man in the audience, she had made a serious mistake tonight. Tabor grinned. He couldn't see the point in telling her that, though. "Fortunate for me that I got a table up close," he drawled.

"Fortunate for both of us, Mr. Stanton." Her lashes swept down in coquettish fashion. "This is a lonely life for a woman. I don't like spending my evenings alone."

"Ma'am." His grin turned devilish. "I can't imagine you spend many of them alone."

Her smile faded a little. What was the matter with him? Any other man would be fawning all over her by now. Men, she'd found, were incredibly easy to deceive. She supposed it never occurred to them they could be outsmarted by a woman. Tabor Stanton, however, looked as if his smoky eyes hid laughter. Well, she knew how to fix that.

Ever so gently she touched the back of his hand with her fingertips. "Too many, Mr. Stanton," she whispered. "I hope this won't be one of them."

"Oh no, ma'am." His flesh heated under that simple touch even though he knew it had been deliberate. Delilah, he remembered from his Sunday-school days, delighted in finding a man's weaknesses. He was quickly developing a few new ones for this Delilah. "I can't see any reason it should be," he told her.

"Dinah, what in heaven's name made you do such a thing?" Delilah paced around Dinah's bed.

"I didn't know anyone would attack me," Dinah sobbed. "I just wanted them to like me as much as they do you. Hardly anybody misbehaves when you're onstage. And if someone does, the rest of the crowd tosses him out." She stopped to blow her nose. "They all laughed and treated me like a—"

"Don't say it. Don't think about it." Delilah stopped her pacing and sat at Dinah's bedside. "You have to realize those men were half-drunk. They thought you were really an Indian girl. Men don't think they have to be polite to Indian girls."

"I want to go home," Dinah whimpered.

"We will go, precious. In the morning."

"What about the man you found here?"

Delilah looked surprised. She hadn't mentioned finding Stanton. Loo must have. A terrible pain filled her heart. She *had* made a mistake bringing Dinah along. Dinah was too young and too vulnerable to be exposed to this life.

The muscles in her throat tightening, she answered Dinah's question. "Don't worry about him. What I have in mind won't delay us. By tomorrow he'll wish he'd never set foot in Yuba City."

Delilah said good night and, not wanting Dinah to be alone, sent Loo in to stay with her. She had an idea she was sure would work. She was sure, too, that she could handle Stanton easily enough.

"Seth, Todd," she said. "We'll follow the same plan. Serve dinner, then see we're not disturbed. Have the coach ready to leave at dawn."

The men agreed, asked a few questions about the details, then set about doing as she'd asked. Meanwhile Delilah hurriedly arranged the dinner table and lit the candles in her room.

An hour. Tabor watched the pendulum swing inside the clock in the hotel lobby. Why did a woman need an hour to get dressed to be undressed? A courtesan's trick? His look of annoyance eased into a smile. Maybe she knew what she was doing. Waiting wasn't cooling his fever any.

At two minutes until midnight he put on his hat and

mounted the stairs. There wasn't any mistaking Delilah's room. The two dandies from her show stood like sentries on either side of the threshold, now sporting tooled black leather holsters and pearl-handled pistols. Very pretty. He wondered if either of them could shoot.

"Hey!" he called before they had him in view. Two hands zoomed toward leather, respectably fast. So the men were more than decoration. "Easy," Tabor called, remembering he'd left his hardware in his room. He stepped through the alcove and into the hall. "It's me, Stanton. I'm expected."

"Sorry, Mr. Stanton," Seth said, relaxing. "We don't take chances with Miss Delilah."

"No, I don't imagine the hired help does," Tabor mumbled under his breath as Todd tapped the door and announced him.

"Send the gentleman in, Todd," Delilah's silvery voice called.

Tabor found himself in a candlelit room potent with the essence of spicy perfume. There was a table set for two, champagne, a canopy bed lined with rose-colored satin, everything a man might dream about, except Delilah.

"I'll be a minute, Mr. Stanton." The voice drifted out from behind a clothes-laden dressing screen. "I had trouble making up my mind about which gown to wear."

Tabor smiled lazily. "You shouldn't have gone to any trouble. I'm certain to like anything you have on."

"That's sweet of you, Mr. Stanton." Her laughter trilled. "But when I'm dressing for a special occasion, I like to be sure everything is exactly right."

She stepped from behind the screen wearing a dress

of pale pink overlaid with black lace. The effect, at first glance, was that black lace was all she wore. The sight almost took his breath. She was perfection, skin white as a winter moon, sapphire eyes full of secrets, and the hair—he thought it was the hair that beguiled him most. It glowed like a fiery sunset. She'd loosened a strand and let it fall over one shoulder. Did she know how much he wanted his hands in that hair? How much he wanted to bury his face in it?

He knew what she had been saying downstairs. Her life didn't allow time for the pre-mating rituals. She had to sidestep them. Of course she would want what semblance of it could be fitted into a night, the civilized dinner, conversation. He didn't mind. Those things, too, heightened the anticipation. Only the way his body was reacting just to the sight of Delilah, he wasn't sure he could be civilized for long.

"Good evening, Miss Delilah," he said, forcing smoothness into his voice.

Smiling, he removed his hat. As he did, the silver medallion on the band flashed with the light of a candle. Delilah saw it and gasped. Suddenly weak-legged, she caught hold of the table to steady herself. For an instant everything in the room turned black and she was once again a young girl surrounded by riders. The medallion and another like it shone from the stirrups of one of those riders. A man named Stanton. *This man.*

Stanton had started to get off his horse and help. But his noble thought had been quickly crushed. She wondered if he had any regrets. If he even remembered what he had done that night.

"Ma'am? Delilah?" Seeing the color wash out of her face, Tabor started toward her. "Anything wrong?"

"No. N-not really," she stuttered. "I . . . I twisted my ankle. I'm fine now."

"Here. Sit down." Before she could resist, he helped her to a brocade-covered settee and insisted she get off her feet. "Let me have a look."

"Oh no. Really. It doesn't hurt now."

But he was kneeling before her and gently massaging one ankle. Tiny shock waves started through her.

"Not that one," she said, snatching her foot away. It was a useless defense. He immediately set about massaging the other ankle, with exactly the same result.

"Better?" he asked. Black silk stockings. Trim ankles. Curvy calves. Pink satin slippers. The hour's wait would be worthwhile. He'd enjoy peeling off the silk and satin and lace.

"Much better." Wanting to break the physical contact, Delilah got hurriedly to her feet, but immediately found herself swept into Tabor Stanton's arms.

"Good," he said, his lips muffling her objections. The kiss, brief but thorough, stunned her and sent unwarranted pleasure spiraling through her body. For a few seconds afterward Delilah stood speechless.

The first words to come back surprised both her and Stanton. "You low-lyin' side . . ." She stopped short, her eyes incredibly wide. What was she saying? She could ruin everything. Delilah quickly turned her back so he couldn't see the confusion registered on her face. "I'm sorry, Mr. Stanton." It galled her to pretend politeness, but she didn't want him losing interest so soon. She softened her voice. "I'm not accustomed to a man being so forward."

Tabor arched a brow. *Low-lyin' sidewinder?* Something a boom-town woman might say, but from the well-bred Delilah, more of the puzzle. "I owe the apology, ma'am," he drawled. "Guess I misunderstood your invitation."

She kept her back to him, completely missing the disarming grin on his face. His words were right but the tone lacked conviction. The arrogant bastard. He thought she was nothing more than a well-dressed whore. Incensed, she braced herself to remain calm, swearing the mistake would cost him.

Eyes twinkling, and with a new hold on her composure, Delilah looked over her shoulder at Tabor. "Maybe not, Mr. Stanton," she cooed. "A lady needs a little time to make up her mind about a man, a little time to anticipate. Let's see how we both feel later in the evening."

Tabor dropped a hand on her shoulder. The skin was warm and smooth. He turned her around. The lady liked games. Fine. He supposed it affronted her dignity to fall into a man's arms without a few preliminaries. Damn, she was good to look at. A magnificent woman. Full breasts almost spilling out of her dress, a waist he could reach around, eyes that were hard to look away from. The lips had been soft and sweet. Maybe he could wait—awhile.

Heat waves started where his hand rested. She felt a tiny shudder, not of revulsion but of enjoyment. This was inexcusable, to feel anything resembling excitement from this man's touch. She abhorred the thought of it. She couldn't let herself be distracted just because he had a handsome face. That medallion on his hat reminded her he was a man without courage or conviction, a man with a hollow heart.

She breathed in a deep breath. Self-command was imperative. "Some champagne, Mr. Stanton," she said smoothly.

"Call me Tabor, please. Formalities have always been a nuisance. May I?" He offered to open the bottle. When the cork popped and a stream of foam shot into the air, they laughed together. Before much of the champagne was lost, Delilah got the glasses.

"Ummm. This is good." She sipped contentedly. "I adore champagne. Do you, Tabor?"

He nodded. "Mostly bubbles. But it'll do."

When Seth knocked and said he had the supper tray, Delilah was still sipping her first glass, Tabor, at Delilah's prompting, his third.

Halfway through the meal Delilah realized Tabor was staring at her in a peculiar way. Those intense gray eyes made her edgy. A slow flutter of panic started down in her stomach. He couldn't possibly suspect . . . No. It had to be something else. She gathered courage and spoke. "Is something bothering you, Tabor?"

Tabor shook his head. "Not a thing." Without warning he clasped the hand she rested on the table, finding it warm but slightly shaky. "I was just sitting here wondering how you tell a beautiful woman she's beautiful in a way she hasn't heard a hundred times before."

Delilah sighed and relaxed a bit. Her smile was purely theatrical. "You've done just that, Tabor." She wrapped her fingers around his hand and squeezed. "Thank you," she said. Silently she congratulated herself. He wasn't so different after all. He wanted her. A man in that condition was like a rutting deer, blind to everything but his lust. The fact that he had stirred her a little only made her angry. Tabor Stanton would topple like the others. She would enjoy watching him fall.

Seth came in later to take the supper dishes. When the door clicked shut behind him, Delilah turned her charm on Tabor full force.

"It is warm in here isn't it?" She lifted the curls from her neck and fanned herself with a silk Japanese fan. "I wonder if you'd pour me another glass of champagne? It does make me feel cooler." Tabor complied. When he handed her the glass, she looked up at him with wide blue eyes. "Do you play poker, Tabor?"

"I've played a few games." The long months at sea, he'd occupied many hours playing poker and had gained an expertise that kept his fellow officers low on funds most of the time.

"I find a few hands relaxing after dinner," she said innocently. "Would you indulge me?" The long reddish lashes swept her cheeks. "I promise to make it worth your while."

His desire for her intensified. "I like the stakes," he responded.

Delilah dealt the first round in her clumsy, misleading way. A few rounds later she had lost a sizable stack of gold coins.

"Oh!" Delilah showed her hand and then Tabor his. Her lips went into a soft pout. "You are entirely too skilled for me, Tabor. You've won again."

"Looks that way." He grinned. He should be complimenting her on her skills. She was quite a woman. Every word, every gesture, every glance designed to ignite a man's passion. And it did. For the last hour he'd felt that he had a volcano inside him. If she wanted him at a fever pitch when they made love, she would have her wish. With every minute that passed, he was more fascinated with her. She was a better poker player than she let on, too good to lose every hand. That too had to be deliberate. Maybe she thought it swelled a man's pride to win.

"More brandy, Tabor." She stood for a moment and refilled his snifter, brushing her arm against his shoulder as she placed it on the table. "You aren't by any chance a professional gambler, are you?"

"Not at cards," he returned, feeling a jolt as her flesh touched him and the scent of her perfume invaded his nostrils. That was the third glass of brandy she had forced on him. He could swear she was trying to get him drunk. But why? If she opened another button on her bodice, he would gladly do anything she asked. Maybe she wanted to be sure she could stay in control of the situation. His easy grin widened. "I do enjoy the excitement of taking risks. How about you?"

"Oh, I rather like following the tried-and-true. Maybe that's why I so seldom win."

"At cards?"

Annoyed, Delilah almost forgot to smile. She wasn't accustomed to having a man tease her. The problem was, Tabor held his liquor too well. He wasn't the least bit tipsy and now he'd stopped drinking. At least she'd learned enough about him to feel confident her hasty plan would work. He'd been in the navy until recently and evidently never in Mexico. The detective had done a poor job tracing Stanton. He seemed to have no roots. He mentioned no family. As best she could tell, he drifted around living on what was left of his navy pay.

"You haven't touched your brandy," she said as she dealt another hand.

He lifted one eyebrow devilishly. "I don't like drinking alone."

"We'll have to remedy that." Delilah quickly rose to her feet and poured herself another snifter of brandy. She wished she'd added the powder when she poured his. Maybe she could distract him and slip it into his glass at the table. She didn't want to prolong this encounter. She didn't like the way those smoke-gray eyes looked as if they could see right through her. She didn't like the way that grin softened his face and made it look so . . . appealing. She wanted to be done with Tabor Stanton as soon as possible.

Damm! Delilah swore under her breath. The little

silver snuffbox with the powder wasn't in her pocket. She'd been so upset about Dinah, she'd forgotten to get it from Loo. She felt like crying. This might be a long night after all. She had no choice but to get Tabor genuinely drunk.

"Drink up," she said, and took a generous swallow of brandy. "Let's play another hand. My luck might change."

"Or mine might," he quipped.

She lost, again and again. Looking forlorn, Delilah cast her luminous blue eyes on him and said a bit thickly, "Pour me another brandy."

Tabor got unsteadily to his feet. "Brandy's all gone," he reported. "Champagne too."

Delilah watched him bump the chair and breathed a sigh of relief. "Sherry, then, and tell me about the Admiral."

"Which one?"

"The four-legged one. The one you spent your severance pay on."

Tabor grinned. "You ought to see him. Black as midnight, almost seventeen hands at the withers, long powerful legs, good bloodlines, and he's smart, smarter than most of the scalawags I sailed with."

"And you spent all your money to buy this horse, the Admiral?"

Tabor settled back in his chair. Christ! His head was swimming. Was she trying to stroke his passion or put it out? "All I could save from the last five years of navy pay. When a man's had nothing steadier than a rolling deck under him for years, he wants a good horse. The Admiral's the finest piece of horseflesh west of St. Jo."

"Would you sell him?"

His heavy dark brows flew up. "Sell him? Hell, no!

I've got plans for the Admiral." His words slurred, "Ranch. . . . a few good mares."

"A ranch costs money." Tall plans for a man who was little better than a saddle tramp. The Admiral was probably a flea-bitten nag. But the horse was apparently the only thing of worth Tabor Stanton owned. And that wouldn't be for long.

He clinked the coins from his stack of winnings and slid most of them into a vest pocket. "A few more poker games and who knows."

She knew. Delilah fumed beneath her pasted-on smile. He had a high opinion of himself. And this encounter had gone on long enough.

Delilah placed a hand to her temple to steady her head. How much could one man drink? She could handle perhaps one more glass of sherry. Tabor was several ahead of her. She hoped one more would be enough to drop him.

"A toast to luck," she said, sporting a sugary smile. The glasses clinked.

"Always ready to drink to luck," Tabor told her. "Your deal."

He started to pick up his cards, but Delilah stopped him. "Let's change the stakes," she suggested. "Make the game more exciting. Let's wager something we value."

"What would that be?" he asked, mesmerized by what he saw glistening in her sapphire eyes.

"I believe I have something you'd like to possess," she said. Tabor slowly nodded. "Suppose you wager the Admiral and your winnings against"—she paced out her words—"anything you'd like from me."

"Anything?" He felt the jolt of desire in his loins. Damn, she knew how to make a fire hotter. "Do I have to name my pleasure before we play?"

She moistened her lips. "That would make it more interesting. What would you like?"

But if you love Delilah, there's a terrible price . . . Tabor flooded his lungs with oxygen. Christ! It was all in the song. What a game she played. The lady was a spider. She built a man up, then snatched the ground out from under him. If he had the picture right, she'd win the next hand, have his horse, then call those two buffoons to drag him out. She didn't want to make love to him. She wanted to castrate him. Damn her! All his passion turned to raw fury. It was time Delilah met a man she couldn't geld.

He nodded his consent and gave a smile the devil would have envied. "I'm going to remember this game the rest of my life." He paused while he rolled a cigarette and lit it. "What I'd like is to have Delilah as my love slave for one entire week." He exhaled a smoky breath. "Agreed?"

She didn't hesitate, though she would have liked to scratch his eyes out for even thinking such a thing. "Agreed," she said, and winked. "Sounds tantalizing." The dolt! He'd remember this game the rest of his life, all right.

Slowly Tabor and Delilah picked up their cards and looked at the hands dealt. Delilah frowned. Tabor hardly restrained himself from bursting out with laughter. She'd dealt him a pair of kings and a pair of queens. She wanted him to fall hard. Her frown deepened. She was a magnificent actress.

"Cards?" she asked, sounding worried.

Tabor rubbed his eyes and reeled in his chair. She wanted him drunk. Let her think he was. "I'll hold what I have," he mumbled. "Go ahead."

Her former clumsiness with the cards vanished. She handled them with expertise and finesse, discarding and quickly dealing herself two more.

Her expression changed from one of worry to one of joy. "I believe my luck has changed, Tabor," she said sweetly.

The corner of his mouth twitched. She just didn't know how right she was. "I'm sure it has," he replied. "No changing the ante?"

"No changing." Delilah stroked beneath her chin with one slender finger. "Shall we do this together?"

"By all means."

In unison they spread the cards on the table. His eyes went to the full house she'd dealt herself.

"You lost." Her eyes glowed with triumph.

"I'll be damned!" His fist slammed the tabletop. "Never saw anything like that. Well, hell." He nodded complacently. "Fair's fair. I reckon you'll want a written claim for the Admiral. You'll find him down at the livery. Just promise you'll treat him good. He's a fine horse."

"I'll get paper and a pen," she responded, turning her face away from him to conceal her haughty smile. At the dresser she opened a drawer and removed the needed articles. She quickly scrawled out a few words, then laid a paper before him which lacked only his signature. Tabor hastily signed his name to it.

Delilah folded the title and tucked it in her bosom. Being sotted obviously made him more agreeable. She couldn't believe he wouldn't offer more fight if he were sober. If she could get him to take one more drink she was sure he'd pass out. Then she could carry out the remainder of her plan.

"I don't suppose you're going to give me a chance to win the Admiral back?" he mumbled, sliding down in his chair a bit.

"Maybe," she lied. "Let's have another drink while I think it over."

He staggered to his feet. "Don't mind if I do."

Spilling half of it, Tabor attempted pouring sherry in his glass, and failing, forgot the glass, picked up the nearly empty bottle, and stumbled across the room toward the bed. He downed the amber liquid, unsteadily deposited the bottle on the bedside table and himself on the bed. His eyes snapped shut.

Delilah watched. "Tabor?" She got no answer. Imagine that. And so easy. She approached him. "Tabor?"

Delilah stood over the sleeping cowboy a few moments, listening to his heavy breathing. One of his arms hung off the bed, the other sprawled across the opposite side. He looked amazingly different with his eyes closed, boyish, harmless. Had she called him passably handsome? Now she had to admit he was much more. The dark shadow of a beard covered his chin. Not sure why, she ran a finger over the fine bristles and got a surprising ripple of delight.

Angry at herself, Delilah quickly drew her hand away. The gold coins were in his vest pocket. They had been part of the stakes. She reached for them.

A flurry of silk skirts whirled over the bed. Tabor, moving like lightning, trapped Delilah and pinned her beneath him, his arms holding hers above her head on the pillows. Outraged, she spat out a profanity and glared at the diabolical face above her.

"You took your time," he whispered, smiling.

"Let me go, you mangy bastard!"

Holding both her wrists with one hand, Tabor clamped his other one over her mouth. A devilish look flared in his eyes. "Watch that gutter language," he warned. "You'll spoil the illusion of Lady Delilah."

His taunting gave her time to think a little more clearly. She tried a calmer approach and her most ladylike tone. The hard glare in her eyes softened as her voice did. "You are making a mistake, Mr. Stanton. I implore you to let me go."

He gave a scornful laugh. "This is the mistake," Tabor reached inside her bodice and searched for the paper he'd signed. Delilah gasped as his hands probed where they would. He found the paper, snatched it out, and tossed it to the bedside table.

"I won that horse!" Her face was a mask of fury.

His expression was one of amused tolerance. Now his hand roamed to her pocket and snatched out several playing cards.

"You cheated," he said tonelessly. Before she could shriek a denial, he clamped his hand over her mouth again. "Which means the Admiral still belongs to me. So does the gold." His smile struck terror in her eyes. His voice fell low and husky. "And for the next week, Delilah belongs to me too."

She nearly exhausted herself struggling, to no avail. Tabor settled himself over her, his weight pinning her tightly to the bed. His mouth replaced his hand over her lips. Again she fought as something intense and frightening ignited within her. Disgust? No. Desire? Impossible. She refused to admit it. She hated Tabor Stanton.

His free hand tore the puffed silk sleeve from one shoulder and slid to the soft swell of her breast. She gasped her horror at his action and her reaction. A quick rush of heat filled her. She'd never been touched that way, never been forced so close to a man. The shame of it was that half the emotion she felt *was* desire. How could she? How could she have turned wanton? For him?

As his hand moved lower, she fought a new surge of passion but felt herself weakening. Delilah shut her eyes. It was a mistake, heightening the other senses to his nearness. His lips, ravishing hers, still held the taste of sherry. The scent of him, maleness and leather, intoxicated her . . . the sound of his heartbeat and breathing drummed in her ears. His body against her was hard and strong as steel, his mouth unrelenting.

Her body turned renegade, responding to him, wanting to give in to him, softening under his pressure. "Tabor . . ." she moaned as his tongue slid past her lips.

"You won't regret losing this time, Delilah. I promise," came his hoarse whisper.

His words were ill-timed and reminded her who he was. When he released her arms, she struck at his shoulders with her fists. But as his mouth reclaimed hers, the fighting ceased and she clutched at his leather vest instead. Lost, she wrapped her arms around his neck, pulled him closer.

"Delilah," he whispered, kissing her face as he plucked the pins from her flaming hair. Fingers laced in the loosened silk strands, he continued exploring the velvet warmth of her mouth, stopping only when he felt her struggle for breath. Damm, how he wanted her.

His mouth crushed down hard on hers again, savoring the honey taste of her lips. His tongue swept once more into the soft hollows of her mouth.

Delilah's arms locked around him, holding him close when she would have pushed him away. Oh, God help her, she was kissing him back, joying in the feverish press of his lips.

"Nooo," she moaned when he took his mouth away. Her eyes locked instinctively with his.

"Yes," he corrected, his hands never leaving her. Warm rough fingers slid from her hair to her throat, over her shoulders, downward to tease beneath the restricting lace-covered bodice. With what seemed like infinite slowness, he unbuttoned each tiny black pearl stud. When all were free, he parted the garment, moaning as the rose-tipped mounds spilled out.

He drew a ragged breath. "Christ, you're a bitter-sweet woman, Delilah. So damn beautiful. So bad." His palms made slow circles over the tightening peaks. "I think you need taming. Am I right?"

"Yes," she whispered breathlessly. Her pulse pounded in her ears, drowning out logic and thought. "Yes."

Tabor stripped away his vest and shirt and flung them to the floor. His eyes lingered on her milk-white flesh. She had a small dark mole on the left side below her breast. He found it provocative, a tiny secret for his eyes only. Whispering her name, Tabor eased himself down on her, crushing her softness against his hair-glazed chest. Both moaned at the maddening contact. Face buried in her fragrant hair, he slid his mouth lower until he found the velvet flesh and the marble-hard peaks he craved.

Her loins ached in a way she had never known. Delilah, jolted beyond reason by a host of new and shattering emotions, cried out his name as his hand probed recklessly beneath her skirts. Warm fingers drifted maddeningly past silk stockings and satin garters, caressing smooth, soft skin, stopping only when his hand reached that intimate part of her. Soft cries came from her lips as he probed the soft, springy curls there. Her body felt hot and fiery as a new star, waiting, wanting to be unleashed into the heavens. She had completely lost her senses and she didn't care. She didn't care about anything but his touch and the consuming burn of desire.

Tabor rolled away and started to unbuckle his belt. Hell! He'd wanted to go slowly, to savor. But it wasn't going to happen this time. The flames leapt too high. He needed her now.

With his weight gone, Delilah pushed up on her elbows and saw what he was doing. By all of heaven, what was *she* doing letting this man make love to her . . . wanting him to? She must be mad to have let herself go, to have let him . . . Paling as she suddenly realized how perilously close to disaster she was, Delilah edged away.

Tabor had only a second to glance up and see the sherry bottle aimed at his head. He heard more than felt the blow as it impacted with his skull. The next second, he tumbled to the floor.

4

"Honestly, Walsh." Delilah, wearing a deep wine velvet traveling costume and a matching bonnet, wrung the embroidered handkerchief in her hands. "You don't mind if I call you Walsh?" Long tawny lashes rimming her eyes, she glanced up like a frightened child pleading with a trusted elder. "I feel we've become friends."

Walsh Peregrine's heavy cheeks reddened. "Why, no, Miss Delilah. I'd be honored."

Delilah dabbed at an imaginary tear. "I don't think I've ever been more frightened. It was an honest game— Seth and Todd were there." Behind her chair Seth nodded. "I just don't know what came over the man. I told him I thought we ought to stop. He'd lost all his money." She sighed. "He insisted on one more hand and wanted to bet his horse."

"A man can get that way about gamblin'," Peregrine said.

"I never would have agreed to a game with Stanton except that he insisted, and we do have a mutual friend. I never thought . . ." Again she broke off and sobbed in her handkerchief. "When he lost his horse, he went absolutely wild, drew his gun, and threatened me in the most horrible ways. If it hadn't been for Seth . . ." She sniffed, covering her face with her hands but peeking through her fingers to read Peregrine's reaction.

"Now, you just hush, ma'am. Stanton'll be in my jail a mighty long time." Huffing, Peregrine pushed back from his desk, scrubbing chair legs on the floor. Chest expanded, he stood.

Delilah's head dropped. "But, Walsh, how can you hold him? I just couldn't face him in a courtroom." She lifted her frightened eyes to Peregrine again. "Not after what he said, what he threatened."

Peregrine patted Delilah's shoulder. "No need for you to ever set eyes on that no-good wrangler again. You just sign this deposition and leave everything to me. I'm the law and the justice here."

"Oh, Walsh! You're the finest man I ever met!" Eyes amazingly dry, Delilah sprang to her feet and hurried around the marshal's desk. Putting her hands on his cheeks, she pulled his burly head forward and kissed a surprised Peregrine right on the mouth. He almost lost his balance. "Where do I sign?" she asked.

Outside on the dark street she wiped her mouth with the back of her hand. "I swear that buffoon had a whole plug of tobacco in his mouth." With Seth escorting her, she bypassed the main door of the hotel and made her way to the back entrance. She stopped just outside. "Seth," she said briskly. "Take this claim down to the livery. Get Stanton's horse and hightail it out of here. We'll meet you where we planned."

"Yes, ma'am." Seth tipped his hat, took the paper, then, scattering little clouds of dust in the darkness, hurried to the livery.

Delilah slipped inside the hotel and up the back stairs to Dinah's room. Dinah and Loo, dressed for traveling, sat on the settee, Dinah asleep with her head resting on Loo's shoulder. Remorse flooded Delilah's senses. Dinah was such an innocent. Being manhandled by a drunken cowboy was an experience she should never have had.

"How is she, Loo?"

"She will be fine when she wakes up. You'll have to help me get her down the stairs, though. Todd has the coach ready and all the trunks on board." Loo eased herself away from Dinah and stood. "How are you?"

Delilah thought the question over. She was too stirred up to know how she was. Her escapade with Stanton had been unnerving at best.

"I'm fine," she offered. "Just anxious to leave here." Gently she massaged her temples. "And I may never take another drink."

"What happened in there?" Loo's dark almond-shaped eyes probed for the truth. She knew Delilah better than anyone else, and Delilah definitely wasn't fine. She seemed to have the jitters instead of the euphoria that was usual after a successful operation.

"Nothing," Delilah said hastily.

"Nothing?" Loo's look demanded more. "The room was a mess. The men had to put Stanton's clothes on him. Your black lace dress was ripped and—"

"I ripped it getting out of it in a hurry. Nothing happened." She couldn't look at Loo. "Nothing important," she added.

Nothing. Warm color in Delilah's face contradicted her. She had almost allowed that reprobate to make love to her. That was all. She hadn't stopped shaking yet, nor could she get the image of him out of her thoughts. That look on his face when he'd seen the sherry bottle coming. Rage. The threat in his eyes still blazed in her mind. She hadn't lied to Peregrine about that. Tabor Stanton had told her with that last look what was in store for her. Thank God the blow had rendered him unconscious. Her lips closed tightly together. She was also thankful she would never see him again.

Or was she? Another image of Stanton stole into her mind. His face after he kissed her and when he whispered her name. The way his eyes turned a soft gray. The way she felt then. Butterflies fanned velvety wings in her stomach. If only he hadn't been one of the men on her list.

No. She shook her head in dismay. That was unthinkable. She loathed him for touching her, for making her respond, for making her want him. Nervously Delilah swallowed a gulp of air. Stanton *was* done with. What had happened never would have occurred if she hadn't had so much to drink. She refused to think about it more. She refused to think about him.

"Delilah?" Loo took her arm. "Are you sure you're all right? You have not heard me call your name twice."

Delilah hugged Loo. "I'm sorry." A note of weariness sounded in her voice. "I'm just tired." She forced a soft smile. "Come on." Holding Loo's arm, she led the way to the settee to wake Dinah. "It's over. We can go home."

Two hours later, amber and rose bands lined the morning sky. Todd pulled the team of horses to a halt and shouted in the window, "Seth's up ahead."

Within moments Seth galloped up, leading a snorting, high-stepping black stallion. Delilah leaned out the window and watched the approach. The animal's black coat shone in the early light, his mane streamed and shimmered like long satin ribbons. Tail held high, the Admiral tossed his head and whinnied a greeting to the mares in the team. Seth led him up alongside the coach.

"He's some horse, ma'am," Seth told her. "Ain't no wonder that Stanton fellow didn't want to lose him. Look at those shoulders and withers. A horse like that could run all day and never tire out."

"He is a beautiful horse," Delilah declared, reaching out to stroke the Admiral's nose.

"Wouldn't do that, ma'am." Seth quickly pulled the stallion's head out of reach. "He's an ornery cayuse. Don't do nothin' he don't want to. Couldn't even get the saddle on him. I left it at the livery. That all right?"

"Of course." Delilah smiled smugly. Tabor Stanton ought to be awake by now—behind the bars of the Yuba City jail. It might be a while yet before he knew the horse was gone. She'd like to see that arrogant face now. He wouldn't have much use for a saddle if he ever did get out.

But as it had several times in the past few hours, another image of Tabor's face intruded in her mind. With it came a sudden flush of heat beneath her skin. She shuddered. The memory of his touch, his hands, his lips, haunted her. Damn him! She wished she'd thought of a way to get him hanged.

"Where to, ma'am?" Seth asked.

"Sacramento," Delilah said, settling back into the coach. "Where there's a decent hotel. I'll pay you boys off and you can head for that ranch you're so fond of."

"Yes, ma'am." Seth waved to Todd. "Head 'em out to Sacramento."

Delilah managed a few hours of restless sleep during the long journey. Tired, her thoughts disturbingly unsettled, she welcomed the end of the rough ride as the coach drew to a halt just outside of town. During the hour's wait while Todd rode in and rented a buggy, she and Dinah and Loo got out and stretched their legs. When Todd returned, Delilah issued more instructions to the men before climbing into the new conveyance.

"Get three tickets to San Francisco and ship that one trunk on for storage. Todd, you see the coach gets back. Wait at least an hour after we drive into town. Get a freight car for the horse and hire someone to look after him on the trip. I don't want anything happening to that animal."

"We'll take care of it," Todd told her.

"I know you will," she said, finally feeling herself grow calmer. "I can always depend on you boys to do what's needed." She smiled, thinking that if she'd had brothers she would want them to be like Seth and Todd. "Come to my suite when you're finished and we'll settle up."

Loo pushed a folded garment into her hands. Delilah opened it up and slipped on a plain linen cloak and lifted the hood over her hair. As soon as Dinah and Loo donned similar cloaks, Seth started the team. A few minutes later the buggy rolled into Sacramento. With the ladies safely on the sidewalk in front of the Sacramento Hotel, Todd unloaded the valises, then drove away. An hour afterward the empty coach rumbled in, the Admiral and Seth's horse tied behind.

From the registration desk, a wiry little man with spectacles and sparse gray hair addressed the travelers. " 'Afternoon to you, Misses Alden," he said. "You ladies had a long visit with your aunt."

"Yes, we did, Mr. Ridgley," Delilah responded to the clerk without approaching the desk. "And we've had a long ride. We're hot and dusty and very anxious to get to our suite. If you'll just give my maid the key."

"Right here, miss." His words were for Delilah. He barely glanced at Loo as he handed her the key. "Everything's just like you left it. Want me to send up hot water right away?"

"How thoughtful," Delilah said softly. "Yes. In half an hour, Mr. Ridgley. Good day."

Ridgley watched the three women climb the stairs, the two Misses Alden and the Oriental maid. Must be mighty rich, he thought, renting the biggest suite in the hotel permanently and using it only every now and then. Quiet ladies too. Especially the older one. Kept to themselves. No visitors except those two cousins who came by once or twice. When the three passed the first landing, Ridgley slipped through the curtains behind the desk.

"Maggie," the clerk called. "Put some kettles on. The Alden women are back and want water for a bath." He paused and put a hand to his ear. "Maggie? You hear me?"

"I hear you," came back a grating voice. A clanking of metal followed as Maggie filled kettles and slammed them on the stove. The Alden women, a prissy, fancy pair. Good tippers, but not much on conversation. Kind of suspicious, if you asked her. Running in and out of Sacramento. Never a word about where to reach them. Never any mail. Made a person wonder. With four kettles on and heating, Maggie slumped back in her chair beside the broom closet and closed her eyes until the whine of the kettle spouts sounded an alarm.

At Maggie's knock, Delilah eased inside one of the bedrooms. Loo, wearing a plain black dress and starched white apron and cap, answered the door.

"Hello, Maggie," she said. "Come in."

"Reckon I will," Maggie retorted, seeing no reason to be overly polite to a maid. "I've got the hot water."

"In here." Loo directed Maggie to the dressing room, where a brass hip tub sat. While Maggie emptied the kettles and went back for more, Loo hung fresh linen bath sheets on the towel racks and tore the paper wrapping off a cake of imported lavender soap. When Maggie returned, Loo was handing two silk dressing gowns on pegs.

"Everybody wonders where it is you and the Alden ladies go."

"Everybody?" Loo returned. Maggie had a curious streak and Loo would bet her buttons the cleaning woman was the one who had carefully gone through the armoire and dressing-table drawers while they were away. She must have found the locked Saratoga trunks frustrating.

Maggie poured the water slowly. "Well, you have to admit it's peculiar, keepin' a suite you hardly ever use."

"It's merely a convenience," Loo said. "The ladies enjoy a respite in a fine hotel now and then." Loo lowered her voice as if revealing a confidence. "The Alden family is a large one. The misses have eight brothers. Their mother's dead. Sometimes they just have to get away from all those men telling them what to do and who to see. It drives the misses half out of their minds."

Maggie nodded knowingly. "Guess they don't want the menfolk knowin' where they go."

"That's right," Loo answered in the same conspiratorial voice.

"I won't tell," Maggie whispered back, then, raising her harsh voice again, said, "Got two more kettles to get."

With Maggie gone, Loo broke into laughter and Delilah slipped from her listening post behind the door.

"That was a fantastic story! I predict it'll spread over Sacramento by nightfall."

"I'm afraid you're right." Loo smiled. "I had to tell her something. She snoops. I think she's been through the wardrobes."

Delilah sighed. "It doesn't matter. She won't find a thing to make her believe your story isn't true. But as a precaution we'll find another base for next year."

Loo agreed, looking up at Delilah as she poured fragrant bath salts in the steaming water. "Smells divine."

"It looks divine. We'll draw straws and see who gets in first."

"Let Dinah," Loo said softly. "She needs pampering."

"You're right.' Delilah's smile vanished and once again she felt a sinking in her heart. Dinah had hardly opened her mouth since they left Yuba City. She absolutely refused to talk about what happened after her solo act. "Tip Maggie well and have her bring up a couple of extra kettles," Delilah added, having lost the liveliness in her voice. "I'm going to need plenty of hot water to wash this henna out of my hair."

Downstairs Maggie called Ridgley to the back where she stood pumping water. "The Alden women got eight brothers and no mother. They came in here just to get some privacy from a house full of men."

"That right?" Ridgley said, his ears perking up as he stepped closer. "Learn anything else?"

"Nope," Maggie said, throwing more wood in the stove. "Eight brothers telling them what to do. Kind of makes you feel sympathetic." She touched a patch on her apron. "If it wasn't for all that money."

*   *   *

"Christ!" Tabor's hand went to the aching part of his head, expecting to find it crusty with blood. It wasn't, but just the lightest pressure on the goose egg swollen beneath his hair made him wince. He blinked his eyes several times, failing to convince them to focus clearly. Where the devil was he? His last memory wasn't of a lumpy mattress or a cracked ceiling or bars. Bars?

Moaning, he struggled to a sitting position. A cell? He was in a cell? No, that wasn't right. Had to be a dream. He clenched his eyes tight and flicked them open again, only to be greeted by the same view, rows of iron bars. He rubbed his eyes, hoping to clear the fog a little. Where was that rose-patterned wallpaper and that soft feather bed and that pretty face he'd been seeing until the moment he woke up?

"Been out awhile," came Walsh Peregrine's gravelly voice. "Reckon that fancy cowboy packed a fancy punch." A robust laugh followed.

Tabor's vision cleared quickly as a man with a face like an old bulldog's strode up to the cell, a wide grin showing his tobacco-stained teeth. A dented but shiny star hung on his chest.

"What the hell? Marshal?"

"Yep."

Tabor made a mistake and stood up. The action made his head feel as if it were taking punishment all over again. He stayed on his feet only a few seconds before he slumped back to the bunk. Half pain, half the aftermath of all the liquor Delilah had poured down him, he decided. *Delilah.* Only vague memories bobbled in his mind, but Delilah had to be the answer to this.

"Marshal." Tabor spoke slowly. "Why am I locked up?"

" 'Cause you were lucky enough not to get killed,

mister." Peregrine hooked his thumbs in the arm openings of his vest. "I thought about puttin' a plug in you myself."

"I must have been rotten drunk," Tabor said, holding his head steady with his hands.

"Don't go layin' what you did off on drink. A man don't treat a woman like that in Yuba City, drunk or sober."

A cloud of uneasiness darkened Tabor's face. "Just what is it I'm supposed to have done?"

"You ain't supposed to have done nothin', cowboy," Peregrine barked. "I got a signed deposition on my desk says you *did* draw a gun on a lady and threaten to kill her. Maybe would have if her hired man hadn't got you." His eyes bulged as his anger mounted. "We don't take to a man mistreatin' a lady, or to a man welshin' on a bet."

"Delilah," Tabor mumbled as a line of her song echoed mockingly in his mind? *If you love Delilah there's a terrible price* . . . He was finding out what that price was.

"I see you ain't denyin' it," Peregrine growled.

"I sure as hell am denying it." Tabor stood and grabbed the bars, too mad now to feel the pain. "The lady whacked me with a sherry bottle while I was in a vulnerable state. She also cheats at poker."

Peregrine grabbed Tabor by the shirtfront and jolted him against the bars. "Watch your filthy mouth, Stanton. Miss Delilah ain't the kind of lady to compromise herself with the likes of you."

"Lady, my eyetooth."

Peregrine shoved. Tabor hit the wood-framed bunk like a cannonball. "Now, don't go makin' me madder, Stanton." Peregrine's eyes threatened to pop out of his head. "Wouldn't take much for me to make you a permanent resident of the Yuba City jail."

Tabor groaned and heaved himself to his feet. He wisely avoided approaching the bars again. "Does that mean you're not holding me long?"

"It means I ain't holdin' you permanently," Peregrine responded. "Six or eight months ought to be enough to make a better man out of you." He started to leave.

"Wait a minute, Marshal," Tabor called, for the first time realizing the severity of his situation. It wasn't going to be easy to reason with the marshal, not after that redheaded witch Delilah had worked a spell on him. He'd have to think of something. Meanwhile Curtis down at the livery would be expecting him to come for the Admiral. "I need to send word to the livery about my horse," he said.

Peregrine stopped at the door, turned, and grinned. "You ain't got no horse. Miss Delilah took *her* horse with her."

"Good-bye, Misses Alden." Ridgley edged out from behind the desk to offer his farewell. "Hope to see you again soon."

"Perhaps that will be the case, Mr. Ridgley. My sister and I always enjoy our stays here." Delilah gave Ridgley one of those smiles that made a man forget almost everything else on his mind. Wearing a dark blue bonnet and a traveling dress of the same shade, she had her hair concealed by a brown wig. Still smiling, she dropped several fat envelopes in Ridgley's hand, one for each member of the hotel staff who had served the suite. She considered the money a good buffer for questions, should anyone come along asking them. Ridgley quickly pocketed his envelope.

Dinah, outfitted in green and also wearing a brown wig, told Ridgley good-bye as well. Loo, in her

black maid's uniform, merely nodded as she passed
him by.

A short walk took the trio down the street to the
train station. Seth and Todd had ridden out of Sacramento the night before, shortly after collecting their
pay.

Dinah remained uncharacteristically quiet. Delilah
was worried about her, but until they were settled in
the Pullman car and the noise of the engine building
speed leveled off, refrained from attempting to persuade her sister to talk.

When the train was under way she looked under-
standingly at her sister. "Dinah," Delilah said softly,
looping an arm around the younger girl's shoulder, "I
know this tour has been hard on you. I'm especially
glad for your sake it's over."

"For my sake?" Dinah's morose mood quickly
changed to anger. She shrugged Delilah's arm away.
"All this is for your sake, isn't it? You've had your
revenge on two more men. Now that it's over for a
year, you can worry about little Dinah."

"Dinah!" Bewildered, Delilah stared at her sister.
"How can you say that? I'm not doing this for me. I'm
doing it because these men deserve to pay for what
they did to our papa. And to others. It isn't right they
should go unpunished when they made so many suffer.
You can't believe I like—"

Suddenly repentant, Dinah threw her arms around
Delilah's neck and clung to her. "I'm sorry," she
cried. "That was awful of me. I didn't mean it."

Delilah stroked Dinah's soft cheek and brushed a
tear from her face. "I know. And you have every right
to be upset. I've been thinking that perhaps next year
you should stay home. Loo and I—"

Dinah straightened up and adjusted her bonnet.

"We'll decide on that next year." She deftly changed the subject. "How long to San Francisco?"

"Not so long," Delilah told her, and for the first time in days felt a genuine sense of relief. Tomorrow the madness would be completely over. The brown wigs could be discarded. Delilah and Bright Moon and the Alden sisters would vanish from California. She and Dinah could step back where they really belonged and resume living the life they loved.

"Lilah! Dinah!" Clement Damon rolled his wheelchair into the crowd on the platform of the train station. Following closely behind him came a black-clad Chinese man. "I'm here."

"Papa!" Lilah and Dinah said in unison as their eyes turned in the direction of the familiar voice. They spotted their father and hurried toward him. His joyful smile gave no hint that Clement Damon was a man often racked by pain, nor did it indicate any bitterness at being confined to an invalid's chair.

Determined to always see the bright side of life, Clement considered that if he had not become an invalid he might still be in the hills with a pick and a pan waiting to strike it rich. Not many of his acquaintances who had stayed with prospecting had ever found that mother lode. Unable to continue that sort of rugged life, Clement had sold out the Damon Star Mine and set himself up as a banker and storekeeper.

He'd come a long way from hiding bags of dust in holes dug in a dirt floor. Today the Damon Bank was among the largest in San Francisco. His dry-goods store, started out in a mule-skinner's wagon, was the biggest in town. The lumber company up in the Sierra Nevada and the other half-dozen businesses he owned had made him a wealthy man. And that wasn't counting his greatest assets, Lilah and Dinah.

"How are my girls?" Clement asked, extending hands to both daughters. "It seems you've been gone forever."

"To me too, Papa," Dinah said as she knelt beside her father's chair and dispensed kisses and hugs. "It's wonderful to be back."

Lilah Damon offered her share of hugs and kisses from the other side. Finally Clement waved them back, insisting he was being smothered.

"It's your fault, Papa," Lilah told him. "We didn't expect to see you at the station." Her brow furrowed. "Are you sure you feel like being here?" She took a step back and made a careful study of her father's appearance, then smiled. "Actually, you look splendid. How are you feeling?"

"I feel fine." His elder daughter had a tendency to dote on him if she thought he was the least bit under the weather. Thankfully today he did feel splendid. "I may decide to roll myself home," he added.

Dinah laughed too, dislodging her green straw bonnet. "Oh, Papa, you are outrageous. I think you would, if someone dared you."

"It won't be today," he said, joining her laughter as he took her hand again. "I want to ride with my daughters and hear all about the trip to St. Louis."

Dinah's smile faltered for a few seconds and she cast a look of uncertainty at her sister. Lilah, however, returned a look of encouragement which quickly restored Dinah's confidence.

"What do you think, Dinah?" Lilah said, blue eyes twinkling mischievously. "Shall we make him listen to every detail, even down to the shopping excursions?"

Clement winced. His daughters' weaknesses for shopping constantly amazed him. He was convinced such a propensity for bonnets, slippers, gloves, and gowns had been deliberately instilled in them during the years they had spent in London with their mother's sister, Emily Dearborn. He had given up accompanying them on such expeditions long ago, finding even the mention of such an ordeal tiresome. Now he simply gave each daughter a generous allowance and a free hand to do what she would with it.

"Later," he said, hoping to postpone that accounting indefinitely. He glanced around the platform. "Where is Loo?"

"She wanted to be certain all the trunks arrived," Lilah answered, also looking around. "She'll be along. Where has Ching gotten to?"

Clement twisted around in his chair. "He's right behind me. Or he was." He shook his head. "He's somewhere near. You know Ching. He never lets me out of his sight."

At that moment both Ching and Loo appeared, Loo from the direction of the train, Ching as if by magic. While Loo gave Clement a warm greeting and a kiss on the cheek, Lilah and Dinah hugged a resistant Ching.

"You are making a spectacle," the Chinese man said, patiently enduring their attentions but never changing his stoic expression. Only a pair of twinkling black eyes revealed how glad he was to see the girls.

"That's all right. We don't mind a spectacle," Lilah teased.

Nodding to the women to follow, Ching rolled Clement's chair through the station, and when outside, with assistance from the driver, helped him into the carriage. Dinah climbed in beside her father, while Lilah and Loo sat across from them.

"Well, Loo," Clement said, looking fondly at his daughter's companion. "Did you enjoy St. Louis as much this time as you did on the last visit?"

Loo gave an implacable smile. "I've had a very interesting trip."

"You did get our letters, didn't you, Papa?" Lilah queried innocently.

"Oh, yes," Clement acknowledged, his expression carefully blank. "Two from you. Two from Dinah. Very vague, very hastily written. Makes me wonder why I paid all that money for schooling." He drummed his fingers on his knee, but neither daughter offered any explanation. "I don't suppose either of you met any marriageable young men."

"Papa!" Lilah blurted out, her cheeks warming. "Dinah's only sixteen and I'm—"

"And you're old enough to be thinking about providing me with grandchildren." He sighed. "I suppose I'll have to put my money on Barrett. He's the only man you'll give the time of day to," he said to Lilah.

Barrett Fenton worked as her father's assistant and for the past three years had gradually assumed more and more responsibility at the bank and in the other Damon businesses. It had been more or less understood for the last year that Lilah and Barrett would marry. The only hindrance was Lilah herself, who kept postponing the engagement. Barrett, a mild-tempered man, didn't press her on the matter. Lilah had no real objection to marrying Barrett, understanding he was the perfect choice to eventually take over her father's businesses. She simply wasn't yet ready to start explaining her actions to a fiancé.

Dinah, her smile leaving at the mention of Barrett's name, hurriedly glanced out the window as Lilah responded to her father's pointed hints.

"I don't see why you have to be in such a hurry," Lilah answered. "Barrett and I aren't."

"I hope you'll consider getting in one," Clement said, smiling. "I'm not a young man anymore. By the way, I've invited Barrett to dinner. Maybe he'll propose."

"Oh, Papa!" Dinah wailed, and turned an anguished face on her father. "Did you have to invite him our first night back? Couldn't we have had this night alone?"

Surprised by Dinah's outburst and wondering how he had managed to do anything so wrong, Clement clasped her hand. "I'm sorry, princess. I didn't think you'd mind. You've always liked Barrett."

"It's not that I don't like him," Dinah said, her cheeks suffused with color. "It's just I'd rather not see anyone tonight. I wish you hadn't asked him," she added, withdrawing her hand and crossing her arms over her chest.

Clement gave Lilah a puzzled look. Lilah, though, not as new to Dinah's moodiness, understood it no better than her father. She merely lifted her brows in response. She couldn't imagine why Dinah should object to Barrett's visit either.

The carriage rolled up a tree-lined lane to Damon House, one of the largest and finest mansions in San Francisco. Built only a few years before, the house sat atop a hill looking down on the city. A mass of gables and dormers above rose-colored brick walls, Damon House contained twenty-five rooms and was supported by numerous outbuildings, including a stable built of the same brick. White trim and railings edged the sweeping porches and high balconies of upper-story bedroom windows.

Clement had designed the house himself. Inside it he could move around with a minimum of help. The entrance had been built only one step above ground level. Instead of a step up, however, a low brick ramp to accommodate Clement's chair led to the door.

The driver halted the team of matched bays in front of the mansion. Almost immediately two Chinese men ran to meet them, helped the ladies out of the carriage, then assisted Ching in getting Clement and his chair on the ground.

For Lilah, Damon House was a welcome sight. Of all places, it was where she most preferred to be.

She whirled around. It was good to be home.

5

"I have a surprise for you, Papa." Lilah, dressed in a pale blue watered-silk gown with handmade lace cuffs and collar, caught her father's eye.

"What's that?" For a better view of his elder daughter, Clement looked around a gleaming silver epergne centerpiece laden with fruit. "Ching," he said from his chair at the head of the table, "have someone take that confounded thing off so I can see."

Ching muttered a few words in Chinese and a servant appeared to do as he'd asked, removing the epergne and opening the view from one end of the long dining table to the other.

"I said I have a surprise for you," Lilah repeated. "But you will have to wait until morning to see it."

Clement laughed. "If it's a bill for all your purchases, I might not be able to face it in daylight."

"Papa. What a dreadful thing to say in front of Barrett," Lilah responded. "He'll think I'm a spendthrift."

Clement raised a finger to his lips. "I must be careful. I wouldn't want Barrett to learn that so soon."

A blond-haired man sitting at the center of the table directly across from Dinah raised his head. "Did I hear my name spoken? I was talking to Dinah and didn't understand—"

"Pay no attention to Papa, Barrett," Lilah interrupted, laughing lightly. Her father's good spirits heightened her own. "Papa's trying to provoke me, but I refuse to let him."

Dinah, whose mood had undergone another remarkable change, lifted a beaming face to the others. Any annoyance she might have felt about Barrett's presence seemed to have dissipated. Looking older than her years in a moiré silk gown of lemon yellow, she wore her hair pinned high on her head with a pair of tortoiseshell combs. Dangling emerald earrings brought out the light in her deep green eyes; her smile had been constant.

"She's a rare woman, Barrett. Not a trace of a temper," Clement said. "Nothing ever gets her ruffled. You'll appreciate that in years to come, I'm sure."

Barrett smiled at his future father-in-law. "Yes, sir," he agreed. "There's never a surprise from Lilah."

Lilah's and Dinah's eyes caught knowingly for a moment, but neither face registered what they thought. Barrett and her father made her sound like a docile old horse, which was about as far from the truth as it was possible to be. But since neither man was slated to know the other side of her nature, Lilah smiled serenely and didn't refute the assessment. Clement Damon had no idea how many times in the last four years she had nearly bitten her tongue off rather than say something which might upset him. His infirmity was burden enough for a man to bear. Lilah always tried to spare him any other.

"I suggest we retire to the library for our coffee," Clement said. "We can all be more comfortable there."

Ching immediately rolled out Clement's chair and led the way to the library. Barrett followed, Lilah on one arm, Dinah on the other. Like all the rooms Clement used, the library was on the main floor. Paneled in dark oak and furnished with a large desk and leather-upholstered chairs, the library also served as Clement's study. In addition to an excellent selection of books, the room contained Clement's business papers, those that were not kept in the bank's vault.

Clement also had his collection of ivory and jade figurines from the Orient displayed in the library. Elsewhere in the house he kept an extensive collection of Indian pottery recovered from old burial grounds, some pieces undoubtedly hundreds of years old.

With Ching's assistance Clement moved from his wheelchair to one of the leather chairs near the fireplace. A warm feeling filled him as his eyes went to Lilah and Dinah. He hadn't realized just how empty Damon House had been the three months his daughters had been away on their excursion to St. Louis. He never forgot how much they meant to him. What he had told Barrett was true: a man couldn't ask for two more even-tempered young ladies. Admittedly, Dinah was a bit sulky at times, but no more than any other young girl trying to grow up.

If he had a complaint about either of them, it was that they were too temperate. Their mother had been a fiery woman whose red hair was a warning to tread lightly around her. Neither Lilah nor Dinah had inherited Marie's volatile nature. As a child Lilah had promised to be a firebrand like her mother, but the ten years she had spent under Emily Dearborn's care had converted her into a mild and perfectly mannered lady. He couldn't recall ever hearing her raise her voice during the years she had been back in California.

That had been a pleasant surprise. He had expected the girls to have their seasons in London, marry, and remain there. But Lilah had refused all offers of marriage and insisted on returning to her father in California. Seeing she was determined, he'd had Damon House built. And he had no regrets, unless it was that he hadn't brought them home sooner.

Barrett removed a newspaper from the arm of his chair. The paper was open to an article about a woman singer who had created a sensation in mining and cattle towns. He laid the paper on the table separating his chair from Lilah's.

"Did you hear about her in St. Louis?" he asked, observing Lilah's awestruck look as she read the prominent caption.

"Who?" Lilah mumbled, passing a warning look to Dinah.

"Delilah, Flame of the West. She's all the talk. A stunning woman, if her picture does her justice."

"There's a picture?" Lilah paled.

"Only a drawing." Barrett, who prided himself on staying abreast of all the news, flipped the folded paper over. He pointed to the drawing of Delilah in her silver-and-black costume. "Apparently this Delilah refuses to be photographed or interviewed. It's darned clever of her," he added. "Keeps her in a cloud of mystery." He held the paper for Lilah. "There's talk she'll perform in San Francisco."

"Really?" Lilah remarked as she studied the drawing and decided it was a poor likeness. The color came back to her cheeks. "Perhaps you would take me to see her."

"Certainly not," Barrett said quickly. "This Delilah doesn't give the kind of performance a lady should see."

"Does it say anything about the others in her troupe?" Dinah asked, bounding out of her chair.

Barrett reluctantly handed Dinah the paper. "Not much. There's mention of an Indian girl and a pair of cowboys who do rope tricks," he said. "Apparently no one notices much in the show except Delilah."

"Bring me that paper, Dinah."

Dinah, her lower lip protruding slightly, did as her father asked.

"Oh, Papa." Lilah's cheeks grew pale again. "Surely you aren't interested in reading about Delilah."

Clement laughed. "I believe I've shocked my strait-laced daughter," he said to Barrett. "She doesn't think I could be interested in a look at a fine woman."

"You might as well have a look too," Dinah said sourly, handing the paper to Clement. "Everyone else does," she mumbled beneath her breath.

The room grew quiet as a servant arrived and poured the coffee. Clement read the article about Delilah, scrutinized the drawing, and then put the paper aside. "The reporter says she has a fine voice." He glanced up. "Not as good as yours, Lilah, I'll warrant." He gave her a fond smile. "Perhaps you'll sing for us once we've finished our coffee."

"Oh, Papa. Not tonight," Lilah protested. "We're comfortable in here. We'd have to move to the music room, and I really don't feel like singing." She hastened on, "I'm sure Dinah doesn't feel like playing either."

"Of course I do," Dinah returned quickly, flashing her eyes defiantly at her sister.

Taken aback, Lilah felt a surge of temper and had one of those occasions to bite her tongue. Dinah surely understood she didn't want to sing tonight, not for days yet, maybe weeks.

"Another time, Papa," Lilah offered sweetly, glancing around at Barrett and touching his hand. "Barrett, you don't mind, do you? I'm tired. I'd like to retire early." She almost added that Dinah was tired too, but didn't, guessing she might again find herself without her sister's confirmation.

Barrett shook his head. "You do look a bit flushed," he answered. "And I still have some figures to work on tonight. I ought to go." He stood, thanked Clement for the dinner invitation, and said good night to Dinah.

Lilah rose quickly and slipped her arm through Barrett's. "I'll walk you to the door," she told him.

Lilah apologized again for cutting the evening short, all the while hoping her father hadn't dropped too many hints in Barrett's ear about setting a wedding date. She still wasn't ready for an engagement and she didn't want to be forced into inventing new excuses.

A large gilt mirror hung over a table in the foyer of Damon House. As she and Barrett passed it, Lilah caught a glimpse of Dinah hurrying out of the library and up the staircase. She and her little sister were due a serious talk. Dinah's deliberate obstinacy and moodiness were beginning to wear on her nerves.

Barrett paused at the door, slipped his hands to Lilah's shoulders, and looked expectantly at her. She lifted her face for his kiss. It came, a quick brush of the lips, affectionate but devoid of real passion. Lilah had an unconscionable memory of the last time she had been kissed, of the way her whole body had burned from the crush of Tabor Stanton's lips.

Shocked at herself for even making a comparison, she whispered a good-night to Barrett and watched him walk to his carriage. She much preferred Barrett's undemanding kiss, she told herself. No question about it.

Hurrying past the library, Lilah climbed the stairs

quickly, hoping to speak to Dinah before she got into bed. A rap on Dinah's bedroom door received no response. Lilah entered the room. Dinah hadn't heard because she stood on her balcony blowing kisses to the moon. At least that was what Lilah assumed until she stepped onto the balcony and saw Barrett below, just climbing into his carriage.

"Dinah."

Dinah spun around. "How dare you come in without knocking!"

Lilah gasped, surprised at Dinah's abruptness. "Is this a new rule?"

"Yes, it is," Dinah snapped back. "I'd like to think I can have my privacy."

Lilah's brow creased. "We've never locked doors between us."

Dinah tossed her head and hurried back into the bedroom. "I'm sure you'll be locking doors between us when you marry Barrett. Why postpone it?"

Lilah's heart softened. At last she understood. Dinah was jealous of Barrett. And most likely afraid of being alone. After all, Lilah had been both mother and sister to Dinah most of her life. Of course Dinah was upset over the prospect of losing someone she loved. But that need not happen. Lilah and Barrett could make their home at Damon House. Papa would like that too.

She spoke softly. "I've been thinking that Barrett and I might live here after we've married." Lilah placed an arm around Dinah's drooping shoulders. "That way, nothing much would change. I would still be here with you and Papa."

"Oh yes it would change," Dinah sobbed. "Nothing would ever be right again."

Lilah and her father sat in an open carriage in front

of the Damon stable. Clement's love and appreciation for horses hadn't diminished despite the way he'd incurred his injuries or the fact that he could no longer ride. He boasted one of the finest stables of saddle and carriage horses around. His breeding stock was of the best quality, their offspring bringing premium prices.

Lilah didn't completely share her father's love of horses. She did, however, love her father enough to overlook her reticence about anything that made him happy. She could hardly wait for him to see his surprise, and didn't intend to let anything spoil it, not even Dinah's perplexing behavior, though she couldn't understand why her sister had refused to come to the stable to share in the event.

"Cover your eyes, Papa. I don't want you looking until everything is ready," Lilah said with evident glee in her voice.

"I feel ridiculous holding my hands over my eyes," Clement retorted good-naturedly. Lilah, he understood, took it as another of her duties to keep her father cheerful. She was forever surprising him with things she thought would add to his comfort and happiness. He thought back. Just last year there had been an upholstered rocking chair with a music box built into the armrest, a frisky spaniel named Squire, and a bottle of rather repulsive Egyptian massage oil. He dared not guess what she was foisting on him now.

"You're determined to peek, but I'll take care of that." Lilah laughed and whipped off her broad-brimmed straw bonnet and held it in front of Clement's face. "Bring him out, Gus," she called.

The thump of hooves on flinty earth brought an exclamation of interest from Clement Damon. "Lilah, what have you been up to?"

"Grand things, Papa. You'll see." Slowly she lowered her hat, fearful a sudden move might startle the tall black stallion standing stretched out only a few feet away. "What do you think of him?"

"I'll be damned!" Clement said, leaning forward as he did at those times he consciously wished he could walk. "What a magnificent animal! Where did you get him?"

"In St. Louis," Lilah said, deliberately avoiding her father's eyes lest he see the lie hidden in them.

"Take him in a circle, Gus." Clement, smiling broadly, watched the horse's power and clean, solid moves as, neck arched, he pranced around behind the stable man. "An animal like that must have cost a fortune," he mumbled. "Lilah!" Suddenly his eyes were on his daughter. "How did you pay for that horse?"

"With my allowance, Papa," Lilah said sweetly. She caught Clement's hand. "I suppose I'll have to do without a few gowns, but it's worth it to see you so happy."

"Sweetheart . . ." Clement said, creases lining his brow. He had never put any limits on Lilah's spending, but if she intended making more purchases like this, he would have to come to a new understanding with her. "Six months of your allowance wouldn't pay for that animal."

"He wasn't nearly that much, Papa," she answered, still avoiding her father's eyes as she hugged him. "I got him at a bargain price. The man who owned him had no idea of his value. The horse isn't well-broken. Why, it's hard to even get a saddle on him. The owner was glad to be rid of him." The smile on her face came from a deep-seated sense of satisfaction.

Clement saw the strange light in Lilah's eyes and wondered about it, but he was much too entranced with the horse to give her expression any serious thought. He shook his head in disbelief.

"Take him around again, Gus. This time in a wide circle." Gus led the horse completely around the carriage. "Pick up the pace a little," Clement called. Gus speeded up, and the stallion followed in a trot, moving proudly, as if he knew he was being admired and knew he deserved that admiration.

"You like him, don't you, Papa?" Lilah asked softly, pleased by the look of delight on her father's face.

"He's one of the finest animals I've ever owned." He squeezed her hand. "Does he have a name?"

"Indeed he does," Lilah returned, the peculiar brightness once more in her eyes. "I call him Rogue."

Tabor scrubbed his chair back from the bars of his cell and stood and stretched his muscles. A light breeze drifted in the small window and he had to admit his own odor was a bit ripe. Peregrine had allowed him only bucket baths. He and both sets of his clothes were in need of a good wash. The marshal didn't seem to mind, though. Tabor wondered if being made to smell like a carcass was part of his punishment. Still he managed a smile as he tossed his last hand of cards through the bars to the marshal.

"Damn!" Peregrine said. "Reckon I better try again."

Tabor shook his head. "Hell, Walsh. You're wearing me out. Why don't you forget about winning and just admit I'm too good a poker player for you?"

The marshal, his bulk straining a wooden straight chair, used his foot to push a small table away. " 'Cause you ain't been here but two weeks and I got plenty of time to outsmart you yet."

"Now, that's another thing, Walsh." Tabor ventured into a subject he'd avoided until now. In two weeks he had gotten to know the marshal rather well. Odd as it was, the men had become friends of a sort.

"Didn't you tell me you were one of the best poker players in town?"

"That's right." Peregrine leaned the chair back on two legs and propped his feet on the rough wood table where the cards lay. "Not a man in town can get the better of me, and that's not just because I'm wearin' this badge." He reached into his shirt pocket for his tobacco pouch, and finding it empty, asked Tabor for a smoke. Tabor obliged.

"You haven't won a game with me."

"I reckon I know that." Peregrine filled a paper with tobacco, licked it, and formed it into a lumpy cylinder with his stubby fingers. "You've damned near cleaned out my tobacco money. Had to ask my wife for two bits to buy lunch today."

"Doesn't that tell you something?"

Peregrine frowned. "It ought to tell me not to play another hand with you." He struck a match on his boot sole and lit his cigarette. "But I mean to get my money back."

The marshal threw back his head and barked a laugh. Having Stanton in his jail and listening to his tales about naval voyages to Japan and Hawaii made the time pass better, gave him something to talk to his wife about too. She had even sent the boy a slice of apple pie. Stanton offered such a believable account of native girls in grass skirts doing a dance called the hula that Peregrine could almost see brown-skinned hips shaking.

"Ever played poker with a woman?" Tabor asked.

"Nope." Peregrine puffed on his cigarette. "Never seen a woman who knew a jack from a king. Anyhow, women are too emotional to play poker. They'd give away a hand every time."

"You ever seen me cheat?"

"Nope. You don't have to."

"Think I'd lose a game with a woman?"

Peregrine guffawed at the thought. "Nope," he said. "You'd have a woman in tears in—" He abruptly dropped the other two chair legs on the floor and drilled Tabor with a pair of deep-set eyes. "What're you gettin' at, Stanton? Are you claimin' Miss Delilah lied?"

Tabor backed away a few feet, remembering how the marshal had once slammed him into the bars. "Think about it, Walsh," he said matter-of-factly, hoping he was leading Peregrine where he wanted him to go. "Do you believe I'd lose a game to any woman?"

Delilah had left Yuba City two weeks ago. Her spell on Walsh Peregrine had faded but not died. "Aw, I don't know," the marshal said, scratching his chin as he thought about it.

"Would you lose a game to a woman?"

"Hell no!"

"See what I mean, Walsh?"

"Yeah, you got a point, but I still can't believe Miss Delilah told a lie."

Tabor pressed on while he had Peregrine thinking. "I'm not saying she told a lie. I don't think she really understands poker. Most likely she thinks she had the winning hand. But women are . . ." He decided on Peregrine's own word. "Emotional. And when they get that way, they don't know what they're doing."

Peregrine nodded slowly as he remembered a recent disagreement with his wife after he had told her the biscuits were too dry. She had snatched his dinner plate from under his nose and fed the contents to the dog, then sent him packing out of the house to find his own meal. His eyes nearly got lost in the deep furrows of his brow as he frowned. Stanton was right. Women were unreasonable when they were upset.

"Well, what about you pullin' a gun on the lady?"

He stood and tugged up the gunbelt that liked to slip under his potbelly. "Was she wrong about that too?"

"Now, Walsh." Tabor wanted to tell the marshal what a thick head he had, but couldn't risk losing whatever advantage he had gained. "I don't wear a gun when I visit a lady. You got my holster and guns out of *my* hotel room the same day you picked up my bedroll." He made fists of the hands he longed to wrap around Delilah's neck. "Hell! I don't know. She was hysterical. Maybe she *thought* I had a gun."

"Yeah. That could be it." Peregrine tossed the smoldering butt of his cigarette into a sand-filled bucket. "Trouble is, she ain't comin' back to say what she thought after she calmed down. And I still got a signed deposition says different."

Forgetting his caution, Tabor gripped the cell bars. "The judge won't be here for another six weeks."

"So?"

"So when he gets here, you're going to have to tell him you locked me up because I pulled a gun that was in another room. What's he going to think?"

Peregrine rubbed his bristly chin. "You know, I been thinkin', Stanton. You can't always put store in what a woman says when she's hysterical."

"Uh-huh," Tabor mumbled, afraid to say anything that might sway the marshal another way. A few days ago Peregrine had mentioned an old quarrel with the judge. Tabor had stored the information away for later use, thinking it might come in handy.

"I reckon two weeks is long enough to keep a man locked up for bein' drunk and disorderly."

"Two weeks is about right," Tabor agreed. His entire body tensed. He could see freedom almost at hand. All he could think about was what he was going to do when he found Delilah.

Peregrine got up and scuffed across the office to his

desk. " 'Course, I'm going to have to fine you. You bein' a guest of the jail so long."

"How much, Marshal?" Tabor scowled as he watched Peregrine pull a ring of keys from his desk drawer. He could still have a problem. Delilah had emptied his pockets before carting him over to the jail. The only money he had was the twenty dollars he'd won from the marshal.

Peregrine jangled the keys. His wide grin worried Tabor. "Say about as much as you won from me playin' poker. Don't forget, I staked you that first game."

"Marshal, I got to buy a horse to leave town."

Tabor's crestfallen look must have stirred a little sympathy loose in Peregrine. "Yeah. I reckon you do," he drawled. "Look, I'm sorry about you losin' your horse. How was I to know I was dealin' with a hysterical woman?"

Tabor swallowed his anger. He didn't expect to be without the Admiral for long. He smiled. "No hard feelings, Marshal. It's not your fault. You did the only thing you could."

"Yeah. I reckon I did. I've always believed in givin' a lady the benefit of the doubt."

Tabor gritted his teeth and nodded. The lady who had put him in this predicament was a scheming, man-hating, red-haired witch. She was going to wish she'd never heard of Tabor Stanton. Hell! Who was he kidding? By now she'd probably left another half-dozen witless victims in her wake. Most likely she didn't even remember his name.

"So you're going to drop the fine?" Tabor asked hopefully.

Peregrine started to agree, then thought of asking Martha for more spending money. "I'm droppin' it to half," he said.

Tabor opened his mouth to argue, but quickly assessed the likelihood of doing more harm than good. He wouldn't get much of a horse for ten bucks, but if he rubbed Peregrine the wrong way he wouldn't need one.

"That's fair, Marshal," he agreed.

"That's what I figured you'd say." Peregrine's grin widened as he slid the key in the lock.

"Curtis . . ." Tabor spoke to the livery owner he had left the Admiral with two weeks back. "You remember that black stallion I rode into town."

Curtis smiled. "The one Miss Delilah won from you in that poker game?" Curtis remembered. The stallion was one of the best-looking horses he'd ever seen. Temperamental, though. He hadn't ventured into the stall with that one.

"Right." Tabor fumed. He supposed he had been the laughingstock of Yuba City since that night. Being reminded of it didn't help his outlook any. "Who took him out of here?"

"One of them dandies led him out. Couldn't saddle him. Left your rig here. Reckon you'll be wanting it." Curtis disappeared into the tack room, returning shortly with the saddle. He dropped it at Tabor's feet. "Got anything to go under it?"

"No," Tabor said, galled to have to ask for a horse and knowing he was going to be laughed at again when he told Curtis how much money he had. "I need a mount."

"No problem about that." Curtis pointed to a gelding at one end of the barn and at a mare nearby. "Thirty dollars will git you either one of those."

"What've you got for ten?" Tabor mumbled.

"Ten!" Curtis spat tobacco juice on the ground. "For ten I can git you a rocky horse."

Tabor, blood throbbing in his temples, knuckles stretched tight, looked at the ground, afraid that if he looked at Curtis he'd soon find himself back in Peregrine's jail. The sight of his saddle gave him an idea.

"All right," he said slowly when Curtis showed no sign of letting up. "How about a trade? My saddle for a horse and an old saddle of yours."

Curtis glanced at Tabor's saddle. "Well, I don't know," he said, poking his boot at the saddle. "It's a good saddle, but it ain't *that* good. Let's say you throw in the ten bucks you got and it's a deal. I'll even hand you back enough for a little grub."

"It's a deal," Tabor agreed, kicking his saddle toward Curtis. A black look on his face, he dipped a hand into his pocket and pulled out the ten dollars he'd won from Peregrine. Curtis counted the money, then handed him back a few dollars. Under his breath Tabor mumbled the thoughts he couldn't voice. He knew now how outlaws were made. A little more humiliation and he'd be ready to resort to holding up the Yuba City Bank. He could bear it only because he knew someday he'd get even with Delilah.

"You come back late this afternoon and I'll have a horse ready," Curtis told him.

"Thanks. I'll be back." Saying thanks to Curtis put a sour taste in his mouth, but he didn't figure he'd get a better deal anywhere else.

" 'Bout forgot," Curtis said. "Been a fella here askin' for you. I told him you was in jail. Did he look you up?"

"No." Tabor scowled. "Was it Wilkins?"

"Some other fella. Didn't git his name." Curtis picked up Tabor's saddle with a lot more care than he'd shown in throwing it down. He laughed. "Reckon he don't like the inside of a jail neither."

Tabor's lips thinned with anger but he reminded

himself he had no reason to blame Curtis for his predicament. That credit went to Delilah.

Curtis laughed again. "And here," he added, flipping Tabor another coin. "Git yourself a bath, on me. Don't want the horse thinkin' he's carryin' a polecat."

The saddle rode like a fence rail, the horse had a gait that made Tabor suspect it had one short leg. At least he was clean, and his clothes were too. He had coffee, a little bacon, and some beans. He rode out of Yuba City with nothing more guiding him than a mention that Delilah's coach had pulled out in the same direction.

Fat Jack back in the saloon hadn't been able to supply him with much more information than he already had about that devil-woman. Knowing Yuba City was the end of her tour wasn't encouraging. She could be on a ship heading to Europe. Or on a train east. He figured his best chance of tracking her down was to follow her coach to the next stop. Somebody would know where she went from there. A woman like Delilah couldn't pass through a town without being noticed.

When he came to a fork in the road and had to decide on a direction, he thought of flipping a coin. Since he didn't have one, he let the horse, an old mare named Beetle, choose.

His bad luck held. Inquiries in the next town assured him nobody had seen Delilah. Everybody had wanted to. Two more days of riding brought him no leads. Eventually he found himself backtracking. It was possible Delilah had done the same, circling around Yuba City and heading out in the opposite direction. Over a two-week period he rode back to the last three towns she'd performed in, finally getting a lead. The coach she used was hired and one of the men who had helped unload her trunk happened to know the company had offices in Sacramento.

Encouraged but low on grub and tired of eating jackrabbits, he sidled into a saloon and with some sharp talking found a man willing to stake him in a poker game. His winnings paid for grub enough to get him to Sacramento, with a few dollars left over.

Tired and dusty, Tabor entered the offices of the Logan Stage Lines in Sacramento. The young clerk looked up and asked if he could be of any assistance.

"I'm trying to find an entertainer called Delilah."

The clerk nodded methodically. "You and a thousand other men."

Tabor shot him a withering look. "You mean other people have been here looking for her?"

"I do," the clerk said. "You aren't the only one who figured out she rents a coach from us." He closed the ticket drawer since it was obvious he wouldn't be making a sale. "Thing is, Logan Stage Lines can't help you. One of her agents makes the arrangements. All we know is somebody picks up the coach, somebody brings it back. Nobody here has ever seen Delilah."

"You don't keep records or have an address even on the agent? Isn't that risky?"

"Not when the customer pays double rate like Delilah does." The young man pulled a pencil from behind his ear. "If that's all, I've got work to do."

Disappointed but still determined, Tabor left. Sacramento might be another dead end, but a hunch told him it wasn't. He decided to check the hotels in town. Following another hunch, he decided not to ask for Delilah by name.

"I'm looking for lady who might have stayed here recently," he said to a maid at the Sacramento Hotel, figuring she might know more than the desk clerk about who occupied the rooms. "A pretty woman, fire-red hair, fancy clothes."

"Your sweetheart or your sister?" Maggie asked.

"My . . . ah . . . sweetheart," Tabor said. "You see, I upset her and she ran out on me. Now I want to tell her I'm sorry and I can't find her. I was hoping you might have seen her."

"Does your sweetheart have a name?"

"Rose," he said. "Her name is Rose Smith."

Maggie's eyes showed her disappointment as she shook her head. She fancied the idea of reuniting a pair of broken hearts. "There hasn't been a Rose Smith here."

Tabor frowned. "I have reason to think she might use another name. Has anyone been here who fits Rose's description?"

"No," Maggie said. "I don't remember anybody with fire-red hair."

Tabor swore silently. She could have told him that to begin with. He was about to thank her and leave when she volunteered something else.

"I don't suppose you could mean Miss Alden."

"Miss Alden?"

"Miss Alden and her sister stay here sometimes, but neither one is redheaded."

"Tell me about these Alden sisters."

Gossip being Maggie's favorite pastime, she needed only that encouragement to tell all she knew. "Now, there's a pair. Miss Alden keeps a suite here permanent. Just uses it when her and her sister want to get away from all those brothers—eight brothers. To begin with, I thought you might be one of the brothers checking up on them."

Tabor wasn't sure just why, but what he was hearing about the Alden sisters made him want to hear more. "When were they here last?"

"Must have been three weeks back."

Tabor smiled. The timing was right.

Maggie guessed his next questions. "They left by train. I don't know where."

"Thanks," Tabor said, hurrying out of the hotel.

"Good luck," Maggie called after him.

The stationmaster remembered the Alden sisters and their destination. San Francisco. He also remembered a horse of the Admiral's description being loaded on a boxcar headed for the same place. Tabor bought a ticket for the next day, then left the station. He needed a good poker game and a livery man who couldn't see too well, one he might convince to take Beetle off his hands.

If Delilah and the Admiral were in San Francisco, he would find them. If the trail led on, he would follow, as soon as he had taken care of his other business in that city. He had a letter to deliver to someone named Clement Damon.

6

"I had an absolutely abominable journey," Emily Dearborn professed over tea with her niece. A small woman with china-blue eyes and blond hair that hadn't yet gone gray, Lilah's aunt had arrived a week earlier. "Lilah," Emily continued, "why you want to live in this savage land is beyond my understanding."

"San Francisco isn't savage, Aunt Emily. It's not London, of course, but it is my home."

Lilah couldn't imagine what her aunt had seen since arriving that brought her to such a conclusion. Lawless areas existed not far away, but Aunt Emily had seen only the port and the posh sections of the city. Lilah smiled indulgently. Why, just a glance around her sitting room, a look at the handmade Aubusson rug, the lace curtains, and the pink moiré lambrequins at the windows should make her aunt feel as comfortable as she would in her own London town house.

"I'd like to change your mind about that," Emily said, revealing a little of the strong will beneath her delicate appearance. "My intent is to persuade you and Dinah to return to England with me."

"You won't succeed," Lilah said, pouring tea, then taking a small second slice of poppy-seed cake. "Neither Dinah nor I intend to leave Papa again."

Emily chose to ignore Lilah's remark. "That young Charles Rutherford who proposed to you has never married."

"I have a fiancé, Aunt Emily," Lilah said. "Almost."

She guessed her aunt's thoughts. Charles, although untitled, was from a prominent family and had been Emily's choice for Lilah's husband. Lilah remembered the handsome Charles Rutherford well. His father, who had made a fortune in trade, favored the match even though Lilah was American. She might have been tempted to accept Charles's proposal if she hadn't felt so strongly about her personal obligations.

"A bank clerk," Emily went on indignantly. "You could do better for yourself." She gave a long, discontented sigh. "You know it broke my heart when you refused Charles and left my house. I still question your decision and why you choose to live in a wilderness."

Lilah lowered her eyes and thought about Emily's motives. She loved her aunt and was indebted to her. Emily, whose husband had died only a few years after their marriage, had no children of her own. When she had taken on the task of raising her sister's children, she had done so wholeheartedly. And though she had taken two unruly mining-camp waifs and transformed them into fashionable young ladies, Emily would not be satisfied until she saw them successfully married. To Emily's mind, no American man could possibly have a family background that measured up to her standards.

"First of all, Barrett isn't a bank clerk," Lilah said gently. "He's Papa's assistant and is being trained to oversee all the Damon enterprises. Second, America isn't a wilderness, at least not all of it. Last of all,

Aunt Emily"—Lilah spoke her aunt's name with great
affection—"I love it here. I could never be happy in
London again."

Emily frowned, fearing defeat before she even got
started. "I can't bear to think I've failed Marie," she
said sadly. "Bringing out her daughters and arranging
good marriages seemed the least I could do for my
sister." Emily directed a stern and assessing look at
Lilah. "I haven't heard you say you love this Barrett."

For Lilah the conversation was getting tiresome.
She hoped it wasn't to be repeated often during Emily's visit. Her mind was made up and she wouldn't
change it. No doubt her aunt would soon despair of
trying and direct her persuasive talk at Dinah.

"I'm fond of Barrett and he is of me," Lilah said
softly. "We'll have a good marriage," she continued
with a string of evasive chatter. "You must remember
that my mother chose to follow my father into the
goldfields when this country really was savage. Don't
you think she would be happy about her daughters
being here now?"

"I suppose you're right, dear." Emily's chin trembled slightly. This journey to San Francisco was her
first venture out of England, unless she counted Paris,
which was only a little less civilized than London. The
Bret Harte stories she had read and the proximity of
the Californians who had shared her table on the ship
hadn't left her with a favorable impression of Lilah's
home. And though she was willing to admit that Damon
House and what she had seen of San Francisco were
pleasing, she suspected most of the inhabitants were
like those men on the ship, ill-dressed and with the
table manners of pigs.

"I'm happy to hear you agree," Lilah said.

Though Emily had never accepted the ease with
which her sister followed Clement Damon first to Penn-

sylvania and then into the unsettled West, she realized they had shared a strong love.

"Even as a child Marie had a daring streak," Emily said. "She coveted adventure." She looked at Lilah, seeing much of Marie in her. "Your mother could be very unladylike at times."

Lilah's smile brightened. "As unladylike as I was when I first came to you?"

"Indeed not." Emily laughed. "I thought for a time Clement had sent me a wild little red Indian. As I recall, it took a week to brush the tangles out of your hair, even longer to induce you to wear shoes. And your language. I was horrified."

Lilah laughed too, remembering what a hard time she had given her aunt and how much patience it had taken for Emily to mold her into an acceptable young lady.

"Papa thinks you worked miracles."

Emily smiled. Her niece was everything she had hoped for, beautiful, gracious, and much more demure than her mother had been. Marie would be proud of her daughter, of both of them.

Emily's smile became a laugh. "My dear, when I remember you then and see you now, I am inclined to agree."

Tabor spent most of a day at the San Francisco station interviewing workers who might remember either the stallion or the Alden sisters. His only success was in checking the freight arrivals of the day in question. The horse, he was told, had been claimed shortly after being unloaded. The story was the same as at the stage company—no name, no address given.

His small success was learning that a trunk registered to M. Alden had been delivered to a storage company. The lead, however, raised only false hopes.

The storage company refused to allow him a look in the trunk unless he produced the required claim. They did supply him with a post-office number from which payments and instruction were received. Inquiries at the post office, however, brought him to the end of his trail. The rent on the postal box had been prepaid for a full year and no worker could remember placing any mail inside it for months.

Tabor decided he had two options. He could watch the post office indefinitely, waiting for someone to use the box, someone who might or might not be the person he sought. The other choice was to admit a temporary defeat in his search for Delilah. Either way, he stood to lose. A muscle twitched in his tightly clenched jaw. He hated losing.

He settled for posting a letter to M. Alden. Someone surely checked the box periodically for mail. He might get a response to his request. A few hours later Tabor sent off a wire to his aunt at the Cooke ranch near Los Angeles. Sending that message wasn't the easiest thing he had ever done, but he had put it off as long as he could. By now Sarah would be wondering what had happened to him.

Tomorrow he planned to look up Damon and finish what his father had asked him to do. When that was done, he could get back to looking for the Admiral and Delilah.

He found a moderately priced hotel and settled himself in. It wasn't just a matter of pride, he told himself, tracking down Delilah. The Cooke ranch couldn't afford the loss of the Admiral. With most of its capital tied up in cattle, the sale of the Admiral's colts brought in much-needed working cash.

Boots off and stretched out on a soft bed, he couldn't suppress a facetious smile. He had gotten himself in one hellacious fix, but a man didn't ever need to lose the ability to laugh at himself. The smile dimmed as his thoughts rambled on. Sarah wouldn't be laughing if he came home without the stallion. She owned part interest in the animal and would most likely take her share out of his hide. He'd had to swallow a lot of pride before he wired her for money.

Relaxing more, he closed his eyes and got a vision of a blaze of red hair. He could almost smell that exotic scent Delilah wore, something from the East, Oriental and exciting. He remembered how much he had liked that perfume and the way it had seemed to grow more potent as she responded to his touch. The memory almost overshadowed that of her deceit.

Delilah was some woman, a she-cat if ever California had one. The lady didn't like losing any better than he did—but she had lost the bet they made. She owed him, and her debt was more than the return of the stallion. She owed him a week of bowing to his will. He aimed to collect.

The answering wire from Sarah arrived the following morning. With money from the bank draw she authorized, Tabor bought himself a suit of clothes and hired a saddle horse for the day. Tracking down Clement Damon wasn't nearly as baffling as tracking Delilah. It seemed half the storefronts in San Francisco bore the Damon name. He bypassed the Damon Lumber Company and Damon Dry Goods Store, concluding the best chance of finding the man would be behind a desk in the Damon Bank on Montgomery Street.

Tabor considered himself correct when he saw Damon's name listed on the dedication stone as bank president. He entered the building and approached the only teller who wasn't occupied with a customer.

"Is that Clement Damon?" Tabor asked, observing a prominently displayed portrait of a man around fifty with silver-touched temples and a face that showed strength and character.

The teller looked up from a line of numbers he had been figuring. "Yes. And a fine man too," he responded. "May I help you, sir?"

"Maybe," Tabor answered, bending down to look into the teller's cage. "I'd like to see Mr. Damon."

The teller shook his head. "I'm sorry, sir. Mr. Damon comes in only once a week, on Friday."

Tabor frowned and straightened to his full six feet, two inches. "That's three days. I don't plan on being in town that long," he said. "Do you think there's a way I could get a message to Mr. Damon to ride in and see me tomorrow?"

"I'm sure you could send a message," the teller answered. "Mr. Fenton, our vice-president, goes out to Damon House twice weekly to report on the bank's business. He generally carries personal messages for Mr. Damon as well. He'll be going tonight. You could have a reply in the morning."

"Any chance I might find Damon at the lumber company or at the store today?"

"That's unlikely. Mr. Damon rarely comes into town more than once a week."

Mouth set in annoyance at another delay, Tabor accepted the loan of the teller's pencil and wrote out a message on a piece of notepaper. He didn't want to waste time on Damon when he had more critical things to do. On the other hand, he was anxious to be done with delivering his father's letter. He wondered, as he folded the notepaper and returned it to the teller, what link his father could have had with Clement Damon. Clearly Damon was a person of wealth and importance. It stretched Tabor's imagination that his father and that distinguished man in the portrait could ever have been friends.

Tabor spent the afternoon visiting theatrical compa-
nies and dance halls, people he figured might know
Delilah. Several theater proprietors were almost as
anxious as he was to find the Flame of the West,
having calculated what a draw she would be for their
establishments. Hearing half a dozen other men tout
her beauty and talent didn't sit well in Tabor's craw.
By evening, when he joined in a poker game, his
mounting temper made him a brutal adversary. A
pocketful of winnings helped to cool him down and by
morning he was ready to turn his attention in another
direction. He returned to the Damon Bank.

The same teller he had spoken with the day before
presented him with an envelope closed with a gold-foil
seal. Tabor took a seat on the customers' bench in the
bank lobby and read Clement Damon's response. The
note expressed Damon's regret he could not meet
Tabor at his hotel; however, if it was agreeable, he
requested Tabor come to his home at three the same
afternoon.

Tabor got directions to Damon House from the
teller. At exactly five minutes until three he rode up in
front of the Damon mansion. A Chinese boy ran out
to meet him and to take his horse. Another Chinese
boy, dressed in pajamalike clothing, like the first one,
led him up a low ramp to the front door. The boy
pulled a rope and Tabor heard the sound of a chime
from inside the house.

Again it was a Chinese servant who greeted him.
With a sharp eye Tabor spotted numerous Chinese
men about the grounds. Knowing something of Oriental ways, his guess was that the unimposing Chinese
were guards, guards who required no more than their
hands for weapons.

"You are Mr. Stanton?" the man answering the
door asked. Tabor nodded and the Chinese did the

same. "My name is Wan. Please come in, Mr. Stanton. Mr. Damon is in his library. He expects you."

Tabor followed past a spiral staircase and into a wide hall. He stopped when the Chinese did and waited for a response to the man's knock on the library door. Tabor had a mental picture of Clement Damon as a strong and powerful person. The luxury of the mansion confirmed it. He was unprepared for the man in the invalid's chair with his legs covered by a wool lap rug.

"Mr. Damon?"

"Clement Damon," the man responded, rolling his chair forward. "Your message said you were Stan's son." His eyes were strangely pain-filled as he searched Tabor's face. "I knew he had a boy. I never knew what became of him."

They met and shook hands in the center of the room. Out of the corner of his eye Tabor saw another Chinese man almost in the shadows at one side of the room. His eyes too lingered on Tabor's face, but unlike Damon's, held a warning.

Damon rolled himself behind his desk and offered Tabor the chair in front of it.

"Were you a friend of my father's?" Tabor sat, acutely aware the Chinese man had silently moved to a position behind him. "I'm afraid I don't know much about him. He and my mother parted company almost fifteen years ago. I grew up south of here. Never saw my father all that time until last year."

"I see," Damon said, not bothering to answer as he exchanged a glance with the Chinese man. "I believe your message said you wished to give me a letter from your father."

"That's right," Tabor responded, withdrawing a creased and soiled envelope from his coat pocket. "He requested I deliver this to you. Here it is." Tabor placed the envelope in Damon's hands. He sensed the tension strung among the three of them in the room, and though he had no idea of the reason, his muscles tightened with anticipation.

Clement held the envelope a few minutes without opening it. "You asked if your father and I were friends. We were once. But that changed a long time ago. I have to admit I'm surprised to be hearing from him."

Tabor's eyes narrowed. He had the feeling his visit was opening old wounds. "I don't think you understand, Mr. Damon," Tabor said, his voice flat. "My father died a few months ago. He wanted that envelope delivered to you. I don't know what's in it and I can't say I care. It's a hard thing to admit to a stranger, but I had no use for my father. He let my mother down and she never got over it. I'm honoring his dying request to deliver that letter, but it's more for her sake than for his."

Clement's face went blank. He tore open the envelope and slowly read the contents, then looked up. "This isn't a letter. It's a mining claim to a piece of ground east of here. Your father signed it over to me. Is it worth anything?"

Tabor shrugged. "My guess is no," he said bitterly. "Not much my father had anything to do with was. But whether that claim is or isn't is your business. I brought it to you. That's all I have to do with it."

Clement laid the claim and the torn envelope on his desk. He thought he understood what had happened to the older Stanton's life. A man could lose many things and survive. But when he lost his self-respect, he wasn't much good to himself or his family. Stan had been that way. He had participated in an act of violence his conscience couldn't bear.

"You didn't think much of your father, you say."

"I didn't have much reason to," Tabor answered. "He deserted us, wound up a drunk. He was no account to anybody, including himself. I can't find a thing to admire about him. If he was indebted to you and paid up, that's probably the only honest thing he ever did."

Clement stared at Tabor. The younger Stanton resembled his father. Looking at him, it was difficult not to remember the betrayal he had felt learning that a man he called friend was among his attackers. He and Stan had agreed to work some claims together until they had differed over the treatment of the Chinese laborers. Even now Clement couldn't believe Stan would have joined the attack if he hadn't been pressured by Hoke Newell and his cohorts. Stan hadn't really hated the Chinese, he had just been afraid to take a stand. Clement shrugged. The memories hurt. He wanted to stop remembering.

"I guess Stan thought he owed me something," he said, still staring at Tabor. "We had a business agreement once. Things happened. I wouldn't have held him to it. You may be right that this property is worth nothing. In any event, I don't need it. I think it ought to go to you." He pushed the papers toward Tabor.

Tabor refused them. "My mother would never let me say a word against my father. I had to watch her die slowly, of grieving for him, always thinking tomorrow he'd ride up or there'd be a letter. It would have hurt her if I hadn't done what he asked. That's the only reason I'm here. Worthless or not, the property's yours. Keep it."

Clement opened a desk drawer and put the papers inside. "I'll send someone to take a look at it someday. If you change your mind . . ."

"I won't."

"Papa!" The library door burst open. A girl in a

light green dress swept in but stopped abruptly when she saw her father had a guest. "I'm sorry, Papa. I should have knocked."

Clement found a smile for his daughter. "I remember telling you that several times, Dinah," he said. "Can what you have to say wait?"

"Yes, Papa," Dinah answered. She had gotten a good look at her father's face just as she came in. His expression puzzled her, but she quickly forgot her dismay when her eyes came to rest on Tabor Stanton. Her father's tall, handsome visitor was about the most virile-looking man she'd ever seen. He glanced back at her at the same moment, gave a half-smile, and nodded politely as she backed out of the room and eased the door shut.

Clement waited until he heard the latch click, then returned his attention to Tabor. The hard light that had shone in the older man's eyes was gone. He had suffered because of Stanton, no doubt about it. Over the years he had come to the conclusion that suffering made a man stronger, though it didn't sound like that had been the case with Stan.

Clement took a deep breath. He hadn't gotten where he was easily. Accepting what had happened to him had taken as long as learning to live with his physical infirmities. Still, he had overcome what he had lost, though he had never forgotten the men who had harmed him.

The man before him apparently didn't know what had changed his father from a decent, hard-working husband and father into an aimless drunk. Clement decided not to tell him.

Dinah's unexpected appearance had reminded him of his blessings. He had two daughters he loved and who loved him in return. Suddenly it seemed clear to Clement that what he had lost had been much easier to live without than what Stan had lost. Seeing the hate and bitterness of that night spill over into another generation saddened Clement. Still, it surprised him to hear himself defending Stan.

"Most men have a little good in them, Stanton." Both of Clement's silver brows lifted. "Even a man like your father. Sometimes you have to look a little deeper to find it."

Tabor found his thoughts thrown back to a time he didn't want to remember. He stood quickly. "Mr. Damon," he said. "I didn't mean to stay so long. I thank you for taking the time to see me. I'm sure you have other appointments." He extended a hand to Clement.

Clement waved it off. "Sit down, Stanton. I'm not nearly as busy a man as you seem to think. Truth is, I'd appreciate it if you'd have a drink with me. Ching," he said, nodding to the Chinese. "Get the whiskey, will you?"

Ching moved in his silent way to the liquor cabinet and poured whiskey from a glass decanter. Tabor dropped back into his chair. He wasn't opposed to having a drink. It was, in fact, exactly what he thought he needed.

Dinah raced up the stairs to Lilah's sitting room, hoping her father wasn't upset that she had interrupted him. If he was, he might not agree to allow her to spend the Saturday and Sunday with Deirdre Kittring. The Kittrings' house was only a few doors down from Barrett's, and Dinah was sure she could arrange to bump into him while she was there. She probably should have waited until dinner to ask Papa anyway. Her other worry was having forgotten she was to join Lilah and Aunt Emily for tea. Dinah bit down on her lower lip. It wasn't really her fault she kept forgetting things. She had a lot on her mind.

"Dinah, I wondered where you were," Emily said as Dinah hurried into Lilah's sitting room.

Lilah smiled but her eyes said all the accusing things Dinah knew were true. She had practically ignored Aunt Emily the last few days. She did hope she hadn't actually been rude. She just hadn't been in the mood for company.

"I'm sorry," Dinah said sweetly, pausing to kiss her aunt's cheek. "I was downstairs. I had to see Papa for a minute."

"And did you?" Lilah asked.

"Yes." Dinah plopped down on the settee beside Lilah. "He looked quite peculiar."

Any indication her father wasn't feeling well was cause for concern to Lilah. "Is he ill?" she asked, putting her teacup aside.

"Oh no. Nothing like that," Dinah answered, helping herself to tea and cake. "Papa was talking to a man I've never seen and he had the most peculiar look on his face."

"You're sure he isn't ill?" Lilah clutched her fingers tightly together in her lap.

"I told you he isn't," Dinah said. "Do you think he'll agree to let me stay a few nights with Deirdre?"

Lilah's voice dropped in volume. "I hardly think that would be polite while Aunt Emily is here."

Dinah's cheerful expression turned wistful. She knew her sister was right, but it meant she would have to postpone her plans for weeks. "I don't mean to be rude, Aunt Emily," she said, bouncing over to her aunt's chair. "It's just that I really don't think of you as a guest. After all, you are one of the family."

Emily smiled at Dinah's exuberance. She wished Lilah had a little of that vivaciousness. She imagined

Dinah and Deirdre wanted to talk about the dancing partners they hoped to have at the ball Clement was giving in her honor the next week.

"Go and visit your friend if your father will allow it," Emily said, patting Dinah's hand. "I won't be offended. I suspect you and Deirdre have important things to discuss."

Dinah kissed her aunt again. "You always understand me, Aunt Emily. I want you to help me choose a dress for the ball."

Pleased, Emily agreed. This was just the sort of things she wanted to see her nieces interested in. Girls who were concerned about ball gowns and dances soon had husbands.

"Lilah, do you want to come with us?" Dinah asked, urging Emily to her feet.

Lilah declined. "I'm going down to see Papa. You and Aunt Emily go ahead," she said. "I'll call for someone to take the tea things."

"You said you grew up south of here, Mr. Stanton. I presume that was on a ranch."

Tabor smiled. The whiskey went down smooth as silk, and only a few swallows of it relaxed him. "My mother and I went to live with my aunt and uncle. He had a cattle spread. My Aunt Sarah runs it now. We've started breeding horses too since I got back."

"Back?"

"Sorry." Tabor grinned. "I tried a naval career for a while until I got a yearning for the smell of horses and trail dust. I've been back at the ranch two years."

Ching quickly refilled Tabor's empty glass. Clement took a refill too. He enjoyed talking with a man who shared his interest in horses. That was his one complaint of Barrett Fenton. His assistant had an exceptional business head but couldn't seem to think of horses as anything more than a necessity for travel.

"I've got what I think is a fine stable," Clement told Tabor. "I'd enjoy showing it to you. You could stay for dinner too, if you don't have plans."

Tabor finished his second whiskey. Damon amazed him. In spite of being crippled, the man teemed with enthusiasm for life. He would have accepted Clement's invitation if he hadn't remembered the trail he was following was getting colder by the minute.

"Thank you, Mr. Damon," Tabor said, setting down his glass. "I'm sorry I can't say yes. Maybe another time."

"I understand," Clement assured him. "A young man in San Francisco doesn't want to spend his evenings talking about horses."

Tabor's smile passed for silent agreement. There was one horse he would like to hear talk about, but he didn't think Damon would be of any help to him on that one. He had a few more livery stables to visit, and counted on finding the Admiral in one of them.

Clement followed Tabor to the library door and past Ching. Tabor thanked his host for the whiskey as he walked through the long hall with white marble floors. He glanced around appreciatively at his surroundings, particularly at the remarkable mahogany-and-marble staircase that curved to the second floor.

The sight of the young woman descending the stairs made Tabor suddenly stop and stare. Clement stopped too and watched both his daughter and his guest with some amusement. Lilah's eyes were on faraway thoughts; Clement wondered what had her in such distraction that she didn't notice them below.

Tabor wondered if the stairs didn't go all the way up into the clouds. The woman in the white lace dress wore an angel's face. Her softly curled hair was pale red-gold, her skin fair and delicate. She moved with such grace she seemed to float down the white marble steps. She was almost to the bottom stair when she looked up in surprise and saw him. As if stunned, she stopped in mid-step and grabbed the rail. She saw her father almost at the same time.

"Papa? Who . . . ? What . . . ?" Lilah's free hand flew to her throat. Suddenly queasy, she stared back into the storm-gray eyes watching her so intently. Surely her eyes deceived her. The dark-haired man in the light gray suit and maroon silk vest couldn't be Tabor Stanton.

Clement, witnessing the rather dramatic exchange, suppressed a chuckle. He'd never seen Lilah flustered about anything, particularly not a man. Seeing she could be undone by a handsome face as any normal female gave him a curious sense of relief.

"Lilah," Clement said, smiling. "I'd like you to meet Mr. Stanton, a new friend. Maybe you can change his mind about staying for dinner." He looked at Tabor. "Mr. Stanton, this is my elder daughter, Lilah."

She wouldn't have to say a word about dinner, Tabor realized. He had changed his mind already. Lilah Damon had him captivated. She was easily the prettiest woman he'd ever seen, the kind who inspired a man to be humble and noble at the same time. He made a step toward the stairs, unmindful that he was staring. She made a good case for love at first sight.

Lilah looked helplessly at her father, panic deafening her to his words. It *was* Tabor Stanton. He had found her. She was about to be exposed. Her father was about to know everything—if he didn't already. All at once the stairs beneath her feet seemed to quake—or was it her legs losing strength? She gasped once as the blood drained from her face. Suddenly there wasn't enough air in the room and she felt as if she had plunged through a trapdoor into void black space.

"No," she mumbled, and for the second time in her life, Lilah Damon fainted.

Tabor saw her knees buckle and her eyelids quiver just before they closed. Only a step away, he rushed forward and caught her before she collapsed to the floor. With Lilah limp as a rag doll in his arms, he turned a bewildered face to Clement.

"Thank God you were here," Clement exclaimed as Tabor brought his daughter close. He hastily felt her cheeks and checked her pulse, determining from the clamminess of her skin and the erratic pace of her pulse that his daughter was in a dead faint. "Her room's at the top of the stairs," he told Tabor quickly. "Wan will show you. I'd appreciate it if you would take her up. Ching," he said, turning to the Chinese. "Get Emily and send for the doctor."

Tabor carried Lilah Damon to her room and placed her on the half-tester bed. He was there only a moment before an older woman arrived and shooed him out.

"Just a faint," she told him. "Tell Clement it's nothing serious."

Tabor relayed the message to the anxious man downstairs. Before leaving Damon House, he gave Clement the name of his hotel. Clement insisted he come to dinner the following night. Tabor accepted and hoped the hours passed quickly. Lilah Damon had felt as if she belonged in his arms.

7

Tabor wouldn't have thought anything could diminish his determination to find Delilah and the black stallion. Until he met Lilah Damon. He couldn't get her out of his mind. How ironic that he had met her when he was looking for the infamous Delilah, a woman who was Miss Damon's opposite in every regard.

All morning and afternoon as he rode from one livery stable to another asking if any had recently acquired a black stallion, he kept picturing Lilah Damon's angelic face. She had come to a little just before he put her on the bed, treating him to a glimpse of her vivid blue eyes. She had mumbled a word that sounded a little like his name, but he credited that to his imagination, just as he did the feeling that he already knew her.

He hoped her illness hadn't been serious and wouldn't keep her from joining them at dinner. Ladies like Miss Damon were inclined to have delicate natures, but when they were as beautiful as she was, it was easy to overlook.

Tabor headed his horse to the outskirts of town. At the last livery, he had learned of another stable, one of the few left he hadn't visited. He rode up to it, dismounted, and went inside, walking by the rows of stalls but not holding out much hope he would find his stallion. Nate, a black-skinned man who identified himself as the owner, asked his business. Tabor described the Admiral.

"Shucks no," the man said, putting his pitchfork aside. "Ain't been no horse like that here. You best keep lookin'. Tell you what, though, if I see him I'll send word."

Tabor left his name and hotel address. Disappointed again, he thanked Nate for his trouble and started back into town. He had a few hours before he was due at the Damons' and had his mind set on a bath and a barber-shop shave first. He hadn't traveled far when another rider galloped up, then slowed his horse to keep pace with Tabor's. Tabor didn't pay the man much attention. He was still thinking of Lilah Damon.

"You Stanton?" the fellow asked after a few minutes.

Tabor looked over at the other rider, a sandy-haired man only a few years older than himself. Unlikely as it seemed, he supposed Nate had remembered something and sent this man to tell him.

"I'm Stanton," he answered. "Tabor Stanton."

"You're Stan's son?"

"That's right." Tabor frowned and gave the rider a closer look. The fellow looked as if he'd just come in off a long ride. His clothes were dust-covered, his face and cheeks dark with several days' growth of whiskers.

Hell, he wouldn't be surprised if his father had left a passel of debts behind. His guess was he was about to be accosted by someone wanting payment for one of them.

"Glad you got out of jail," he said. "My name's

Chapman." He was more than glad. Having his face plastered on a few wanted posters, there was no way he could have approached young Stanton when he was behind bars. He was taking a risk on getting caught, just coming out of the hills. But if he got hold of that claim, he'd soon have enough money to bribe his way out of his troubles.

Next to a mention of his father, a mention of his jail stay was the quickest way to make Tabor mad. A cold, hard look settled on his face.

The man grinned, trying to melt Stanton's anger. He had hoped the young Stanton would be as spineless as his pa, but that didn't seem to be the case. "Been trackin' you a couple of weeks," he said pleasantly. "Your pa and me did some prospectin' together a while back. I heard he died and left what he had to you."

Chapman didn't add that it had been a blow from his shovel that had sent Stan plummeting into a gully, leaving him with a broken neck. Chapman cursed silently. He hadn't meant to kill him before he got what he wanted from him. Right after he hit Stan old Wilkins had come over the hill toting his shotgun, and Chapman had to light out or chance getting caught. Later he had searched Wilkins' cabin but failed to turn up the claim. Fearing Stan might have lingered long enough to tell Wilkins what happened, he'd laid low a few months before going back to the cabin.

Damn his luck! The lost time had been for nothing. Wilkins didn't even know Stan had been murdered. He had told about the envelopes and Stan's son for a bottle of cheap whiskey. Chapman shook his head but kept grinning. No need to rub young Stanton the wrong way if he could help it. Hell! If he had known what was in that ground he never would have sold out to Stan for a handful of nuggets.

Tabor glared at the stranger. "You heard wrong," he told Chapman. "My father died owning about as much as he had when he came into the world. What little he did have he apparently owed to somebody."

His answer didn't set well with Chapman. "That somebody was me," he said testily. "And the something was a claim. Your pa and me staked that spot together. We had an understanding that if one of us went, the other got the claim."

Tabor didn't want to get caught up in any more of his father's unfinished business. He didn't like the tone of Chapman's voice either.

"Well now, Chapman," he said flatly, "I reckon you're wrong. I didn't see your name on anything my father left behind." The claim he had given Clement Damon had been legally signed over and registered. Clement had shown him the seal.

"What the hell does that matter?" Chapman growled. "In the hills a man's word carries more weight than any paper. Your pa and me had an understanding. I expect you to abide by what your pa wanted."

Tabor pulled the roan he was riding to a halt. "Chapman," he said in a low voice, "whatever understanding you had or didn't have with my father died with him. I've got nothing to do with it. I suggest you put that horse of yours in a trot and ride on."

Chapman's hand edged toward his gun, but he changed his mind and slapped his thigh instead. He didn't know how good Stanton was, and besides, fighting face-to-face wasn't the way he favored.

"Hell, Stanton," he said, grinning again. "The claim's worthless. I just want to put me a shack up there because there's water on it. I'm not askin' you to give up anything."

"That's good," Tabor acknowledged, not returning Chapman's grin. "Because I'm not giving up anything."

Unperturbed, Chapman pressed on. "That place is mine by right. Why don't you just hand it over and save us both the trouble of goin' before a judge?"

Tabor's eyes narrowed. He hadn't been looking for a fight but he was getting just about ready for one. His voice dropped to a near-growl. "You're wasting your time, mister. I don't even have this claim you're so hot to get. My father used it to pay an old debt." He put his heels in the roan's sides. "Build your shack somewhere else and stay away from me."

Chapman's caution fled. He urged his horse on and caught up with Tabor. "You're lyin', Stanton," he snarled, and whipped out his revolver. Both men reined their horses to a sudden stop. "I been polite. Now I'm telling you: hand over that claim!"

Anger boiling inside him, Tabor met Chapman's eyes with a stone-cold stare. At the same instant, he eased his foot out of the stirrup and kicked out at Chapman's gun hand. The hard toe of his boot connected with Chapman's elbow. Tabor heard the joint pop. Yelping with pain, Chapman released his gun. While he grabbed his injured arm, Tabor grabbed his shirtfront and jerked him off his horse.

Seeing Chapman scramble in the dust for the dropped gun, Tabor swung out of the saddle and kicked the weapon into a thicket beside the road. Chapman leapt to his feet and charged. Tabor dodged a swinging fist, but still took a sturdy blow on the jaw. He rallied with a hard punch to Chapman's midsection and heard a groan. A second punch to Chapman's jaw rolled the man to his knees.

Cursing, Chapman shook his head to clear it. Thinking Chapman meant he had taken enough, Tabor stepped back. It was a mistake. Chapman yanked a knife from his boot and jumped up, mouthing another string of curses.

"Let's see how you like the taste of my blade, you thievin' bastard." Face contorted, he sliced the air in front of Tabor's belly. Tabor sprang back out of the way. Chapman lunged again, mising a second time. "You'll get tired of doin' them dance steps," Chapman growled. "Then I'll cut that claim out of you."

Chapman's third swipe hit Tabor's upper arm and drew blood. It was only a scratch, but enough to send Tabor into a reckless rage. Yelling and spinning around, he shot out a kick that pounded into Chapman's shoulder, a move he had learned from a Japanese warrior while in the Far East. The impact caught Chapman completely by surprise and toppled him to the ground. Before he could rise, Tabor stomped the hand that held the knife. Chapman quickly let it go.

"Get up, you beggar!" Tabor jerked Chapman to his feet and delivered two fast punches that quickly returned the man to the ground. This time Chapman made no effort to rise.

Tabor grabbed the knife and stabbed the blade into a tree trunk, breaking it off near the shank. He recovered the gun from the thicket and slid it beneath his gunbelt. With Chapman still lying groaning where he had fallen, Tabor unsaddled the man's horse and tossed the saddle down beside him.

"I'll leave your horse a mile or two down the road," Tabor said. "Make sure our paths don't cross again." With the toe of his boot he lifted Chapman's chin. "Agreed?"

Chapman nodded affirmatively, hatred for Tabor Stanton boiling in his blood.

Two hours later Tabor stepped into a steaming tub of water. Chapman's fist had left a small purple mark on his cheek. He didn't like the thought of going to dinner at the Damons' with bruises on his face, but there was nothing he could do about it. He consoled himself that Chapman would be sporting a couple of shiners for a while. The cut on his arm was worse than he had thought, but a tight bandage had stopped the bleeding, and the pain was about gone. At least that wound wouldn't show. He didn't think Lilah Damon would be impressed by a man who got in gun- and fistfights. For some reason he didn't try to explain to himself, he wanted to impress Miss Damon.

The barber across the street from his hotel gave him a shave and trimmed his thick black hair into what he assured Tabor was the latest in men's fashion. Dressed in the gray suit, maroon vest, a new shirt, and string tie, his boots freshly polished, Tabor rode out to Damon House.

"Lilah, are you certain you're well enough to be up?" Emily Dearborn, who knew quite well that a woman who had fainted should remain in bed for at least a day, found her niece's restless energy perturbing. Lilah had stayed in bed less than an hour after her swoon. During the night Emily had come in to check on Lilah and again found her niece up and pacing the floor in her nightdress.

"American women are hearty, Aunt Emily," Lilah responded to her aunt's objections. "I don't think I really fainted at all."

"Nonsense," Emily insisted. "You were white as sheep's wool and your skin like ice. You definitely had a case of the vapors."

Lilah shrugged. "Well, it's all over now. I do wish you would let me go downstairs. I want to see Papa. I'm sure he's been worried."

Emily smiled. "He was until the doctor assured him

you had no serious malady. Clement found it rather amusing that Mr. Stanton affected you so."

"That's ridiculous," Lilah sputtered, her cheeks warming with a quick rise of heat. "Mr. Stanton had nothing to do with it. Bess laced my corset too tight and the exertion of going down the stairs took my breath. It's that simple."

"If you say so, dear," Emily agreed.

Admittedly, Lilah was healthy as ever today, and much more animated than usual. But having seen Tabor Stanton herself, a spectacularly handsome man, tall and quite strong, Emily might have managed to faint in his arms had she been a young girl. The smile he had given her as she ushered him out of Lilah's bedroom had been enough to melt her heart and start her questioning her negative opinion of American men. If all of them were like Mr. Stanton, perhaps Lilah wasn't wrong to prefer this country.

"I *am* going down for dinner," Lilah said, turning and resting her hands on the cool marble top of a turtle-backed table near the window. She stared out at the treetops until she was sure the high color she didn't want Emily to notice had left her face.

"You do know your father has invited Mr. Stanton to dinner?"

Lilah nodded and delayed turning around. That worried her. But with almost a day to think about it, and from what she considered careful questioning of Ching and Dinah, she had concluded that only a twist of fate had brought Tabor Stanton to Damon House. She had immediately recognized him and assumed he knew her too. Fortunately she had been wrong. He had no idea the genteel Lilah Damon was in fact the woman who had left him unconscious and jailed in Yuba City. How could he?

Why her father was being friendly to one of the men

who had injured him was also perplexing. Still another troublesome thought hit her as she at last turned around. How had he gotten out of jail? That fool Walsh Peregrine had promised Delilah that Stanton woud spend the good part of a year behind bars.

She sighed resolutely. He was out and there was no help for it. She was quite certain he hadn't recognized her yesterday, but how long could she count on her luck to hold? She dreaded joining her father and Mr. Stanton for dinner. But she needed to know how long Tabor would be in San Francisco. And she needed to assure herself he actually did not realize who she was.

Her dread vanished as her lips curled into a smug smile. If he didn't know she and the nefarious Delilah were one and the same, she could make sure he never did. If necessary, she would instigate a plan to hasten his departure from the city. She would play the pampered-banker's-daughter role so cleverly Tabor would never guess who she was. After all, she was Lilah Damon, rich, soft-spoken, the perfect lady. Delilah, with her brazen, seductive ways, was only a disguise—one soon to be discarded forever.

Dinah fortunately had never seen Stanton and had never been told the names of the six men on Delilah's list. Given her addled state of mind lately, Lilah decided not to tell her tonight's dinner guest was one of those men. Loo was still away visiting friends in Chinatown. Lilah, however, had no doubt she could handle Mr. Stanton alone. Hadn't she done so once before?

Emily, alarmed by Lilah's evident distraction, came up to her niece and placed an arm around her waist. "You seem too stimulated, dear. Perhaps you should rest a little longer if you plan to be up all evening."

Lilah straightened her shoulders and brightened her face. She surprised her aunt by agreeing. "I will," she said softly. "Since we're having a guest, I definitely want to look and feel my best."

Emily left Lilah's room smiling to herself. She believed her niece had been affected by Mr. Stanton, even if she did deny it. In high spirits, Emily entered Dinah's sitting room. She had promised the younger girl to help her learn some new embroidery stitches. Emily was glad Dinah learned quickly and the lesson wouldn't take long. Lilah wasn't the only one who wanted to look her best for Mr. Stanton.

Dinah put away the square of white linen she had been working on and got out her practice sampler when Emily came in. "Is Lilah better?" she asked. Dinah had her straight red hair smoothed back and fashioned into a large bun on the back of her head. The severe style made her look all of eighteen, which was exactly what Dinah wanted.

"Your sister is fine," Emily told her, seating herself in a biscuit tufted chair and reaching for the sewing basket she had left beside it earlier. She took out cloth and needles and selected the silk threads she wanted. "Lilah isn't actually engaged to Barrett Fenton, is she?" Emily asked, deftly executing a French knot in her sampler.

"She's as good as," Dinah said, and followed with a squeal of pain as she pricked her finger making a stitch.

Emily, who missed having her chatty London friends at teatime, lowered her voice as she would delivering a tidbit of gossip to that group of ladies. "I wouldn't be surprised if the engagement never occurred."

Dinah lost interest in her stitching and dropped her sampler into her sewing basket without even anchoring the needle. The green of her eyes deepened. "Why do you think so?"

Emily looked up. "Yesterday when I was giving her smelling salts, she said Mr. Stanton's given name several times."

"Oh," Dinah remarked.

Emily nodded. "So I think Lilah is smitten with Mr. Stanton and doesn't realize it. Why, when I met Mr. Dearborn I had almost the same reaction. He was so dashing and handsome in his cavalry uniform, it absolutely took my breath and made me quite giddy, as I remember. I fell in love with him that very minute."

"Did he feel the same?" Dinah's eyes glowed brightly. Aunt Emily had planted the seed of a remarkable idea in her head.

"Not as dramatically." Emily smiled and gazed into the distance, remembering Giles Dearborn as he had looked that day. She had loved him deeply and known when he died she could never give her heart to another. With a sigh she went on. "Men don't. But he proposed only a few weeks later. So you see, my feelings were right from the first."

For a moment Dinah deliberated on what Emily had said. If Lilah did fall in love with this Tabor Stanton, it would solve all her problems. She tapped her chin with her forefinger. "You said you knew you loved Uncle Giles the moment you saw him. Has Lilah said she loves Mr. Stanton?"

"No, no, dear," Emily said indulgently. She didn't really expect someone as young as Dinah to understand these things. "Your sister is much too reserved. If she did have feelings for Mr. Stanton, she would deny them to herself and everyone else." Emily folded her stitching in her lap and smiled to herself. "I imagine I'm being fanciful. Mr. Stanton reminded me a little of Giles and put romantic notions in my head. Why, we don't know a thing about the man except that he's handsome. Here it's very difficult to know a man's background."

"Papa must like him," Dinah said encouragingly.

"Oh, Clement. What does he know about such things?" Emily sighed as she considered the enormity of the problem. "There's really no order at all in America. Mr. Stanton may very well be a . . . a cowpoke." The term was one she had heard bandied about by the men on the ship. Emily had no idea what a cowpoke was, but it sounded to her like a man of low station. She laughed lightly. "And here I am matching him with your sister."

Dinah laughed too as she retrieved her sampler from her sewing basket. "Show me the feather stitch again, Aunt Emily. I'm not satisfied with the way mine looks."

Lilah dressed for dinner with exceeding care, choosing tiny pearl ear studs, a simple gown of white lawn with only a touch of lace at the throat. She pinned Marie Damon's cameo just below the high collar and ordered Bess to style her hair simply. She wanted to look prim and innocent for Mr. Stanton. There must be nothing about her to remind him of Delilah.

"Bring me that bottle of lemon scent, Bess," she requested of the Irish maid, one of the few servants at Damon House who was not Chinese. Bess had been Lilah and Dinah's maid in London and had traveled to San Francisco with the sisters when they returned to their father.

"Why, Miss Damon," Bess responded in surprise. "You've always said you didn't like that perfume."

"Oh, I know, Bess." Lilah dabbed the scent behind her ears and on her wrists. "I'm simply in the mood for something different tonight."

"I declare you look almost like you did as a little

girl," Bess told her, stepping back and taking a good look.

Lilah laughed, pleased at Bess's assessment. It assured her she had successfully created the illusion she wanted. "Is Papa in the library?"

"Wan said he was just before I came in to do your hair." She made a circle around Lilah, looking carefully at her mistress's trim waist. "I haven't laced your corset too tight tonight, have I? I wouldn't have you fainting again."

"No, it's fine. I have bundles of room. And thank you, Bess, for taking such good care of me. You run along now. I'm going down early. I haven't seen Papa in a whole day."

Bess left and Lilah allowed a smug smile to steal onto her face. She believed she was actually going to enjoy tangling with Tabor Stanton again. He might have gotten away from Walsh Peregrine, but tonight she would learn enough about him to find a way to put him behind bars for good. Flushed with excitement, Lilah started for the stairs. Tabor Stanton wasn't due for another hour. She hoped to feel her father out on his interest in the man.

She found the library excessively warm. Clement sat in his chair before a small fire. Poor circulation in his legs often caused him to feel chilled, and when that occurred he ordered a fire on even the warmest of days. Ching, eyes closed, sat in a Louis XV chair in the corner. Lilah didn't delude herself the Chinese was actually asleep. She knew that somehow he watched through those closed lids as she tiptoed up behind her father and surprised him with a hug.

Clement spun his chair around to look at her. "I see my princess is well and fit again."

"I feel wonderful, Papa. I hope you didn't worry

about me." She gave him a series of kisses on the face.

"I certainly did," Clement responded as if offended. "You give me so little opportunity to worry, I indulge myself when the opportunity arises."

"Papa! You're impossible," Lilah cried in a girlish voice. "I think you would like it if I swooned and fretted and fussed constantly."

"I most certainly would not." Clement laughed freely. "I like my daughters just the way they are. Don't change one bit."

"I won't, Papa." Lilah pulled a chair close to her father's. "Tell me about Mr. Stanton," she said, hoping her voice sounded natural. "I like to know just a little about our dinner guests before they're at the table."

Clement winked at his daughter. "So you want to know all about Mr. Stanton, do you? He's attractice, unmarried . . ."

Lilah blushed, more out of exasperation than embarrassment. She already knew those things about Tabor Stanton. "You know that isn't what I mean."

"Do I?" Clement raised his brows.

"Have . . . have you known Mr. Stanton long?" Surely her father hadn't forgotten Tabor Stanton was one of the men responsible for crippling him. She couldn't understand why the man had even been allowed in the house.

Clement shook his head. He never spoke of the accident. Lilah had suffered nightmares about it for years afterwards, and he didn't want to reawaken the memory.

"I met Mr. Stanton for the first time yesterday." He made a conscious effort to keep his expression cheerful. "A long time ago I knew his father. Stan died a few months back and left a letter to be delivered to me—a sort of payment for an old debt. The young Mr. Stanton came here to deliver the letter and carry out one of his father's last requests."

Lilah fell back in her chair and gasped softly. Tabor Stanton was the *wrong* man. His father, dead even before her encounter with Tabor, was the guilty one. Her pulse fluttered wildly. How could she have made such a mistake? Dear heaven! How could she make up to Tabor Stanton what she had done?

"Lilah . . ." Clement's voice carried concern. "Are you feeling faint again? You've turned pale." He wheeled about, ready to call Ching to attend her.

Lilah caught his arm. "I'm all right, Papa," she said weakly. "It's too warm in here with the fire."

"Oh," Clement said, relieved. "Is that it? I'll have Ching put it out." He looked around at Ching and nodded. "Stanton's a likeable young man. Sounds like he really knows horses. If he does, I'm thinking about offering him a job. You know Gus is leaving next month and I'll be without a trainer." Seeing Lilah's face blanch even more, he stopped. "Lilah . . ."

She rose quickly. "I'm going out for some air, Papa. I'll see you at dinner." Trembling uncontrollably, she hurried out, aware both her father's and Ching's eyes followed her every step.

In the downstairs parlor Lilah rang for tea and paced from window to window until it arrived. With shaking fingers she took the cup the servant poured, finding some solace in sipping the warm, fragrant brew.

What a grand mess she had created. And all for nothing where Tabor Stanton was concerned. Her father was thinking of offering him a job. Her mind jumped from thought to thought. How could she allow that? Maybe he wouldn't take it. What if he did? She couldn't let that happen even if she had wronged him.

If he saw that stallion . . . Lilah shuddered as the ugly consequences reared their heads. She had to make sure Tabor didn't go near the stables.

By hell's fire! She gulped her tea. The stallion was Tabor's. But how could she possibly take back the horse she had presented her father? She couldn't. What she could do was make sure Tabor Stanton left Damon House tonight and never came back. Later she could find a way to pay him for the animal and to compensate him for the time spent in jail.

Her chaotic mind raced on. She only needed to get his address, and the money could be sent anonymously with a note explaining a mistake had been made. That should satisfy him. The thought calmed her a little. Now she only had to think of a way to make him leave. That was the solution. If she simply kept her head, she could straighten everything out.

Whatever the cost, she couldn't allow her father to find out how she got that horse or that she was Delilah. Since her return from the tour, her father's doctor had confided his concern that Clement's heart had weakened. He was not to become overly excited. She couldn't possibly let him learn the daughters he valued above everything else had danced and cavorted in saloons throughout California. Or that his elder one had entertained men in her hotel rooms. It would be too much for him. Lilah clamped her teeth and clenched her small fists. Somehow she *would* make sure Tabor Stanton's visit tonight was his last to Damon House.

Her eyes narrowed as she remembered the way Tabor had lured her to the bed that night in Yuba City, pretending to be asleep. She remembered how he had pressed his advances on her, covered her face and breasts with kisses, touched her in forbidden places. A warm and wicked shiver rippled through her flesh. She could almost feel his hands and lips touching her again. No. Lilah stiffened her spine. She refused to admit that she liked his touch or that her mounting excitement had anything to do with a desire to see him again.

Her only interest in Tabor was to get him away from the Damon family, permanently. She rubbed her hands together thoughtfully. She knew the perfect way. As attracted as he was to loose women like Delilah, he wouldn't know what to make of one who was virtuous and respectable and had her cap set on marriage.

Lilah's sly smile belonged on Delilah's face. Tabor Stanton would turn tail and run the minute he realized a woman had singled him out for matrimony. Her brows curved wickedly. Especially one who would lose her fortune by doing so. She would give him a strong dose of that bitter medicine tonight.

When the door chime sounded and Wan showed Tabor into the drawing room where Lilah waited with her father, Dinah, and Aunt Emily, she was quite ready for the next melee.

Dinah wore a deep-cut gown of bottle green, and dangling emerald earrings. Emily was dressed in blue taffeta set off by a sapphire-and-diamond brooch. In her high-necked, long-sleeved gown of pristine white lawn fashioned with a modest bustle, Lilah looked subdued beside them. If she could have managed to appear mousy without arousing suspicion, it would have suited her better. Subdued, however, would have to do.

Clement introduced the women properly, since all had met Tabor in awkward circumstances the first time around.

"This is Emily Dearborn, Lilah and Dinah's aunt from London," he said to Tabor. "My daughters lived in London with Emily for ten years. I must credit her with forming them into the lovely creatures they are."

Tabor smiled at the small-boned blond lady, whose mannerisms were typically English. She looked like a pleasant woman and he detected a keen mind behind her proper face.

He kissed Emily's hand. Lilah couldn't help fuming as she recalled he had once casually done the same to her.

"You must have been little more than a girl yourself ten years ago," Tabor said, releasing Emily's hand.

Emily blushed. "What wonderful flatterers you Americans are."

"And this," Clement went on, rolling closer to Dinah, who stood nearest him, "is my younger and sometimes quite impulsive daughter, Dinah."

Tabor smiled at Dinah Damon, a lovely green-eyed girl with hair a brighter, deeper color than her sister's. Clement seemed to treat her as if she were a child but she looked almost as old as Lilah.

"If you are referring to the interruption when we were in your library, I found it a charming distraction." Tabor nodded to Clement. "Miss Damon," he said, lifting Dinah's hand to his lips. "This time is also a pleasure."

"Are you French?" Dinah asked, her eyes glittering with interest. He was attractive, in some ways more than Barrett. How could Lilah help but be drawn to him?

"A little, perhaps, back along the line," Tabor answered, his eyes lingering on Dinah in the way of a man who knows how to enchant women. "Actually I'm second-generation American. I did live in Paris a year. I adopted some of the customs I most admired."

Lilah's brows flickered. Mr. Stanton was more worldly than she had realized. It really didn't matter, though. She knew his suave manners did not run deep. Underneath was an insolent boor. He did have a certain manly appeal some women might find attractive. Devoid of his tan and dressed in a tailored suit, he might be able to pass himself off as a gentleman. She, however, found his rugged looks offensive. Barrett, fair-skinned and slim, was by far the more attractive man.

Of course Barrett didn't cause her heart to lurch, or goose bumps to form on her skin. But why should he? she questioned as Tabor stepped closer. Barrett hadn't placed her entire family in jeopardy.

"I'm sure you remember Lilah," Clement said, eyes twinkling as he watched this second meeting between the two. He definitely thought he saw sparks flying between them. Lilah was embarrassed, he supposed, about having tumbled into a stranger's arms.

"Indeed I do," Tabor replied, taking Lilah's hand and pressing it between both his own, pleased to feel a slight tremble in it. "I'm happy to see you recovered." He squeezed her hand lightly, then quickly released it.

Lilah blushed, though she had sworn she would not. Why had he spared her a kiss on the hand? Did he find Dinah and even Aunt Emily more attractive? And why was she complaining? That was what she wanted, wasn't it? That Tabor not find her appealing.

"I'm glad you could come to dinner, Mr. Stanton," she heard herself saying. "I'd hoped for a chance to thank you properly for sparing me a bad fall."

Tabor's breath caught in his throat. Just being near Lilah Damon made him feel like a foolish schoolboy. Yesterday he had thought she looked like an angel. Tonight confirmed his impression. She was stunningly sweet, soft, and gentle. She wasn't the kind of woman who usually appealed to him. In days past, he had known his share of sporting women and had always been careful not to involve himself with anxious virgins or ladies who had their wedding veils ready.

He had better watch his step. Lilah Damon made him feel like breaking every rule he had ever set for himself. Those innocent eyes, that melodious voice, the shining red-gold hair—he felt as if he had known her a long, long time. Other warm feelings long lost inside him stirred to new life, some he had thought he would never feel again, those for family, children, a lifetime love.

8

"So you were a naval officer, Mr. Stanton." Emily Dearborn and Dinah kept the conversation clipping by asking Tabor so many questions Lilah began to wonder if both had forgotten their manners. With the added exchange between Tabor and her father, she learned an amazing amount about the man she had wronged.

"A lieutenant, ma'am," he said, offering Emily a special smile.

"With the Union," Clement supplied.

Tabor nodded. "My ship was part of the Atlantic Blockading Squadron until it was sunk. Later I was part of the American embassage in France for a year. When the war was over I'd had enough of the sea and politics. I resigned my commission."

"I presume you speak French," Emily said, her eyes resting admiringly on the dark-haired young man.

How unlikely, Lilah thought, remembering the difficulty she and Dinah had learning the language. Irritably she tapped her toe on the carpet beneath the table.

Tabor had both her aunt and her sister sitting up and taking notice. What could they possibly see in that cowboy that made them act like a pair of coquettes? Aunt Emily was actually flirting. Thank goodness Dinah hadn't gone to those lengths. As it was, Lilah's attempt to make Tabor feel uncomfortable at Damon House was being thwarted. But now Emily was about to embarrass him by making him admit to his lack of education?

"Yes, ma'am," Tabor answered, and gave Emily another melting smile. "My mother raised me alone. My father went his own way before I was half-grown. Mother kept me to the books. She was an educated woman and thought her son should be too. I suppose I was reading the classics when other boys my age were romping and hunting. Of course my uncle saw I got to those things too. Now I'd like the chance to thank my mother for her perseverance. I put up quite a fuss about having to learn French, but it did get me the assignment to Paris."

"So your mother is no longer living?" Emily asked.

He looked briefly sad. "She died a number of years ago. She was a fine lady. I miss her."

"Yes, I understand," Emily remarked, thinking of her late husband. "I'm sure your mother would be pleased at the man you've become."

"I like to think so," Tabor said gently.

Lilah gritted her teeth, tense with guilt and frustration. Clearly Tabor and his mother had been separated from his father many years. It sounded as if Stan Stanton had deserted his wife and child. If that were true, both Tabor and his mother had also been victimized. That made her offense against Tabor even worse. She prayed the talk wouldn't lead into an account of his father. If it did, Dinah might guess who he was. Nervously she searched her mind for a new topic.

Fortunately Dinah spared her the necessity of finding one. "The political life in France must have been terribly exciting," Dinah chimed in. "Don't you agree, Lilah? Please tell us some of your experiences, Mr. Stanton."

Tabor complied, giving Dinah an amusing account of a minor crash between the American and Spanish ambassadors' carriages.

Silently thanking Dinah, Lilah listened as she stared down at her plate and the dinner she had all but neglected. Tabor Stanton was full of surprises. Occasionally during the evening she too made a comment, but she was careful not to present herself as too clever or interesting. Mostly she bit her tongue as it became clearer and clearer that Tabor was no empty-headed cowpuncher. When she had met him as Delilah, she had assumed he'd been an ordinary sailor and had only the few dollars in his pocket. Now she knew he had been a commissioned naval officer, an embassy aide, and owned part of a cattle ranch near Monterey.

"How fascinating," Dinah said as Tabor finished his story.

Lilah sighed deeply, inadvertently drawing the unwanted attention of everyone at the table. She had to immediately smile to assure everyone she wasn't bored. How she wished she had given the detectives time to ferret out all this information about Tabor, instead of learning who and what he was too late. It was good to know Tabor wasn't in need of a job. But that wouldn't stop her father from offering him one. If Clement was impressed with a man's ability, he was unremitting.

Tabor, seated beside Lilah, heard her sigh, then responded to her smile. She wasn't a chatterbox like her younger sister and her aunt. She spoke only if she had something of significance to say. He liked that.

Nothing annoyed him more about a woman than constant talk about nothing.

To Lilah's delight, during dessert the conversation waned a little. She didn't think she could bear hearing Dinah remark "How fascinating," another time. After dinner Clement invited the party to his library and called for coffee for the ladies. A servant poured brandy from a decanter for the men. As Tabor drank, Lilah fought the memory of his brandy-laced kisses. She was quick to notice the ease between her father and Stanton. That worried her. She didn't want them building a lasting friendship. She decided she had better create a distraction.

Her chance came sooner than expected. Clement glanced at his watch. "Nine-thirty," he said. "I didn't realize the time. Ladies, I hope you'll excuse me. I promised to show Tabor my horses. I particularly want him to see Rogue, the new stallion."

Lilah's throat constricted. Her heart thundered. She had worried that her father would try to persuade Tabor to work for him. This was much worse. Once Tabor saw Rogue, disaster would fall. She gave a choked cry and half-rose to her feet, almost spilling her coffee.

"Papa, you can't!"

Clement looked at his daughter in amazement. "Why not?" he asked, wondering what had put a bee in her bonnet when she had been as quiet as a sleeping cat all night.

Lilah thought quickly. "Papa, it's night. It's dark."

Clement half-turned his chair around, swearing Lilah had taken leave of her senses, attributing the condition to his guest.

"It won't matter," he replied, handing his empty glass to Ching. "The moon is full and the stable is well-lit—as you know."

"But, Papa," Lilah pleaded, putting her cup aside and hurrying to his chair, "I had my heart set on showing Mr. Stanton the conservatory."

"The conservatory?" Clement stammered. "Lilah, Tabor is a horse breeder. He's not intersted in seeing flowers and ferns . . ." He trailed off as he noted a look pass between Tabor and Lilah. Slowly the old man exhaled a breath, his eyes moving purposefully from one to the other, then to Emily. "I guess maybe he is," he said softly.

With her arm hooked through his and her heart beating double-time, Lilah led Tabor to the conservatory. On Clement's orders, servants had hurried in and lighted a few lamps. Long wispy shadows lay on the floor and walls, deeper masses of dark shadows filling the corners. Most of the light in the glass-domed room spilled in from the moon and stars. The windows were flung open and a warm breeze floated through, rippling leaves and lifting perfume from the blossoms.

Lilah paused beside one of the ferns Clement had referred to. Next to it a bunch of violets grew in a clay pot. Lilah plucked one of the tiny blossoms.

"This is my favorite room," she said quietly, turning her wide blue eyes on Tabor. "I'm very fond of flowers. I often have tea here on winter mornings. It's quite nice, like being in a garden." She looked away shyly. "I do like flowers, especially roses, white roses. Do you like flowers, Mr. Stanton?"

"Tabor," he said, thinking her face the sweetest he had ever looked on. "Call me Tabor."

Lilah gave a demure smile. "And you may call me Lilah."

Tabor smiled back. She looked more delicate than a flower and more beautiful than any of the exotic blossoms in the conservatory. It was fitting she should prefer the white rose. She was just as lovely as one, her skin almost as fair. Surely if Lilah Damon were a flower, she would be a white rose, the purest, most fragrant, most desirable of all.

Faintly Lilah lifted her brows, reminding him he hadn't answered her question.

"Yes, I do like flowers," he said, feeling an odd tightness in his throat. "My Aunt Sarah has a rose garden beside the ranch house. When I was a boy she often had me weeding and watering. White roses are Sarah's favorite too."

Lilah didn't give a hoot which roses were his aunt's favorite. The fact was, nothing she had said since entering the conservatory was true. She didn't like white roses any better than red ones. She certainly didn't like being alone with Tabor Stanton, not knowing how dangerous he could be. Of course nothing like what had happened in that hotel room could ever happen again. She reminded herself how much she had drunk that night. Otherwise she was sure she would have been repulsed by his touch.

Lilah lowered her lids shyly. His hand rested on the wooden top of a fern stand. She touched it lightly, sending a current up his arm.

"I'd like to ask you a most personal question, Tabor." She pronounced his name slowly, taking time to emphasize the syllables. "You won't think I'm too forward, will you?"

His smile widened. She seemed to find it difficult to express herself. He supposed she hadn't had much experience around men. Her father was probably protective—certainly protective. What man with such a beautiful daughter wouldn't be? And Lilah with her gentle, soft-spoken ways gave a man the feeling she needed protecting.

"I'm sure you could never be forward, Lilah," he assured her. "You're too much a lady for that."

"Thank you, Tabor," she continued softly. "You do make me feel at ease. I usually don't around men." She blushed at the baldness of her lie. "You aren't" —pausing, she took a breath— "engaged or . . . or promised to anyone, are you?"

"Why, no. I'm not," he answered, stunned.

"I'm so happy to hear it," Lilah whispered, shutting her eyes as if in prayer. "Because the first minute I saw you I knew . . ." Twirling the violet stem in her fingers, she let her words dangle, hoping he would draw the conclusion that she had been enraptured by him. "Let me . . . go back to the beginning." Deliberately stumbling over her words, Lilah turned her back to him and timidly dropped her head.

Tabor gently caught her shoulders and turned her about. "Is something wrong, Lilah? You seem upset."

She tried to ignore the warmth where his hands rested. So far, he was reacting exactly as she had hoped. Now that she had him almost in her trap, she would ready her snare. Hesitantly she placed her palms on his chest.

"Oh, yes," she answered breathlessly. "Everything is wrong. You see, Papa insists I marry a man he has chosen for me." She closed her lids as if covering tears. "I know Papa seems kind and wonderful to you. But he can be dictatorial where Dinah and I are concerned."

"I'm not sure I understand what you're saying." Tabor's voice was husky. Having her so close, smelling the light scent of her perfume, quickly sent a wave of passion through him. He had to take a deep breath to ward it off.

"What I'm saying, Tabor"—she lifted her luminous blue eyes, pleading—"is that since I've met you I know it would be wrong to marry the man Papa has picked." Her voice fell to a strangled whisper. "I can't."

"Why not?" he asked, forgetting himself and drawing her improperly close, sliding his hands down her back to her waist.

"Don't you know?" she whispered, clutching at his silk vest. "I could never marry anyone else. I couldn't." She slyly stole a look at his face, then went on. "I couldn't. Even though Papa will disinherit me for disobeying him. Even though I would have to leave this house with only the dress on my back, I couldn't marry anyone else—not now that I've met you."

Lilah braced herself. Her flesh burned, her breathing quickened. She hadn't expected that being close to him would feel so pleasurable. Purposely she had taken nothing stronger than coffee tonight. But she wouldn't have to endure his nearness for long. She had said the words that would send him packing. He might allow a woman to throw herself at him, but he wouldn't want to cope with one who would be penniless and who expected marriage.

"Lilah," Tabor whispered hoarsely. "Beautiful Lilah." He plucked the violet she held from her fingers and tucked it into a reddish curl above her ear. "It hurts me to see you sad. What can I do?"

Lilah's half-closed lids flicked open. *What could he do?* Was he thick-headed? "I . . . I don't think you understand what I'm saying," she stammered, now geniunely distressed.

Tabor crossed his arms over her back, and though not conscious of it, pressed her closer against him. "I understand," he whispered, surprised at the emotion in his voice. "I just don't think *you've* taken time to think about what you're saying. We've only just met. I'm afraid you look at me and see only freedom from something you feel your father is imposing on you."

"No. That isn't it," Lilah insisted, feeling a measure of panic sift into her blood. "I . . . I have feelings for you. I do."

Tabor had to pull in another deep breath. She fit so beautifully against him. The style of her dress, flat in the front, bustled in the back, allowed him to feel the press of her thighs against his. The softness of her breasts nudging his chest was almost too much to endure. He had to give himself a strong reminder the woman he held was a lady, one who would be shocked if she felt how her nearness aroused him.

"Lilah, my sweet." The endearment came without thinking. "I hope what you're saying is true. I know I have feelings for you. But we'll have to give this time to grow, time for us to be sure. I wouldn't be much of a gentleman if I didn't give you time to be sure."

Lilah stiffened. What was he saying? He hadn't a particle of a gentleman in him. Not the Tabor Stanton she knew. This was going wrong, awfully wrong. Desperate, she wrapped her arms around his waist and laid her head against his chest.

"I don't want time. There isn't any time. We have to act tonight. We'll run away. I know a minister who will marry us—tonight."

God! She had his blood running hot. All along he had been afraid of this, that he had fallen in love with Lilah Damon the minute he laid eyes on her. To hear she felt the same was too good to be true. He had heard that love made a man a fool. He believed it. Here he was ready to forget everything that had ever mattered to him for a woman he had known only a day. Whispering her name, he brought his hands to her face, gently cupping it and forcing her to look up at him.

"Do you mean that, Lilah? Would you go away with me right now? Leave all of this forever? Would you?"

"Yes, yes," she whispered, terrified by what she saw in his eyes. "Papa would try to find us. He would want to have you killed."

Tabor nuzzled the soft red-blond curls at her temple. "I'm not afraid of your father, Lilah. Or of what he might try to do."

"You wouldn't care if I had no money?" Lilah trembled. His hands were gentle. She had the maddening wish that he would kiss her. What was wrong with her? She couldn't even think of backing away from him.

He must have read the thought. He kissed her temples, her eyelids, her cheeks, his mouth finally coming to rest at her ear. "I wouldn't care," he whispered, his breath fanning the tendrils around her face. "I wouldn't care about anything but loving you."

A tingling started in the pit of her stomach. At the moment, Lilah cared about nothing else either. Completely forgetting her purpose in initiating the charade, she lifted her face to Tabor, offering her softly parted lips. He took them with incredible gentleness, knowing the swift urgency he felt building inside would frighten the virginal Lilah Damon. He pledged to himself to treat her gently, now and on their wedding night. He had no doubt there would be one—if he ever hoped for another sane moment in his life.

Lilah had kept her passions about everything so contained all her life that once ignited they leapt into flames like a raging bonfire. It was she and not Tabor who deepened the kiss. Her body ached not only for his lips but also for the intimacy of his embrace. Moaning softly, she wrapped her arms around his neck. Soon his arms again formed a tight circle around her. Wanting to get closer, Lilah twisted within the circle, bringing herself firmly against his aroused manhood. Tabor groaned, realizing she had no idea that if she continued to move she would drive him beyond control.

"Lilah, don't," he whispered hoarsely. "Be still, please."

His words fell on ears deafened by passion. In another moment he was beyond pleading with her to stop. His hands slid to her hips and lifted all her weight against him. At the same time his tongue slid past her lips. She eagerly accepted it inside the softness of her mouth. Breaking that bond for a gasp of air, Lilah cried his name, realizing somehow within the fog of her desire that both of them had gone past all constraints.

When he let her down, her legs were jelly, and had he not supported her, she would have fallen hard to the brick-lined floor. He did not allow that. He did let her sink to her knees. With his mouth joined to hers, he did likewise, falling back on his heels and pulling Lilah against him. Not until his hands eased beneath her skirt, skimming to the bare flesh of her thighs, was Lilah aware she was no longer on her feet.

Pulling her mouth from his and throwing her head back, she sighed with pleasure as his fingers moved like hot sparks on her skin. The tight nubs of her nipples strained at the soft fabric of her bodice. Tabor rubbed his cheek against them and, urged on by her response, closed his mouth over one taut peak, gently sucking fabric and all. Lilah cried out in sweet agony.

From one of the garden windows a red-crowned head appeared above the sill. Dinah's view from behind Tabor's back showed her only the positioning of his mouth. That alone was enough to cause her chin to fall and bump the windowsill. She quickly ducked, but another red-crowned head appeared, this one belonging to a ginger cat who had no second thoughts about bounding through the open conservatory window. Seeing her mistress, the cat meowed loudly.

Tabor, faster to react than Lilah, quickly rolled her out of sight under a table. Finding herself suddenly beneath Tabor on the cool floor shocked Lilah back to awareness. Horrified that someone had come in and found her allowing him to take such liberties, she furiously pulled away. When she saw the intruder was only Lotus, her cat, her temper exploded.

"You beast," she cried as Tabor hurriedly got to his feet and pulled her up too.

"The cat?" he said, smiling.

"I mean you, Mr. Stanton." Ice hung on her words. "Taking advantage of a lady that way. I don't know how I could ever have been so misled." She glared at him, her hands covering the wet spot at her breast.

Surprise registered in his face. Not because of her words but because a recent memory he couldn't pin down spun through his mind. Lilah dropped her head and sniffed. Good God! She was crying. But what could he expect? She had every right to be devastated. She was a delicate lady who had led a sheltered life, not some chippie to be treated commonly. He grimaced at the thought of what he had done.

"Lilah, I'm sorry," he said, his voice full of entreaty. "I never meant to get so carried away. It's just that having you close . . . Lilah, I wouldn't have harmed you for anything. Believe me."

Lilah wiped her dry eyes. "Believe you," she hissed. "Well, I don't. You're nothing but a beast!"

Her slap stung his cheek. He knew he deserved it. He said nothing as she whirled and like a white blur ran from the room.

As soon as he composed himself, Tabor returned to the library. So overwrought with guilt he could hardly speak, he thanked Clement for his hospitality and said he would have to be on his way.

Good-naturedly Clement shook his head. "Looks

like I've missed out again on showing you my horses. You will come back for that, I hope."

"I don't know, Clement," he answered dully. "I may be leaving town tomorrow. Perhaps the next time I'm in San Francisco."

Clement's disappointment showed. He liked Tabor. He wasn't sure just why. He thought maybe the young man reminded him of himself in the days when he had been whole and strong.

"You're welcome here," Clement told him. "Come back anytime you can."

Hiding his sadness, Tabor said good-bye to Emily Dearborn. Dinah had already gone upstairs. He figured this was his last visit to Damon House. After tomorrow he doubted he would ever be welcome again. Somehow, though, on the way out, he couldn't pass the staircase without stopping and thinking of seeing Lilah there the day before. He shook his head. How could he have been so careless with something as precious as Lilah's affection?

Outside, he had a minute to wait while his horse was brought up from the stable.

"Mr. Stanton . . ."

Tabor spun around, surprised to see Dinah Damon hurrying down the ramp. He forced a smile, certain she had come out only to bid him good-bye.

"Lilah asked me to give you this," she said, slipping a folded paper into his hand. Without waiting for a response, Dinah turned and hurried back into the house.

Almost afraid to look, Tabor opened the note and read the flowery handwriting.

Tabor,
    Please join me for a picnic lunch tomorrow noon. I'll expect you then.

                                        Fondly,
                                        Lilah

"I'll be damned," he mumbled to himself, breaking out in a grin that lasted for another hour. He would never understand women. Now he knew exactly how a man destined for the gallows felt being reprieved at the last hour. The note meant Lilah had forgiven him.

Whistling and allowing the horse to plod along at a slow pace, Tabor made a promise not to give Lilah reason to regret offering the second chance. Tomorrow and in the times that followed, he would be the perfect gentleman. He wanted her trust and knew that even though her body had answered every demand of his, that too must seem a betrayal to her. Undoubtedly he was the first man ever to make her aware of her passions. The way he had gone about it had frightened her.

With Lotus in her lap, Lilah rested on the velvet-tufted chaise longue in her sitting room. An empty saucer rested on the floor beside the chair. Lotus deserved the treat of cream. Lilah shuddered to think what might have occurred if the cat hadn't made a surprise visit to the conservatory. Tabor Stanton would have been her undoing. She believed he exerted some dark charm over her, because truly, this time she couldn't blame strong drink for her foolishness. Thinking it over, though, she decided her weakness last night was entirely due to the guilt she felt for having mistaken him for his father.

She no longer felt that way. Besides, what choice was there but to be a little devious about ensuring he never came to Damon House again? Certainly she had no reason to regret striking him afterward. He definitely had enjoyed himself beforehand. Diffidently Lilah wrung her hands. How had they wound up on the floor? She couldn't remember. But how clearly she remembered the delicious feel of his hands and his mouth. What a warm, heavy feeling just the memory brought her. Lilah shuddered in alarm. How was it he turned her into a wanton woman? Thank goodness she would never see the man again.

Lilah whispered a word of thanks to Lotus. The episode had been almost as costly as before. Tabor Stanton was a worthy opponent. Unlike others of her experience, he had a bent for doing the unexpected. At least he hadn't been dull. In a week or so she would arrange a substantial payment sent to him at his ranch and then the whole Stanton matter could be put to rest. She could then complete her plans for the destruction of the Penn brothers, the last two men on Delilah's list.

Smiling complacently, Lilah stroked Lotus' silky fur. Last night she had been too agitated to sleep, but now she felt herself drifting off. She had managed to appear calm when she had gone down in her nightdress and wrapper to say good night to Papa. But it had required all her dramatic skills. It was all very strange the way she had reacted to Tabor, considering the way she really felt about him. Very strange. Sometimes she felt there were two women living inside her, two women at odds with each other.

Lilah's hand stilled on Lotus' back. Her soft breathing rose and fell in harmony with the cat's purr. An annoying succession of taps at the door aroused her.

"Lilah!" Dinah's mirthful voice called her name.

"Come in," Lilah responded sleepily. Dinah entered carrying a wicker picnic basket covered with a blue gingham cloth.

"What's that?" Lilah asked, swinging her feet to the floor and disturbing Lotus in the process. The cat jumped from her lap and quietly curled up beneath a window.

"Your picnic lunch." Dinah's joyous smile confounded Lilah, but she much preferred it to all the frowns over the last few weeks. "Yours and Mr. Stanton's." Dinah traipsed across the room. "He's here early. He came in a buckboard, so you won't need to call for ours."

Lilah jumped to her feet. "Dinah! What is this ridiculous prattling about Mr. Stanton? If this is a joke, I warn you I'm not in the mood."

"It's no joke," Dinah said. "Papa is at the bank today. Mr. Stanton's waiting in the parlor. Do you want me to tell him you've changed your mind?"

"Changed my mind about what?" Lilah snapped.

"About inviting him on a picnic."

"I did *not* invite him on a picnic."

"No," Dinah said. "I did in your behalf."

Lilah's mouth fell open. "Dinah! How could you? I detest the man!"

Dinah giggled. "You didn't look as if you detested him last night in the conservatory." Her green eyes got enormously wide. "Really, Lilah, if Papa had any idea . . ."

Lilah's face blanched. "You had no right to spy on me."

"Oh, don't be silly, Lilah. I was chasing Lotus and I happened to pass by the window. How was I to know . . .? Anyway, when I overheard him telling Papa he might be leaving San Francisco tomorrow I knew you would be disappointed. So I wrote a note inviting him on a picnic and signed your name." Dinah's lower lip poked out. "I thought you would be pleased, but I see I was wrong. I'll tell Mr. Stanton you don't want to see him."

"No." Lilah felt her heart sinking like a capsized boat. Was there no way to be rid of the man? "I'll take care of this myself," she said crossly.

Dinah's smile burst out again. "I'll take the basket down," she said, grabbing it and hurrying from the room before Lilah had a change of heart.

Thankfully she had dressed simply in a dark blue skirt and a white silk blouse with satin collar and cuffs. She had no time to waste changing clothes, not if she hoped to get Tabor out of the house before Papa was back. She couldn't risk Papa once again urging Tabor to take a look at his horses.

Arriving in the downstairs parlor, Lilah learned that Dinah had given Tabor the picnic basket and that he had taken it out to the buckboard. If she thought Dinah had any inkling of the setback she had caused, well, she would pull out all her younger sister's hair—at the least. But of course Dinah had only tried to be helpful. She was just young and foolish enough to think her surprise was romantic.

Lilah did wonder how Dinah managed so easily to overlook the fact that she and Barrett were practically engaged. Regardless of her good intentions, Dinah was due a good talking-to when she got back.

Lilah's mind, ever quick with a solution to a dilemma, had concluded the best thing to do would be to pretend she was going on the picnic. Once she got Tabor away from the house, she would tell him everything had been a mistake.

She hadn't decided just how to say it, so she sat quietly as Tabor climbed into the buckboard and drove off. He didn't look as if he'd had a sleepless night. His eyes had no circles. He was fresh-shaven, his black hair neatly combed. She recognized the leather vest as the one he'd been wearing on their first meeting. The blue shirt was different, though, and looked quite appropriate with the black string tie.

Tabor pushed back the black hat with the silver medallion pinned on the band. "I'm happy you wanted

to see me again." He gave what she assumed was
supposed to be a contrite smile. "I want you to know
I'm very sorry about upsetting you."

"I'd rather not talk about it," Lilah said coolly.

Tabor slowed the horse and turned to look at her,
his eyes insistent. Lilah felt a dangerous tingle start
inside.

"I understand," he said softly. "You're embarrassed,
naturally." His hand closed gently over hers. "Just let
me apologize and I won't remind you of it again."

A shiver crept down her backbone. Lilah felt herself
weakening. Riding out alone with him in the buckboard hadn't been a good idea. How could he do this
to her? She didn't even like him. Did she? Even if she
did, she had to send him away. Even if she managed
to keep him from seeing the stallion, his stallion, in
time something she said or did would remind him of
Delilah. He'd put the pieces together and know who
she was. The thought of Papa finding out was incen-
tive enough to restore her resolve.

Tabor pulled the horse to a stop beneath the shade
of a tree. He helped Lilah down and spread the gingham cloth on the ground. She looked nervous and
troubled. He felt worse than ever. It must have taken
a lot of courage for her to invite him on a picnic today.

Lilah unpacked the food—cold chicken, cheese, corn
cooked on the cob, apple pie, and root beer. Dinah
had outdone herself on the menu. Lilah insisted Tabor
eat, although she could only pick at her food. When
he was finished and leaning against the trunk of the
tree, it was all she could do to forget how much she
wanted him to kiss her again.

"Tabor," she said, dropping her gaze from his, "I
realize what happened last night wasn't altogether your
fault." Where had that come from? she wondered.
What had happened to her ease at lying? "I was upset

with Papa and his demands. I threw myself at you for the reasons you said. I'm the one who has to apologize. Papa only wants what is best for me. As his daughter, I realize I must concede to his wisdom. I . . . I realize too I only aimed my attention at you as an act of defiance."

"Lilah . . ." He didn't like what she was saying. Somehow he couldn't believe she was giving up so easily on capturing what they had both felt last night. She might have been frightened by the feelings he awakened in her, but he couldn't believe she could actually deny them. His gray eyes darkened like storm clouds.

"Please," she interrupted. "Let me finish while I can. This isn't easy for me. Given what happened, what I allowed to happen, I would appreciate it if after you take me home, you go away—for good."

Tabor's brow wrinkled. Inside his chest, his heart thudded to a halt. He had lost her. "I don't believe you want that."

She didn't believe it either. Her mind did, perhaps, but her body, as it was subject to do around Tabor Stanton, longed for the crush of his arms, the demand of his lips, and the unknown magic that came afterward. She was learning she didn't know Lilah Damon so well after all.

She forced herself to say the next words. "I do mean it, Tabor. Please take me home and drive away. Please spare me any more pain. I beg you."

Grim-faced, Tabor restrained himself from trying to change her mind. Plainly she had agonized considerably over just seeing him again today. Maybe with time and distance she could learn to think kindly of him once more. That was all he could hope for. He cursed himself. He knew how to treat a lady.

How the hell had he let himself forget Lilah Damon was one?

Half an hour later he watched her walk into Damon House, afraid he was seeing her for the last time.

9

The closing of the front door shut him out of Lilah's life. With a slow shake of his head Tabor took a last look at the rose-colored brick set against the deep blue sky. He should have left for good last night. Coming back and seeing Lilah today only deepened the hurt. He hardly felt the blaze of the sun on his back as he climbed into the buckboard, cursing his luck. Lately it was all bad.

Tabor snapped the reins, urging the horse into a trot. His sense of loss weighed heavily on both heart and mind. Before checking out of his hotel he would arrange to have a gift sent to Lilah. Perhaps a delicate porcelain figurine, something to mirror her exquisite beauty. Maybe she would even keep it. Maybe it would leave her with a somewhat better memory of him.

He couldn't think of a good reason to stay in San Francisco. Delilah's trail had disappeared and he really didn't have the same desire for revenge he'd had in the beginning.

He did still want to recover the Admiral, but he was

having no success at that either. He decided his next best move would be to advertise a description of the stallion in newspapers over the state and to offer a reward for information. As much as he hated to admit it, the time had come for him to swallow his pride and head home to the Cooke ranch. Without even a lead, he couldn't justify staying away any longer. Even though Sarah was perfectly capable of operating the ranch without him, she deserved some help.

Intent on his worries, Tabor didn't notice Clement Damon's carriage heading toward him on the lane. Not until Clement's driver shouted did he look up and realize he was being hailed to stop. He tightened the reins.

"Ho! Tabor," Clement called.

Tabor, not feeling at all sociable, merely nodded.

Clement was not put off. "Glad I caught you," he said, smiling. "This time I won't take no for an answer." He beckoned Tabor to climb down and join him in the carriage. "Leave the buckboard," he added. "I'll send one of my men back for it."

Tabor gave him a puzzled look.

"Come on, get in," Clement urged. "I insist you take a look at my stable. I've been waiting weeks to show off my new stallion."

Tabor shook his head. Being cordial, especially to Lilah's father, was the last thing he felt like doing. Fortunately he had a legitimate excuse for saying no.

"I'm sorry, Clement." He shrugged his broad shoulders. "I promised to have this buckboard back an hour from now. It's rented to someone else for the rest of the day."

Persistence was one of Clement Damon's strongest traits. He wanted Tabor to see his horses and refused to allow such a minor obligation to deter him from having his way.

"Don't concern youself about that." Clement waved dismissively. "My man will drive it back. I'll lend you a saddle horse, then you can stay as long as you like." Tabor opened his mouth to offer another excuse, but Clement wouldn't even hear it. He raised his silver brows. "You're not going to disappoint me again, are you?"

Seeing it meant so much to Clement, Tabor reluctantly agreed to see the horses. Clement had been inordinately hospitable, particularly after leaving the impression he had never been an especially good friend of Tabor's father. Resolving he wouldn't stay long, and offering himself the assurance that Lilah wouldn't even know of his visit, he jumped from the buckboard. Having made up his mind, he quickly led the horse off the road and tied the reins to a bush. A couple of minutes later he joined Clement in the carriage, which proceeded up the lane to the Damon stables.

"Most people think me foolish to take so much interest in horses when I haven't been able to ride in years. But as a man who shares that interest, I'm sure you can understand how horses get in your blood. I'm thinking of starting an annual race and putting up the fastest horse in my stable. This new stallion looks good." Tabor nodded. Encouraged, Clement went on, "I like watching my horses run and I like seeing the foals every spring." He smiled happily. "You're going to like Rogue. He was a gift from Lilah."

"Lilah." Tabor's interest perked up. He didn't hear Clement's quiet laugh at his reaction. Somehow he couldn't picture Lilah picking out a horse for her father. He wasn't even sure she rode. Many ladies didn't. He concluded she had arranged for someone knowledgeable about horses to choose the animal.

"I'll save Rogue for last," Clement said once Ching and the driver had helped him from the carriage and into his chair. He gave orders for a man to drive the buckboard back to the livery, then wheeled around and started into the stable, Tabor following.

The brick building with a hayloft overhead had stalls for forty horses, a tack room for harnesses and one for saddles, and carriage wells attached at the sides. Two grooms had quarters in overhead apartments. Half the stalls were filled. The others were used to contain the animals of guests or visitors at Damon House.

Going from stall to stall, with Clement giving Tabor a history on each of the mares and the foals she had produced, took more than an hour. Four matched bays, geldings, especially stood out to Tabor. Clement was particularly proud of the team of carriage horses and called each by name, getting an answering whinny from them all. The last two animals in the barn were a pair of saddle horses. One, a sorrel with a blaze face, belonged to Dinah. The other, a gentle white mare named Darling, belonged to Lilah.

So she did ride. And what a pretty sight she would be on the dainty mare. Nevertheless, mention of Lilah made him restless. After all, he had promised her he would leave.

Remembering he ought to be courteous, Tabor glanced at his host. "I don't think I've ever seen so many good bloodlines in one man's stable. You've got a right to be proud."

"Thanks." Clement smiled broadly.

Tabor stroked Darling's muzzle. She was a friendly little thing, with fine legs and long silky mane and tail. The vision of Lilah riding the mare came back. He breathed out a heavy sigh. He really ought not to be at the stable.

"Clement," he said, making his voice sound cheerful, "you had better show me the stallion you've been keeping hidden. I've got to be leaving soon."

"He's in the paddock out back." Clement, smile deepening, speeded up his chair. "Rogue kicks up too much fuss in the barn." He looked over his shoulder and winked. "Got an eye for the ladies. Guess all males do."

Tabor followed, not able to manage even a polite laugh. Clement's horses were worth seeing. He wished he had just half of them as breeding stock for the Cooke ranch. But that notwithstanding, he liked to think he was a man of his word. He had told Lilah he would leave. He should have refused the invitation and taken the buckboard on into town.

The stable's back doors were shut. Tabor helped Ching and the groom roll them open. Outside in the paddock, the big stallion, getting a sudden whiff of the mares he was anxious to court, threw back his head and neighed.

"Well, by damn!" Tabor said when his eyes adjusted to the bright sunlight and he saw the powerful black horse circling the enclosure.

"I could sit here and watch him strut all day. Ever see a more beautiful sight?" Clement asked, rolling up beside Tabor.

Tabor removed his hat and ran his fingers through his hair. He didn't know whether to curse or laugh.

"No, sir," he answered in all honesty. "Can't say that I have." He meant what he said in more than the literal sense. That black stallion Clement called Rogue was a sight he had given up on seeing for a long time, maybe ever. He replaced his hat and pressed his lips tightly together. A suspicion he couldn't yet give credibility nagged at him. "You did say the stallion was a gift from Lilah?"

"She likes surprising me," Clement offered, drawing a lot of satisfaction from Tabor's evident admiration of Rogue. "She outdid herself this time."

"She sure did," Tabor agreed, his voice grinding low. "Did she tell you how she happened to find this particular horse?"

"Not how, but where," Clement answered. "She and Dinah and their companion made a trip to St. Louis. She bought the horse there and had him shipped home by train."

"Recently?" Tabor didn't like what was starting to take shape in his mind.

"I've had him six weeks or so," Clement said offhandedly. "Trouble is, I haven't had much luck finding a man who can ride him."

Tabor's mind was still on Lilah and the trip to St. Louis. "You mentioned a companion," he said, recalling something he had heard in Sacramento. "Was that an Oriental woman?"

"Loo Wong," Clement answered. "She's half-Chinese. Loo lives with us part of the time. Actually she's more than the girls' companion. Lilah and Dinah think of her as another sister." He noted the puzzlement on Tabor's face. "Loo's been away lately or you would have met her. You must have heard Lilah mention her."

"I might have," Tabor responded, knowing quite well Lilah had never mentioned Loo Wong. He stared alternately at Clement and at the stallion. Until he knew more about how Lilah had bought Rogue, he guessed he had best keep quiet that the stallion actually belonged to him.

The Admiral hadn't gotten wind of him yet. If he had he would have come thundering up expecting to have his head scratched. Tabor tried telling himself finding the Admiral in Clement's stable was coincidence. But his mind kept repeating two names. Lilah and Delilah. So similar. He shook his head. And so. different. What he was thinking just couldn't be. But Clement's words kept reminding him Lilah had been away in St. Louis while Delilah made her tour. And then there was the little detail of the Alden sisters being accompanied by an Oriental maid.

Was he looking for three women or one? His mind insisted on tying them together. Was it possible? He didn't see how. The physical descriptions didn't fit. Delilah had flaming red hair, Lilah's was pale red-gold, and both the Alden sisters had been described as having humdrum brown hair. Wigs? Possibly. But Delilah hadn't worn a wig. That he knew for a fact. He still remembered lacing his fingers in that sweet-smelling flame-colored hair. Lilah's hair was her own too. So how could they all be the same woman?

It was possible the Admiral had been taken to St. Louis and Lilah had found and bought him there. There had been time. But he couldn't discount his sudden and deep attraction to Lilah Damon. Had that happened because she was a woman he already knew quite well? He thought of how she had responded to him in the conservatory. That wasn't the way of a shy, high-bred lady. There had been no timidity, either, in how she kissed him. But did Lilah's soft lips also belong to Delilah? He had to know.

Tabor turned an inscrutable expression on Clement. "You did say you're having trouble finding anyone who can ride . . . Rogue?"

Clement's shoulders sagged slightly. Too much excitement tended to tire him quickly. The trip into town and the tour of the stables had him exhausted. Ching quickly noted his listlessness and took over propelling the chair.

"That's what I said," Clement answered as Ching pushed him back through the stable. "I've had four men try. He threw them all, and none of them would get on him again."

Tabor quirked a brow and voiced a thought he'd been tossing around in his head. "I think I could break him for you."

Clement's face lit up. He signaled Ching to stop. "I'd be happy for you to try. He hasn't got much value as a stud if I can't show he's been broken."

Tabor's eyes darkened like the sky before a storm. He smiled. "I won't make any guarantees. But I've got a notion that big black horse will take to me."

"I hope you're right," Clement said, frowning. "He's too fine an animal not to be trained."

Tabor nodded. "Just make me a promise, Clement." He laughed. "So I don't make a fool of myself, let me give it a try before you tell anybody I'm undertaking breaking this horse."

"You've got a deal," Clement agreed.

Tabor rode off on the borrowed horse. His head felt as if a floodgate had been opened inside it. He recalled the mystery concerning Delilah's astonishing disappearance at the end of her tours, the speculation that she was a titled Englishwoman who immediately left California and resumed her dual life on another continent. Just maybe everyone was wrong and Delilah didn't leave the country or even the state. Just maybe the answer to how she managed a vanishing act was right here in San Francisco—at Damon House.

All Tabor knew for certain was that he'd located his horse and that the burning desire to find Delilah was back as strong as it had been when he'd found himself jailed in Yuba City. Half of him hoped Lilah was as innocent as she seemed. But if that red-haired witch, Delilah, had changed from scarlet to lily-white he was going to have one hell of a fine time showing her true colors.

At a most undignified speed Lilah raced up the stairs to her room. She needed complete privacy for a few minutes, long enough to laugh and think about what a fool she had just made of Tabor Stanton. She flew to the window in time to see the rented buck-board rolling away from Damon House. It hadn't been the easiest thing she had ever done—there had been the unwelcome longing he made her feel. But that would pass, and the cocky Mr. Stanton was out of her life for good.

Lilah closed the lace curtains at her window and called for Bess to prepare a bath. She felt like a good long soak. A relaxing bath would be a good idea before she had that talk with Dinah. Barrett would be coming for dinner. Thankfully she had been able to rid herself of Tabor before adding the inconvenience of a jealous fiancé.

Afterward, clad in a golden silk dressing gown, with her hair loose on her shoulders to dry, Lilah went to Dinah's room. Aunt Emily was napping, so it was a good time to talk to Dinah alone. She found her sister making charcoal sketches.

"I see you're already dressed for dinner," Lilah remarked, noting Dinah's new gown of mist-green satin. The gown's bodice had a scoop neck and cap sleeves, and down the front, tiny tucks stitched with seed pearls. Dinah looked lovely, Lilah thought with sisterly pride. She did wonder when Dinah's behavior would mature to catch up to her appearance.

"I was modeling this dress for Aunt Emily and decided not to change," Dinah said, hastily closing her drawing pad and putting it away before Lilah saw all

the sketches were of Barrett. Lilah's blue eyes sparkled but Dinah couldn't tell whether happiness or
annoyance lighted them. She hoped it wasn't the lat-
ter. She wasn't in a frame of mind for another of her
sister's holier-than-thou lectures. Unquestionably she
had taken a sizable risk in arranging the picnic with
Mr. Stanton. Behind her back Dinah crossed her fingers and wished for the best.

"Did you invite Mr. Stanton to dinner again?" she
asked hopefully.

"Certainly not," Lilah answered coolly, dashing Dinah's hopes. "Mr. Stanton is returning to his ranch. I
doubt we'll ever see him again."

"Oh." Dinah's face fell into a pout. "I was hoping
he would be around a long time."

A flush of pink sped into Lilah's cheeks as she
erroneously guessed the reason for Dinah's unortho-
dox conduct. The thought repelled her. Imagine. Dinah romanticizing about Tabor Stanton.

"Well, he won't, and it's good riddance." Lilah
spoke a little more harshly than she intended. "Unrefined men like Mr. Stanton are out of place in our
society, Dinah. I'm sure he realizes that."

"He seemed nice to me," Dinah returned, unable to
keep her disappointment from showing. "Aunt Emily
didn't find him unrefined. And he is handsome."

"Only superficially so." Now Lilah lapsed into the
maternal tone she used when she felt Dinah needed
the benefit of her wisdom. "He's the kind of man
whose attractiveness would wear thin if you knew him
any length of time."

Dinah looked defiantly at her sister. Lilah's tone of
voice was enough to make her scowl. "Then why did
you invite him for a moonlight walk in the conservatory?"

Lilah bit her lip and grasped for an excuse. "Because . . . because I knew Papa needed to rest instead

of going to the stables. You know he doesn't sleep well if he becomes too stimulated late at night."

Dinah huffed out a breath. Lilah used Papa's infirmity as an excuse for everything. "That doesn't explain why you and Mr. Stanton were—"

"Dinah! Honestly! You misinterpret everything. I can't imagine what you think you saw."

Dinah got out of her chair and sashayed across the floor. She wore an impish smile. "I saw you and Mr. Stanton on the floor, and he had his mouth on your—"

"Dinah!" Lilah pulled herself ramrod straight. Nevertheless, more color stained her cheeks. "There was water on the brick path. What you saw was Mr. Stanton helping me up after I slipped. Really, your imagination is incredible."

Dinah frowned. "It didn't look that way from the window."

"I don't care how it looked from the window," Lilah said tartly. Was there to be any end to the complications Tabor Stanton added to her life? Before meeting him, she could keep the two sides of it separate. Now it seemed her entire life was becoming a lie. But what else could she tell Dinah? She continued with the same tartness, "And in the future, if you find yourself attracted to a man, don't use *me* to ensure you'll see him again."

"What?"

Lilah forcefully calmed her voice. "I am referring to your dim-witted scheme. I suppose you thought I would invite you along on that picnic you arranged. Or did you think I would refuse to go and you could accompany Mr. Stanton?"

Dinah, who usually didn't try to control her temper the way her sister did, bit back her anger and sat silently for a few minutes. Who did Lilah think she

was, always correcting and giving orders? She didn't
believe any of that story about slipping on the bricks
in the conservatory. Something had been going on and
Lilah certainly had looked as if she were enjoying it.
Whom was she fooling, pretending she didn't like Mr.
Stanton? She was probably angry at him because he
was leaving and she couldn't change his mind.

Lilah didn't love Barrett. Not that Dinah doubted
her sister was fond of him. She had decided to marry
her father's assistant with the same calculating shrewd-
ness she used to plan her revenge on their father's
attackers. Marrying Barrett was convenient for the
Damon enterprises, for Papa. That was all that concerned Lilah.

Dinah was certain Barrett didn't really love Lilah
either. Maybe he thought he did. He was almost as
adamant about pleasing Papa as Lilah was. The only
time he talked about anything but business was when
he sat on the tête-à-tête in the parlor with her. Dinah
liked the way Barrett's brown eyes glowed at those
times.

Of course, she couldn't forget that by marrying Lilah
Barrett would gain access to the Damon fortune. That
had to be quite an attraction in itself. Dinah's expression turned smug. She supposed he deserved that.
Having a wife as bossy as Lilah would demand some
compensation.

Still, if Barrett knew about what had happened in
the conservatory, he might change his mind about
marrying Lilah. She had half a mind to tell him. But
she wouldn't. Barrett ought to find out a thing like
that by himself. She would let matters stand as they
were. If Lilah thought *she* was attracted to Mr. Stanton and that was the reason for planning the picnic, let
her.

Having reasoned it all out, Dinah, every bit the

actress Lilah was, dropped her eyes and assumed a repentant look. "I'm sorry, Lilah," she said softly. "I didn't mean any harm. I thought it would be fun."

Seeing Dinah's sorrowful face, Lilah immediately regretted her harsh words. She lifted Dinah's chin, then hugged her. "I know, Sissy. I'm not angry at you. It's just that Tabor Stanton is much too old and wordly for someone your age. Besides, I'm sure saloon girls are more to his taste."

Dinah sighed and refrained from reminding Lilah not to call her Sissy. "I suppose so."

Lilah reproached herself. She really had been neglecting her responsibilities concerning her sister. Dinah was old enough to be thinking of having a beau. Lilah offered a suggestion. "Why don't we invite that Holmes boy to Aunt Emily's party? He's always been rather sweet on you."

Dinah suppressed a groan. "Yes, I think we should," she said, willing to agree to anything that would pacify Lilah. Of course, Dave Holmes was only nineteen and inordinately silly. He was gawky and hardly had more than peach fuzz on his face. Hadn't Lilah any idea her sister was much too grown-up to be interested in a boy like Dave Holmes?

"I'll see that the invitation goes out today," Lilah assured her. "Oh, dear," she said, noticing the hour on the French clock on the mantel. "Barrett was to come an hour early so we could talk before he sees Papa." She frowned, realizing she couldn't possibly meet him on time. "I still have to get Bess to dress my hair. I won't be ready."

Dinah smiled consolingly. "Don't worry. I'll sit with Barrett until you come down."

"Will you?" Lilah smiled too. "Then I won't hurry. I have a new style in mind, and it may take Bess a while to get it right."

Satisfied everything was as it should be between Dinah and herself, Lilah returned to her room and called her maid. As she had anticipated, the new hairstyle took some time. When she arrived in the downstairs parlor, Barrett had already gone into Clement's study and Dinah had returned to her room. Lilah occupied herself with a walk in the garden until the dinner hour.

"You look spendid, dear," Emily said, observing Lilah's eye-catching new coiffure. Bess had pulled all her hair to one side and pinned it so that the mass of curls tumbled over one shoulder. "Don't you like her hair dressed this way, Barrett?"

Barrett Fenton, a man of conservative tastes, attempted a diplomatic reply. "I find it daring," he said, taking a studious look. He set his thin lips in a smile. "Perhaps just a trifle theatrical."

Somewhat miffed, Lilah looked up. The new style had been chosen for his benefit, as had the yellow-and-blue-striped taffeta gown with the wide flounce at the hem. She supposed she should have remembered Barrett liked simple styles, like the neat bun Dinah wore. But such severity didn't suit her, which was just as well, since it was next to impossible to confine her curls in a sleek style.

She forgave Barrett during dinner, however, finding in his presence a kind of reassurance that life at Damon House could once again get back to normal. If unexciting, Barrett at least didn't have her in a tizzy all through dinner, wondering if he would reveal her carefully guarded secrets. And if she went for a walk in the moonlit conservatory with Barrett, she wouldn't find her emotions running out of hand. He was safe. She understood that Aunt Emily thought her fiancé-to-be dull, but he wasn't actually. It was simply that he already had his niche in the Damon family. Marriage to Barrett would require only a small adjustment on her part, and small ones, after all, were the best kind.

"By the way, Lilah," Clement addressed his daughter. "I ran into Tabor Stanton as he was leaving today."

"Did you, Papa?" Lilah gave a sunny smile, masking her displeasure that Tabor's name had been mentioned. She would much have preferred Barrett not hear of him. "I'm glad you had a chance to say good-bye to Mr. Stanton."

Clement gave Lilah a curious look. "I didn't say good-bye to him. Why should I? I took him to the stable to have a look at my horses. The man's quite knowledgeable about horseflesh."

A terrible feeling of foreboding crept over Lilah. The color drained from her face. "He saw all the horses, Papa?" she asked in a small, weak voice.

"Certainly," Clement answered slowly, his eyes on Lilah's pale face. What was the matter with the girl? Was she going to have another fainting spell?

"Even Rogue?" Lilah croaked.

"Rogue too."

Lilah gripped the edge of the table. Her heart hammered unsteadily. All afternoon she had been congratulating herself on successfully duping Tabor again, when all along she had been found out. What would he do? Papa couldn't know yet, not as calm as he was.

"What did he say?" Lilah's voice sounded thin.

"Lilah, are you all right? You look ghastly." Clement's question brought everyone's eyes to Lilah and added to her discomfort.

"I'll be all right, Papa," she answered, giving a fleeting smile. "Did Mr. Stanton like the stallion?"

"I should say he did." Clement grinned. "He's agreed to break the animal to the saddle."

Lilah gasped, and though Clement didn't think it

possible, turned paler. If he could have stood, he would have rushed to her side.

"Emily," he said, his eyes wide with anxiety, "take that girl to her room and see that she gets whatever she needs. Send for the doctor again if you think it's necessary."

Emily hurriedly got to her feet, holding back a suspicious smile. She did believe Lilah was smitten with Tabor Stanton. Just the mention of his name, and the girl went vapid. Emily certainly preferred him over Barrett Fenton. Clement's assistant hadn't a romantic notion in his head. If he had, he would have married Lilah by now.

"Don't you worry, Clement," Emily assured her brother-in-law. She hastened to Lilah's side and assisted her niece from the chair. The girl was shaking. "I'm sure it's nothing," she went on. "In this heat it's a wonder all of us don't have the vapors."

With Lilah in her bed, a cool cloth resting on her forehead, Emily asked the question she had been burning to ask. "Are you going to tell me what's upset you?"

Lilah wished she could. It was one of those moments when pouring her heart out to someone would have made her feel immensely better. But she couldn't tell Aunt Emily the cause of her distress. She couldn't tell anyone, except perhaps Loo, and Loo wouldn't be home for weeks yet.

"I really don't know," Lilah offered weakly. "I think maybe it is the heat." Another lie. And soon she would need another to follow that one. The thought of it sickened her.

Emily frowned. "I mentioned the heat for Clement's sake. I certainly know better. It's Tabor Stanton who has you in this state. What is it, child?" She sat on the bedside and took Lilah's hand. "Are you in love with the man?"

"No!" Lilah gasped, but in another moment saw Emily's suspicion as an avenue of escape. "I mean, I don't know. There is Barrett, you see."

Emily undid her frown. It was all clear to her. "What you mean is, since you've met Mr. Stanton, you aren't sure about your feelings for Barrett. Is that it?"

"Yes," Lilah stammered, wishing she could pull the sheet up over her head. She didn't like deceiving the people she loved. But once started, there was no turning back. "You see, I thought Mr. Stanton was going away. That would have settled everything. Now that I've learned he isn't leaving, I don't know what will happen." She inhaled deeply. "I wish he had just gone away."

"Of course you do," Emily consoled her. "Then you wouldn't have to take a close look at yourself. You wouldn't have to decide whether it's Barrett Fenton or Tabor Stanton you care for."

Lilah pulled the sheet up to her nose. "You may be right, Aunt Emily."

"Undoubtedly so," Emily responded. "And don't you think Mr. Stanton knows it too? Don't you think that's why he's found a reason to stay around? I saw the way he looked at you. I don't believe he heard a word your father said in the library last night. Certainly he's not still here because of a horse."

Lilah groaned and let Aunt Emily ramble on. She had stretched her limits as far as attributing favorable qualities to Tabor Stanton went. He couldn't have seen the stallion without knowing the horse was his. Was it possible he hadn't yet concluded Lilah Damon and Delilah were one and the same? If so, how long before he figured it out?

Papa had said Tabor would be training Rogue. That meant he would be at Damon House regularly. What did he expect to gain by that? She shivered as her mind explored answers to the question. Had Tabor kept quiet about the horse belonging to him out of regard for her father? Or was he just waiting until he could exact a sweeter revenge?

10

Tabor packed the clothes bought in San Francisco and the old ones that had been sent out and laundered. When all his belongings were together, he called for a porter to have them sent to his new address. This hotel had been fine until now, but for what he had in mind, more luxurious surroundings were required.

A visit to the Misses Alden's post-office box revealed that the letter he had sent was still waiting to be picked up. He had small hope it would be. A few hours later, Tabor watched as a valet unpacked his bag in one of the finest suites of the Fontaine Hotel. With few garments to be hung, the task took only a few minutes. Tabor tipped the valet and sent him away with instructions for the hotel chef concerning the dinner party he was giving the next night.

When alone, Tabor seated himself in a wine velvet chair behind a lacquered desk and, using the quill pen and ink he found inside it, wrote out a note. That done, he pushed back the chair and propped his feet on the desk's shiny top. Smiling, he methodically rolled a cigarette and struck a sulfur match on his boot sole. While he smoked, he read what he had written.

Satisfied that his words would have the intended effect, he folded and sealed the note in an envelope. Two days had passed since he had found the Admiral in the Damon stable. He had told Clement he needed a couple of days to tie up some business and then he could start breaking the horse.

Two days should be long enough for Lilah Damon to stew, wondering how much trouble he would cause her. He still hoped she wasn't guilty of anything more than buying a good horse. But the information he had carefully elicited from Clement didn't leave room for much doubt. Lilah, Dinah, and Loo had made a similar trip to St. Louis the previous year, at a time that corresponded to Delilah's first tour. There were too many coincidences, including the young Indian girl with green eyes and freckles just like Dinah Damon's.

What he couldn't figure out was why Lilah did it. Not for the money. Clement Damon had more than enough for his daughters to live opulently all their lives. By observation, he was extremely generous with both of them. Tabor's guess was she liked the excitement. Compared to Delilah's, Lilah Damon's life must seem bland. But how did she justify involving Dinah? To his surprise he had learned Clement's younger daughter was only sixteen. What kind of sister would expose a girl of that age to the unsavory activities in saloons?

He did have a few doubts left. He still didn't know how Lilah could change the color of her hair. But he put nothing past Delilah. If she and Lilah Damon were the same woman, plenty of explanations were due. And no shrinking-virgin act would get Lilah out of his grip this time.

He knew one way to make certain, provided he

couldn't get a confession out of her. Below her left breast, Delilah had a small mole, one exotically dark spot on the whitest of flesh. If Lilah Damon had the same mark, it would remove his last uncertainty. The problem was, he would have to undress her to find out. If Lilah didn't have the mark, he would have compromised a lady. The irony was, he didn't know if he preferred finding it there or not.

Two days of worry, and now this. Lilah paced the floor of the drawing room. Angrily she crushed the torn envelope bearing the lion crest of the Fontaine Hotel into a ball and tossed it into the fireplace.

Tabor Stanton's invitation, quite clearly for her alone, was for a small dinner party in his suite. She couldn't imagine how he could afford the Fontaine or whom he knew in San Francisco to invite to a dinner party. By his own admission he had no friends in the city. She supposed he had been there long enough to make new ones. Surely they weren't persons of her acquaintance. That was some consolation.

What had he been doing the past two days? He hadn't made any accusations since seeing the horse. Why? The man wasn't a complete fool. Maybe he had accepted that the animal was lost to him. After all, she had proof of ownership. He had signed the stallion over to her. On the other hand, she couldn't be sure of Tabor. Maybe he was waiting for her to make the first move. He might simply want her to pay him for the horse—or return it.

Did she dare refuse the invitation? His note asked that a response be sent by evening. Whatever was she to do?

"I swear, miss, I've never known you to fret about your age." Bess untied the linen strips that had Lilah's hair set in sausage curls. "You hardly look as old as Dinah with those ringlets."

"They're just the way I want them, Bess." Lilah turned to get a view of both sides and the back of her head in the dressing table's triple mirror. "Pull them back and tie the ribbon in."

Bess did as asked, tying up the little-girl curls with a blue satin ribbon. When done, she stood back and shook her head in dismay. What had gotten into her mistress?

"Bring the white watered silk, Bess," Lilah said, touching just a hint of lemon scent to her wrists and throat.

"Are you sure, miss?" Bess believed those fainting spells had set her mistress back a little. She wondered if she should tell Mrs. Dearborn how strangely her niece was acting. An infantile hairstyle, and now a dress that had been out of style last year. It wasn't like Miss Damon to wear anything that wasn't the latest in fashion.

"I'm sure, Bess," Lilah said, giving the maid a reassuring smile. "And no, I haven't lost my senses. I'm having dinner with people who aren't . . . Well, I wouldn't want to make anyone feel uncomfortable."

Relieved, Bess smiled. That explained it. The mistress didn't want to make others feel she was above them by dressing too stylishly.

Lilah smiled too, seeing the concern leave Bess's face. The lie about her choice of dress came so easily she wasn't even aware she had told it.

Bess hooked the last of the buttons on the bodice and adjusted the folds of the bustle, then hooked a string of pearls around Lilah's neck. The gown had long sleeves cuffed with ivory lace and a square but modest neckline. It did absolutely nothing to flatter Miss Damon. Bess said she looked more appropriately

dressed for a morning in church than for dinner at the
Fontaine. But since a look of innocence was her goal,
Lilah was satisfied.

The night was too warm for more than a light shawl.
Lilah called for a white one and as an afterthought
draped it over her head. She took a final look in the
mirror as she pulled on her gloves. Just a trace of a
smile curved her lips. With the addition of a rosary,
she might be mistaken for a nun.

"Lilah, welcome." Tabor opened the door of his
suite and showed her in. He contained a laugh. Not
that she wasn't as beautiful as ever. It was just that he
had entertained a thought that the fiery-haired Delilah
might be the one to accept his invitation. He was
somewhat unprepared for the maidenly white gown
and the virtuous expression an angel would envy. "Let
me take your shawl," he said politely.

While he put the shawl away, Lilah's eyes roamed
the room. Seeing a small table covered with a lace
cloth set for four eased her skepticism somewhat. She
didn't completely trust Tabor, and the invitation for
dinner in his hotel suite could easily have been a ruse
to get her alone. But it did look as if he expected two
more guests.

Had she missed them? Perhaps they had stepped
into another room of the suite. She looked around
again. This time her eyes took in every detail. The
room had a warm red-on-red wallpaper, gold-and-red
carpet, and black Italianate chairs at the table. Red
velvet curtains, layered over lace, accented the tall
windows. The same deep red was to be found in the
upholstery of the settee and armchairs. It was a beautiful room, as were those she could see through the
open doorways. What they lacked were people—other

than Tabor and herself. She saw no sign of anyone, no other wrap on the rack.

"Your other guests appear to be late," she said, skepticism returning.

Tabor grinned. "I'm sure they will be here any minute." He ushered her to the settee but to her relief did not sit down beside her. "Perhaps you would like a glass of sherry while we wait." He lifted a bottle and started to pour.

"I never drink it," Lilah responded.

"Perhaps you prefer brandy." A smile flashed on his lips.

"No, thank you. I don't partake of spirits in any form."

"How admirable." Tabor's eyes twinkled as he poured a glass of sherry for himself. "You won't mind if I have a drink? I find a glass of sherry before dinner stimulates the palate."

"I have no objection," Lilah said, sitting stiffly erect.

"I do appreciate your tolerance." Tabor seated himself on the armchair nearest her and sat staring and smiling. As the seconds grew into minutes, Lilah became more and more edgy and more and more suspicious.

"Mr. Stanton," she said when at last she could not separate the beat of her heart from the tick of the mantel clock, "you *are* expecting other guests?"

Tabor's smile widened at the use of his surname. Her patience had lasted a little longer than he had expected. "Why, Lilah," he said, pretending offense, "you don't think I would lure a lady here under false pretenses?"

Lilah steamed beneath the surface. She thought exactly that, but she didn't dare say so until she was sure no one else was coming. She didn't want to anger him without good reason. Too much was at stake.

Hands folded in her lap and feet crossed at the ankles, Lilah gave him a prim look. "It seems odd that they have not yet arrived."

"It does at that," he agreed, looking crestfallen.

Another stretch of silence ensued, Lilah finding the passage of it intolerable. When it was clear Tabor would not break the uneasiness, her brows lifted suspiciously and she presented another question.

"Just who are your other dinner guests?"

Tabor finished his sherry before answering. "Two ladies I'm sure you'll have much in common with. Miss—"

"Ladies?" Lilah sputtered. "What ladies?"

"Are you sure you wouldn't like a glass of sherry? It's very calming and you seem a trifle nervous."

"I told you I didn't care for any," Lilah said slowly, attempting to remain civil but losing the fight. The very idea of inviting her to a private dinner party with two of his lady friends. She wouldn't be suprised if they were residents of a bordello. A rosy flush bloomed on her throat. Flinty sparks gleamed in her eyes. "What ladies, Mr. Stanton?"

Tabor gave her an indulgent look. He would almost be willing to let the stallion go to know what was running through her mind right now. A bemused smile ruffled his lips. "Lilah." He spoke her name softly. "We do know each other better than that. Call me Tabor. Please."

Lilah slid to the edge of the settee, ready to spring to her feet if need be. Her anger at the insult overswept the reason she had accepted his dinner invitation to begin with. How malicious of him to refer to that dreadful episode in the conservatory. What a scoundrel he was. Did he actually think she would sit down to dinner with two lowly trollops?

Her voice crackled. "What ladies, Tabor?"

"Didn't I say?" he asked smoothly.

"You know you didn't."

"Why, Lilah," Tabor said, cocking his head to one side to study her expression. "I believe you're angry." He smiled as he might at a disagreeable child. "I think I understand. You expected to be my dinner partner. Well, you need not be jealous, you'll have no competition for my attention."

Seething, Lilah rose. "You are despicable, Tabor Stanton. I don't know what this is about, but I won't stay here and be insulted. You may tell your ladi—"

"Excuse me," Tabor interrupted, and left her standing mouth open as he crossed the room to answer a knock at the door.

Lilah was relieved to see the person seeking entry was only a bellman delivering the dinner. She quickly turned her face away, deciding it was better if the young man could not identify her. She heard Tabor tell him they would serve themselves. The door clicked shut and Lilah whirled, ready to leave. She gasped softly as she saw Tabor standing guardlike in front of the door.

Lilah marched to the brass coat rack and whipped her shawl from the hook. Tossing it over her shoulders, she marched defiantly toward Tabor. Giving him a look of outrage, she wagged a finger at him.

"I don't believe you actually invited anyone else, Mr. Stanton."

"Tabor, please," he reminded as he gently plucked the shawl from her shoulders and folded it over his arm. "I assure you I did." Lilah stepped back. His cold smile terrified her. "Another young woman of impeccable background, like yourself," he continued. "And a performer you may have heard about." Tabor took Lilah's arm and led her to the table, helping her to be seated.

The tiny hairs on the back of her neck stood up in dread. "Who is that?" she asked weakly.

"A charming woman." Tabor paused until he had also seated himself. Dark amusement filled his eyes. "I've actually met Delilah. I do confess I haven't had the pleasure of meeting Miss Alden."

Looking every bit the damsel in distress, Lilah trembled under Tabor's harsh stare, teetering on the verge of hysteria. The shadow of panic crossed swiftly over her face, but was chased away by her rising anger. Tabor had set a trap worthy of Delilah. If she could have found any kind words for him she might have commended his tactics. But her mind quickly sped to those she wished to protect: Dinah, Loo, Papa. As much as she wanted to storm out of the room, she had to stay.

"What is it you want, Tabor?" Her voice took on a trace of huskiness, her movements a languid grace.

"That's amazing," he said, noting the change in her. "A slant of the eye, a curl of the lips, a slight change in the voice, and Lilah Damon is gone. I wonder what Miss Alden is like."

Her eyes flashed and she threw her head back proudly. "Miss Alden is merely a name on a hotel registration, a convenience for making a transition. You know that, of course."

"I assumed it," he corrected. "You are remarkably good at what you do, Lilah . . . Delilah." He laughed. "I don't know which one of you I'm talking to."

"We are one and the same."

"I'm still not certain of that," he said, reminded he had done himself out of the more intimate confirmation. "If it hadn't been for seeing the horse, I would never have known."

"About the horse . . ." she said.

"My horse."

She sighed. "Your horse. I suppose you want him back or to be paid what he's worth." Tabor didn't respond so she went on. "You've seen how Papa feels about the stallion. If it's all the same to you, I prefer to buy him."

He let her wait because she did it so poorly. "It isn't," he said.

Nibbling at her lip, Lilah realized she had to try to change his mind. The thought of taking the stallion from Papa was painful.

She spoke softly. "I'll make it worth your while. I'll pay you twice what he's worth. I'm sorry about having you jailed. That was a mistake."

Tabor continued to stare, fascinated by the shifts of personality he observed. Delilah demanding. Lilah pleading. Which woman was actually here? Which one was real?

"You can keep the horse."

"Keep him?"

The amazement in Lilah's voice, the girlish smile almost undid Tabor. But he couldn't quite give himself up to it.

His voice hardened. "You can keep him provided you live up to the terms of our bet: you as my love slave for a week. That's more than fair, considering I could keep the horse and collect on your debt too."

She tensed, feeling her blood run cold. "You can't mean what you're saying."

"I can. I do. Either make good on Delilah's bet or give me back the horse. I'll explain to your father myself."

"No!"

Tabor grinned sardonically. "I was right, wasn't I? Clement knows nothing about his daughter being Delilah, Flame of the West."

"You must not tell him," she said, panic lifting her

voice. "Papa has a weak heart. The shock might bring on an attack. It might kill him."

Tabor shook his head. "I won't tell him." He paused until she relaxed a bit in her chair. "Not unless you refuse to honor the bet."

Lilah paled and looked helpless as a lost lamb. "You don't know what you're asking."

He shrugged away a pang of guilt, recalling her skill as an actress, finding it difficult even then to remember that the deceitful Delilah lurked behind that guileless face.

"I'm asking that you honor a bet made in good faith. If anybody has a reason to be upset about this, it's me. To begin with, you cheated in the card game. After that I had a knot on my head for a week. I spent that week and another in Walsh Peregrine's jail. I lost my horse. And if that wasn't enough, I got duped again just trying to do the honorable thing by a woman. You owe me that week, Delilah."

"Lilah," she said weakly. "I'm Lilah. I told you it was all a mistake. I'll pay you three times what the horse is worth."

Tabor's stony gray eyes held hers. "I don't want money," he replied tonelessly. "I want satisfaction."

"How can I?" she demanded. "What would I tell Papa? How could I possibly go away with you for a week?"

She looked near tears, but Tabor refused to be swayed. "A woman who can spend months touring California saloons while her father thinks she's in St. Louis shouldn't have much difficulty coming up with an excuse."

"This is different," she said weakly.

Tabor smiled. "We'll talk out the details after we eat."

He lifted the silver covers from the several dishes of

still-steaming food, enough for four. She hoped he
didn't expect her to eat it all. She had no appetite
whatsoever.

Back on the settee where the disastrous evening had
begun, Lilah accepted a snifter of brandy. She had no
reason to keep up the pretense she was a teetotaler.
Tabor knew otherwise. Besides, this time he had elected
to sit beside her and, listening to what he proposed,
she felt the need of strong drink.

Tabor crushed out the cigarette he had smoked after
dinner. "I'll have my Aunt Sarah write a letter inviting
you to stay at the Cooke ranch. It's about a two-day
ride from here."

Lilah immediately began calculating ways to shorten
the time. Two days down on a stagecoach and two
days back. That left only three days she actually had
to spend with him. She might even find a way to cut
down on that.

She sat rigidly. Tabor's nearness caused a whir of
uneasy emotions. "I can't possibly make a trip before
Aunt Emily leaves for London. Papa would never
allow it."

Tabor scowled. He doubted there was anything Lilah
couldn't get her father to agree to. But it would be
rude of her to leave Damon House while she had a
guest. And it might arouse suspicion.

"How much longer is she staying?"

"Two weeks," Lilah said, adding a few days to the
actual departure date.

Tabor rubbed his chin. "I can wait that long. I
promised your father I'd break the stallion for him.
That ought to take about two weeks."

Lilah finished her brandy but continued to hold the
empty snifter. "He's already broken." She didn't like

the idea of Tabor spending much of the next two weeks at Damon House.

"Only for me. Your father wants him so anyone can ride him."

She couldn't disagree with that. She supposed she would have to put up with him for a while. At Damon House she could manage to avoid him.

"I wonder," Tabor shifted his position to get a better look at her, "if you have any idea how intriguing it is to sit here and look at you in that prudish dress knowing there's a sultry, provocative woman underneath." His voice dropped dangerously low as he unfolded her fingers from the empty glass and set it aside. "What would it take to make you become Delilah right now?"

The sensations she felt confused her. She decided the shiver slithering down her spine was fear, fear that Tabor had decided not to wait the two weeks.

"Delilah isn't really anyone at all," she said weakly, sliding toward the arm of the settee and away from him. "She's like a character from a play. She seems real but she isn't."

He slid closer, making up the distance she had put between them. "You play Delilah to perfection. Like Samson, I expected to be missing my hair when I woke up in that jail cell."

Lilah trembled when he took her arm. His darkening eyes hypnotized her and she offered no resistance when he reached for the satin ribbon that held her curls off her neck. He untied it slowly, allowing the tight cluster to fall over her shoulders. When his fingers slid into the curls and started smoothing them, she held her breath.

"You haven't told me how you changed your hair." He bent his head close. She shut her eyes tightly, thinking he was about to force a kiss. But Tabor only lifted a handful off red-gold hair against his cheek. "I like Delilah's perfume better," he said.

She opened her eyes to find him grinning at her.

"I don't." She snatched her hair from his hand. "I used henna to darken my hair and my brows. With rouge on my cheeks and kohl on my eyelids, it's a rather effective feminine disguise," she added.

He gave her a measuring look. "Everything else is you, I trust."

His sarcasm smarted. Why did he bother to ask? He had made quite sure of that before she knocked him unconscious. But why should she be the only one feeling miserable? She could give as good as she got. She lifted her chin.

"It puzzles me, Tabor," she said, offering a wry smile, "how your aunt could debase herself by helping with your sordid plan. Just what kind of woman is she?"

She thought for a minute her words had hit their mark. Tabor's mocking grin changed to an angry frown. "My aunt is a fine woman. Don't think otherwise," he warned.

"So fine she doesn't mind if you abuse a woman in her house?"

He realized what she was up to. His grin returned. Seeing defeat, her sapphire eyes shot hot sparks at him. He had wondered how long before Delilah broke through Lilah Damon's icy control.

"Sarah doesn't interfere in my private affairs and I don't interfere in hers. You won't be embarrassed." He cupped Lilah's chin in his hands and looked directly in her eyes. "And you won't be abused, sweetheart," he said softly. "You'll belong to me for a week, but I won't do anything you don't want me to. You have my promise."

"Your promise?" What was that worth? She hoped

he couldn't feel her unsteadiness. "Then I might as well not go," she said boldly. "I can't stand the sight of you."

Tabor slid his hands around her throat, holding them there briefly. Many hours he'd thought of placing his hands there, of what he would do. Purposefully he slid them to her shoulders. He felt her quivering.

"Then you'll have to keep your eyes closed," he said huskily. "Because I'm certain you don't feel the same about me touching you."

Lilah inhaled sharply as she caught the full measure of passion smoldering in his dark eyes. Then she did shut her lids again, afraid what she saw in his eyes would spill into her own. But as her lashes fluttered down, she knew she had acted too late. The sensations Tabor seemed to turn on at will raged full and hot in her veins.

"I don't," she mumbled, thinking this was a fine time to give up her lies. "I wish I did, but I don't."

He touched her lips so softly she thought it only her imagination. Her tiny moan of response brought more gentle pressure from his lips. How was it the man who brought her such despair was also the man who gave her the sweetest pleasure? By some dark trick of fate she had become the victim of her own justice. The hardest thing about it was that she wasn't fighting him, she was fighting herself. And finding it increasingly difficult to understand why.

She refused to open her eyes. As long as she kept them shut, it seemed like a dream that her arms encircled his neck and that she liked the feel of him so much.

Tabor teased at her lips until she let him past that barrier and inside. His hands at her waist pulled her into his lap. For a few moments he buried his face against her throat and in the soft curls tumbling over her shoulder. Had he promised not to touch her to-night? He didn't think so. One hand explored the hollows of her back, the other slipped buttons through tiny silk loops. He would have to be careful of the promises he made. They were proving difficult to keep.

Lilah felt the warmth of his kisses against her neck and strained against him. His lips continued to explore her satin flesh, searing a trail past her shoulders and to the neckline of her gown. Behind her his hands parted that garment and slipped it from the path of his lips. She moaned at the new-felt freedom as he uncovered her breasts. His lips touched like whispers, warm and moist on her skin. She was aware he set her on her feet and partially aware that he skimmed the white silk gown from her body. Shortly she was back in his lap and his mouth again was teasing the rosy crests of her breasts.

"You know I want you, sweetheart."

"Yes," she whispered. His want was apparent, throbbing and insistent against her hips.

"I need for you to tell me it's all right."

Her head swirled inside. Half of her shouted no. A lady should never allow a man to touch her so intimately, so boldly. The other half of her shouted yes. Take what you want. Live by your own rules.

"It is," she whispered, making her choice—if she had ever had one, the way his hands rested so provocatively on her thighs, the way the stroking of his fingers sent a pulsing warmth through her.

Tabor tucked his arms beneath her and stood, Lilah in his arms. Whispering loving words in her ear, he carried her to the bedroom and the high-backed chest-nut bed draped with warm red velvet covers. Giving in to the temptation of one more kiss, Tabor yielded to the softness of her lips, then eased her down on the covers. He stepped back to disrobe.

Lilah could keep her eyes closed no longer. She opened them and viewed Tabor shedding his tie and vest and then the silk shirt. He slid off his boots and unfastened his trousers and pushed them down. Lilah's eyes grew endlessly wide. Her imagination, grand as it was, had never shown her such a picture as this, the male animal, strong, virile, and in a full arousal. Self-consciously Lilah pulled the edges of her camisole over her breasts. Were all men like this? So imposing. So big. Could she possibly accommodate such a man? Could she, even though her body burned and shook with wanting.

Her eyes lingered on Tabor as he stepped free of his trousers. He was quite beautiful, for a man. She was surprised to see the richly tanned skin went farther than his neck and wrists and that even those areas generally untouched by the sun were a dark gold color. She forgot his imposing size as the wonder and wanting overtook her.

But when Tabor eased back into the bed, suddenly her Victorian upbringing squashed her reckless abandon.

"Wait!" she cried, scurrying back against the pillows. "Wait! I've changed my mind."

"The hell you have," Tabor growled, his eyes flashing her a warning that he wouldn't be toyed with.

Lilah gave a choked, desperate cry and slid across the bed and off the other side. "I'm not ready for this," she whispered.

"The hell you aren't," he said, coming after Lilah and backing her into a corner.

Lilah crossed her arms over her chest and fell back against the unrelenting wall. "You don't understand," she croaked. "I'm scared."

"You damn well ought to be." His menacing voice sent a chill over her skin. "Not that I think you are.

Delilah invited many men to her hotel room. Men who didn't wake up in jail."

"You're wrong," she cried. "I never . . ."

"You're wrong," he echoed. "I know about the mirror trick. I reckon you were a little more kindly disposed toward the men who didn't catch you cheating. I reckon they left Delilah the next morning thinking empty pockets were worth the experience."

"No!" she gasped. "No!"

"You said yes, and I'm holding you to it," Tabor growled, grabbing her by the waist and tossing her back to the bed. He fell across her, holding her down with ease. Lilah fought him furiously, but Tabor, overcome with passion didn't register that her resistance came from fear and not defiance. He ripped her camisole away and would have done the same to her petticoats had she not covered her eyes with her hands and started to sob. Angrily he pulled back. "You little witch. Don't think you'll get away with that another time." But when her sobs continued, Tabor let her loose. He wouldn't take a woman by force. "Go on," he shouted. "Get out of here. Get dressed."

Lilah flew from the room and pulled on her discarded gown as fast as she could. Tabor, cursing her bitterly, pulled on his trousers and stood scowling and watching from the doorway of the bedroom. Humiliatingly conscious of his eyes, Lilah fumbled with her gown. Why had she chosen one that buttoned down the back, one she couldn't fasten herself? It appalled her, but after long minutes of trying on her own, she had no option but to ask him to fasten it for her.

Tabor was no more pleased about the task and did it as quickly as he could. But somehow his fingers seemed to have lost their dexterity and he struggled with the buttons. When that arduous work was finished, she found the blue ribbon and attempted to put her hair back the way it had been before. It was hopeless.

Tabor brought her shawl and draped it over her shoulders. His scowl hadn't eased in the least. Lilah's hand clutched nervously at her throat and discovered to her horror that her pearls were missing. She balanced their value against Tabor's disposition.

"Please return them to me when you come to Damon House again," she said, not daring to postpone her departure long enough to look for them.

Tabor shot her a withering glance but said that he would. Lilah hurried to the door with every intention of letting the evening end at that, but Tabor wouldn't have it. He followed and spun her around before she could leave. Lilah whimpered pitiably as his mouth closed angrily over hers. But as before, she was powerless to stop him. It seemed to Lilah that other someone inside her took over, clutching him to her, drinking in his kisses, spinning with him into a dark, pulsing blackness. His hands, as rampant, as threatening, left every part of her smoldering from their touch. When he released her the fire of his mouth still burned on her lips as if the fiery tail of a comet swept across them. Her breath came in pants. She wondered if her legs would carry her down two flights of stairs.

Tabor's dark eyes cut her in two. "My bet was with Delilah," he said. "Not a sobbing schoolgirl. No more games. It's Delilah I want in my bed, or the agreement is off. Delilah. Not a pale shadow of her. Remember that."

11

"I've heard a few men have that kind of magic," Clement Damon said quietly to Gus. "Guess I never expected to see it firsthand."

"Me neither," Gus agreed, slowly shaking his head as he watched Stanton haul a saddle right up alongside the stallion, Rogue. He and his men had tried that and wound up getting a good saddle trampled just to escape the stallion's flying hooves.

Rogue whinnied like a colt and alternately stamped his front feet. Tabor rubbed a hand over the stallion's soft muzzle, slipping a chunk of apple into Rogue's mouth.

"The horse likes him," Clement remarked.

"Damned if he don't." Gus propped his elbows on the paddock fence. "Let's see if he'll take that saddle."

Tabor stroked beneath the thick mane. The stallion was in superb form. He had put back the weight the trail had taken off him. His coat shone like polished ebony. His eyes shone with excitement at seeing his master.

"Reckon we're going to have to put on a little show, Admiral," Tabor whispered to the stallion. "Guess I'm going to have to start calling you Rogue, huh?" His hand progressed over a muscled shoulder. "Think you can kick up your heels some?" The horse nudged Tabor's side with his nose. "A little ruckus when I put this saddle on would be good." Gently he stroked Rogue's withers. The horse flicked his skin as if trying to unseat a fly. When Tabor tossed a blanket on his back, Rogue snorted.

"Watch him. He can kick a mile." Gus broke out in a grin as Rogue sidestepped when Tabor lifted the saddle. He hoped the boy could get the girth cinched and get astride for a ride. For anybody else to saddle Rogue, the horse had to be maneuvered into a chute. For the length of time anybody stayed on him, the saddling hadn't been worth the trouble. He didn't want to see Tabor hurt, but a good bronco ride provided entertainment for an old wrangler.

Tabor slung the saddle on Rogue. The horse shook, but not hard enough to knock the saddle from his back. Tabor quickly stepped in and pulled the girth beneath the sleek belly, cinched it, and hooked it tight. Rogue, who never took kindly to the saddle at first, made a couple of hopping steps with his rear legs. Tabor stepped back, knowing the horse would settle down in a few minutes.

"Need a blindfold on him?" Clement asked, pulling a bandanna from around his neck.

Tabor stroked the black muzzle again, then stepped to the horse's side. He paused before fitting his foot in the stirrup. "I think a blindfold would scare him."

Clement retied his bandanna and chuckled. If he were mounting Rogue he'd want the blindfold for himself. "Take it easy on my horse," he called.

Tabor smiled, figuring both Clement and Gus thought

his success so far was pure luck. His real worry was that the stallion wouldn't cooperate in this sham. Hopefully he touched his heels to a sensitive place on Rogue's sides. Usually contact there started the stallion bucking. Rogue snorted and stomped his back legs. Tabor frowned, wondering if the horse's tolerance was because he was glad to see him. He dug his heels in deeper.

Rogue answered with a shrill cry and a cavorting buck worthy of any wild range pony. He sunfished, spun, dived his head, and shot his rear hooves high. Tabor had all he could do to stay in the saddle and was glad when he had hung on long enough to impress even a skeptic. To calm the stallion, he whispered a few soothing words. Rogue, who had enjoyed frolicking with his master, obediently settled into a gallop. Tabor took him several turns around the paddock. When finally pulled to a stop, the stallion crooked his neck around and took a long look at his rider. Tabor, catching his breath and making sure his bones weren't rearranged, could have sworn the horse grinned.

"That's enough for today, boy," Tabor said. "Wouldn't want anyone to notice how quick you're catching on to this."

"Good ride!" Gus shouted, giving Tabor a smile of approval. He waved the stableboys, who had poured outside to watch, back to work.

"Looks like you've got the worst of it over," Clement said as Tabor rode the horse up close.

"Sure hope so." Tabor swung down from the saddle and sidled up to the fence. "Much more of that I'd need a new set of teeth."

Clement laughed. "He's strong and he's smart. I think he figured out I wouldn't let him near the mares until he was broken. Lucky for you he decided that today."

Tabor nodded, glad he and Rogue had managed to put on a convincing performance. "I'll be out every day to work with him. He's smart, like you say. I'll start getting him used to different riders. In a couple of weeks I think I can have him gentle enough for the ladies to ride."

Ching walked up and handed Tabor the black hat that had sailed over the fence when Rogue took off. Tabor noted Ching's eyes taking in the symbol on the silver disk. It wasn't the first time he had felt Damon's companion was sizing him up. Smiling, he thanked Ching, dusted his hat, and put it on, wondering what thoughts disturbed the Chinese's mind.

"You know, I really appreciate this, Tabor." Clement talked as Tabor unsaddled Rogue and handed him over to a groom, who cautiously led the horse into the stable for a rubdown. "If you hadn't offered to break him, I might have been forced to geld a fine stallion."

Tabor grinned, hoping Rogue appreciated being rescued from that fate. "He'll give you good colts," he said to Clement.

"And you get the first pick of them." Clement raised his hand to silence the refusal he saw coming. "You'll have earned him by the time you gentle this stallion. Since you won't let me pay you for the job, I insist."

"Well, then, you've talked me into it," Tabor said. He liked Clement. The man was generous to those he employed and to his friends. His questions at the hotel had all brought about the same response: Clement Damon was a fine, honest man. In Damon enterprises, a man, any man, got respect and the best wages around. Of course, those same sources described Lilah as the untouchable Miss Damon who had broken more hearts and turned away more suitors than any other woman in San Francisco.

What confounded Tabor was that Clement had turned

out such a daughter, one who clandestinely led a dual life right under his nose. The poor man would likely be devastated to learn what she had been doing while he thought she was in St. Louis. He sure wouldn't tell him and break the old man's heart. But he didn't see why Delilah—Lilah—should know he thought that much of her father.

Clement rolled along on one side of the fence while Tabor walked along the other. "I'd like for you to come and stay at the Damon House while you're working with the horse. It'll save you a ride out every day."

Tabor turned and looked at Clement's face. The kind eyes, the sincere smile, jabbed at his conscience. He came close to turning down the offer, but the thought of being so conveniently close to Lilah stopped him. He told himself he wanted the chance to know more about her; perhaps figure out what need drove her into a secret life as Delilah. He wasn't yet ready to admit, especially to himself, that his interest in her ran deeper than simply satisfying curiosity and evening up a score.

"That's thoughtful of you." Tabor stopped and propped a leg on the lowest fence rail. He took out his cigarette makings, lapsing silent as he rolled up the tobacco. "I'll bring my gear along tomorrow when I ride out." When he had the cigarette lighted, he cocked his head to one side and spoke offhandedly to Clement. "I thought maybe since Lilah gave you the stallion she'd be out to watch the first ride."

Clement's easy smile returned. He had a feeling Tabor Stanton was set to give Barrett a run for his money over Lilah. "Horse breaking's a mite too violent for Lilah. She's a quiet girl and she's skittish around even well-behaved horses. Had a bad experience as a child," he said, but didn't elaborate. "Darling's about as gentle a horse as they come. Lilah doesn't much like riding any other."

"I see," Tabor responded, again thinking Clement hardly knew his daughter at all if he thought her a quiet type. He wondered how she would take to having him as a houseguest. He asked Clement about it. "You don't think Lilah or Dinah will mind if I stay at the house?"

Clement chuckled. "I'm sure they will both be happy to have another guest. Emily's leaving at the end of the week," he added. "We'll all enjoy having someone to liven up the place. Which brings me to another thing. I'm giving a party for Emily on Thursday night." His smile deepened as he thought what an interesting night that would be, when Tabor met Barrett. "You'll attend, of course. It's a fancy to-do, the kind of thing Emily's accustomed to in London. Dancing and such. You dance?"

Tabor half-smiled. "I do a reasonable step or two."

"Good." Clement patted the arms of his chair. "You can cover all my obligations on the dance floor."

"Papa." Lilah's anxious eyes met her father's twinkling ones. "Where will we put another guest?"

He exhaled a long breath. How many times had he remarked that Lilah never got flustered? And here she was getting fitful over having one more houseguest. He believed he would enjoy having Tabor at Damon House. Lilah was attracted to Tabor, and Tabor to Lilah. Neither one of them seemed to know what to make of the situation. However, the rather static courtship between them was proving to be amusing.

"This house has twelve bedrooms," he said flatly. "Surely one is available for Mr. Stanton."

"We do have other guests staying the night of the ball," Lilah reminded.

"I know. Five couples who will require five rooms. By my count, adding the four already occupied, that leaves three vacant bedrooms. Is something wrong with those three?"

"No, Papa," Lilah said sheepishly. "It isn't that. It's . . ."

"What?" Clement rolled his eyes. "Don't tell me all this fuss is because you can't decide which one to give Tabor."

Lilah gave up, realizing she had no valid reason to offer her father for not wanting Tabor in the house. If he had to be in Damon House, she would put him as far away from her as possible, in the suite on the third floor.

"I'll have the maid make a room ready," she said listlessly. "I suppose Tabor will be at dinner every night while he's here."

"I suppose he will," Clement said, holding back a laugh. "And at breakfast and at lunch. I don't expect him to go hungry at Damon House."

Clement felt sure Lilah was afraid of her interest in Tabor. The girl was so methodical about everything she did, that now the slightest interruption of her plans threw her into a dither. She needed to learn you couldn't plan the way you'd feel about someone the way you planned the outfit you'd wear. He rather hated seeing Lilah suppress all the liveliness she'd had as a child. He'd like to see that bright spirit shine through, as it had in her mother.

Maybe Lilah was concerned about offending Barrett. But she wasn't officially engaged yet. Later, perhaps, he would tell her the story of his and Marie's elopement, how her mother had broken an engagement and scandalously run off with the man she loved. In the meantime, a little competition would do Barrett some good. Having to overcome a few obstacles be-

fore getting his hands on the Damon fortune would
help toughen Barrett. Yes. Clement's laugh broke out.
He was surely going to enjoy having Tabor around.

The royal-blue Worth gown was a gift from Aunt
Emily, the sapphires and diamonds a present from her
father on her eighteenth birthday. Bess pinned Lilah's
curls high and helped her slip on the long silk gloves.
Lilah had her mind made up to spend the evening at
Barrett's side. She considered briefly telling Barrett of
Tabor's sordid demand on her, but decided Tabor
would simply counter by revealing she was Delilah. In
the end she would lose her fiancé and put her papa at
risk. But she would be cool to Tabor as she had been
the few days he'd been at Damon House.

The family, as was the custom before such events,
met in the drawing room for a few moments alone
before guests began arriving. Lilah's smile fled as she
saw that her father had invited Tabor to join them.
Nevertheless, she hastened to Clement's side and told
him how elegant he looked in his evening clothes.

"I had hoped Barrett would arrive early," she said
quite loudly and primarily for Tabor's ears. "Mr. Fenton
is my fiancé," she went on, directing a haughty look at
Tabor.

"He isn't really," Dinah piped in. She wanted that
fact clear to Tabor. "Lilah keeps putting him off."

Color flared in Lilah's cheeks, though nobody saw
or appreciated it but Tabor. He smiled to himself. "In
that case, Lilah"—he let her name roll slowly off his
tongue—"you won't feel uncomfortable accepting flowers from another man." Stepping forward, he presented her with a corsage of white rosebuds tied up in
blue ribbon and sprigged with violets.

Dinah hurried up to the pair. "I'll help you pin that

on," she said gaily. "Isn't Tabor the sweetest thing? He had corsages made for all three of us."

While Dinah pinned the corsage at her waist, Lilah glanced at Emily, whose face, like Dinah's, glowed with praise for Tabor's thoughtfulness. Emily wore a corsage of tiny pink roses pinned to her glove at the wrist. Dinah wore one of yellow roses and green ribbons at the waist of her pale yellow satin gown. Even Papa had a white rosebud tucked into his buttonhole. Lilah wondered if Tabor had supplied that one too, as another pointed reminder of the night she had told him white roses were her favorite flower.

"Thank you," she said icily. Dinah led her to the mirror and insisted she look at herself. Tabor's reflection loomed overpoweringly behind hers, his face glowing with a self-satisfied smile. The corsage was beautiful and it complemented her gown, but she refused to say so. Dinah and Emily had compliments to spare for Tabor. He could do without hers.

"I hope each of you ladies will save several dances for me," Tabor said gallantly.

"Of course they will," came Clement's good-natured response. He delighted in seeing his daughters dressed like royalty. His chest swelled with pride as he admired his two beautiful daughters. How he wished their mother could see them, especially Lilah. Tonight she looked so much like Marie—just seeing her brought him a nostalgic ray of happiness.

Lilah spun around. "I'm sorry," she said, shaking her head. "I'm afraid mine are promised."

"Not all of them," Dinah offered. "Barrett promised one to me and, of course, he'll want to dance with Aunt Emily." She smiled sweetly. "So you may save those two for Tabor."

Tabor nodded, convincing Lilah he had every intention of claiming those two dances. With a little huff she turned back to the mirror, but there was his face again, mocking her with a smile. Lilah hastened to the empty seat on the settee beside Emily, the one Tabor had vacated when she entered the room.

"You're very quiet tonight, Aunt Emily," she said, taking her aunt's hand.

Emily's serious expression subsided, but a note of it remained in her voice. "Thinking of leaving you and Dinah and Clement saddens me," she said. "The weeks have passed too quickly. I'll miss my girls so very much. And, of course, I am disappointed you and Dinah won't be accompanying me for a visit in London."

"Perhaps we'll come next summer," Lilah said, disheartened to have caused Emily any sorrow. After her last season as Delilah she might like a visit to England. Or perhaps once she and Barrett were married, they might include London in their wedding trip.

"I'll count on that," Emily said softly, and smiled. "I think what really bothers me is the thought of making that long voyage with only my maid as company. Don't you fret, though," she went on. "I'll find someone interesting on board."

Wan interrupted at that moment, announcing the first of the guests. For the next hour people arrived and Clement personally introduced to Emily each guest she hadn't met already during her stay. One of the last to reach Damon House was Barrett Fenton.

Lilah stunned him with her warm greeting. It wasn't like her to kiss him publicly, but she did so freely when he entered the drawing room.

The exhibition wasn't wasted on Tabor. He felt his blood warming and quickly found himself sizing up Lilah's intended. Barrett Fenton was good-looking if a bit bookish. His evening clothes fit his slender frame to a tailor's perfection and he wore them with much more ease than Tabor felt in his hastily purchased ensemble. Tabor knew from Clement's comments that he thought highly of his assistant.

After what he thought was sufficient time alone for the dewy-eyed pair, Tabor strolled over to them. "Mr. Fenton," he said with a smile when he realized Lilah didn't intend to introduce him. "I'm Tabor Stanton, a friend of Clement's."

"He's mentioned you, Stanton." Barrett extended a hand. He needed only that quick look at the ruggedly handsome Stanton, only a glimpse of the gleam hidden in those sharp eyes, to realize he ought to keep a close watch on what he considered his property. "You're the new wrangler he hired, aren't you?"

Tabor noted the put-down. He glanced at Lilah and registered the satisfaction in the blue depths of her eyes. He shook his head. "Just doing a favor for a friend," he said. "I only work for myself."

"I understand you won't be staying long," Barrett continued, holding tightly to Lilah's hand.

"No," Tabor agreed. "I'll be heading back to my ranch soon. I'm sure Miss Damon has told you she's agreed to pay a visit to the Cooke spread." The devilish smile Lilah despised curled his lips.

Barrett missed it. He cocked his head toward Lilah, his mouth thin-lipped. "What's this? You haven't mentioned going away."

"I . . . I haven't really made up my mind yet." Lilah hooked her arm through Barrett's, but behind his back she gave Tabor a look that would shatter glass. "Anyway, it's not important." Turning aside to Tabor, she lifted her chin. "Will you excuse us, Mr. Stanton," she said acidly. As she and Barrett walked away Tabor heard her saying, "He invited me and I didn't want to hurt his feelings. He is a friend of Papa's. You don't think I'd have any interest in a man like . . ."

Tabor could have kicked himself. Why the hell had he done a thing like that? It was uncalled-for. He was acting like a spurned lover. He had no quarrel with Fenton. And hadn't he sworn he'd keep what he had at issue with Delilah from hurting anyone else? Disgusted with himself, Tabor milled through the crowded room, spotting the prettiest girl at the ball—after Lilah—and making a beeline for her.

After dinner the party moved to the ballroom. Tabor had no problem finding dance partners, but as charming as the young ladies were and as intent as they were on capturing his attention, his eyes kept straying to Lilah. Seeing her glide over the dance floor, most often in Barrett's arms, hearing her soft but demure laughter, he couldn't believe that the same woman bared her limbs and pranced in saloons like a strumpet for miners and cowboys.

She almost had a halo around her head. People old and young flocked to her. Everyone seemed to like Lilah. Not one of the girls he'd danced with had made a catty remark about her. Apparently she inspired friendship and not jealousy, an accomplishment for one who so easily outshone her girlfriends.

He got a queasy feeling in his belly, thinking he might be doing Lilah Damon a great wrong. Maybe what she really needed was someone to help her straighten out who she was. He laughed bitterly at his sentiments as he touched the spot on his head where she had once beaned him with a bottle. Make an honest woman of Delilah? He'd better stick to getting even.

She whirled by in Barrett's arms, shooting icicles at him as she passed. When the music ended, he heard Barrett explain he owed the next dance to Dinah. Before Lilah could leave the floor, Tabor appeared and swept her into his arms.

"This is my dance, I believe."

"Believe what you like, you vulgar . . ." Lilah choked on her words and tried to pull herself free.

"Easy," he whispered. "You're turning heads."

She saw that he was right, and quickly affected a smile for those who were looking. The music started an instant later and Tabor soon had her busy keeping step to a spirited waltz.

"I detest you," she whispered from behind her smile.

Tabor pulled her closer, eliciting a startled gasp from her lips. "Such sweet words," he teased. "I believe Delilah's getting through that sugar facade you have her in."

Lilah met his eyes without flinching. "Don't flatter yourself that you know me so well, Tabor."

He chuckled. "I don't know you nearly as well as I'm going to."

Unable to take any more, Lilah stopped abruptly in the middle of the waltz. Before she could slip from his arms, Tabor clamped his hand around her wrist and led her through the open French doors and into the garden. Other couples who had stepped out for cool air strolled in the torchlight. Tabor pulled Lilah past them and toward a bench in a corner where they could be alone.

"You are an absolute brute!" she cried, anger sharpening her voice.

"You'd be wise not to forget it," Tabor warned. "The dance isn't over until the music stops."

"Barrett will be looking for me."

"Barrett is being polite to your sister, which is no difficult job."

Lilah's eyes froze on him. "What are you saying, you barbarian? I warn you, keep away from Dinah."

Tabor's laugh raked her. "Jealous, Lilah?" She had missed his meaning completely. Hadn't she noticed her sister was honey-eyed over her fiancé?

"Don't be a fool!" She snatched her arm back but Tabor refused to let go of her wrist. "No power on earth could make me jealous of you."

The devilish smile appeared on his lips. The music had stopped, but with her back to the doors and her temper up, Lilah hadn't noticed. Tabor, however, could see another surge of dancers coming out for air. Among them were Barrett and Dinah. They moved past the crowd, but not completely away from it. Dinah, he was sure, had spotted him and Lilah on the corner bench.

"How about one from heaven?" he asked smoothly.

"Not one from heaven or hell," she snapped back.

Tabor leaned close. Lilah felt her heart lurch. "I guess you're pretty sure of yourself," he whispered.

"I have no idea what you're talking about," she remarked tersely, seeing deep lights of desire in his dark eyes, like lightning flashing behind storm clouds.

Her tattling shiver beneath his hand warned Tabor what his nearness was doing to her. Pleased, he shook his head in mock disbelief of her denial. "I think you know I wouldn't look at another woman with you around."

Lilah's senses deserted her when he leaned nearer. "You wouldn't?" Her voice faded to a whisper.

"How could I?" He edged even closer. "Not another woman in the world is as beautiful, as desirable, as kissable as you are."

"Kissable?"

"Very," he whispered, touching his lips to hers as his hands grazed her bare shoulders.

Lilah shuddered and her tawny lashes flickered down. Where was the desire to free herself from his embrace? Gone. Flown away like a night bird at dawn. Her arms, which ought to be holding him back, stretched around his neck. Her lips, which should be protesting his insolence, parted to meet the cloud-light touch of his. Slowly, maddeningly, he deepened the kiss, and the whole world spun crazily away.

She felt a sudden emptiness when he broke the bond. "Tabor?" she questioned, desiring an explanation for what she felt.

"Delilah," he answered huskily. "Sweet, sweet Delilah. You're the kind of mystery that drives a man out of his head." His dark eyes flashed a threat. "I won't be satisfied until I know all your secrets."

Delilah. Delilah again. The name brought her careening back to the present moment and sent a flush of shame into her cheeks.

"You're a devil," she hissed. Quickly Lilah looked around to assure herself no one had witnessed her lapse of sanity. She was horrified to see she hadn't been so lucky. Halfway across the garden, Barrett, with Dinah at his side, stood and stared. Lilah jumped to her feet, but Barrett whirled and rushed into the ballroom, Dinah right behind him.

Lilah spun around and cast a look of fury at Tabor. He shrugged it away. She could think of nothing tame enough to say to him without drawing half the guests in dismay. With an angry swish of her skirts and blood in her eye, Lilah stormed inside. She found Barrett in the drawing room waiting for his hat. Thankfully Dinah wasn't with him.

"Barrett," she cried, rushing up to him. "Please don't go."

Barrett turned toward her, his face drawn with hurt and anger. "What choice do you give me? Every man and woman here knows you and I will announce our engagement soon. Am I supposed to look the other way while some cowboy fondles you in the garden?"

"Barrett," Lilah pleaded. "It wasn't like that at all. It was a mistake. I'm sorry."

"Lilah, I love you. You've let me think you love me. Dinah and I weren't the only ones who saw you kissing Stanton. The others were just polite enough to look away. They won't be polite enough not to spread the news to everyone here. Do you expect me to go back into that ballroom and smile as if nothing happened?"

"It didn't mean a thing." Frantically Lilah caught his hands.

"To you or to him? Lilah, a man doesn't kiss a woman without it meaning something. Listen," he said, the harshness lessening in his voice, "your father's offered me the opportunity to take care of some business in London for him. I turned him down to begin with because I didn't want to be away from you. I've now decided to go."

"Barrett! You can't run away because of this."

"Lilah," he said indulgently, "I'm no physical match for Stanton. If you want someone to fight over you, I'm not the man to do it. I'm not running away. I'm giving you room to make up your mind about what you want. If you marry me, it's got to be because you love me. When I get back I hope you'll know if you do."

"Barrett! No!"

Barrett gripped her shoulders stiffly and kissed her on the forehead. "I'll be sailing with your aunt," he said. "I won't see you again before I go."

Wan arrived with Barrett's hat. Without another word he turned and left her. Lilah gritted her teeth and felt her temper rise and pound in her brain like an angry surf. If she had a knife, she believed she could cut out Tabor Stanton's heart. Damn him! How dare he place himself between her and Barrett? How dared he? Flushed with anger, Lilah would have liked to retreat to the sanctum of her room, but instead masked her wrath behind a shaky smile and returned to the ballroom.

"Where's Barrett?" her father asked. "I wanted to discuss a few things with him."

Lilah glanced anxiously at Dinah, who stood at her father's side. Her sister's face betrayed nothing of what she might be thinking. Lilah, however, felt sure she wouldn't have told Papa about the incident.

"He left, Papa," she said calmly. "He said he'd changed his mind about going to London and needed to begin getting ready."

Clement's brows shot up. "In the middle of the night?"

Lilah took a deep breath and went on, hoping she wouldn't lose track of all the lies she was telling. "You know how conscientious Barrett is, Papa. He won't leave until he's finished up everything here. If he has paperwork to do, he'll stay up all night getting it done."

"Yes, he would," Clement agreed. "Well, Emily will be delighted to know she won't be making the voyage alone. I'll go over and tell her."

As her father wheeled himself away, Lilah decided she would go to her room just for a few minutes, thinking that some cool water on her wrists might soothe her nerves. Dinah declined to join her. Neither Lilah nor her father noticed, as they left Dinah in the ballroom, that she looked exactly like a cat eyeing the milk pail.

Lilah slumped in the chair at her dressing table. The cool water hadn't helped. She wondered why she had thought anything so simple could ease her mind. Barrett was terribly hurt by what he'd seen. She couldn't blame him. Nor could she fathom how she had allowed Tabor to kiss her again. One minute she wanted to claw out Tabor's eyes and the next she was mindlessly entwined in his arms. She hadn't resisted that embrace. Poor Barrett. He deserved better.

Still chiding herself for having hurt Barrett, Lilah left her bedroom. She did have an obligation as hostess of Damon House. Papa expected her to attend their guests. She hurried along, knowing she wouldn't be able to stand herself if she disappointed anyone else tonight. Somberly she stepped through the doorway, but paused as, up the hall, she saw Tabor descending the staircase from the third floor. Lilah hurriedly slipped back into her room and waited for him to pass.

A few minutes later she again left her room, descended the stairs, and rejoined the party. She found Emily breathless from dancing and thirsty for champagne. Emily excused herself from a silver-haired gentleman who had taken most of her dances, by promising him more once she had caught her breath. Lilah sent a servant for two glasses of champagne.

"Are you enjoying the ball, Aunt Emily?"

Emily produced a fan from the folds of her skirt and waved it gently to stir a breeze. "My dear, I am," she said. "I have to take back all the derogatory things I said about California." She laughed and her eyes twinkled in delight. "Why, if Clement had held the ball the first week of my visit, I might not be going back at all."

"I'm really sorry you aren't staying longer," Lilah said, "Dinah and I will miss you very much. Papa too."

"Oh!" Emily said abruptly. "Then you haven't spoken to Dinah."

Lilah looked puzzled. "I did a short while ago. Is something wrong?"

"No, no, dear," Emily assured her. "Dinah has

decided to visit me in London after all. Isn't it just like her to change her mind at the last minute?"

Lilah sat back, momentarily stunned. Dinah going to London. What had brought that about? She had a shadowy thought of something Tabor had put in her mind, but that was ridiculous. Why should she give any credibility to what *he* suggested? Dinah wanted to spend time with Emily. Nothing more.

When Emily's dance partner returned to claim her, Lilah left her chair to wind through the crowd and speak to any guests she might have missed chatting with earlier. Her duty done, she eased out of the ballroom and into a breezeway where she could stand and watch the dancers without being hounded for requests to take a spin over the floor herself. Since coming in from the garden, she had completely lost interest in dancing.

The husky voice of Tabor Stanton assailed her. "You look pensive."

Lilah grimaced and whirled around. "If you come near me I'll scream," she said in a low voice. "Haven't you caused me enough trouble tonight? Forever?"

Tabor propped his shoulder against a marble pillar. "The way I add it up, I'm a good month behind."

"Meaning?"

"Meaning that's less time than I lost being jailed and combing the countryside looking for a double-dealing songstress who caused me more trouble than I can care to recall."

"I told you that was a mistake." She couldn't give him much argument on that. "I've offered to make it up to you."

Tabor grinned. "You will. And soon."

Lilah's anger was thunderous. She started to walk away before it broke loose.

"Leaving?" He caught her arm lightly.

She shrugged away. "Yes. Please take note that I would appreciate your keeping your hands to yourself while you are here. This harassment wasn't part of our deal."

"Harassment, sweetheart? If touching you and kissing you are harassment, you're in for a lot of punishment later on."

Hours later Lilah was pleased to see the last guest leave. She kissed Papa good night before Ching wheeled him away. She was too tired even to think about talking to Dinah about her reasons for going to London. She longed for the peace and darkness of her room. Still, it was a long time later before she fell asleep.

She awoke with a start only a few minutes later.

"You're beautiful asleep," Tabor whispered from her bedside.

Lilah's heart sounded a drumbeat. She scrambled over in the bed, wondering if that darkly handsome face was part of a dream or frightfully real.

"How did you get in here?"

He laughed and seated himself on the edge of the bed. "I like that," he said. "Not a scream. Not a demand I get out, but a question. Didn't anyone ever tell you what curiosity cost the cat?"

Lilah glared at him, too angry to be scared. "You can't get away with this. Not in my father's house."

"Keep calm," he said softly. "My intentions are honorable tonight." Lilah's brows lifted suspiciously. "I came to tell you I'm sorry about upsetting your friend Barrett. I really didn't mean to let my grievance with you affect anyone else."

"That's awfully high-minded of you." She sneered. "If I believed anything you're saying—which I don't."

"Why, Lilah," he teased, lifting the sheet and tucking it under her chin, "I believe you're disappointed. Are you as anxious as I am for our week to get started?"

Lilah saw a look in his eyes she didn't misread as honor. Her heart skipped several beats and her flesh shivered with forbidden excitement. She was dismayed to realize the wayward sense of longing meant she *was* disappointed.

"Go away, please," she whispered.

Tabor laughed and smothered her words with a kiss. Her pulse throbbed in the hollow of her throat. Her skin burned as if she'd been thrown into a fire. Lilah felt herself going dangerously weak as his lips moved with fury on hers. His hand captured one soft breast, his thumb toying with the tiny stiffened peak. His tongue tasted her lips, flicked over her teeth, then plunged on into the dark warm chasm of her mouth, taunting her in a hundred sensuous ways until she was kissing him back and with her deepening response demanding more, more. The kiss was too short, too draining. Tabor pulled away, leaving her whimpering and breathless with passion while he held his ardor in check and smiled down at her.

"Don't worry, sweetheart," he whispered. "It won't be long." He left the curtains at the balcony doors fluttering.

12

"I asked Barrett to Damon House for dinner last night." Clement lingered at the breakfast table with Lilah while Emily and Dinah were upstairs attending to the last of their packing. "He said he was too busy getting his notes and belongings together." Clement's gaze lifted from the muffin he was buttering to Lilah. "I was surprised he didn't make time to see you before he left."

"We said good-bye earlier, Papa." Lilah shifted uncomfortably in her chair, wishing she had gone upstairs with the other women. She had written Barrett a note of apology and received a brisk reply with a restatement of his refusal to see her before his departure. She was thankful Papa didn't plan going along to the docks to see Emily and Dinah off. She fully expected Barrett to board the ship without another word to her.

Clement eyed Lilah carefully. She hadn't been herself since the ball. "I got the impression something unpleasant happened between the two of you. Should I know about it?"

Lilah felt her flesh color as she tried to think of a way to answer her father without telling another outright lie. "Barrett wants to give me time to be sure I want to marry him."

"I thought he knew that." Clement took a bite of muffin.

"He does, Papa. He's just being overly cautious. Check and double-check. You know his ways."

Clement's brows rose a degree. "This has nothing to do with Stanton?"

Lilah fidgeted. "Why would you think that?"

Clement chuckled softly. Lilah's discomfiture was evident. "Because I notice far more than you realize. You may not be aware of it yourself, but something draws you to Tabor. I can see that you're fighting it, but it's there."

"Papa! That's ridiculous." Lilah wrung her napkin beneath the table. Was it so evident? "I have no interest in Tabor Stanton. Certainly not the romantic interest you suggest." She had half a mind to tell her father what his "friend" Stanton wanted of her. Maybe he wouldn't react as badly as she thought to finding out she was Delilah.

Clement started to laugh but ended up in a grimace instead. His face turned red and he drew in several heavy breaths.

"Papa!" Lilah cried.

"It's nothing," he said, pushing back from the table. "Just a pain reminding me these legs aren't completely dead." Once again he breathed deeply. "I'm afraid I've been pushing myself too hard these last few days. Too many trips to town. It's catching up with me."

"Oh, Papa." Lilah hurried to his chair. "You're ill."

"Not ill, just tired," he insisted, signaling Ching to come to him. "I'm going back to bed." Reassuringly, he patted Lilah's hand. "A day of rest and I'll be better than ever tomorrow." With difficulty Clement smiled. "Tabor's trying another rider on the stallion tomorrow. I don't want to miss that."

Wordlessly Ching came and wheeled Clement away to his suite at the rear of the house. Lilah stood stoically where her father had left her. How she wished she had sold that horse instead of giving him to Papa. Tabor might never have known the truth if he hadn't seen the horse.

Lilah's face fell further as she realized she couldn't possibly burden her father with anything else. He had enough to contend with just trying to stay well. Her problem was one she had brought on herself. Rather than upset Papa, she would go through with what Tabor expected. She really had no choice.

Shortly after Ching took her father away, Lilah left the dining room. There was nothing she could do for him that Ching couldn't do better. When he was ill or in pain, Clement preferred Ching's attendance of his needs to even that of his doctors. Ching knew the secrets of many herbs, roots, and other compounds yet unknown to Western medicine. When the pain was acute, he sometimes used long needles to puncture the skin. As much as the use of acupuncture alarmed his doctors, Clement insisted the treatment brought him relief. Lilah, too, occasionally availed herself of Ching's remedies, finding them more palatable and effective than those her doctor prescribed.

She had only a short wait before the servants brought the last trunks down and Emily and Dinah joined her in the downstairs parlor. Emily was understandably pleased that she would have Barrett's and Dinah's company on the voyage. Lilah still didn't understand why Dinah had suddenly decided on going along. However, she supposed she would never understand her younger sister's capricious ways. A bit sad, Lilah took hold of Emily's hands, recalling it might be years before she saw her aunt again.

Emily, who very much wanted to prevent a show of tears at her departure, hurriedly asked after Clement.

"Papa wasn't feeling well and has gone to bed," Lilah explained.

"I won't disturb him," Emily said, her eyes showing the sympathy she felt for her brother-in-law. "He's made the arrangements for the trunks to go on ahead and we said good-bye at breakfast. Is the carriage ready?" she asked, opening the gold watch she wore pinned on her jacket and checking the time.

"Wan will call us," Dinah said, tying the ribbons of a russet-colored bonnet trimmed with yellow and blue silk flowers. When the bow was carefully tightened beneath her chin, she took Lilah's hands fondly. "Tell Papa I love him and he's not to worry about me," Dinah said softly. "I love you too, Lilah," she added in an even softer voice. "Regardless of our differences, I still love you. You won't forget that, will you?"

"What a silly goose you are. Of course I won't forget. We're sisters. Nothing could stop us loving each other." Lilah kissed Dinah's cheek, and having pulled her hands free, wrapped her sister in her arms. She couldn't hold back several tears that splashed onto her lashes. "I think I'm even sillier." Lilah dabbed her tears away with a handkerchief. "I was thinking of having you all grown up when you come back."

"Oh, Lilah. It won't be so long." Now Dinah hugged Lilah, and though her eyes filled with warm tears, she smiled. "You take care of Papa."

Before Lilah could assure Dinah she would, Wan

announced the carriage. Emily and Dinah gathered the things they wanted to carry on board the ship, and with Lilah leading the way, left Damon House.

"Barrett is to meet us before we board," Dinah volunteered as the carriage approached the waterfront. "He came down earlier."

Lilah made no reply, since she hadn't been aware Barrett was waiting for Dinah and Emily. But there he was near the gangplank of the *Serendipity*. Looking solemn, he stood by quietly as she and Dinah and Emily had another round of good-byes. He waited quietly too as Dinah and Emily boarded.

"We won't write, Lilah. I think that's best." A lively wind whipped Barrett's blond hair. He clutched his hat in his hand rather than lose it. Lilah was glad she had added extra hatpins to keep hers secure. Even at that she felt the need to reach up and hold it as the velocity of the wind increased.

"If that's what you prefer, Barrett." The bitterness she detected in Barrett's voice saddened her. At least he had spared her the humiliation of a rebuff in front of Emily and Dinah.

"It is," he said curtly. "Oh, it's not what my heart wants, but it's what my head tells me I should do. All the time I'm away I'll be hoping to find you waiting here on the dock when I return. I'll be hoping to find you'll tell me you want to share the rest of your life with me."

"I'll be here, Barrett," she said over a lump in her throat.

His expression was strained but proud as he took Lilah's hand and pressed it firmly. He made no attempt to kiss her good-bye. After a few moments more with neither of them certain what else to say, he released her hand and turned and walked away.

Dinah, watching with Aunt Emily from the deck of

the ship, observed the lack of affection in the farewell. She smiled and waved vigorously to Lilah as Barrett climbed the gangplank.

Lilah stayed on the dock until the three of them left the deck to go into the ship's salon. Feeling very hollow, she walked slowly to the carriage and climbed in. Sighing, she dropped back against the pleated leather carriage cushions, wondering what was wrong with her that she actually felt relief at not having to concern herself with Barrett or Dinah for a time. Where were her tears that she might lose the man she had planned to spend her life with? She did believe she was becoming callous. In the end she decided her lack of feeling came from the strain put on her by Tabor Stanton. So be it. But as soon as Barrett returned, she would have Papa announce their engagement.

By then Tabor would have had his satisfaction. She would have completed her last tour as Delilah. The tour would be a short one, just long enough to mete out a measure of justice to the Penn brothers. Thankfully, too, Dinah would not be along. She would be safe in London. Lilah was confident Barrett would aid Aunt Emily in looking after her sister.

Clement was three days recovering and getting strong enough to resume his routine activities. Lilah ordered meals prepared and served to Tabor during that time, but took her own meals privately, if at all. She locked her balcony doors each night, though she was positive Tabor hadn't tried to enter her room again. As if he understood her concern, he gave her no additional worries during Clement's illness, spending most of his time at the stable.

The stallion now accepted any rider. Before, he had allowed only Tabor on his back. She heard from the servants that Tabor had begun working with Clement's other horses and that he was overseeing the selection of mares for breeding with Rogue. Thinking it over, and with a haughty slant of her brows, she was sure Tabor found that matter to his liking.

Clement's recovery ended Lilah's reprieve from Tabor. She could hardly avoid him when Papa had ordered a special dinner served in the small family dining room, which meant that the three of them would share a cozy table. Seated at her father's right, she was forced to gaze into Tabor's smoldering eyes all evening. Only the fact that they were celebrating her father's improved health made the meal tolerable.

"I'll want to see Rogue put through his paces early tomorrow morning," Clement said. "Sorry to have held you up here, son. I know you're anxious to get back to your ranch."

Son? Lilah flinched, wondering if her father really was recovered from his illness. How could he, even in a slip of the tongue, refer to Tabor as "son"?

"It's been a pleasure," Tabor replied in an infuriatingly casual way. "All pleasure."

"Glad to hear it," Clement said. "I'm sure Lilah's been a good hostess."

Lilah's back stiffened and she was once again aware that Tabor kept her so tense it was a wonder her spine didn't snap. He took his time to answer, giving her agonizing moments of worry over whether or not he would tell Clement she had avoided him as she would a rattlesnake.

"I won't complain." He could but he wouldn't. Catching glimpses of Lilah as he passed through the house, seeing her hurry away when she saw him, hadn't been easy to take. He'd seen how worried she was about her father, he had even had a desire to tell her how sorry he was that Clement was ill. But he suspected his sentiments would be poorly received. The sharp look she was giving him now let him know he had been right.

"That's kind of you, Tabor." Lilah's eyes glittered with anger. She hoped Papa wouldn't notice.

"Actually there's something I want to ask you," Tabor said, giving Lilah a more intensified moment of dread. "Lilah and I have talked about this and she's agreed." He shot her a fiendish smile. "She didn't think you'd object but, of course, she wants your approval first."

Clement looked at both Tabor and Lilah in surprise. It wasn't like Lilah to allow someone else to do her talking for her. He could think of only one explanation. But surely Tabor wasn't about to ask for Lilah's hand. Things couldn't have moved along that fast. If that were the case, he had no idea what he would say.

"Tabor—" Lilah started in alarm, but Tabor wouldn't let her finish.

"I've written to my aunt, told her about you and Lilah. Well . . ." He hedged, fumbling in his shirt pocket. "What I'm getting at is in this letter." He handed the letter to Clement. "Aunt Sarah has invited Lilah to the Cooke ranch for a visit. She could travel down with me day after tomorrow. We would meet Sarah on the trail the first day out. Lilah wouldn't be without a chaperon. I sure would like for her to come along." He slipped Lilah a wink. "If you're agreeable, that is."

Clement read the short letter. "It's entirely up to my daughter, Tabor. If she wants to go, she has my approval." He turned to Lilah. "How about it?"

Lilah fumed. Tabor had sprung this on her in her father's presence without any warning it was coming. Just when she was beginning to think there was some good substance in the man because he hadn't badgered her while her father was ill, he proved her wrong.

"I'm undecided, Papa." She thought she at least owed herself the chance to call his bluff. "When Tabor and I talked, I didn't know I'd be leaving you alone. But now that Dinah is away, perhaps I should stay with you. You've just gotten well."

"Don't let that hold you," Clement insisted, dashing her thin wall of resistance. "Loo will be back soon and she's almost worse than you about fussing over me." He smiled. "Go if you like."

She bit into her lip to keep from losing control. "I'll think it over, Papa. Perhaps I'll delay the visit a few weeks. I'd like to be sure you're all right first." Lilah knew from past experience that her father's severe attacks were infrequent. He wasn't likely to have another one soon. But Tabor had no way of knowing that. She cut her eyes toward him, daring him to push his advantage any further.

"Maybe Lilah's right," he spoke up, giving her a brief taste of victory. "She could visit later. I won't be bored staying in San Francisco a few more weeks. Why, just the other day I heard a rumor that that gal Delilah, touted as the Flame of the West, would be performing in the city. Have you ever seen her, Clement?"

"No," Clement responded. "But if she does come to San Francisco, you and I will take in the show together."

Tabor looked at Lilah and tipped his head. "Pardon me, ma'am, for bringing up an unsavory topic in the presence of a lady. I'm sure you find a man's interest in a dance-hall miss appalling. And pardon me for adding fat to the fire," he went on, "but has anyone ever mentioned that you bear a slight resemblance to Delilah?"

The sweet taste in Lilah's mouth turned bitter. "No, Tabor," she said sharply, her face whitening with indignation. "No one has." The bastard! He had upped the ante in this game, to stakes she didn't dare match.

Tabor's face fell, but only Lilah knew how false the appearance was. "I'm truly sorry, Lilah," he said remorsefully. "I see I have offended you. I assure you that wasn't my intent. Delilah is a beautiful woman—for her kind."

"I see." Lilah had to choke on the damning words she wanted to fling at Tabor. His not-at-all-subtle mention of Delilah was a warning. He would tell Papa about her if she didn't agree to do as he suggested. "Since I don't ever expect to have a chance to judge for myself if I do resemble Delilah, perhaps we can drop the topic."

Clement chuckled at his daughter's show of disdain for the entertainer. He knew things Tabor didn't about Lilah. That ladylike demeanor she now wore hadn't come naturally to her. He had let her come up free-spirited until he had been forced to send her to Emily in London. Once, as a young girl, she had met Lola Montez. The dark-haired beauty had been impressed with Lilah's quick skill at learning the dance steps and songs she showed her. For weeks afterward Lilah had climbed up on an empty crate and put on a song-and-dance show for anyone who would watch. He supposed Lilah had forgotten that long ago and would be dreadfully embarrassed to be reminded. He sure hoped his daughter wasn't beginning to let wealth and status go to her head.

"My apologies again," Tabor said. "Now, when you get ready for that visit to the ranch, you just let me know."

Lilah barely managed to voice the words she hated having to say: "I've changed my mind, Tabor. Since Papa insists he's feeling fine, I'll be ready to go the day after tomorrow."

His dark eyes told her he looked forward to the next contest.

Lilah awoke in the night with an intuitive feeling that something was wrong. She glanced toward the open window as a muffled noise sounded from below. That part of her room was over the hallway to Papa's suite. Thinking something might be wrong with him, she hurriedly lit a lamp and slipped on a silk wrapper. With the lamp lighting her way, she rushed out of her room and toward the staircase. Halfway down, she paused, hearing another unwelcome noise. Footsteps, two sets, clattered from the direction of the back hall. Lilah quickened her own steps, frightfully aware there could be no good reason for people to be rushing to Papa's rooms.

Darkness filled the hallway. The wall lamp that normally burned through the night had been extinguished. Up ahead she heard the sound of a scuffle before the ring of light from her lamp showed two murky shadows locked in a struggle. Papa was in danger. For a moment she had the same sick, helpless feeling she'd had that last night in the Damon Star camp. Clutching her stomach, Lilah whimpered like a frightened child. From within the struggle, one dark head shot up and caught enough light to reveal the features.

"Tabor!"

Tabor looked up from the fight into a face ghostly white with fear. Lilah! Couldn't she have stayed where she belonged? He hadn't heard the soft rustle of her nightclothes. Damn her! She could only make things worse. He started to shout her away, but already the distraction had cost him. His opponent landed a dizzying punch to his jaw.

Lilah gasped. She could see the other man now. He

had a length of hair braided into a pigtail, which marked him as Chinese. She was sure she didn't know him. Her father had recently hired some new men, but that didn't explain why this one was in the house or why he was fighting Tabor. She steadied her lamp on a window ledge and edged slowly past the pair. Her guiding thought was that her father was in danger and she had to get to him.

Tabor's head hit the wall and the Chinese was quickly on him again. Tabor had a split second to bring his knees up and shove his feet into the Chinese's belly. The man bellowed in pain and staggered back across the narrow hall.

"Stay back!" Tabor shouted at Lilah.

She had little choice. Now she couldn't move without getting between the two men. Trembling, she realized she wasn't completely sure which one was the threat.

Like a big mountain cat, Tabor sprang across the hall and pinned the Chinese to the wall. Suddenly his opponent seemed to have as many legs as a spider. One of his scattered kicks cracked against Tabor's shin. The pain loosened Tabor's hold and the Chinese was free. He raced two steps toward an open window and escape, but Tabor caught hold of his shirt and hauled him back.

The Chinese had tried to escape, Lilah thought. Ching's men would never have done that. She felt a strange wave of relief it hadn't been Tabor attempting to break into her father's room.

Pressed flat against the wall between shelves housing her father's collection of Indian pottery, Lilah held her breath as she saw the savage shimmer of a knife blade in the tangle. One man groaned. In the knotting of arms and legs and dark clothing, Lilah couldn't tell who, nor could she tell which man wielded the weapon.

Her heartbeat faltered at the thought that it might be the Chinese and not Tabor who was armed.

Without thinking how rashly she acted or that it was Tabor Stanton she risked everything for, Lilah grabbed a pottery bowl and ran toward the fray. In the thin light, it was hard to distinguish which man each head of black hair belonged to. Lilah stood with the bowl poised. When she saw what appeared to be the wave of the pigtail, she crashed the bowl against the head to which it was attached. One man slumped on top of the other.

"Never miss, do you?" Tabor climbed from beneath the unconscious Chinese.

"You can be glad of that!" With her fear of the Chinese gone, Lilah's hostility toward Tabor came rushing back. "Who is that man?"

"I guess that means he's not one of the servants." Tabor pulled the knife from the Chinese's hand and tucked it into his belt. He paused to straighten his clothes and run his bruised fingers through his tousled hair.

Lilah took a closer look at the moon-shaped face. "I'm sure I've never seen him. I'd better call Ching."

"No rush," Tabor said, whirling around and giving Lilah reason to wonder if she shouldn't have cracked the bowl on the other skull. Wildly he swung her into his arms and pressed his mouth to hers.

"Don't!" Lilah sputtered her outrage. But as his lips moved on hers, she felt herself growing weak and confused.

"Thanks." Tabor stepped back, noting the glow in her eyes.

"For what?" she mumbled, still dazed.

His eyes sparkled. "For trying to save me. I had no idea you cared so much."

"You simpleminded fool!" Lilah's face reddened. "I

wouldn't have cared if he had cut you into cubes. I was afraid he would get to Papa."

"Now, Lilah," Tabor teased. "Don't be shy."

"You idiot!" In her fury Lilah grabbed another pottery bowl and heaved it at Tabor. He dodged and the bowl shattered at his feet.

Lilah's hands covered her mouth as she realized she had just destroyed another of her father's prized artifacts.

"What's that commotion, Ching?"

Hearing her father's voice from inside his room, Lilah looked quickly toward the now open doorway and saw Ching standing there. She didn't notice that as he folded his arms into his sleeves, he hid the weapon he had held in readiness. She did wonder how long he had stood there and silently watched.

Ching's expression remained unreadable as he knelt and lifted the downed Chinese's head.

"An intruder," he said in answer to Clement's question.

Clement wheeled himself to the doorway. His face ran a flurry of varied expressions. He looked at Lilah, at Tabor, at the unconscious man, the broken bowls.

"Do you know him?" he asked Ching, aware his companion knew most of the Chinese in the city.

By now several of the servants, having heard the strange noises, had ventured into the hall. Ching gave them orders in Chinese. One boy nodded quickly and ran off.

"He calls himself Joe Han. He is a hired man, not one to work on his own," Ching reported in his flat voice.

"I saw him slink out of your library and head down this hall," Tabor said. "When I asked his business, he attacked me."

"Lilah?" Clement wondered how she had gotten into the altercation.

"A noise awakened me. I came downstairs to see what it was," Lilah explained. Standing close to her father, she rested a shaky hand on the back of his chair. "I was afraid for you, Papa."

Clement touched her hand as he looked up at Tabor. "I'm grateful to you for stopping him," he said, then quickly lifted his brow in surprise when Tabor laughed.

"I would have," Tabor said. "But Lilah put him in that state by cracking one of those bowls over his head." He gestured toward the empty spots on the shelves.

Lilah was relieved Clement didn't have a chance to ask what had happened to the second bowl. The boy Ching had sent out returned with two of the Chinese men who usually watched the grounds of Damon House. She couldn't understand a word but knew Ching's staccato orders to take the man away included a strong reproach that he had been allowed to slip past them.

"My men will find out why he was here before they turn him over to the authorities." Clement turned to Ching and asked that he have other men search the house in case Joe Han had not come alone. Ching responded that was already being done. "Let's have a look at the library, then," Clement said.

The party moved up the now brightly lighted hall. Lilah tightened her wrapper around her waist and was conscious of the cool tiles under her bare feet. At Clement's insistence she waited outside with a servant while the men made an investigation in the library. After a few silent minutes she couldn't stand the wait and slipped inside herself. Nothing was obviously out of place in the room. Only a close inspection revealed one desk drawer not quite shut, a painting no longer hanging straight, and several books replaced on the wrong shelves.

Clement cursed more violently than Lilah had ever heard him.

"What did he want, Papa?" She voiced the question all of them had in their minds.

"I had a bag of coins in that drawer," Clement said. "The men will probably find it in his pockets. He seems to have taken a few papers from my desk. Nothing of importance—all those that matter are in the bank vault. Some of the ivory figurines are missing, a piece of the jade too, I think. It doesn't look as if he came for anything in particular. He was a very tidy thief, probably figured we wouldn't notice for some time that he'd been here."

"You don't think he was intentionally headed for your suite?" Tabor asked.

"I doubt it," Clement said. "Most likely he was looking for more small items he could carry away in his pockets. This kind of thieving is happening more and more often around here. That's why I keep guards on the grounds."

"For all the good they did," Lilah remarked.

She saw Ching's slanted eyes narrow. It was all the assurance she or Clement needed that such a thing would never occur again at Damon House. She pitied the guards who would take Ching's full wrath. One of those poor fellows came in a few minutes later and relayed what he had learned from Joe Han. He spoke quietly in Chinese to Ching.

Ching related the entire story without pause. "Joe Han was persuaded to rob this house by a man he met in Chinatown. He was told a crippled man lived here and there would be no danger. For showing him this house, Joe Han was to divide his take with this man. He was instructed to steal papers from the desk and any money he found. Whatever else he took was to remain his. He does not know this man's name, only that he was a white. The man was to meet him a street away half an hour ago. The men are going there now."

Clement frowned. "If he was smart enough not to come inside, he'll be smart enough to know something has gone wrong after this long. I suggest we all get to bed. Ching and his men will see to everything that needs to be done."

Ching, rather than leave Clement alone, called for another of his men to accompany him to his suite. Lilah held her father's hand and walked with him as far as the door.

"Promise me the next time you hear odd noises you'll call for help before you explore," Clement admonished Lilah.

"I will, Papa. I promise." She smiled. "I really don't know what prompted me to come downstairs like that, but I'm glad I did."

"And I appreciate what you did, Lilah. But I'm sure Tabor could have stopped Joe Han. I don't like you risking your safety for me."

"Papa—"

"I mean it, Lilah. Don't you realize what I want in life is for you and Dinah to be happy? I have all I care about or need in my two girls. I don't want you sacrificing yourself for me. What would I have to live for then?"

"All right, Papa," she said obediently. "I'll be careful. For you. Good night." She kissed his cheek.

Until he was satisfied everything was safe at Damon House, Ching had ordered that Lilah be escorted to and from her room. A Chinese guard accompanied her to her bedroom door and waited with her while another went inside and checked both the bedroom and adjoining sitting room. Only then was Lilah allowed to enter. With the guards outside, she closed her door and turned the key in the latch.

"He almost spotted me," Tabor said as he stepped through the balcony doors.

Lilah scarcely gave him a glance. "Go away," she said weakly, dropping down on the dressing-table bench. "I want to be alone."

"You were scared down there, weren't you?" Tabor crossed the room in a few strides. "I thought maybe cracking skulls came as easily to you as breathing."

Now that the danger was over, Lilah felt exhaustion take over. "If that man had gotten into Papa's room . . ."

"Ching would have killed him before he took a step."

Lilah looked up in astonishment. That was undoubtedly true. But for some reason it hadn't occurred to her at the time. Just as it hadn't occurred to her to call for Ching's assistance while Tabor fought Joe Han. Down there in the darkness, caught up in the struggle and danger, she had thought she was the only one who could protect Papa. Now she felt foolish and frightened.

"I wasn't thinking clearly," she said.

Tabor propped one foot on a stool and leaned his elbow on his knee, bringing his face quite close to hers.

"You fuss over your father like a mother hen with chicks. You treat him like . . ."

"An invalid?" Lilah's eyes heated up.

"Your father isn't an invalid, Lilah. He's got more life in him than most men with two good legs. He doesn't need your doting."

"You've known my father a few weeks. Does that give you divine insight into his needs?" she tossed back.

"I know what kind of man he is. I don't think you

do. I don't think you know what kind of woman you are, either."

She lifted her shoulders. "You seem determined to find out."

"I am. Maybe I would have let you out of that bet days ago if I could have settled on just who and what you are. But you fascinate me and I can't be satisfied until I know which part of you is real." He stared into Lilah's eyes, seeking what lay behind them. "Tonight you were a scared little girl. I saw that in your face."

The spell of his eyes held her. For a moment she couldn't think. Not until he raised her chin with his finger did the words come through.

"Anybody would have been scared," she said bluntly.

"It was more than ordinary fear. I almost forgot the Chinese when I saw the look on your face. Nothing about you adds up, Lilah. You're a woman torn into pieces, and every time I put them together, I get another picture."

"Why does it matter to you?" she asked, turning her head so that she freed herself from his touch. "You could have your horse and your money back if you wanted it."

He looped his fingers possessively in her flowing hair. Just touching her started a tightening in his loins. He let go of her hair as he realized touching her also brought alive more dangerous feelings, those warm and tender ones a man could lose himself in.

"I don't know why it matters," he said gruffly, angered at how his body ached for her. "But what happened tonight doesn't change anything. You *are* going with me to the ranch. Just as planned."

13

"Papa, remember to tell Loo to look after Lotus."
Lilah stroked the orange tabby's silky fur a last time,
then took the cat and laid her on a cushion.

Dressed in a fringed jacket over a blue cotton blouse,
a divided buckskin skirt, and high boots, Lilah was
ready for the journey to Tabor's ranch. A brown felt
hat hung loosely on her back, held there by a leather
chin strap. Experience having taught Lilah that her
abundant hair would not hold in a bun when subjected
to the rigors of a long ride, she wore it fashioned into
a single braid that swung over one shoulder.

"The cat won't be neglected, Lilah. Nothing here is.
Now, stop your dallying and tell me good-bye too. Or
is Lotus the only one entitled to farewell kisses?"
Clement had watched patiently for nearly half an hour
as Lilah found an endless string of nonessential tasks
to do.

Out of excuses for delaying her departure with Tabor, Lilah hastened to her father. She knelt on the
floor beside his chair.

"You're sure you don't mind if I go away, Papa? I could still—"

Scoffing at her, Clement brushed cat fur from the sleeve of Lilah's riding jacket. "I want you to go, Lilah. Haven't I always insisted you and Dinah take up every opportunity that comes your way? It will do you good to stay on a ranch, to get another taste of the vigorous life you had as a child."

"I hope you're right, Papa," Lilah said softly, her heart trembling with misgivings.

"Rigorous" was perhaps a better description for what she would expect on this trip. She did hate leaving Papa again so soon, and yet some small mutinous part of her actually relished what lay ahead. It almost seemed that her creation, Delilah, cried out from somewhere deep inside that she would have her way. With a tender look, Tabor made her want to abandon the strong and puritanical values Aunt Emily had instilled in her youthful mind. One gentle touch from him and she was ready to forget her conviction that a woman's virtue must be placed above all else. One kiss from his warm, eager lips and she was ready to live the legend of Delilah and to become, for him, a woman of fire who followed no rules but her own.

Ah, well, she sighed. That was fine when the rules were only the dry old laws of justice. But the rules which governed her body were another matter indeed. She had never held back bending the law when in the end the curve led on to justice. But what would happen if she bent the rules of what was right or wrong between a man and woman? Where would she find herself then? At least as things were now, she knew where the dividing line stood. But where would it be and where would she be once she crossed that carnal threshold?

The dilemma brought Lilah a deep frown and a

rather muddled thought that it was quite unfair she should have to make restitution for one of Delilah's misdeeds. Tabor Stanton was driving her insane, and once again she searched her mind for a way to undo what she had agreed to. Only the memory of how ill her father had been a scant few days ago kept her from blurting out the scandalous thing she was about to do. But, better she sacrifice her innocence than put Papa's heart to the test.

And yet, as she stood and the moment to leave was before her, Lilah prepared to say something—though she had no idea what—something, anything, to break through the compounding confusion in her head. Nervous excitement built inside her like steam in a kettle, needing an outlet. She knew she should be hating what lay ahead, but only part of her did; the other part insisted on rebelling and feeling a strangely wayward elation about it. Truly that was the most frightening thing of all. She almost spilled out her feelings, but looked up and saw Tabor standing in the library door, an intimidating look marring his handsome face.

Clement, unaware Tabor was near, cocked his head and looked curiously at Lilah. Lately she had been as moody and detached as Dinah. "Is something bothering you, Lilah, or are you simply apprehensive about leaving me?"

"Yes. Yes, Papa," she said, partially for Tabor's sake. Finding it easy to blame him for all the turmoil in her head, she gave him a quick and loathsome glance. "Since that man, Joe Han, got into the house, I've wondered if I shouldn't stay home."

Clement considered what she said. "If I thought there was any danger of that happening again, I believe I'd feel better if you were away."

Lilah felt another slip in her composure. That line

of defense had gotten her nowhere. "You're sure Ching has taken care of the problem?"

"One of the guards fell asleep. I'm sure that won't happen again even if the man has to poke pins in himself to stay awake. Don't you worry about me or Damon House. Go with Tabor. Have yourself an adventure." He smiled and leaned forward for Lilah's kiss.

As Lilah hugged her father, over his shoulder she saw Tabor's smirking face. Of course Papa didn't intend it, but she was being manipulated by both him and that black-hearted rogue who worked such mayhem in her life. Once again, just for an instant, she considered telling Papa the truth. She relented. She did have to go. Papa wasn't as well as he insisted. He didn't need the shock Tabor held in store for him should she refuse.

As Lilah sat astride Darling and rode beside Tabor on the chestnut gelding her father had lent him, the reality of her plight took hold. Tabor rode as if he were born to the saddle, completely at home on a horse, which was more than she could say for herself. Green meadows and tall pines rolled by, and here and there a naked hill rose up in the distance. Little plumes of red dust floated out behind the horses' hooves. In the distance the shadowy reaches of higher hills stretched toward the clouds. More often than not, Lilah found herself engrossed in memorizing the lines of Tabor's profile rather than in studying the landscape. One was as strong and rugged as the other, though Tabor's face, as she recalled, could grow soft and sensitive at times.

And when it did, his stormy eyes went gentle, his voice husky and low. It rather pleased her to know she had the power to bring about that change in him. How wonderful it would be if she *could* be Delilah, only Delilah, and do and feel exactly as she pleased. Ripples of excitement flowed through her at the thought of it. Lilah gasped softly as she acknowledged that what had prompted her wishful thinking was desire. That she felt it for a man who wanted her only to prove a point nettled her to no end. But even that didn't stop the uncoiling of her longing for him.

Disgusted with herself, Lilah turned her head away and refused to look at him any more. What she was thinking and feeling wasn't proper even if that wayward part of her kept telling her to give in to it. Admittedly she had played the seductress as Delilah. But that had been only a role, as she had so pointedly explained to Tabor. How she behaved as Delilah didn't truly reflect the person of Lilah Damon. Couldn't he understand that? Mile after mile went by in stony silence until finally she had whipped her anxiety into ready anger and directed it all at Tabor. Eyes glowering, Lilah turned toward him.

"You are the most despicable man I ever set eyes on," she burst out unexpectedly. "I want it clear right from the start that I loathe you for what you're making me do."

Tabor winced, but he was in too good a humor to let her heated words bother him. He tapped her knee and winked.

"Delilah's back, I see."

His quick remark pinpointed exactly what had her in such a state. Lilah's pent-up temper exploded. She swung at him with her riding crop. He caught it before the swing carried through and wrenched it from her hand. Lilah cursed him and put her heels in Darling's sides. The little mare, already jittery from Lilah's nervous hold on the reins, leapt into a gallop. Swearing, Tabor sent the gelding sprinting after her. The nimble mare was fast and quickly outdistanced Tabor's horse. But eventually the gelding's endurance won out and he overtook the mare.

Lilah spat another oath at Tabor as he reached for Darling's reins. She struck at his hand but couldn't prevent him from getting a grip on the strip of leather. In a few more seconds Tabor pulled both horses to a jolting stop. Lilah was too angry to think anything but that he had forcefully bent her to his will another time. With a cry of defiance, she sprang from the saddle and fled up a rocky hill.

"Lilah!" Tabor shouted.

He didn't know if the horses would stay, so he had to take time to tie them to a scrubby tree before trying to catch her, all the while grumbling about the flightiness of women. Lilah was as unpredictable as weather off the ocean. He never knew if his remarks would bring a cool retort or a furious outburst. In her present frame of mind, she was likely to take a harmful fall on the rocks or into any of the small ravines nearby. She was out of sight by the time he had the horses secured, but had left an easy-to-follow trail of dust.

Tabor raced up the hill, stopping at the gnarled crest of it. He spied Lilah scrambling down the other side. She'd lost her hat. Seeing she wasn't in any danger other than from her temper, he stopped to pick it up, then went on after her. He didn't rush, knowing she would soon be winded. When he saw her slow down, he speeded up.

Lilah was breathless but still had fight in her. When Tabor caught her shoulder, she spun around and slapped him hard.

"What's that for?" He clamped her wrists together to spare himself another lick.

"Just for being here," she said venomously.

Holding her firmly by the shoulders, he pulled her

squarely up against him. "Don't make a habit of it," he threatened. "I'm not going to get to like it."

Lilah struggled a minute, but knowing she was too tired to run anymore or to resist whatever he might do, gave it up and went limp in his grasp. She could feel his chest rise and fall with a deep breath. And in her own the rebellious and alarming tingle of desire started to spread.

"I'm not going to like what you do to me either." A knot rose in her throat. "But that won't stop you, will it?"

He bent his head down so that his breath fanned her hot face. "I told you I won't do anything you don't want me to. That still holds."

"I've told you I don't want you." She felt his taut body move against her as he shifted his weight. Her heart skipped beats, her pulse fluttered like a stricken bird.

Tabor crossed his arms over her back, pressing her tighter against his chest and thighs, feeling her tremble. "With words, Lilah," he said huskily. "You've told me with words. But words lie. Actions don't."

"You lie," she said, pretending not to be affected by being held so close she could feel the slightest move in his muscles; denying her trembling came from a growing excitement rather than fear.

Tabor groaned. How could one woman be so much trouble? And why did he enjoy her kind of trouble so much? Lilah felt so good against him, he had to close his eyes a second just to remind himself the time wasn't right yet. He didn't want to make love to her for the first time at the foot of a rock-strewn hill under the hot, blazing sun. His body had other ideas, though, and they were making themselves known.

"I haven't lied to you, Lilah," he said slowly, easing

his grip just a little. "Though God knows it might have made things easier."

Lilah tensed, not knowing what it meant as she felt a change in him. "You told Papa your aunt would meet us before nightfall." She gulped a breath. "That I wouldn't be on the trail alone with you."

"That's true, sweetheart." His hands moved gently on her back, sending a slow, hot ache right through her. "Sarah's a day's ride from here. If you don't keep running off, we'll catch up to her by nightfall."

"I'm not your sweetheart." Lilah pushed back from him while she still had the will to do so. "And I won't make any promises unless you're going to stop provoking me."

"I'll try," he said, letting her go reluctantly, warning himself that even one kiss wouldn't be safe. Not if he intended to keep his word. "But you stay close. You could run into worse than me out here off the trail."

"I doubt it," Lilah sniped. "What could be worse than you?" Still shaky from all the crazy sensations he'd started inside her, she walked away a few steps and picked up her hat from where Tabor had dropped it when he caught hold of her.

"Let's get back to the horses," he said stiffly. He turned and started up the hill without looking back to see if she followed.

Lilah did follow, finding the climb up more difficult than the one down. She slipped several times on loose rocks, but Tabor didn't offer his help. She supposed she couldn't blame him. Running from him had been foolish. If she wanted to get away, she shouldn't have tried it on foot and she should have waited until they were near a town.

Lilah untied Darling and led her away from the tree. As she mounted, she saw Tabor hesitate and study the ground where the horses had been tethered.

"There are tracks here we didn't make," he said.

Lilah tightened the string on her hat. "Why shouldn't there be?"

Tabor dropped down to examine the marks more closely. "Because your side journey took us a mile off the road. I don't know why anyone else would ride out here. There's no water close by."

Lilah held Darling steady while Tabor mounted. She shot him an accusing look. "I think you are trying to frighten me."

Tabor's patience had its limits. "Suit yourself," he said. "Somebody was mighty interested in what we were doing out here. There are three sets of tracks down there. A blind man could see them."

Lilah could too as they rode onto softer ground. She thought of Joe Han and the way Tabor had fought to protect her father. "Who do you think it was?" she asked contritely.

"I don't know." Tabor slid back his hat and wiped sweat from his brow. "Guess somebody got curious about why we left the trail."

He didn't need to tell her again not to wander off. Lilah quickly concluded there *could* be worse dangers than Tabor. For the next few hours she kept Darling's stride in close pace with the gelding's.

"Just where is this ranch of yours?" Lilah twisted in the saddle to get some of the stiffness out of her back.

Tabor laughed. "Are you just now wondering about that?"

Lilah scowled at him. The location of the Cooke ranch had been the least of her worries. "What I really want to know is how far it is. Will we be there tomorrow?" She didn't like traveling with no more than she could carry in a saddle pack. She certainly didn't like riding for more than a couple of hours.

"We could be if you could ride a little harder. I

didn't want to push you, though, so we're taking it slow. We'll camp two nights before we get to the ranch.''

Lilah huffed, all her contrition toward him gone. "If you didn't want to push me, you might have let me take a train or coach to the nearest city.'' Three days on a horse would be torturous. She had only one change of clothes with her. She would be positively grimy by the time they reached the ranch. Hopefully her trunk would arrive there before she did.

Tabor shrugged. "Sarah had to bring some cattle up this way. We'd have missed her if we traveled by train.''

"Besides that, it would have been comfortable,'' Lilah remarked under her breath. She didn't complain aloud, though. If Tabor's aunt really was to meet them, she hoped to make an ally of the woman. Maybe with her help she could talk Tabor out of collecting on the bet.

Several hours and, for Lilah, many sore muscles later, Tabor guided his horse alongside a streambed. The red glow of sunset stained the evening sky with a glorious array of colors, and in spite of herself, Lilah remarked on the beauty of it. She hoped they were near the end of the day's journey, for she was certain she couldn't make another mile. She was overjoyed to see in the distance a chimney of smoke from a campfire.

Tabor assured her the fire was from Sarah's camp and led her through a grove of trees and into a clearing. Just ahead they saw two men sitting near a chuck wagon, tin plates resting on their knees. A woman dressed in scuffed boots, corduroy trousers, a plaid shirt, and an apron bent over the cook pot on the fire. She looked their way when the horses came out of the trees.

"You're late," she called to Tabor, dropping her spoon and wiping her hands on the apron.

Lilah had expected Sarah Cooke to be a sharp-faced shrewish woman who might or might not help her. She was pleasantly surprised to see a kind, matronly face beneath the pinned-up gray-black braids.

"We took our time. Did you worry about me?" Tabor gave his aunt a big smile.

"No, by thunder! If I did that, I wouldn't have a moment's peace."

Tabor dismounted and wrapped Sarah in an aggressive hug. He swung her completely off her feet and set her down a few steps from where he'd picked her up. Sarah laughed and looked over at Lilah.

"So this is the fine little filly you wrote me about." Lilah wasn't sure for a minute whether Sarah referred to her or Darling. "Climb down and introduce yourself. Don't wait for Tabor to help you. He's lost his manners."

Lilah couldn't agree more. She climbed painfully out of the saddle and hobbled over to Sarah.

"I'm Lilah Damon," she said. "Tabor didn't tell me how nice you were."

"Didn't he?" Sarah laughed again. "Maybe I need to look into what he says behind my back." She gestured to Lilah. "Come on over to the wagon. We've got grub ready but I reckon you'd like to have a wash first."

"I would," Lilah agreed. "And a change of clothes. These buckskins have grown to me."

Sarah stirred the cook pot while she introduced Lilah to the ranch hands who had come along on the drive. They were both polite, but Lilah saw plenty of curiosity in the looks they gave her.

Sarah handed her a clean towel. "There's a bucket of water and a little privacy behind the wagon," she said. "Tabor, you can wash in the stream." Grinning broadly, she pushed an empty bucket into his hand. "And bring back some more water," she added.

"There you go, Sarah," Tabor teased, swinging the bucket. "Already ordering me around again."

"Humph," Sarah said. "Don't do it enough."

Lilah pulled her saddle pack down and went behind the wagon, where she found a blanket strung on a line. Moaning a little as she undressed, she shed her blouse and stepped out of her buckskin skirt. She hung the garments on the line over the blanket so they could air out during the night, then turned to get rid of some of the dust she had accumulated during the ride. The water in the bucket was cold but refreshing. Lilah splashed it all over, then dried with the towel.

She had brought along a fairly simple yellow dimity dress. It was rumpled but felt cool and light after her riding clothes. Since she planned to sleep in it, the wrinkles didn't matter much and she didn't bother trying to shake them out. Once the dress was on, she freed the long braid that held her hair, and after combing it, left it in a wavy curtain tied loosely back with a ribbon. She started to slip on a pair of soft slippers, but seeing they would be ruined in the dust, reluctantly kept her riding boots on under the dress.

Sarah had a plate ready and Tabor was back when Lilah came around the wagon. The ranch hands had moved off to bed down for the night. One of them had tethered and fed Darling and the gelding.

Sarah stepped back from the side shelf of the chuck wagon and looked at Lilah anew. "Well, aren't you a pretty thing? I can see why my nephew's gone foolish about you."

A muscle twitched in Tabor's jaw at his aunt's unwarranted words, but the look in his eyes told Lilah he was at least partly in agreement with Sarah. His gaze swept her appreciatively from head to foot.

With his hair sleek and wet and his face still moist from washing, he looked inordinately appealing. Lilah tried to ignore the return of the strange aching inside as their eyes unexpectedly met. Somehow she thought there would be much less danger in giving herself to Tabor if she didn't feel this attraction to him. It confused her badly that on the one hand she wanted the man and on the other hand she wanted nothing to do with him. She didn't know either what to make of the fact that he had kept his word and met up with Sarah by nightfall.

"Have a seat," Sarah said, breaking the spell as she offered Lilah the first plate. "I reckon you two are hungry enough to eat most anything after riding all day, even *my* cooking."

Tabor served his own plate. "You know you're the best cook around Sandy Flats," he said.

"Maybe so." Sarah smiled. "Just don't forget to keep telling me that."

Lilah tuned out the exchange between them and decided to eat standing up, since her saddle-weary derriere needed a rest. The food hadn't much to offer by appearance, and Lilah wondered if Tabor's praise had been facetious. Hesitantly she took a forkful, then looked around at Sarah in surprise. The lunch Clement's chef had prepared for them had been delicious, but it wasn't half as good as Sarah's beef stew and biscuits.

Good as it was, Lilah ate slowly and kept looking for the opportunity to talk to Sarah alone. But Tabor didn't give her any time to be by herself with his aunt. After supper he even helped wash the dishes and set up what would be needed for breakfast. Lilah hid her disappointment as she dried the plates and forks. But

she still had hope. They had two more days before
reaching the ranch, the last two days before the start
of the week she owed Tabor. Before then she would
find a way to talk to Sarah alone.

With all the camp chores done, Tabor spread the
bedrolls on the ground. He stretched Sarah's and Lilah's
beneath the wagon and his nearby. The fire had burned
down to glowing coals, and Tabor added a few chunks
of wood so it wouldn't die out before morning. Sarah
offered them a swig of her homemade wine before
retiring. Lilah refused. But Sarah and Tabor poured
portions into their clean coffee cups. While they sipped
it, Sarah updated Tabor on ranch business.

Lilah felt herself shrinking into her blanket when
the talk turned to what had happened to the stallion
Tabor called the Admiral.

"Losing that horse in a poker game has got to be
the dumbest thing you ever did," Sarah admonished.
"Never known you to take a chance like that with
anything you cared about."

Tabor's dark eyes lit on Lilah, though his words
were for Sarah. "I didn't figure you'd let a mistake
like that go by without mentioning it."

"You're mighty right." Sarah's voice gained strength.
"Not only did part of him belong to me, but the ranch
needed the Admiral's colts."

"I know that, Sarah," Tabor said softly. He hadn't
told Sarah all the details about losing the stallion and
wasn't sure he ever would. She would get too big a
kick out of knowing what Delilah had done to him.
"I've started looking for another stud horse for the
ranch."

"Looks like you could have found one in all the
months you've been gone."

"I had some thinking to do, Sarah." Tabor tossed

the last of his wine into the fire and lapsed into silence as the low flames sputtered.

Through half-lowered lids he watched the tottering fire. Sarah was right. He could have found another stallion, not one to replace the Admiral, but one to produce good colts for the ranch. The truth was, he hadn't started looking even when he had decided to leave the Admiral with Clement. Maybe there was something to Delilah's song. He was a man burned in her flame. Finding the cooler side of her nature in Lilah Damon hadn't healed him. Even now he wasn't sure what he wanted from her. The contest between them had gone way past settling up on a poker bet. And though he had her in his grip, what was going on in his heart made him think he could still turn out the loser.

Sarah picked up Tabor's hat and looked thoughtfully at the silver disk on the band. "You got that from Stan."

"Yes," Tabor said softly, seeing the faded images of his boyhood dreams dance in the fire.

"I hope I wasn't wrong sending you up there to pay your respects to Stan. It just seemed right that if you two hadn't made your peace while he was still living, you ought to do it then." Sarah tossed the hat back to his saddle horn. "I meant well," she said. "But it seems to have changed you."

Tabor gripped Sarah's hand and squeezed it. "You weren't wrong, Sarah."

Lilah was glad when they turned to other topics, like the number of calves and the well being dug on the ranch. She was also relieved that Sarah realized how tired she was and didn't expect her to be sociable. Soon the talking had stopped and the three of them were beneath their blankets to sleep. Lilah didn't know how she could still feel ashamed of any hardship she had caused Tabor. Maybe it was because she had met Sarah and seen how her blunder had interfered in the lives of people she had no right to cause trouble. As much as she despised Tabor, as much as he upset her, she couldn't ignore the fact that she had done an injustice to innocent people.

With those things and the thoughts of what was yet to come on her mind, she found it impossible to fall asleep. Even with every part of her begging for rest, she couldn't stop thinking how wrong things had gone.

Overhead the moon was nearly full and like new silver among the multitude of stars. The sight of it hovering peacefully in the black sky eased her a little. She remembered what Papa had said about getting back to things she had known before. How had she let herself forget how beautiful and free she could feel with nothing between her and the heavens but an occasional drifting cloud? Deciding she wasn't going to get to sleep soon and that the night was too beautiful not to enjoy, Lilah eased out of her bedroll, and with her boots in her hand, walked toward the streambed.

Large rocks sat in the shallow edge of the stream. Lilah waded out to one and sat on the cool stone with her feet dangling in the stream's flow. She used to do that long ago when she had thought Papa's mining camp the best place in the world. Papa would swing her out over the water and carry her on his back as he jumped from stone to stone. One night he'd caught her splashing naked in the creek and chased her all over camp with a blanket. What happy days those had been. And how long ago, back when Papa's legs were still sound, when he could walk and run like any other man.

The wistful smile left her face and suddenly she felt cold, lost, and alone. The trip into her memories had stirred recollections of good and bad times. As always, it dredged up the old pains and fears. Shivering with a self-made chill, Lilah rose to leave her memories and to go back to the wagon before she recalled too much more of the event that had driven her most of her life. Gingerly she slid from the rock and turned back to the bank.

"Don't move!" a gravelly voice warned from within the dark wall of bordering trees.

"Tabor?" Lilah asked hollowly as she listened to the approaching footsteps, knowing she would have recognized Tabor's voice.

A man stepped out of the shadows, just a black image against the white sand. Lilah tried desperately to get a clear look at him, but the wispy moonlight from behind a bank of clouds made recognition difficult. It definitely wasn't Tabor. The man was too short and she could tell his hair was light-colored. She hoped he was one of the wranglers accompanying Sarah. But that hope was misguided. The man was a stranger and had trained on her the biggest pistol she had ever seen.

"How sweet," he said, jabbing her ribs with the gun barrel. "Waiting here for your lover."

Lilah was afraid to even tremble. "No, no I wasn't," she said with much more calm than she felt. "I came out . . ." Lilah stopped herself, realizing she betrayed her vulnerability by admitting she expected no one. Cautiously she moved back a step and smiled weakly. "I'm sorry if I disturbed you. I'll get back to the camp."

"You ain't going nowhere," he growled, turning so that the moonlight struck his face. It might have been attractive if it hadn't been so hard and cynical. He gave her a cold-eyed smile. "And don't think about yellin' for help. You wouldn't be the first woman I shot."

Lilah's mouth felt as if it were full of dust. She didn't want to think about what this grim-faced stranger had in mind. Her eyes strained as quietly, helplessly she watched him untie a bandanna knotted around his neck. With the gun bruising her rib cage, he wadded the cloth into a ball and poked it in her mouth. Lilah gasped for air with the sandy, gritty cloth jammed in her mouth. The man again warned her to keep quiet and forced her to walk backward into the trees. She feared the worst and was actually relieved when he only pushed her against a tree and quickly tied her hands.

"Don't give me any trouble." He glanced around nervously. "I want to get out of here without waking anybody."

Saucer-eyed, Lilah nodded. She didn't know what horrible fate lay in wait for her, but at the moment time seemed the only friend she had. Tears streamed hotly down her cheeks. When he pulled the bandanna from her mouth, she gave a strangled cry.

"What do you want?" she whispered. "I don't even know you."

"Shut up," he warned. "I know you, Miss Lilah Damon. And seein' as how you're so precious to Stanton and that crippled pa of yours, you're gonna get me what I want." Now more frightened than ever, Lilah sniffed. "And don't waste those tears on me," he growled. "I hate a woman who snivels."

Quickly he folded the bandanna lengthwise and tied it over her mouth. It was uncomfortable but not nearly as bad as choking on it. With Lilah tied and gagged, he took her roughly by the arm and dragged her through the trees and away from the camp. Lilah wondered how long before anyone would miss her and come looking. Not likely before morning. By then she could be dead or wish she was. She was surprised when the man pulled her into a clearing where two horses were tied. Apparently she was to be given a little more time. He helped her mount one of the horses and quickly got astride the other. Riding slowly, he led her mount away.

The ragtag clouds blocking the moon drifted on. Silver-white light bathed the camp. Tabor had seen Lilah slip away toward the streambed and had forced himself to stay in his bedroll. He didn't think he could be responsible for his actions if he found himself alone with her after watching and wanting her all day. She wouldn't go far in the dark, he was sure, and most likely she was only answering the call of nature and wouldn't appreciate being followed. But when half an hour passed and she hadn't come back, his thoughts turned to worries. Tabor rose quietly, strapped on his guns, pulled on his boots, and went after her.

Her boots rested, one upright, one lying down, on the stream bank. He checked the sandy ground for tracks and saw that she had waded into the water. She wasn't there now, though, and the stream was too deep for her to have crossed on foot. He scanned the bank farther down, looking for a sign of where she had come out. After a few minutes of searching he found himself growing angry at the thought of how foolish she was to go wandering around in the dark. Didn't she have any idea there was danger from all kinds of animals out here, even man?

When he saw her tracks and another set, he stopped short. The pattern of the steps showed that a man had met Lilah, and then it looked oddly as if she had walked backward into the trees. That made no sense. Whom could she have met out here? A friend? A lover? Or someone she didn't expect? Alarm ripped down his spine as he followed the tracks into the trees, only to lose them for a few seconds. Finally he spotted them again in a patch of light. Lilah's scuffled prints confirmed his fear she had entered the trees under duress.

He didn't know how much time flew by as he lost and found the tracks another dozen times before coming to a clearing where it was plain a couple of horses had been tied. Both were gone and he knew by the plummeting of his heart that Lilah had been on one of them.

"Lilah's gone!" Tabor sounded an alarm as he ran into camp.

Sarah scooted from under the wagon and jumped to her feet. "When and where?" she asked. She had a lantern lit in no time.

"Almost an hour ago." Tabor grabbed his saddle and headed for the tie line where the horses were. Sarah, by now in her boots and hat, followed. "By the looks of things, she didn't go willingly."

"Gabe's horse is missing," Sarah pointed out, lifting up a cut-off length of rope where the animal had been secured. "Do you know who's got her?"

"No." He tossed the saddle on the gelding's back. "But I've got a suspicion it's a fellow who's been following us. I noticed some tracks this morning when we left the horses for a while. I should have been more curious about why they were there."

"Sounds to me like you've lost a lot of the good sense you used to have." Sarah put the bridle on the gelding while Tabor tightened the girth.

"Not now, Sarah," Tabor said flatly. "You can chew me out later. Let me get Lilah back first."

"All right, but you've got it coming." Sarah led the horse free of the tie line. "Are you going alone or do you want me to send the boys after you?"

"I'm going alone." Tabor mounted. "You break

camp and move out in the morning. We'll catch up
with you."

Sarah nodded. "Get going!" she said, and gave the
gelding a slap on the rump.

"The name's Chapman. Judd Chapman," the sandy-
haired stranger said. "I got a score to settle with your
beau, Stanton."

Chapman pulled Lilah's horse up alongside his. He
had both animals moving in a trot. Lilah gripped the
saddle horn with her tied hands, trying to minimize
the pounding of the rough ride. She mumbled something at him but couldn't get any words through the
tight bandanna. Chapman reached over and pulled it
loose.

Lilah coughed. "Tabor Stanton isn't my lover and
he isn't my beau. If you plan on using me to get
something from him, I'm afraid you've made a mistake. He wouldn't care what happened to me."

Chapman laughed bitterly. "He's been hanging
around your pa's mansion for something. If it's not
you, I don't know what."

"It's not me," Lilah insisted. She could see the
sinister gleam in Chapman's eyes and the hungry way
he looked at her. It sent a chill down to her toes. "If
you want something from my father, I'm sure he'll
give you what you want to get me back—safe."

"Well, now, Miss Smarty. Ain't that why I've got
you?" He laughed harder. "As for handing you back
safe, well, whatever damage I do you'll most likely get
over." He grinned as he reached out and roughly
stroked her arm. "I don't reckon you'll mind it too
much." Lilah flinched from his touch and Chapman's
face turned a mottled red. "We'll see just as soon as
we put some distance between us and Stanton."

They rode on for another hour, Chapman not pushing the horses but keeping them above a walk. Lilah felt strength draining from her body. She'd had a long, strenuous ride before being taken away by Chapman. Now fear and apprehension of what awaited her at the end of this one added to her exhaustion. Her stomach felt as if it churned with rocks, and each jolt in the saddle worsened the feeling. After a few more minutes she had to shout to Chapman to stop because she was going to be sick.

He let her get down from the horse on her own. "This better not be a trick to slow me down. I warn you you'll regret it."

"It's not a trick," Lilah gasped, hurrying behind some bushes and giving herself over to her nausea. When the heaves stopped, she drew in several deep breaths, hoping Chapman was disgusted enough by her sickness to stay away from her. Feeling weak but better, she walked back to her horse and started to climb on.

"Don't bother," he said, giving her a canteen of water so she could rinse her mouth. She did so as noisily as she could manage. But nothing took the lurid gleam out of Chapman's eye. He swung down from his saddle. "We'll walk a ways and find a place to camp. I don't think Stanton can find us now."

Icy fear gripped her heart as he pushed her over sharp stones and through patches of briars. Lilah stumbled on, mindless of the damage to her feet, knowing those injuries would be minor compared to the ones she would suffer from Chapman.

14

The gelding was strong and gave what was asked of him. When the trail was clear, Tabor kept him in a gallop. At times when he lost it, he led the horse, often resorting to holding a lighted torch over the ground to find it again. He tried to keep his speed faster than the tracks indicated the pair ahead were moving. He thought he must have made up half an hour of the lead they had on him.

Whatever Delilah—Lilah, he corrected himself—was, he had never meant for her to be in any danger because of him. He felt the rise of a strong protective instinct. It didn't occur to him that in her eyes he might have been doing the same thing as this man who had forced her to leave the camp.

Seeing her out on the trail would be enough to arouse a man's lust. He supposed the man had hung back and followed them most of the day, then waited near the camp until Lilah gave him an easy opening for kidnapping. She was safe as long as they kept moving. Evidently the hombre who had her wanted to put miles between him and a rescue party. Tabor urged the gelding to go faster, calculating how much more stamina the horse had. He couldn't slack off, but he couldn't risk wearing out his horse and winding up on foot either. He knew what any man low enough to abduct a woman would do as soon as he felt safe enough to let his guard down.

He had to find Lilah before that happened. A cold sweat broke out on his brow at the thought of anyone taking her with brutal force. Lilah might not be an innocent, but no woman deserved to be taken against her will. Back by the stream he had seen boot prints. Both horses ahead wore shoes, which meant it probably wasn't a renegade Indian who had snared her. That might be good, though he knew some white men who could be as heartless.

Already this man had crossed the line that would allow Tabor to show him mercy. His hand went involuntarily to the handle of one of the guns at his side. Grim creases cut into his brow; his lips were sealed tight. He knew deep in his heart he could shoot Lilah's captor in the back without a qualm.

The gelding, lathered and nearly winded, but still in a lope, whinnied lightly.

"Easy now. No noise." Tabor laid his hand on the horse's neck and spoke softly to him. He guessed his mount had picked up the familiar scent of Lilah's horse. He rode a few more yards, then dismounted and followed the fresh tracks. Lilah and the man had dismounted too. The gruesome thought that he might not have reached her in time tore at his insides.

Hearing sounds ahead, Tabor tied the gelding and proceeded on foot. The voices came from only a hundred or so yards ahead, muffled but clearly from a man and a woman. He moved toward them but stopped when he saw a bundle of cloth on the ground. Tabor picked it up and felt his blood chill to ice. *Lilah's yellow dress*. The implication cut him in two, still he moved ahead cautiously, not daring to rush in and maybe cost Lilah her life.

Chapman's slap knocked Lilah to the ground and left her jaw feeling as if it had been stung by a hundred bees. Too tangled in her petticoats to jump to her feet, she scrambled into a thicket, hoping to avoid more of his wrath. Chapman, ugly red veins pulsing in his neck and temples, pursued her.

"You're no woman," he ranted.

Lilah pushed herself back along the ground with her hands. "Please," she cried. "I don't know what you want."

He snarled. "I want you to act like a woman. I want you to make me feel like a man."

"How?" Lilah whimpered.

She had an ugly suspicion why Chapman was enraged. Stripped down to his drawers and boots but with his gun in his hand, he was a fanatical sight standing over her, urging his limp, flaccid member to rise.

Breathing raggedly as if he couldn't get enough air, Chapman rubbed his hand over his groin. "I'm warning you. Make something happen."

"Tell me how. Tell me what," Lilah pleaded. She thought she might rather die than follow through with what he said, but maybe if he thought she was willing, he'd put down that gun. And just maybe she could get her hands on it.

"Your mouth," Chapman said. "With your mouth."

Repulsed and feeling the heaves start in her stomach again, Lilah shrank away from Chapman, not realizing how that would anger him.

He planted his foot on the ruffles of her petticoat. "Don't back off from me, gal." The gun waved close to her face. "You don't back away from Stanton, do you?"

"Yes," Lilah said weakly.

Chapman ground her petticoat into the dirt. "Don't lie to me neither. I'm not fool enough to believe Stanton hasn't been shaking the sheets on your bed." He dropped down on his knees. "I reckon you're quick to spread for him."

"No," Lilah whispered, drawing her body into a tight knot as Chapman leaned into her.

Eyes glazed over, he touched the red spot his slap had left on her cheek. "I'm gonna leave my marks all over you," he said. "That's what I do to gals who don't get my cock up. I put my teeth in 'em, Lilah. I bite till the blood runs out. I bite 'em everywhere, Lilah. And them that don't like it, I take my knife to. I ain't gonna have to do that to you, am I, Lilah? Am I?"

"No, no," Lilah whispered, hoping against hope Chapman was only trying to scare her into submitting to him without a fight.

The rough inside of his hand slid down her neck and over her shoulder; then he moved it to his groin. His member hadn't grown an iota. A tic started in his eyelid, turning on the uncontrollable spasms he got every time he tried to take a woman. He damned Abe Wafield for that. The tic had started the same time he had lost his ability to get an erection, back that day when he was nineteen and fucking the hell out of Wafield's daughter.

The little bitch was just fourteen and had a face about as pretty as Wafield's old rabbit hound, but she had been prissing around and leading him on for two weeks, all the time since he'd hired on to help Wafield work his farm. Finally one day she had come down to the barn where he was tending the cows.

"I ain't never had a sweetheart, Judd. I ain't never had a boy to kiss me." Judy followed right behind him while he was pitching hay to the cows. "Pa's gone off to town and Ma's busy in the house with the little 'uns," she hinted.

He stopped for a minute and jabbed the tines of the pitchfork in the dirt. "You wantin' somebody to kiss you, Judy? That why you been swinging your skirts around me? That it?"

Judy turned red to the roots of her hair. "I reckon it is, Judd," she admitted, her stubby-lashed lids going down. "Wouldn't nobody have to know 'cept you and me."

Chapman grinned wide. The little twit. He'd show her about kissing and something else too. "Well, come on over here then," he told her. "Come on over here by the feed room where it's kinda dark."

Judy followed him over there, looking about as stiff and appealing as one of the scarecrows out in the field. But he could see those soft triangles under her dress where her young breasts were starting to bud out. She closed her eyes and lifted up her face for a peck on the lips. He gave her that but got her by the arms and jacked her up against the wall and then he covered those tempting little swells with his hands. Judy got scared and started crying and saying she needed to get on back to the house. But it was too late for that by then.

"Shut up, you slut," he warned her. "You got what you wanted, now I'm gonna get what I want." Feeling a hot surge in his loins, he ripped open the front of her homespun dress and uncovered the dusky breast buds that looked like they were just waiting for him to take them in his mouth. Judy screamed when he did that but he shut her up by slamming his mouth over her lips and driving his tongue in her mouth so far she choked on it.

Hot, sour sweat poured from Chapman's body as he remembered what happened after that. he pushed Judy into the feed room and tore off her cotton drawers and then he busted into her with all the fury he had in him. Judy screamed like a dying owl and he reckoned she fainted after that. But it didn't matter because he just kept hammering into her anyway.

Chapman shuddered and the tic got so bad he had to cover it with his hand. Old Wafield found them on the corn sacks in the feed room and snatched him off his daughter just before he finished with her. Wafield handed Judy out the door to her wild-eyed mother. From what he had heard later, Judy Wafield went soft in the head afterward, couldn't stand to be around a man, not even her pa. Served her right, though, because with him being in no condition to run, Wafield caught him by the neck and threw him down.

Chapman pressed the heel of his hand against his twitching eye. Wafield, red with rage, started bellowing about rape and Judy being just fourteen. Wafield didn't give a shit that Judy had asked for it, had been asking for it. Telling him that just made the bastard madder.

Chapman croaked for air. For a minute he didn't see Lilah cringing there in front of him or hear her pleading for him to let her go. He heard Wafield yelling he'd fix that smart cock, and then the big man took that bullwhip of his and damn near stripped all the skin off Chapman's body. When he was done with the whip, he spread-eagled him and stomped his testicles until Chapman stopped screaming and passed out.

Chapman shuddered convulsively. He hoped Wafield was burning in hell, and that little whore Judy with him. Since that day, no matter how much he wanted a woman, he couldn't drive himself into one. But he kept trying and kept trying to find another way to get the same release. What he did with his teeth to whores and the young girls he sometimes managed to lure off alone came close, but never close enough.

Chapman moved up on Lilah, his pupils cold and fixed as snake eyes. He wiped sweat from his face with the back of his sleeve. "I bet that white flesh tastes sweet as sugar." He groaned. "Untie them ribbons on that camisole. I want to see your breasts."

"I can't." She meant it. Frozen with fear, she couldn't make her arms move.

"Do it!" Chapman warned. He pulled the hammer of the gun back with his thumb.

Lilah, wrists tied, fumbled with the ribbons, opening up the front of her camisole, exposing her cleavage to his mad-dog gaze.

Chapman licked his lips. "That's mighty purty," he growled. "I bit a woman's tit clean off one time 'cause she wouldn't make me proud. You gonna let that happen to you?"

"No, no," she said weakly. Knowing any show of tears would only bring more abuse from him, she bit her tongue and concentrated on the pain.

"That's good to hear," he said, giving a half-sneer, half-smile. He laid the gun to one side and straddled her legs. Lilah rubbed her wrists when he freed them from the tight bonds. Indicating the slit in the front of his drawers, he whispered to her, "Touch me."

Lilah followed the placement of the gun without moving her eyes. God's mercy! She hoped she could reach it in one try, otherwise she didn't think she would want to see tomorrow. She felt her mind going black with terror. But she couldn't faint. Being unconscious wouldn't stop Chapman's wrath. He was a madman, a sexually deficient one, and he expected her to make him a man.

A strangled cry slipped from her lips. Chapman's cruel face contorted more.

"I said touch me," he repeated.

Lilah stretched out a trembling hand toward him. Let him think she was going to touch him. But if she couldn't reach the gun, he would have to kill her first.

Feeling a stir in his groin for one of the few times in all those years, Chapman closed his eyes to slits and groaned in lustful anticipation. At last. He groaned loudly. At last. It was happening to him.

"Get off her, Chapman!" Tabor, his voice a deadly snarl, lunged into view. If he could have fired without hitting Lilah, the bastard would already be dead.

Awkwardly positioned for a fight, Chapman yelled a curse and started to his feet. Trying to get clear of him, Lilah lurched and rolled away, knocking Chapman on his side. Cursing her and trying to straighten out, he belly-crawled toward his gun.

"Move, Lilah! Move!" Tabor shouted, wanting a clear line of fire.

Lilah, still foggy with fear, was slow to realize what Tabor wanted her to do. Ripping her petticoats as she bolted away from Chapman, she had only the presence of mind to mutter a prayer of thanks she had been saved.

Almost blind with pain and fury, Chapman groveled for his gun and found it as the girl bounded past him. He snarled a curse. He needed her for cover to get away, but there wasn't time to grab her before Tabor fired at him and he had to slide behind a fallen tree. The bullet sent splinters of wood and bark spattering into the air. Chapman fired back two shots without even attempting to take aim. The next of Tabor's bullets vented the baggy leg of his drawers. Chapman sent off another two wild shots.

Lilah was between them with the paltry cover of a stump protecting her from Chapman's bullets. Tabor ordered her to flatten out on the ground, a decision he quickly regretted, because it drew Chapman's attention back to her.

Gasping for breath, Chapman stilled himself to look. He could see a shimmer of red-gold hair and aimed at it. "I'll split her skull, Stanton," he yelled. "Throw out your gun."

Tabor plastered himself against the tree trunk that was his cover. "I hope you had a full round in that gun, Chapman, because when you do I'm going to put a hole right through your rotten heart."

Chapman fired at the stump. The bullet whizzed by Lilah's head. She screamed, not because she was hit, but because she was suddenly unsure Tabor was going to give up his gun.

"The next one's gonna give her a third eye. You want to see that?"

"No," Tabor answered hollowly. Lilah heard a thud and wasn't sure if it was Tabor's pistol or her heart falling. "Your choice, Chapman. You've got one bullet left, either for her or for me."

Chapman's laugh sounded like glass breaking. He stood but let Tabor see his gun was still aimed at Lilah. "It's yours, Stanton. I still got a use for her. Step out here, though, I ain't too choosy."

Tabor came halfway from behind the tree. Chapman leveled the gun at his chest and pulled the hammer back. He laughed again. "I like to see a man die sweatin'," he said. "Git over here, gal," he ordered Lilah. "You're gonna watch this too."

Tabor waited until Chapman's gaze was diverted to Lilah. Quicker than a jackrabbit, he dropped to one knee and with his left hand drew his second revolver. The bullet ripped through Chapman's right wrist. The gun flew from his hand and went off at the same time. Chapman's wild bullet grazed Tabor's neck and sent him spinning to the ground behind the tree.

Blood oozed from Chapman's wound. Seeing that Tabor was down, Chapman used the moment to dash for his horse. Getting astride was a struggle, but fear gave him strength. He didn't try to recover his lost gun but rode out as if the devil had called his name.

"Sweet Jesus," Lilah whispered, rising on trembling legs to her feet.

She heard Tabor moaning and hurried through the brush to him. He had his hand on his neck and blood streamed from beneath his fingers. Her tears ran as freely as, amid sobs, she stepped out of one of her petticoats and ripped it down the seam and into strips. She folded the cleanest strips, making one into a pad and then, prying his fingers loose, tied a bandage around his neck.

"Lilah?" His voice was weak.

"It's me," she said. His face was as white as the cloth she had tied on him. She couldn't think of anything else to do but cradle his head in her lap and wipe the droplets of sweat from his brow.

Tabor closed his eyes, though it was difficult not to keep looking at Lilah falling out of her open camisole and bending her care-softened face over him. The wound wasn't too bad. He was sure the bullet had only nicked a vein and that the bleeding would soon stop. He hated to admit it, but he thought he was more scared than hurt—not for himself, but because he had come so close to getting Lilah killed.

"I'm sorry," he whispered, reaching for her hand and not finding it.

"Don't be sorry," she said, catching his hand in the

air and lacing it with hers. "He's gone and we're both alive." Her voice was soft and comforting as a lullaby. "I'm not hurt and I think you're going to be all right after you've rested."

"Lilah, Lilah," he whispered. "I'm sorry I brought you out here and put you in danger." His dark eyes blinked open. "Did he touch you? Did he rape you? I'll hunt him down and kill him for it," he said savagely.

Lilah trembled. She didn't know where she got the insight to explain to Tabor about Chapman. "He wanted to rape me. I don't think he could. Something . . . something is wrong with him. He got raving mad when I couldn't make it . . . happen for him. He told me about horrible things he's done to other women. He's a horrible man. He's crazy." Her voice became more agitated. "He talked about using me to get something from Papa. A ransom, I suppose."

Tabor moaned. He had thought of Chapman as a nuisance at their first meeting and had thought he'd seen the last of him. But Chapman was crazy, as Lilah said. He wanted that worthless claim Tabor's father had left to Clement Damon.

Or was that it? Maybe the land wasn't worthless and Chapman knew it and was willing to kill to get it. He should have warned Clement before, but he had thought Chapman was just another prospector who had lost touch with what was real. Tabor laboriously closed his eyes again and decided he wouldn't tell Lilah about the claim. She was half-scared out of her wits now. But as soon as he got to the ranch he would wire Clement of the danger.

"I'm better, Lilah." Tabor pushed himself up on his elbows. "Let's get out of here and find a better place to spend the night."

"Spend the night?" She thought of the campfire and the secure berth beneath the wagon. She thought of

Sarah's kind eyes. "Aren't we going back to the camp?"

"We can't," he said, saddened to hear the anguish in her voice. "My horse is spent and I doubt yours is up to carrying two. Chapman won't be back. We'll start off at first light, meet Sarah and the boys down the trail."

Lilah shuddered at the mention of Chapman's name. She was afraid to close her eyes for fear of seeing that twisted face and thinking of what he had wanted from her.

Tabor struggled to his feet. Lilah shuffled up after him, tying together the few intact ribbons of her camisole. She walked gingerly behind Tabor as he got her horse and led the animal down the trail to where his mount was tied. All the while, she had to keep her fingers tightened to a fold of his shirt; she couldn't bear the aloneness she felt if the hold broke. To her it seemed a miracle Tabor had come looking for her.

"How did you find me? How did you even know to look?" she asked softly.

With Lilah at his side, Tabor unsaddled and unbridled the horses and hobbled their feet. He wanted them to graze and have enough freedom to reach the small brook below the rise they were on.

"I was awake. I saw you leave the camp. When you didn't come back right away, I followed you. I found your boots by the stream, then saw two sets of tracks."

Lilah placed her arm on his, finding strength in renewing the bond. "I'm glad you went looking," she said.

"Me too," he answered, feeling his voice quiver as he closed his hand over hers. "Chapman's a nasty piece of goods. I'm sorry I didn't kill him."

Lilah's brow lifted at the hatred she heard in his voice. Tabor thought the gesture indicated another question. "My aim's not so good with my left hand," he explained. "Guess I ought to be glad Chapman's memory wasn't so good about what kind of hardware I had."

"He won't come back, will he?" Lilah's heart leapt to her throat.

Tabor assured her they would be safe. "Not tonight. I hope never. He's hurt bad. The wound is going to keep him down for a while, probably ruin his gun arm." Tabor led her away from the horses and spread a blanket for her, then walked a few more feet and spread another. "Just the same, we won't build a fire."

Lilah looked at the big gulf of blackness separating the two blankets. Tabor's interest in her might not be admirable, but he had cared enough to chance his life for her. That was a precious gift from one human being to another. Tonight it was enough to make her forget all the harsh things she felt toward him.

She spoke just above a whisper. "I don't want to be alone, Tabor."

Now it was his heart that caught in his throat. He could see her eyes shining in the moonlight and wished what he read in them meant more than that she was afraid of Chapman. Without saying anything he picked up his blanket and brought it back to hers. They didn't have long to sleep. The sun would be up in less than two hours. After that there was a long ride to catch up with Sarah. She curled up on the blanket. Tabor eased down beside her. Needing more than just knowing he was near, Lilah placed her arm over his chest.

Tabor stared up at the stars, feeling heat radiate from the place she touched. But he knew that link was only for the assurance she wasn't alone. He wanted her, but she had seen the ugliest side of a man tonight. What she needed most was someone to trust.

* * *

Big pink cabbage clouds caught the early rays of the sun. Lilah awoke to the wonder of dawn and for the first few minutes found last evening's nightmare washed from her mind. Without thinking that Tabor's shoulder formed her pillow, she folded herself closer against his side. Her arm still stretched across his chest and one leg rested partially on his thigh.

No shadows lay across her heart in this most glorious time of day. She liked mornings because the day was yet untainted by any of the little sorrows and heartaches that might become a part of it. Dawn was hope, and this one, which she had never believed she would see, was to be cherished. And the man beside her, because he had given her this dawn and all those that would follow, was special too. For now she could bask in the glow of the rising sun, free of resentments, old wounds healed. She owed Tabor Stanton her life, and though they might never again have such a bond between them, today it was there.

How ironic that she had thought Tabor an intemperate, even malicious man. Now that she knew Judd Chapman, Tabor's vices seemed minimal. If too assertively so, he at least demanded nothing that hadn't been promised him. She breathed a soft sigh. The promise, the bet, the debt she owed him—of how little value that was compared with her life.

Like the heat of the sun on her skin, a warm flow of emotions coursed through her veins; a haze of them clouded in her mind. Last night his nearness had soothed her into a quick slumber. She trusted Tabor, perhaps because he made no pretense about what he wanted from her. His honesty, if nothing else, she could appreciate.

The anguish over Chapman had left her the moment he lay down beside her. With sleep-heavy eyes she studied the tanned handsome face so near her own. A heavy black shadow covered the jaw and chin, but the strong lines were evident. His brow was smooth as he rested, his lashes sooty and surprisingly long. She thought she liked his mouth best. It was expressive, a quick signal of his mood. She had seen it set in a hard line and she had felt the gentleness of it against her lips.

Tabor. Tabor Stanton. She twirled the name in her mind as if it were a new one to her thoughts. How had they come to be here, alone together, stripped of all the ordinary human barriers between a man and woman? She felt a curious pull at her heart and mind, as if some thread of understanding should be spun between them. But it was too much to ask of herself when there were so many other mysteries to solve. The sight of him awakened the flames within her, made her want to be someone besides the sedate and proper Lilah Damon. Why was it that only he could quench that fire? That was the thing she had to know. Why?

Tabor saw her eyes, still misted with sleep, open, blue and trusting in the daylight. If she knew how much he longed for her and how much restraint it had taken for him to lie there all those hours enduring the sleep moves and soft caresses she gave, she might be as afraid of him as she was of Chapman.

After a few minutes she saw him watching. He smiled. The ordeal she had been through didn't show in the soft beauty of her face. Her hair, shining like the sun's own gold, hung in loose tangles on her forehead and across her throat. The blue satin ribbons adorning her camisole hung in loops against her ivory skin. He longed to touch her, longed to hold her, to calm the turbulence he felt inside.

"We ought to go," he said, unable to control the

huskiness in his voice. He started to ease himself from beneath her.

"Don't. Not yet," she whispered, feeling all restraint fall away. "Stay here."

She owed him a debt. She was anxious and ready to begin paying. She would give Tabor his week, be the wanton woman he desired. For him she would be Delilah, in body, in mind. She would be all he expected Delilah to be, but she would do it on her terms, not his. And when it was over, she would go back to being Lilah Damon, go back to living within her proper upbringing. Tabor would keep her secret. She knew him well enough now to be confident of that.

There was one worry, though. She knew, too, he was a man who would insist upon doing right by a girl he had spoiled. That she couldn't have. He must never know Delilah the seductress, the siren, existed only in the fancy of her audience.

Lilah smiled softly. Early in her first tour she had let herself listen to Carrie, a jaded saloon girl, bemoaning the ways of men. How her ears had tingled hearing the things a man did with a woman. But she had needed to know if she was to convincingly present herself as a tasty tart. So she had asked the ways that pleased, the ways that excited a man, and Carrie had told her in infinite detail. Tabor Stanton and all California believed Delilah an expensive courtesan. She would make sure that when a week had passed, Tabor believed it still.

There was the problem of her maidenhead. But Carrie said no matter how sweet a man talked or how gentle he started, he knew nothing but his own rutting need when he took a whore.

Would Tabor be different? She hoped so. Somehow it mattered very much that he would. What a quandary. But she couldn't have it both ways. She would have to hope all the myths, all the warnings matronly women gave to young girls were wrong, and that virginity was not such an evident thing that a man really knew if he was the first.

"Lilah," Tabor answered after a moment, "I don't think I *can* stay here. A man can't stay so close to a woman without wanting to bed her, especially one as beautiful as you." His voice broke with huskiness. "I said I wouldn't rush you. Don't make me a liar."

She shook her head gently and spoke from her heart, without thinking, without hearing that her words were not those of a worldly woman. Her fingers slid into the thatch of dark curls on his chest. Her eyes were luminous with desire.

"Show me how beautiful it can be, Tabor," she pleaded. "I need to know. I have to know or I'll be afraid from now on."

Anger ripped through him, but he kept it hidden. She was thinking of Chapman and the perverted things he had threatened her with. It was enough to make a woman afraid to ever give herself to a man again. Once more he wished his bullet had struck the mark. But looking into Lilah's face, he forgot Chapman. Gently he rolled to his side so that her body molded to his, eyes and lips only inches apart.

"Do you know what you're asking?"

"I know. I know you saved my life."

"Lilah." A pain squeezed his heart as he whispered her name. Did she think she had to repay him for that? Did she think she had to repay him with her body? Was that what he had shown her of himself? He thought of his demands on her; he supposed it was. "I don't want you out of gratitude," he said sadly. "I never would have forced you to go through—"

She stroked his lips with her fingers, silencing him.

"It isn't gratitude, though I feel that too. It's more. I know being close to you makes me feel warm and safe. That may not last. Maybe when we leave here everything will be like it was yesterday on the trail. But this time, this hour, is outside all that. I want you, Tabor," she whispered. "I want you to make love to me. I want it to be beautiful."

That was a plea he couldn't resist, not with her hand again slipping inside his shirt and her fingers teasing over his skin. Her voice trembled like that of a shy virgin feeling the first awakening of passion. There was so much about her he didn't understand. Delilah had known other men. He had heard her with one of them. Was it crazy to feel that this woman, so soft and yielding in his arms, was someone else?

Why did he wonder? She wanted him, and for reasons that had nothing to do with those that had hurled them together. For a time they would be a man and a woman with no past and no future hampering what they shared. No matter what might spring up between them later, he knew that this intimacy would be a sweet memory to hold in his heart.

Tabor's stubbled cheek brushed Lilah's smooth one. She laughed as his bristly beard scrubbed her lightly. He'd have to be careful not to mar her soft skin. He hoped he could remember, because when their lips met and sealed together, every other thought seemed to fade back into the night.

Lilah knelt beside him and opened his shirt, helping him slip it off. She giggled as he pulled off his boots, finding it funny that he'd slept in them. The gunbelt was beside him. He had kept one hand on it all night in the unlikely event anyone should disturb them. He pushed it away, not out of reach but where they wouldn't roll on it.

Tabor untied the few ribbons on her camisole that

hadn't worked loose while she slept. His usually dex-
terous fingers seemed to be a handful of thumbs. But
when she was out of the garment, they were nimble as
ever, skimming her flesh, caressing the satiny skin,
learning the curves and valleys of her breasts.

Her thoughts spun in a vortex of her own making.
She had stepped out of reality because what she felt
and what she wanted to make him feel went beyond
all but imagination. She cast off her petticoats and,
unabashedly naked, helped him out of his trousers.
She inhaled sharply. He was the first man she had
seen naked, but this time the sight of his manhood
rising from the dark bush that held it awed rather than
frightened her.

She forced her eyes to look elsewhere, to see all of
him. She saw power and strength his clothes kept
hidden from all other eyes. He was a beautiful man.
Was that a thing to think? That a man could be
beautiful?

Again the sight of that decidedly male part of him
drew her eyes. She lowered her head so that her
tumbling curls hid the sudden blush. He need not
know he was the first nude man she had seen. How
would he know? He thought she had taken many men
before him. She feared he would feel obligated if he
knew otherwise. That would never do. Her future was
set, and it held no room for Tabor Stanton.

Last night she had seen the dark soul of death.
Today she wanted all the brightness of life. She had
chosen this man and this moment for her deflowering.
That was Delilah's right. That was her right.

A smile spread across her lips. Aunt Emily would
be apoplectic if she knew. Emily had done her best to
instill righteousness and morality in her. But here and
now, surrounded by the beauty of a wild land, Lilah
wanted only the laws of nature to show her right and

wrong. Those were the laws she had known as a child. Beneath a Victorian facade, those were the principles that still guided her.

It seemed apropos that she had the decorous guise of Delilah to slip into. From the heart of Delilah she would feel no shame. Tabor was a man. She wanted him. She yearned to be filled with the joy of womanhood.

Lilah lifted her head. Her eyes slanted, the innocence gone from her smile. Tabor, now seated on the blanket, saw her face change. He half-expected her hair to darken to brilliant red. Delilah. This was Delilah. Her moves were practiced, her voice huskier. She knelt beside him.

"Lie back," she whispered, touching his shoulders and giving him a gentle nudge.

Tabor lowered himself to his back. To allow a woman to take the lead in lovemaking was new to him. But Delilah was determined and he was not a man to turn back from the unknown. Resting on her knees, she leaned across him, sprinkling kisses over his face. That was all it took to tighten his loins. Tabor reached for her. But she gently pushed his hands down beside him.

"Hold them here," she said.

Tabor did as she asked, but only by imposing an iron will on himself. Blood pounded in his brain and the pleasure and the passion mounted as her hands moved over him. He had to close his eyes against the thought of her ever having done to another man what she did to him.

Her fingers trembled as she moved them in a sensuous massage over Tabor's lean, rock-hard body. She hoped he wouldn't realize the trembling wasn't as much from passion as from nervousness. Carrie had made it sound so easy to touch a man in this way, but now that she was into it, she was sure her arousal was even greater than his. Not that he wasn't aroused. There was no hiding that manly staff or the heat of it when her hand came near. She hadn't been able to make herself touch him there yet. Oh, she wanted to, and Carrie had told her how a man liked it done. But would she get it right? Where was all Delilah's confidence now?

Tabor moaned as she slid her fingers through the line of hair running from his chest to his loins. Delilah knew her craft, how to tantalize a man, how to drive him near to exploding with erotic strokes and random kisses, her nipples now and then grazing his skin as if by accident. How long did she think he could endure such sweet torture?

Lilah, fortifying herself, eased her hand around his manhood and felt the pulsing heat it contained. Her touch was light but sent a jolt of desire careening through her. A moist, hot flame spread onto her thighs. Should that be happening?

"God's blood, woman! Do you think I'm made of iron?"

She hadn't remembered he could go from perfect stillness to the speed of a leaping deer. But in half an instant she found herself on her back and was held there by Tabor's heavy thigh across her legs.

Tabor moaned as his mouth moved to hers. He kissed her with much less vigor than his passion demanded. But somehow within the fire he remembered the damage his heavy beard would do to her skin. He was gentle too as he moved his mouth to her breasts, letting the velvet warmth of his tongue ply her tender, smooth flesh. He moved lower, his lips nuzzling the soft, flat plane of her belly.

She couldn't stop an outcry of pleasure. Carrie had never told her about this unbearable longing, this fire licking unceasingly at the core of her.

"Tabor, please." There were no ready words to explain what she wanted, but he would understand. He must understand.

And he did. Tabor nudged her legs apart and knelt between them. He hadn't let himself look at the fiery red curls on the gentle swell above her thighs. Now he couldn't keep his eyes and hands away. He touched her gently, separating, massaging, tugging the down curls, teasing that sensuous place, driving her to the peak of ecstasy. Lilah's soft moans told him when to stop. She cried his name when his hand left her.

Their eyes met as he eased down on her and probed at the warm, wet center of her. Only one small boundary separated them. Lilah longed with all of her being to have it shattered. Her hands cupped his buttocks, urging him on. She could think of nothing but unlocking the woman inside her, the one who so longed to know all the mysteries of love. Her whole body felt as if it were ablaze with need for him.

Tabor was surprised by her tightness, but too sodden with passion to think of it as more than another of her treasures. With her nails cutting into his flesh and a moan on his lips, he plunged inside her. He felt the tearing as the virginal membrane gave way. He heard her muffled cry of pain but she was soon thrusting high to meet him and he was plunging with her into the dark flames of passion. Now her soft cries were of pleasure, her rhythm as fast as his own, as ecstasy consumed them both in the hottest of fires.

"Oh, love," he cried. "Lilah, my love," as the flames took him.

15

Bare as a babe, Lilah stretched languorously. The sun had risen high in the blue sky while she and Tabor lay quietly in each other's arms. She felt freer, lighter, and so much more womanly than she could have imagined. The pain had lasted but a second; the joy lingered like the fragrance of rich perfume.

She felt Tabor stir beside her and smiled. For her the smile had secret meaning. She had heard it said a man received a rare treasure when he took a virgin. Well, here she was feeling as if she were the one blessed. This new power of womanhood was a priceless gift. Tabor had given it to her. The irony was, he knew nothing about it. He hadn't noticed the rending of her maidenhead. Oh, she felt a little sad about that. Such a wonderful event, surely the most wonderful of her life, was worthy of a celebration, and she had to hold back her happiness.

"I'll get some water," he said. "We should have been on the trail hours ago." He picked up his trousers, and with them draped over his arm, stood above her, noting the wistfulness in her soft eyes, and for a moment he was hesitant to leave. But before the temptation grew too strong, before he lay down to again intertwine himself with her beneath the blanket, he turned away.

Lilah allowed herself an unchallenged view as he walked off toward the creek. He was a pleasure to the eyes. Powerful calves and thighs carried him smoothly over the ground. Muscles flexed in the firm buttocks and rippled in his shoulders as he swung his arms. She marveled at the way that strong frame had found the gentle harmony of hers and how together they had sung nature's sweetest song. Who could have dreamed of such a perfect fitting? She thought it no small marvel that Tabor's body matched and moved with hers as if he had been cast to the mold.

He was back before her wandering thoughts settled, handing her a canteen. She rolled from beneath the woolly cover and bared her skin to the sun. Again he stood and stared for a moment; her beauty took his breath away. His eyes followed the twist and turn of tangled red-gold curls which hung down her back like trailing tendrils of wild vine. His eyes strayed onward to the V of darker curls, those which had been soft as down beneath his probing fingers. The stir of desire began anew within him, and a mellow warmth filled his heart. Lilah accepted his admiration and stood before him like a proud Venus. He wondered how much false courage that took.

"I'm afraid there's nothing to wash with. Maybe one of your petticoats," he suggested.

Lilah took the canteen and poured the cool water over her shoulders, shivering beneath the cleansing rivulets that ran over breasts, belly, and thighs. Grinning, Tabor politely turned away as she attended more delicate places. It was then she noticed the tenderness

between her thighs and the flakes of dried blood cling-
ing to them. Hurriedly she washed them away, certain
Tabor had failed to see those reminders of her virginity.

Done with bathing, Lilah took his suggestion and
used her remaining petticoat as a towel and dried her
skin, saving a part of the garment to use as a clean
bandage for his wound.

While she washed, Tabor tucked his shirt into his
trousers and slid his feet into his boots. By the time
Lilah was finished bathing, he brought her the yellow
dress he had found last night. She slipped it on, then,
on tiptoes, reached up to untie the strip of cloth around
his neck.

The wound was closed but she wanted to cleanse it
before rebandaging. "You'll have to kneel," she said,
soaking a piece of cloth with water from the canteen.
"You're much too tall for me to do this properly with
you standing."

A light twinkling deep in his gray eyes, Tabor knelt.
Delilah had brought him to his knees. All along, hadn't
he feared that was what she would do to him? Hadn't
that been his worry while he had chased her all over
the country like a man in pursuit of a big-game animal? The prey had turned on the hunter. Here he was
the one downed, a man with an arrow in his heart, and
for a lying, two-faced woman.

He almost laughed out loud. She had been a virgin.
And she had tried to pass herself off as a man-wise
strumpet. He had half-believed she was a strumpet
and had totally enjoyed playing along with her deceitful game. Hell! What point in fooling himself? He *had*
believed her a fancified harlot until that last sweet
moment when he pushed inside her.

Lilah's hands were gentle as she dabbed his wound
with the wet cloth, her fingers warm against his skin as
she tied the fresh bandage around his neck. He didn't

like the thought of what he had done. Why the devil hadn't she told him to begin with that she was a virgin? Didn't she know that would have made a difference? Why was she still keeping quiet about it now?

"All done?" he asked softly as she tied the ends of the bandage.

Lilah nodded and folded the scraps of her petticoat. Tabor sighed. Was she going to confess her deception? Or was she waiting for him to mention the fact? Facing her, he stared questioningly down into sky-blue eyes and saw the doors behind them closed tight. The truth of the situation came to him. She wasn't going to say a thing. For some reason, the conniving wench wanted him to think she was a tarnished woman.

Having noticed the scratches and bruises on her bare feet, Tabor bade her to wait while he got the horses.

Lilah felt let down. Why did he keep looking at her as if he wanted to laugh? Was this the way a man treated a woman he had just made love to for the first time? Did the tenderness last only until a man's blood cooled? And what about all the loving things he had whispered to her? Where were those adoring words now?

Tabor saw her throw back her head and imperiously heave out her chest. She was playing Delilah to the hilt. A quick surge of heat hit his loins. He supposed she knew just how provocative she was, standing that way. Damn her! If she didn't want him to stay here all day making love to her, she'd better tone down the act.

Tabor refilled the canteen and tied it to his saddle, then led Lilah's horse to her. "Let's get moving," he said brusquely.

She interpreted the terseness in his voice as impatience. She didn't like at all the ease with which he could switch his mind to other things, like catching up with Sarah. She supposed that was the way it was when a man finished with a loose woman. But it didn't seem fair that she still felt all warm and achy inside, just looking at him.

"I'm waiting for you," she responded crisply as she grabbed the saddle horn and tried to swing herself up, though she could barely reach the stirrup.

Tabor hurried to her side. "Let me help." His hands closed around her waist, but instead of lifting her to the saddle, he pulled her aside and into his arms. "One kiss won't hold us up too long," he said softly. Crushing her to him, he kissed her long, savoring the honey-sweet softness of her mouth.

Lilah felt her knees weaken and all the little glass shards of temper melt like butter inside her. It gave her a grand sense of satisfaction to know he wasn't immune to her at all.

"Sorry there's no food," Tabor said. "But cutting across like this, we ought to meet up with Sarah in another two hours."

Lilah sighed wearily. She felt as if she would wear the imprint of a saddle the rest of her life. Riding had never been one of her favorite activities, and this horse lacked Darling's smooth gait. She much preferred traveling by coach or train, and here she had spent the last two days astride a horse, this last day after almost no sleep. She was hungry and she was tired. Coupling that with the two experiences that had taken her to the depth and height of a lifetime, she wondered that she could even stay on the animal. How could she possibly last another day on the trail?

Tabor's eyes were on her as he decided that his preoccupation with Lilah was the reason Chapman had been able to follow them yesterday without his being aware of it. What was there about her? He had known other women almost as beautiful, but none had ever taken over his mind the way Lilah had. Hell! Half the instincts he depended on to survive were gone. Yesterday he couldn't think for wondering how it would be to make love to her. Today he couldn't think for remembering how heavenly it had been.

His expression became almost somber but he still couldn't take his eyes off Lilah. She had him bewitched, all right. He had thought making love to her would lessen his fascination. But now he wanted her again, more than before, enough that he was contemplating stopping the horses and . . . Tabor sighed heavily, trying to release some of the madness. If he didn't break this spell Del . . . Lilah had on him, he wasn't going to be much of a man by the end of the week.

"There's the wagon!" Lilah shouted. "Oh, Tabor," she moaned. "Tell me we're going to stop and make camp right away. Please. If we don't, I think you'll have to find a place for me in the chuck wagon."

Too concerned about Tabor and Lilah to keep traveling, Sarah had already made camp. She was measuring out grain for the mules and horses when she saw riders approach. Noting the shotgun at her side, Tabor called out a greeting.

"By thunder! I've been worrying my hair white! Just sent the boys back up the trail to look for you." Sarah put down the wooden bucket and took the reins of Lilah's horse. Her eyes took in the girl's appearance, not missing the tears and stains on the yellow dress. "Are you hurt, child?"

Grateful for Sarah's assistance, Lilah got off the horse and welcomed a hug from the older woman. "I think Chapman scared a few years off my life, but Tabor found me in time," she answered.

Sarah kept her arm around Lilah's shoulder and led her to the wagon, noting that her young friend limped. "Are you sure you aren't hurt?"

Lilah insisted she wasn't. "My feet are sore, but only because I didn't have my boots out there."

Sarah had a small straight-backed chair she kept tied on the side of the wagon. She hurriedly pulled it down and set it before Lilah.

"You sit down here," she ordered. "I've got some water heating, and with a little of my liniment in it you can soak all the soreness out." Sarah fetched the dishpan and a cork-topped bottle filled with a dark malodorous liquid. "Sure glad nothing is hurt but your feet," she said as she poured hot water and liniment in the pan. "Who's this Chapman varmint who hauled you off?"

"One about half as nice as a polecat, Aunt Sarah," Tabor interceded. He didn't want Lilah thinking too much about Chapman before she had a chance to rest. "He won't be bothering anybody for a while. He's nursing a bullet hole."

Sarah looked up and frowned. "Something wrong with your aim, boy?" That wasn't the only thing she wondered about, but she held her tongue. Tabor didn't call her "Aunt" unless he had serious things on his mind.

Tabor grinned. Sarah never missed pointing out his mistakes. "I'll tell you about it later," he said, looking hopefully toward a couple of steaming pots and pans. "You got anything to eat on this chuck wagon?"

"Chicken and dumplings," Sarah answered with a mischievous smile. "And hot biscuits on the fire." She rinsed her hands and dried them on her apron. " 'Course I had to use a rabbit for the chicken, but you won't notice that."

Lilah didn't. She was hungry enough to have eaten

it raw and to forget the dainty attitude toward food that Aunt Emily had instilled in her. What would Emily do if she saw her niece licking gravy from her fingers and wiping her mouth with the back of her hand? Lilah laughed softly. She would brand herself a failure, that was what.

"Oh, Sarah." Lilah looked down at her clean plate. "I've never tasted anything better."

Sarah's grin stretched the limits of her mouth. "Thanks," she said. "You've sure got a rippin' appetite for a city girl. I was expecting some persnickety miss who kept her corset laced tighter than a drum."

"I usually do," Lilah told her. "Papa says it'll be the death of me and he fusses because I spend so much time and money on my wardrobe." Thinking she might have cast her father in an unfavorable light, she explained further. "Oh, he likes for me to dress prettily and it isn't as if he can't afford my tastes. But he remembers my mother panning for gold beside him and wearing trousers and one of his old shirts. I think he's always been afraid being brought up in London society might have made me forget the hard, plain way things were for us then."

Sarah took the plate from Lilah's lap. "I think he's worrying for nothing. You've got pluck, girl. Being able to smile after what you've been through tells me there's more to you than any society girl can boast. You aren't put together from lace and perfume. No sirree, you've got pluck!"

It was a strange compliment but Lilah liked it. Even the terrible ordeal with Chapman hadn't dispelled the good feeling she had about being out in the open land. She felt like a hothouse plant given a change to grow out in the garden. Life would never be even or smooth out in the wild. But it was free and exhilarating.

"Pluck or not, I think Lilah needs to rest." Tabor

finished a second helping of Sarah's mock chicken and dumplings.

He had been quiet while they ate, letting the women have their say. Still he considered Sarah's description of Lilah. It was one more line of the riddle about her. He already knew the Damon family were leading members of San Francisco's high society. Lilah fit into it like she did her dressmaker gowns. As Delilah she didn't let slide any luxury either. But to see her happy as a lark when she was dirty, tired, sore-footed, and a long way from a soft bed, well, that was a surprise. He had figured she would do well just to make the ride to the Cooke ranch. And by damn! It didn't make her one whit less appealing.

"I could do with a bath. A big tub of hot water," Lilah said dreamily. She winked at Sarah. "But I guess I can make do with a washpan and a towel. Just look at this dress." With thumbs and fingers she lifted the stained and torn skirt a few inches. "Guess it's back to the buckskins for me."

Sarah gave her a washpan and a towel and all the privacy the blanket on the line could provide. After Lilah had scrubbed off the trail dust and changed her clothes, she set to work on the tangles in her hair. That took quite a while. When she emerged, looking as changed as a butterfly out of a cocoon, Sarah had a pallet laid out in the shade of a tree.

"You get in a nap," she said. "The boys will be back here by dark. I'll wake you then for supper."

Lilah looked at the blanket and smiled, thinking of the one she had shared with Tabor the night before. The memory stirred a strange and restless yearning which completely overtook her. She glanced up at Sarah. "I'd like to talk to Tabor about something first. Do you know where he is?"

Sarah pointed at the woods. "There's a small pool not far from here. He went to wash up."

Lilah started off in the direction Sarah pointed, aware she really had nothing to say that couldn't wait, but somehow knowing she wouldn't be able to sleep until she had seen him again. Up ahead she heard water splashing and a noise that resembled singing.

"Hurt yourself?" she asked, surprising Tabor in the waist-deep water. She hadn't expected to find him undressed, but decided not to retreat. After all, Delilah wouldn't.

He whirled around and frowned as if offended. "I take it you don't think I'm good enough for the stage."

Soft laughter floated up from her throat. "Not as a singer," she told him. "But if we could get an audience of ladies together, we could parade you around like that."

A slow smile ruffled his mouth. Lilah's eyes ranged down from there. The dark mat of hair on his chest lay against his skin in damp curls. She remembered the crisp but silky feel of it under her fingers. A band of it tapered down in a furry trail over his belly, then thickened around his manhood. He was broad-shouldered, trim-waisted, and bands of muscles showed hard and strong beneath his skin even when he was relaxed as he was now. The clear water in the pool hid none of him from her eyes. She was a little dismayed that just looking at him could send a shiver of desire through her so quickly.

"And ladies would pay to see this?" Tabor waded out of the pool.

"Oh, I think they would," Lilah said.

Tabor gave a carefree laugh. "Why aren't you resting?" He dried himself with one of Sarah's towels, bending, stretching, treating her to an exhibition.

Lilah's voice caught in the back of her throat. "I'm

too full to lie down," she said, denying it was a longing to be near him that had made her restless. "I
needed to walk around first. And . . . and I wasn't
sure I'd thanked you for saving my life."

Tabor tossed the damp towel onto a bush limb. Still
naked, he sauntered up to Lilah and stood very close.
He could see the flush in her cheeks and noted the
indecisive movements of her hands. At the moment
she was having a little trouble being the bold Delilah,
and that pleased him. Without warning he reached out
and touched her shoulders with his damp fingers and
ran his hands lightly down her arms.

"You thanked me plenty, sweetheart," he said huskily. "But if you want to do it again, I won't complain."
Tabor's hands drifted from her arms to her waist, then
up her rib cage, stopping only when they cupped her
full breasts.

Momentarily stunned, Lilah swallowed hard as Tabor squeezed gently. She was aghast at the thought
Sarah might walk up at any minute and find him
fondling her. How embarrassing that would be. Sarah
thought she was a proper lady, and Lilah would just as
soon maintain that illusion. As much as she wanted to
link her arms around Tabor's back and yield to the
sensations his caresses aroused, this wasn't the time to
let herself go. She had to be careful not to get tangled
in those wayward feelings he turned on at will. She
reminded herself that when this week was over, she
wanted to forget Tabor and resume her life without
him.

"Lilah?" His hands moved in magic circles. She
realized his last statement had been a question of
intent.

"No," she said hurriedly, stepping back and blushing in full color at the change she saw in him. "Not

now," she stammered. "I mean . . . I only want to talk."

Grinning, Tabor pulled her against him. "Talking about it is no fun, Delilah."

"Don't call me that," she said breathlessly, and backed away. "I don't want Sarah hearing it. You be sure you don't slip and call me that name in front of her."

"I'll call you 'sweetheart,' then." He caught her again and wrestled a resistant Lilah into his arms. His voice went low and throaty. "You're sure you just want to talk?"

"Yes," she whispered, feeling him against her, conscious of a rebellious lurch inside herself. She would have to be careful about toying with him. He got out of control too quickly; to say nothing of herself.

Tabor acted as if he hadn't heard her reply. He lifted her in his arms and lowered his mouth to hers, teasing her with his lips until a whole new series of shivery delights flooded through her. She was shocked at how she responded to his kiss. As if pulled by an unknown force, her arms curled around his neck. She moaned softly under the heated press of his lips. He held her tightly in his embrace until time stopped and her consciousness ebbed and she would have agreed to anything he wanted.

Disappointment washed through her when he set her down.

"Well, if you're sure," he said. "I guess I'll have to wait."

Her legs were so weak she had to find a place to sit while he dressed. He stopped after donning his pants and boots and came and sat beside her. Lilah's heart raced.

Tabor gave her a guileless smile. "You wanted to *talk* about lovemaking, I think."

"No!" The word popped out. "Not exactly. I want to talk about us."

"It's perfect with us," he said, looking into her eyes. "The way you move when I'm inside you is . . ."

Lilah's cheeks flamed redder than her hair. "Not exactly that either," she said stiffly. "What I want to talk about is me being Delilah. I don't want anyone else to know, ever."

"Didn't I assure you I wouldn't tell anyone you're Delilah?"

"Yes, but . . . well . . ." She blushed again. "I don't want anyone to know Lilah Damon isn't as virtuous as she seems either."

"I see." Tabor reached for his shirt, deciding he needed a cigarette. He set about rolling one. "I suppose you have a good reason for being two people."

"I do," she said, pleased that he was being so cooperative. "But I can't continue to be two women much longer. Next year when I marry Barrett I'll have to give up being Delilah. So you can understand how crucial it is that I maintain my secret now."

The casualness of her remarks struck him like a slap. So she still planned to marry Fenton and live an aristocratic life in one of those hillside mansions in San Francisco.

"I suppose you intend to pass yourself off to Fenton as a snow-white virgin. Or has he already sampled your wares?"

"Certainly not! How dare . . ." She caught herself. Why wouldn't he think that about Barrett after she had made love to him with such abandon? No doubt he believed that was the way Delilah spent every night of her tour. "Barrett *will* think he has married a virgin."

Tabor's mouth crooked up on one side. "Aren't you afraid he'll know the truth after his wedding night?"

Her smile was condescending. "I'll just have to make

sure he doesn't." The idiot. She *had* fooled him.

Tabor blew out a smoke ring and decided to play along, letting her believe he didn't know he was the first man to make love with her. "I've heard of whores doing that."

"Doing what?" she asked sharply.

"Using chicken blood and sponges to produce a show of virginal blood. Some of them sell themselves as virgins over and over. Is that what you have planned?"

Lilah became silent. Blood? Was he hinting that he had noticed the blood? Had he? Surely he would have said so.

"Is it?" he asked again. Judging by the sudden paleness in her cheeks, he had her wondering if he had been aware of her scheme to trick him.

"I may do that," she answered weakly. "Or something else. The important thing is that you not let Sarah or anyone else at the ranch know about our . . . lovemaking. I don't want to give Barrett any more reason to be upset with me."

Tabor had to clench his fists to prevent himself from throttling Lilah. She was the most stubborn, most headstrong woman in California. He planned on giving Barrett plenty of reason to be upset.

"What do I get for keeping *this* secret?" he asked casually.

Lilah's eyes opened incredulously. "Why should you get anything else?" Wasn't making her a love slave for a week enough for the man?

Tabor dropped his hand onto Lilah's thigh. She gasped. "You don't realize how habit-forming you are, sweetheart. After one time, I know a week with you won't be enough. Once in a while I'll want to visit you in San Francisco."

"Oh, no!" Her eyes blazed at him. "Once I'm married, there won't be any other men sharing my bed. I'll be true to my husband."

She sure would. Tabor sensuously slid his hand along her thigh. He figured he had a week to change her mind about who that husband would be.

"Tabor! Lilah!" Sarah's voice brought Lilah to her feet, but not before Tabor's wandering hand had rekindled her longing for him.

"Promise me," she whispered.

Tabor stood. "I promise your reputation will be no worse when you leave here than when I met you."

"Good," she whispered, then lifted her brows suspiciously. That didn't sound like what she meant.

"I got nervous when you and Lilah didn't come back right away. Am I interrupting something?" Sarah, carrying a bucket, joined them by the pool.

"No!" Lilah said too quickly. "We were just starting back." She smiled sheepishly. "I think I'm ready for that nap now."

Tabor took the bucket from Sarah. "You two go ahead," he said quietly. "I'll get the water."

Lilah was asleep when he got back to the camp, her face angelically reposed. He watched her for a while, wondering what drove her in so many directions. He still hadn't uncovered anything that explained why she had taken up the life of a saloon entertainer. If anything, after discovering her virginal state, he was more confused than before.

Perplexed, he walked back to the wagon and got a cup of coffee. While he sat alone drinking it, something occurred to him that he might have thought about sooner if she hadn't kept him so rattled. She hadn't been making love to those other men she invited to her room. It didn't make sense to go to so much trouble just to fleece a few men out of their money as she had done with him. She wasn't exactly the man-hater he had thought either, not the way she had responded to him. So why did she feel the need to live that life, then try to keep it a secret? The woman was a paradox. A virgin singing a temptress's song. An innocent and a fraud.

He strengthened his resolve to find out the truth about her. The socialite Lilah Damon, the shadowy Miss M. Alden, the tempting Delilah, Flame of the West, his woman. She had given herself to him and the little liar thought she had pulled that off without his being the wiser. Tabor rested his head against the spokes of a wagon wheel, a grin wide as the Rio Grande on his face. She burned him up with curiosity, but he was having one hell of a good time learning about her.

"What happened out there?" Sarah dragged her chair up close to him and sat down. "Who's this Chapman?"

Tabor let his smile go. "I'm not sure about any of it, Sarah. Chapman's loco. I met him back in San Francisco. He contends a piece of property my father had a claim to by right belongs to him. Trouble is, that's the same property I handed over to Clement Damon."

"Clement Damon," Sarah mused. "That's Lilah's father?"

"Do you know the name?"

"Seems like I've heard it." Sarah searched her mind but came up with nothing clear. "Must have been a long time ago. What was his business with Stan?"

Tabor shook his head. He hadn't been interested in his father's business. Now he wished he had been. "I don't know," he answered. "It went back a long time. Damon didn't say much about it. I think he was more than a little surprised when I showed up and presented him with that claim."

"The one Chapman says is his?"

"Right. Chapman confronted me about the claim after I had given it to Damon. I told him he needed legal proof he had any right to it. We wound up fighting. I thought that settled it and I'd seen the last of him. I sure didn't think he'd try anything as crazy as kidnaping Lilah."

"Was he planning to kill her?"

"Worse than that," Tabor said sourly.

Sarah nodded slowly. "He'll be back, won't he?"

Tabor's guess was that he would be as soon as that bullet wound healed. But as loco as Chapman was, he wouldn't give up. He'd keep trying to even the score. Tabor wished he could assure Sarah otherwise. His voice was bitter. "Yes. But not soon. And he won't surprise me the next time."

"And I take it you won't miss when you draw on him."

"Not likely."

Sarah got up and threw a couple of pieces of wood on the cook fire. "You had better warn Damon. Chapman might show up there."

Tabor got to his feet and brushed the dust off his pants. "I'll stop by Sandy Flats tomorrow and send a telegram."

Together they walked to the tether line to check on the horses and mules. "Can Damon handle a man like Chapman?"

"Not alone," he said. "Clement is crippled, confined to an invalid's chair. But he has men to protect him. He'll be safe." Tabor's brow wrinkled as he thought of the break-in at Damon House. "Thinking back," he said, "it may be Chapman's already paid him a visit—in a way. I caught a Chinese fellow breaking in while I was there. He talked about a partner. That could have been Chapman."

Sarah's eyes lit up. "Now I remember about Damon,"

she said. "Back ten or fifteen years ago he took the part of some coolies who had been driven out of a town. Put them to work in his mine. The Chinese resentment was high then. People didn't appreciate Damon helping those Chinese. I don't remember all the talk, but a short time later there was an accident. Damon got trampled by a herd of horses stampeding through his mining camp."

Tabor shook his head. "Somewhere I got the idea he was crippled by a fall from a horse." Though what Sarah had said explained why Clement's Chinese employees were devoted to him.

"No," Sarah said thoughtfully. "I'm sure Clement Damon is the one. It was in the papers back then. But that was years ago. I guess I remember because it was about the same time you and your mother came to live with us."

And about the same time my father deserted us, Tabor thought. Sarah was too kind to put it that way.

"Damon's a fine man," he told Sarah. "He seems to have done well for himself since then."

"Just the same, you keep a close watch on that girl. Damon's had enough loss in his life. Besides, I've got a feeling Lilah Damon is mighty special to you too." She gave him a contemplative look. "You planning on getting hitched?"

Tabor's grin returned. "Sarah, you're too nosy for your own good."

Sarah laughed loudly. "I don't have to be nosy to see you looking like a moonstruck calf."

Hours later the stars shone down on the quiet camp. Tabor had awakened Lilah and the two of them sat a little way apart from the others, balancing bowls of Sarah's soup in their laps. As he finished a slab of cornbread, Tabor watched Lilah nibble at hers.

"Sarah told me about how your father got hurt."

Lilah clumsily dropped her cornbread on the ground. "Sarah knows my father?"

"No." Tabor tossed the dropped bread away and gave Lilah his remaining slice. "She remembers reading about his accident a long time ago. Your father was a brave man to have taken a stand for the Chinese back then. I admired him already, and even more now. Clement handles himself well. You must be proud of him."

"I am," Lilah said, unabashed. "Papa's the most important person in the world to me."

"You must have been quite young when that accident happened."

Her expression turned serious. Accident? What had happened to her father had been no accident. His father had been there that terrible night. But she couldn't let him know that. It would start him asking questions about the other men involved. Too much interest on his part might cost her the chance to bring justice to the last two of those six.

"I was," she said hesitantly, trying to force the memory out of her mind. "Very young. I . . . I hardly remember it." It didn't set easy with her either that her justice had been misguided where he was concerned. But surely she was making it up to him now.

Tabor took her hand gently. "I'm sorry," he said, looking into her stricken face. "I'm upsetting you. Sarah will take a stick to me for that."

God! She could pull the strings of his heart, looking that way. He found it gratifying, though, that as skillful an actress as she was, there were some emotions she couldn't hide. Lilah Damon had many soft spots in her heart. He had just hit one of them.

He could wait to ask her why she needed to be Delilah part of the time. Another day or two of wondering wouldn't hurt him. Talking about it might unlock painful secrets. Out here in the wilderness she was his responsibility and he didn't want her going to sleep with unhappy thoughts on her mind.

Smiling, he kissed her softly on the cheek and was happy to see her face brighten. Near the campfire one of the cowhands started picking a guitar and singing. Tabor pulled Lilah to her feet and led her over to join in the fun.

16

Shortly after the party stopped to eat the noon meal, Tabor rode into Sandy Flats to send a telegram to Clement and to report the incident to the sheriff. Sarah told Lilah they weren't far from the ranch and that by the time Tabor got home, she could have had that bath she'd been talking about and be sitting on the front porch drinking lemonade.

With the possibility of a real bath and a real bed to sleep in at hand, the Cooke ranch sounded like the promised land. A surge of energy rose in Lilah's tired body. And though the bumpy ride in the chuck wagon rattled her almost as much as being in the saddle, she knew she could hold out a few more miles. At last the trip was nearly over and soon she could change her soiled riding clothes and boots for one of her luxurious gowns. Lilah rubbed her arms, thinking how good silk would feel on her skin. Never in her life had she worn the same grimy outfit two days in a row. Thank goodness there wasn't a mirror around. Her face must look as if she had traveled the entire Overland Trail.

While she was daydreaming, Sarah nudged her arm. "Of course if Tabor runs into Sally Ann Caufield in town, he may be late getting home."

Jiggling the reins, Sarah shouted to the mules to get moving while Lilah pondered what she had said. Sarah wasn't much for chitchat, so Lilah supposed she wouldn't have mentioned that name if it wasn't important. Suddenly she was wide-awake.

"Is Sally Ann Caufield a friend of Tabor's?"

Sarah grinned. "Sally Ann's had her fishing hook set for Tabor since she was old enough to notice the difference in girls and boys. Well, maybe before then— she's still just a kid. She lives over on the next ranch. It's closer to town than we are, so she's there in the tearoom almost every day."

"I see."

Lilah wasn't prepared to feel jealous of Tabor but she couldn't account for the sudden agitation she felt any other way. She couldn't imagine why she should feel the prick of jealousy's sharp barbs. Why should it matter to her if Tabor was pursued by another woman? She determined not to let it bother her. Her mind was made up that this week was one to be enjoyed.

Oh, she knew sharing a man's bed wasn't moral, but plenty of things in her life had taught her there were times you had to adapt to a different set of standards. And there was no doubt that once this week was over, she would be through with Tabor for good. Maybe some people would think she was decadent. But what did she care? This week she wasn't truly Lilah Damon. She was Delilah and she meant to get the most out of it.

She had meant what she said about being a faithful wife. A woman owed that to her husband. But since she didn't love Barrett in the romantic way, she deserved her fling first. Tabor excited her in a way

Barrett never would. Certainly she and Barrett cared for each other, but that didn't discount the fact that their marriage was primarily a business arrangement. Oh, she knew Barrett would never put that in words. It was true, though. She was his assurance of getting his hands on the Damon empire. He knew her father had been grooming him for the job. She doubted Barrett was even very worried about what her decision on the marriage would be when he returned from London.

She mulled that over. He knew she would put her father's concerns above her own and that she would never marry a man who wasn't prepared to do the same. That wasn't terribly flattering, was it? Barrett had gone away to save face, but he must have considered that if Lilah chose someone else he would lose all he had worked for. He must be awfully sure of himself.

Or did Barrett know the kind of marriage he offered was what Lilah preferred? Perhaps he knew her better than she thought. In truth she was convinced that high-flung emotions like love and jealousy only got in the way of a successful marriage. Just look how miserable a little jealousy was making her feel now.

As she pondered those things, Sarah spoke up again. "I'm telling you about Sally Ann because she's sure to show up at the ranch. She's dropped by every week since Tabor's been gone, asking when he would be back. Soon as she knows he's here, she'll be around. And when she sees you, she'll have her claws out. She's never has any competition. At least not around here."

"I wonder why Tabor hasn't mentioned her," Lilah said coolly.

Sarah contained her grin. "Don't get me wrong. Tabor hasn't encouraged Sally Ann. Leastwise not that I know of. He just humors her a little. Takes her to a dance once in a while. This idea there's something between them is all hers."

Lilah's dander was up, with wondering if Tabor and Sally Ann ever did more than dance. The barbs of jealousy bit into her again and her eyes narrowed. "I hope you don't think there's anything binding between me and Tabor."

"Isn't there?" Sarah turned the mules through a wooden gate built post-and-lintel style. The board overhead had "Cooke Ranch" burned into it. On either side was a Circle C. Sarah identified the symbol as her brand.

"Why, no," Lilah answered stiffly. "We're friends, that's all. Really this plan for me to visit the ranch was something he worked out with Papa. My father thought I ought to see this part of the country."

"I guess maybe I got the wrong notion about things," Sarah said. "But consarn it, the way that boy looks at you, I thought . . . Anyway, I'm sorry if I've embarrassed you with my presumption."

Lilah moaned to herself. She hadn't meant to be short and hurt Sarah's feelings. Besides, what else could Sarah have thought? Tabor might have indicated as much, as a way of explaining why he was bringing her to the ranch. Maybe she should have let Sarah keep thinking there was something between them. Admittedly, she was glad to learn Tabor didn't make a habit of inviting girls to visit.

"Of course I do like Tabor a lot." Lilah offered the words cautiously. "And you never know what might happen." There. That ought to smooth out the wrinkles. "Thank you for letting me know about Sally Ann," she added calmly.

The ranch house came into view, a whitewashed frame structure of two stories with an outdoor staircase running to a porch on the back of the second floor. The house was no mansion like Damon House, but it was larger than Lilah had imagined and had an inviting hominess to it. The rose garden Tabor had told her about was inside a picket fence on one side.

Sarah drove right past the house and on down to the barn. A wrangler ran out to welcome Sarah back and to take the mules. After Lilah had been introduced to the few ranch hands who were around the barn, she and Sarah walked back to the house.

A wide and airy shotgun hall ran from front door to back. Within it, a sturdy staircase climbed up to the second floor. A cheerful blue paint covered the walls, and white trim bordered the door and window frames. The floor of scrubbed planks showed the indentions of many boot heels. A wooden clothes rack hung just past the front door and held an assortment of hats and jackets and one gunbelt.

Lilah peeped into a parlor, only to be startled by the glass-eyed stare of a stuffed bear head above a new-looking medallion-back settee. The room looked as if Sarah and Tabor had fought over the furnishings and ended up in a bizarre compromise. A bowl of silk flowers sat on an occasional table, a stuffed bird on another. A frilly green fern filled one corner while a carved wooden Indian stood ground in another. Lilah decided Sarah's parlor was indeed the oddest room she had ever seen.

The kitchen, bigger than the parlor, was clearly all woman's domain. No sign of Tabor glared at her there, save a pair of polished boots resting by the fireplace. A blackened cast-iron wood stove occupied a big share of the room. Between it and the fireplace rested a box heaped with split wood and kindling. The cupboards were open shelves lined with pottery bowls and glass jars filled with dried beans or apple butter or other delectable samples of Sarah's culinary skill. A tin-lined sink hung against one wall alongside the dry sink and a marble-topped counter for bread-making. Even without a fire going the atmosphere was warm and cozy, and Lilah guessed Sarah and Tabor spent as much time here as in the parlor.

Sarah had no maid, so Lilah helped start a fire in the stove and helped heat water for her bath. The bathtub turned out to be a large wooden washtub Sarah dragged in from the back porch, but it was clean and big enough to accommodate Lilah. After three days of bathing from a washbowl, Lilah found the oak tub every bit as delightful as the big brass hip tub at Damon House.

After her bath, however, Lilah received the bad news that her trunk hadn't yet arrived at the ranch. Since she had no clean clothes of her own, Sarah offered one of her best calico frocks. The dress was bigger than Lilah's waist by a good six inches and the red print was horrendous with her pink slippers. Laughing at herself, Lilah donned it anyway and cinched one of Sarah's starched aprons around her waist to tighten up the fit. She would have hanged herself before going out in San Francisco clad as she was, but since no one was likely to see her on the ranch, she accepted Sarah's invitation to sit out on the porch.

"Maybe Tabor will pick up your trunk while he's in town. It's probably at the stage office in Sandy Flats, but they haven't gotten around to sending anyone out to tell us."

Lilah groaned. "I certainly hope he does. If my trunk has been lost, I don't even have a decent outfit to wear into town to shop for new clothes." She saw amusement in Sarah's black eyes. "Oh, I don't mean your dress isn't decent, Sarah," she hastened to say. "I'm only complaining about the fit."

"No need." Sarah chuckled. "I understand. You're

much too pretty a girl to be covered up by an extra two yards of calico."

Still smiling and thinking how much she liked Sarah, Lilah lifted her damp hair off her neck so it would dry more quickly in the warm breeze. She noticed Sarah looking toward the gate. "Do you see something?"

"Looks like a buckboard coming in," Sarah replied, getting to her feet and shielding her eyes as she strained to see who it was. "It's leading a horse. Tabor must have rented one to bring your trunk."

"Thank goodness," Lilah responded, standing and joining Sarah on the edge of the porch. She could see the buckboard clearly, and there definitely appeared to be a trunk in back. Tabor's black hat identified him. Lilah was distressed to see that he wasn't alone. "Who's that with Tabor?" she asked.

"By thunder! It's Sally Ann," Sarah said as the buckboard rolled around the last bend in the road.

Now Lilah could make out the womanly figure close beside Tabor on the driver's seat. All at once the tiny hairs on the back of her neck stood up catlike. She could also see the young woman was not a kid, nor the plain-faced country girl she had imagined. Lilah took a quick glance at herself dressed like a bunkhouse cook in Sarah's attire. She was all set to dash in the house and wait to meet Sally Ann when she was properly outfitted. But there wasn't time.

"Hello!" A feminine voice lifted out of the thin cloud of dust the buckboard scattered in front of the porch. "I've brought the prodigal home."

Tabor gave Sally Ann a forbearing smile as he hopped from the buckboard and tied the horse to the hitching post. He unhooked his saddle horse from the back of the conveyance and tied him to the post as well. With both horses taken care of, he returned to the back of the buckboard for Lilah's trunk.

DELILAH'S FLAME   **321**

"Hello, Sally Ann," Sarah replied. "That was nice of you."

"Well, he had that heavy trunk to bring for your guest." Sally Ann's smile flagged as she realized Tabor was struggling with the trunk in question and had forgotten about helping her from the buckboard. "I guess that must be you."

Her perusal of Lilah was sharp and quick, her eyes telegraphing her conclusion that this ill-clad city girl with wet, lank hair wouldn't prove much of a rival. Giving up on Tabor, she climbed down by herself and walked up the steps.

Carrying Lilah's trunk, Tabor edged past the women on the porch. The tension in the air was almost tangible. He gave Lilah a hasty smile, aware he hadn't made the wisest choice about transportation. Then he pushed through the front door, anxious to get out of harm's way.

Lilah was intent in canvassing Sally Ann Caufield, but she found a second to shoot a furious glance at Tabor as he passed. Accustomed to her wardrobe being the envy of her peers in San Francisco, Lilah was colossally put out at meeting another young woman while dressed as she was. Sally Ann observed her discomfiture and immediately called attention to her stylish teal dress by brushing an imaginary speck from the draped skirt.

Lilah reeked with indignation at being made to feel inferior. Sally Ann's gown with its covering of Chantilly lace over a front yoke and a panel of the bustle definitely made her feel dowdy. Like the top hen in the barnyard, Sally Ann swished her way across the porch to offer a hand to Lilah. As she extended a gloved one, Sally Ann tilted her head to reveal the impressively large diamond studs in her ears and to show off her rich brown hair so fashionably pinned up with silver combs.

"This is Miss Lilah Damon of San Francisco, Sally Ann." Sarah pulled up a third rocking chair for the young woman as Lilah shook that gloved hand with her own sunburnt one. "She's visiting with us for a while."

"Nice to meet you. I'm Sally Ann Caufield." Her green eyes flashing regally, Sally Ann gave a lofty smile as she let go of Lilah's hand. "My father owns the Bar Z. It's the biggest spread in these parts."

"How nice," Lilah said, attempting to be polite, though Sally Ann's patronizing looks prodded her quick temper.

"You must be a friend of Sarah's," Sally Ann remarked as she accepted a glass of lemonade.

Lilah tensed. The little snip was hinting she wasn't attractive enough to interest Tabor. Her chin went up. "Tabor invited me," she said boldly. "He's been a guest at our house for several weeks. Now he's asked me down here for a visit."

Her words delivered the intended implication that she and Tabor hadn't been ready to part company.

"How long will you be staying, Miss Damon?"

"She'll stay as long as she likes, Sally Ann." Expecting at any minute to see the girls' backs curl up like angry felines', Sarah stepped in. "I'll invite you and your mother and father over for dinner one night and you can all get to know Lilah."

Sally Ann sneered, not pleased at Sarah's hint to run along. "I'm not sure we have many evenings free," she remarked dryly. "But you can ask anyway."

"I'll do that, Sally Ann. And thanks for bringing Lilah's trunk out. I'm sure she appreciates it."

"I certainly do," Lilah said icily. "It's been a pleasure meeting you."

"Whew!" Sarah exclaimed as Sally Ann snapped the whip over the horse's head and drove away. "I sure am glad you don't have any personal interest in my nephew. I'd be right upset to find myself caught between two jealous women fighting over a man."

"You don't have to worry about that." Lilah tried to keep her voice calm, but her words crackled anyway. After all, this wasn't Sarah's fault. "Where is Tabor? I'm surprised he didn't come back to say good-bye to Sally Ann."

Sarah laughed aloud but didn't say what she was thinking, that a man developed a cowardly streak when two females were furious at him at the same time.

Lilah excused herself and went upstairs to the bedroom Sarah had prepared for her. She found her trunk in the middle of the floor. She hadn't noticed Tabor downstairs. The doors to the other rooms were open and she peered into all of them but he wasn't to be found. She assumed he had ducked out and down the back stairs, then had taken his horse on to the barn when Sally Ann left. That was fine with her. She had nothing to say to him. Not when he had been so discourteous as to bring another woman visiting when he knew she didn't have a thing to wear.

Lilah unpacked her dresses and hung them in the pine armoire, never thinking that Bess usually attended to such tasks for her. She looked at her beautiful gowns, any of which would have put that catty Sally Ann Caufield to shame. Her fine red-gold brows arched sharply. The next time they met, she wouldn't look like a vagabond.

Still fuming at Sally Ann and Tabor, Lilah took off Sarah's dress and got into one of her own. By the time she had her other things unpacked and her hair dressed, Sarah was calling her downstairs.

The look Tabor gave her took away all her unease

about being overdressed for supper in the ranch kitchen. She hadn't been thinking about that when she chose the ivory satin and the garnets she wore. She had been thinking something totally foolish, that she wanted Tabor to acknowledge she was prettier than Sally Ann Caufield. He just had.

Her appetite was less hearty than it had been on the trail. Tabor's seemed to have picked up. He ate several slices of ham and two helpings of potatoes. She lost count of the biscuits. She also lost sight of most of the caustic things she had wanted to say to him, and by the time supper was over and Sarah had taken them to the parlor, she was all smiles.

Sarah poured glasses of wine for everyone, then left Tabor and Lilah alone while she went back to the kitchen to do the dishes. Lilah felt bad about that, but as Sarah pointed out, she wasn't dressed for dishwashing. But, Sarah agreed, she could have the chore the next night.

"What do you think of the ranch?" Tabor asked, looking for safe ground. He knew she had been miffed at him for bringing Sally Ann out unexpectedly. Dammit! He'd tried to avoid that little nuisance in town, but she had caught him coming out of the sheriff's office and followed him to the stage company. Once she saw he had a trunk to cart home, nothing he could say would stop her from lending her buckboard.

"The ranch is nice. Bigger than I thought." Lilah decided the wine had made her giddy when one more inane comment slipped from her. "I like the house." It took her a few minutes to realize that what really had her nervous was wondering if Tabor planned to slip into her bedroom during the night—and knowing she hoped he would.

"You and Sarah seem to be getting along fine." He couldn't get used to seeing her sitting in the parlor where he had spent so many nights with Sarah and his mother. It still amazed him that Lilah took to this life with ease. She hadn't complained once since that first day on the trail. No. He reconsidered the moment of change. Since he had made love to her she had been a different woman.

"I like Sarah," Lilah said, interrupting his recollections.

His eyes hung on her, maybe rudely, but she was beautiful as a mountain sunset and so desirable he ached to sweep her into his arms and carry her up the stairs to his room. But she was too concerned about her reputation to stand for that. So he smiled in a way that let her know what he was thinking. Banked fires of passion lit her sky-blue eyes in response. His sweet strumpet was torn between doing what she wanted and doing what looked right. Making love to her was permissible only if it was done in secret.

The little firebrand was afraid to acknowledge what he aroused in her. But why should he worry over it when she was so warm and willing in his arms in secret? Couldn't he be content with that?

Tabor finished his wine and took his glass to the cabinet near the front window. He stood there a moment, staring into the inky darkness. She might not say so, but she acted as if she felt differently toward him than when they had started out. Or was that an act too? He sure had messed up today, bringing Sally Ann by the house. Trouble was, he didn't know if that killing glance Lilah had given him when he carried her trunk in had been because she was embarrassed about being caught in Sarah's dress or because she was jealous of seeing him with Sally Ann. With a woman it was difficult to tell which was more important.

She didn't seem mad now, though. He wondered if she would put up a fight if he slipped into her room later. He didn't want her feeling embarrassed around

Sarah, so maybe he shouldn't push it. Dammit! He sounded spineless as a milksop. Why didn't he just ask her? Tabor spun around, but the words died on his lips. Lilah lay slumped against the back of the wing chair, sound asleep.

Sarah helped Lilah into bed. Tabor waited for her in the parlor, disappointed that tonight he wouldn't have anything more real than his dreams to keep him company.

"She's sleeping like a lamb," Sarah said, rejoining him in the parlor. "The girl's been needing this rest since you got her away from that no-good Chapman."

Tabor frowned. He hated bringing it up, but this was as good a time as any to tell Sarah what he had learned from the sheriff about Chapman.

"Roscoe had a poster on him," he said. "It was an old one, so he had to go through a stack, but the name rang a bell with him and he wouldn't quit until he found it."

"What's he wanted for?" Sarah didn't like the look in Tabor's eyes.

Tabor shook his head, because even now, even after what had almost happened to Lilah, he couldn't believe a man capable of such a crime. "Turns out Chapman once took up preaching about five years back. Even had a little church and a congregation that thought highly of him. He passed himself off as a sinner back in the fold, ready to lead others to salvation. Trouble was, nobody bothered to ask just what Chapman's sins had been."

"I don't like the sound of this," Sarah said flatly.

Tabor sighed wearily. "It doesn't get better. Seems his 'weakness of the flesh' is just that. He likes to molest women, usually young girls. He sweet-talks them off somewhere alone and . . ."

"What?"

"The man's a lunatic, Sarah. He strips them down and bites them all over. He's never raped anybody, but what he does is worse. The last one, at least the last one anybody knows about, was a young girl in his congregation. He used a knife on her too. The poor kid died of shock, but not before she identified Chapman. Later others came forward and told a similar story, but too late. Chapman got away and just disappeared."

Sarah said nothing for a long while, just sat thinking how close Lilah had come to meeting that same fate. "You told Lilah about this?"

"No and I don't think I will right away. I wrote to Clement about it, though, and told him I'm keeping a guard out all the time."

Again Sarah sat for a long time without speaking. "You should have killed him," she said at last.

"I know." A little while later Tabor breezed out, heading down to the bunkhouse for the smoke Sarah didn't allow in her parlor. He also wanted a drink of something stronger than homemade wine.

"Is Sarah gone?" At midmorning Lilah showed up in the kitchen just as Tabor came in the back door for a refill of coffee. "I've called and looked through the house. I was about to see if she was down at the barn." Her eyes and voice were still heavy with sleep.

Tabor half-turned from filling his cup at the stove. In moss-green muslin she looked as cool and fresh as the first leaves of spring. Her red-gold curls were piled loosely on top of her head, and already tendrils twisted and trailed from the knot. He was right back where he had been last night, with the yearning for her leaping through his body. He had waited around, thinking maybe he would tell her about Chapman, but with one look he postponed it again.

"She's gone." He set the coffeepot back on the stove top, forgetting to offer Lilah a cup. "Bris Franklin's wife, Millie, is in labor with her first child. Doc Flynn is out of town, so they sent for Sarah to midwife."

"She does that?"

Tabor crossed to the kitchen table. "She brought in half the babies, calves, and foals around here. She'll be gone all day."

Lilah found the coffeepot on the back of the stove and poured a cup for herself. Tabor had drawn a chair out from the table and straddled it. Lilah seated herself in another one. "How do you know she'll be gone all day?"

He supposed she wouldn't know much about such things. A girl in her station would be shielded from such gritty realities. He smiled softly.

"Because first babies take a long time, and then she'll stay around until she's sure Millie's all right. She won't be back before nightfall."

Lilah's skin prickled at the thought of the empty house, Tabor, and no one to disturb them. She forgot all about wanting breakfast. Tabor looked wildly appealing in denim pants and a faded blue shirt. His black hair gleamed, lit by a bright stream of light from the kitchen window behind him. Days on the trail had darkened his skin to an even deeper golden color. His smile was placid, but a faint glow of hunger shone in his dusk-gray eyes.

A wave of longing swept through her, banishing all the wrath she had once held for him. Her heart sang out like a caged bird that had been set free. With Sarah away she had no need to hold up a false front. How stimulating it was to simply drop her pretenses and to do what she felt.

Her face must have involuntarily shown what she was thinking, for suddenly Tabor put aside his tin cup and rose from the chair. He strode toward her, taking the half-empty cup of coffee from her hand and leaving it to cool on the kitchen table. As if he were inviting her to dance at a cotillion, he took Lilah's hands and drew her to her feet.

Tabor whirled her around on the kitchen floor where a patch of sunlight spilled through a window. Lilah laughed wholeheartedly, caught up in the excitement of his surprise, hearing music in her ears.

"We must look ridiculous," she insisted as he waltzed her around his abandoned chair.

"Do you feel ridiculous?"

She laughed again. "No! I feel wonderful."

"I used to watch you onstage and wish you would dance into my arms," Tabor said, twirling her from the kitchen through the hall and into the parlor. "I watched you drive men to a fever pitch. I saw them looking at you so hard their eyelids wouldn't blink. Every one of them as starved for you as I was, and hoping the light of that mirror would shine in their faces. You're a witch on that stage, Delilah. Do you know it? A beautiful, enchanting witch." He spun her around, her feet and skirts fluttering in the air.

"No one ever called me that." She smiled gaily. She felt like a witch, a wonderfully light one flying through the darkness, but with nothing sinister in her heart.

"I kept coming back to see you, hoping to catch the eye of the magnificent Delilah, to have her choose me as her man."

She didn't mind that he called her Delilah again. Perhaps Delilah *was* a witch. If so, Lilah Damon was as much under her spell as any of those men Tabor spoke of. She was pleasantly surprised to hear he had felt more than an ordinary attraction to her before that night in Yuba City.

How thrilling to learn he had been there by choice

and not by chance. Of course he wouldn't know she
never really saw the individuals in her audience. From
the stage those faces were blank spheres, and always
someone had pointed out the man to shine her mirror
on. But had she seen Tabor watching in the way he
described, she was sure she would have selected him
herself.

"And so you did catch my eye," she reminded.

Laughter shook him. "And so I did," he repeated.
"But I didn't have the night of ecstasy I believed the
reward for Delilah's man." Tabor stopped the dancing
but continued to hold her in his arms. "You haven't
yet explained that."

In his mind he was giving her a chance to admit why
neither he nor any other man had enjoyed such a night
of pleasure with Delilah.

The gay smile slipped from her lips. The freed bird
felt the tug of a restraint, as if a string had been tied to
her leg, allowing her to fly just so far from the cage.
Here she was cast back on her sea of lies, reminded
she had more secrets to keep then the single one Tabor
knew. The strongest feeling was regret that this bliss-
ful morning might end on a sour note. She wanted to
recapture that bounteous free spirit she and Tabor had
shared only a moment before.

"We don't have to discuss that now," she said softly.
"It isn't even part of the bargain. Let it wait."

"Let it wait," he agreed when she turned those
sapphire eyes on him.

Just the start of a hard line on that lovely face
melted his curiosity. Let the hundred questions on the
tip of his tongue wait. Let everything wait that might
interfere with the promises shining like stars in a field
of deep blue. He wished he hadn't mentioned the
subject at all. Just recalling that she was in his arms
only because he could expose her as Delilah took some

of the joy out of the swell of passion inside him.

Most women of his experience made a fuss to get his attention. The thought that none of what he read in Lilah's sparkling eyes might be true wounded him to the quick. And why he had an unyielding desire to untangle his emotions and hers still bewildered him. She was fire and brimstone inside a gossamer angel skin, maybe too much trouble to tame.

If he wanted a woman outside a brothel, Sally Ann Caufield was his for the taking. If he wanted a woman who would be a good wife, a woman who knew his ways and cared about them, Sally Ann was the sensible choice. But he wanted Delilah, Lilah Damon, and the feelings she aroused in him wouldn't let him consider being sensible.

Her eyes darkened and he couldn't read anything in them at all. He contented himself with making them mirrors of his own deep thoughts. A heavy sigh issued from him. He burned with enough passion for both of them. If her ardor was make-believe, it wouldn't stay that forever. He alone had tasted the rich sensuality in Delilah. The memory of slipping inside the satin sheath of her body ignited a hot flame of desire in his loins. He had no intention of sharing her with another man.

Delilah was his woman, his alone. His mind swirled, spinning his emotions like straw in a whirlwind, lust for a flame-haired witch, jealousy over any other man who dared to want her, possessiveness because he alone had awakened her erotic nature. For other men she had worn her shimmering costumes and sung her provocative songs. But that part of her which only one man could claim, she had given to him. She was his woman. In time she would know it too.

Without warning, Tabor's mouth came down on hers. But, oh, how she wanted the crush of his lips. His hands wrapped the creamy expanse of her throat,

stroked the gentle slope of her shoulders, and swept
away the troublesome sleeves of her gown. She loved
the feel of his hands sliding over her skin. Onward
they sped to the soft swells of her breasts, thumbs
flicking the nipples through soft cottony muslin. Lilah
felt the tiny buds tighten as a hot flush swept her.

Tabor's lips moved on her soft, trembling mouth
and gently, gently demanded more. His tongue darted
to and fro, tracing the outline of her lips before urging
them to open. When her lips yielded, his mouth rav-
aged, his tongue plundering and looting the sweet
treasures inside.

"Do you want me, Lilah?" he whispered, his mouth
at her ear and as untamed there as it had been on
her lips. He teased and taunted that smooth shell, his
breath warm and intimate on her skin. Words of love,
words of desire came in a soft, sweet murmur.

Lilah moaned. She was free again, free to tread on
her lies and speak the words of truth in her heart. "I
do want you. Oh, Tabor, I do."

Swept along in the tide of her passion, she held
tightly to Tabor, afraid that without him as anchor her
quivering flesh and bones would fail her and she would
sink as if into the fathomless depths of the ocean. But
if he were by her side she wouldn't mind the deep,
dark waters. She knew that instinctively as his body,
lithe and lean as a whipcord, pressed into hers. The
unsteady hammering of his heart drummed in her ears
as her head lay still against his chest. The tight hard-
ness of his loins against her thigh stoked the fires
within her.

Tabor's hands plucked pins and combs from the
tresses she had so carefully styled. Loose, it tumbled
over her shoulders in strawberry-blond curls. Bent
backward with his fingers laced in her hair, Lilah gave
herself to the assault of his mouth on the sensitive

flesh at her throat and yielded willingly as he sought the soft hollow between her breasts.

Tabor flicked the buttons of her bodice loose, exposing the twin rose-tipped peaks to his hungry eyes. As his mouth took one flushed tip, a storm of sensations sped through her veins like the unleashing of tiny bolts of lightning. His eyes glittered with passion and wanting as his mouth moved on her wildly. Lilah cupped his head in her hands, pulling him ever closer. She cried his name angrily when he pulled away, only to be swept into his arms.

Carrying her, he bounded up the stairs and down the hall to the farthest bedroom. He gave the door a kick, swinging it open. It was a man's room, devoid of any frills. The one item of luxury was an oversize four-poster bed. Balancing her on his knee, Tabor flung back the wool Indian blanket and laid Lilah on the soft sheets underneath. He cast off his shirt and boots, and Lilah felt for her morocco leather slippers, discovering she had lost them somewhere on the trip up the stairs.

Tabor joined her on the bed, fighting through a bevy of petticoats to locate one slipperless foot. His hand carefully traveled the length of a shapely calf and knee to find the garter which held her silk stocking. Slowly he rolled the stocking down into a neat silken ball and tossed it to the pillows, then repeated his work on the other.

Lilah was astonished when he kissed her toes and the sensitive arch of her foot, for he seemed to know, as she did not, that there were many surprisingly erogenous spots on a woman's body. With so many to choose from, Tabor stayed not long on that one. He hurriedly rid her of the muslin gown, leaving her clad in a thin and lacy chemise.

When she would shed that garment, he stopped her.

"This time, sweetheart," he whispered huskily, "I want to have my way with you. Lie back and let me."

Passion-laden, Lilah did as bidden, though it was difficult to contain herself when he stripped away his trousers and stood within her reach so temptingly displayed. She smiled, but mostly out of dismay that he had the power to stoke such a wantonness in her. Once again she feared the new sensation and knew a trace of maidenly fear. But with Tabor easing into the bed beside her, his aroused manhood nudging at her thigh, the last small vestige of misgiving abandoned her consciousness.

He kissed her slender fingers, the soft palms of her hands, the delectable bend of her elbow, her smooth forehead and feather-light eyelids, her perfectly shaped nose and proud little chin. His mouth played fervidly with those more neutral zones, his hands splayed over her pale soft skin, heating her flesh through the gauzy chemise. Lilah shivered and gasped with delight.

When he paused to look into her eyes, she whispered to him, "The way of a man with a woman is a very beautiful thing."

He kissed her gently. "And the way of a man with a beautiful woman is a wonderful thing," he mocked.

Lilah smiled in pure bliss as he wriggled down her body and knelt at her feet. Forbidding her to move, Tabor edged her chemise slowly up above her knees, his lips following his hands in a sensuous parade of ecstasy. His carnal mouth teased the satin flesh of her thighs, slowly, provocatively inching upward, sliding the chemise away ahead of his fevered kiss. Lilah moaned deep in her throat, urging Tabor on. She didn't noticed that his hands blazed on ahead until his fingers trailed feathery strokes over her breasts, his palms rotating slowly over the nubile peaks.

His mouth stayed low, touching those womanly places

in a way which seared her soul. Lilah writhed and shivered beneath him. At times his teeth sank gently into her flesh, his tongue courted the tiny center of pleasure half-hidden in her womanhood. She could feel her heart pounding, her breath grabbing in her throat, her lungs tight and straining. Her whole body felt as if it were on fire, as if hot sparks stung her skin. She cried out in surprise. She hadn't known, hadn't guessed it could happen this way, that with his mouth he could bring her this wonderfully sweet shock of pleasure.

"Is that surprise?" Tabor asked, lifting up, straddling her, seeing the wide look of wonder in her eyes. "Surely I'm not the first man to fulfill you that way."

"No," Lilah stammered, remembering he thought her experienced in the ways of love. How many more thing were there she didn't know? How many more ways could he make the fire grow within her? How many more ways could he make her burn in the golden flames of passion?

As he plunged inside her, igniting her again, Lilah swore she would learn them all.

17

An hour before sunset, Sarah Cooke returned to the ranch, her heart filled with the joy of having helped bring a new life into the world. As was customary, she entered by the kitchen door. The stove was cold but there were signs Lilah and Tabor had found the plate of ham and the fresh loaf of bread she had left in the cupboard. She started a fire and got the coffee brewing, and for the first time since arriving home from the drive, had a chance to sit back and contemplate just why Tabor had been so all fired anxious to have Miss Lilah Damon at the Cooke ranch.

She liked the girl, and that on top of admitting she had expected Tabor to eventually settle down with Sally Ann. Shucks. Maybe she was losing her instincts about things. Lilah had as good as told her she wasn't interested in Tabor. Perhaps Tabor was just doing her father a favor and keeping her out of San Francisco for a time. Could be the girl had been keeping company with a fast crowd and Clement Damon hoped a change of scene would slow her down. Or maybe he was trying his hand at matchmaking because he wanted some new blood to bolster that citified crowd in San Francisco.

Trouble was, she couldn't see Tabor leaving the ranch to live in town. Not when he had already given up a sterling naval career to come back and run the place. The coffee boiled. Sarah poured a cup and sat at the table enjoying the hot, bitter brew. Where were those two? The boys at the bunkhouse said they hadn't seen Tabor since early morning. She supposed he had stayed around and kept Lilah company. She hoped the girl wouldn't be offended about being left alone her first day at the ranch.

Her coffee finished, Sarah left the kitchen and started up the stairs to her bedroom. On the third riser she felt something beneath her feet. Bending down, she discovered one of Lilah's soft leather slippers. The mate was a few steps farther up the stairs, lying upside down. Sarah picked that one up too and felt a quick tingle of alarm. What in heaven's name would have sent Lilah up the stairs so fast she lost her slippers? Anxiously Sarah hurried up the steps to investigate, but as she reached the top, soft laughter rippled from down the hall and after it Tabor's deep voice. Sarah smiled to herself and reinstated her faith in her instincts. She also felt a twinge of sympathy for Sally Ann.

"Oh, my!" Blushing crimson, Lilah stopped so fast a cloud of green skirts and red-gold hair swirled around her.

"Did I startle you?"

"Yes!" A lump thickened in Lilah's throat. She had forgotten the time. They both had. It must be nearly dark. What would Sarah think, finding her running down the hall barefoot, dress held high, her hair flying free? Fortunately she didn't know her lips were still puffed from the fervor of Tabor's passion or that her blue eyes still smoldered. "I thought you would be much later," she blurted out. "Tabor said . . ."

"Where is that slacker?" Sarah handed Lilah the lost slippers without a word about where she had come across them. "The boys said he hadn't done a lick of work today."

Lilah stammered for a reply, but before she found one, Tabor appeared from his doorway, dressed presentably, which wasn't how she had left him, in his denim pants and faded blue shirt. His face was beaming and Lilah was aghast to see he wasn't embarrassed in the least.

"How's Millie?" he asked as if he had met Sarah at the front door.

Sarah meandered along to the door of her bedroom. "Millie's fine. Had a strapping boy. Named him Carl Bristol Franklin. She's proud as punch and still not half the fool over him his pa is."

"That's fine news," Tabor went on. "I reckon you're all tuckered out."

"Heck no!" Sarah laughed. "Why should I be? Millie did all the work. The worst job I had was keeping Bris Franklin from worrying both of us to death. The man mighty near paced a rut in the parlor floor. You'd have thought he was the one in labor."

Lilah slipped into her shoes as unobtrusively as possible, and realized as she did that her silk stockings were somewhere in the tumbled sheets on Tabor's bed. Her blush came back faintly, but evidently, if Sarah saw anything amiss in her appearance or behavior, she didn't intend to mention it. Lilah compared that with how her Aunt Emily would have reacted. By now the arrangements would have been under way for a quiet wedding.

"We were just going down to the parlor, Aunt Sarah. Are you coming back down?" Tabor gave his aunt a one-armed hug just to let her know how proud he was she gave so much of herself to others.

Sarah laughed behind her straight face. Tabor had called her "Aunt Sarah," a dead giveaway he wasn't as calm and collected as he made it appear. She had a good guess about how the two of them had spent the day. Tabor's slip of the tongue, not to mention that lazy look of satisfaction on his face, betrayed him.

"Let me clean up a little," she said. "Bris Franklin drank everything in his house that had a kick to it. I sure could do with a glass of my wine."

"I could turn to stone and never regret it," Lilah whispered to Tabor as they trekked down the stairs together. "Anybody could look at me and see I just crawled out of your bed."

"You look beautiful," Tabor assured her. "And anyway, Sarah isn't a prude. She has a lover herself."

"Aunt Sarah!" Lilah's eyes went round as wagon wheels. "How could you even say such a thing?"

Tabor's face split into a wide grin. Those tight Victorian values were showing again. "Sweetheart," he said, "a man and a woman don't stop needing what they can give to each other just because a few hairs turn gray. You ought to be aware of that. Weren't some of your lovers older men?"

"Why, yes," Lilah stammered, unable to stop her cheeks from reddening. She had to stop speaking like a schoolgirl. "Yes, they were. You're right, of course. It's just that I can't think of Sarah that way."

"Sarah's a warmhearted woman, Lilah. She's got a lot of love in her. Wouldn't it be a shame if she didn't have anyone to share it with?"

"I suppose it would," she said slowly, thinking through the wisdom of what he had said. She really was naive about such things. Truthfully she had never thought of people her father's and Sarah's age having needs. And yet she would be the first to say what she and Tabor shared was too glorious to miss. Suddenly it occurred to her he might be making it up as a joke. "You aren't teasing me, are you? Sarah wouldn't be appalled if she knew how you and I spent so many hours today?"

"She wouldn't be appalled and she wouldn't say a word. She'd probably be happy for both of us. I'd bank on it. Sarah's always believed in taking happiness where you find it."

"Are you happy?" Lilah asked, the question surprising her even as she uttered it. "Do I make you happy?"

"If you made me any happier, sweetheart, I'd be blind with it. And don't you worry about Sarah. She's not going to brand you a scarlet woman and turn you out in the world. Sarah's a special kind of person. She usually understands things about people before they do themselves."

His reassurances did make her feel better. She knew Sarah Cooke was a special woman and that growing up under her influence, Tabor had to have some of the same good qualities. Once again she felt a pang of regret that what they shared couldn't last. Somehow she knew she wasn't likely to find the same depth of feeling with Barrett. Oh, dear, Barrett. This was no time to be thinking about him. Lilah looked wistfully into Tabor's eyes, wishing she could tell him what she felt and wondering how she had gone from hating him to questioning how much she cared for him.

Star-crossed lovers. That was what they were. Two people on a island of time who must eventually be separated because an event in the past ruled what could be between them. It seemed unfair that she knew about that past and he didn't, but she reaffirmed her decision to keep the secret. She couldn't take the chance of telling him. He had come so very close to destroying all her plans already. Whatever her needs, whatever the personal cost, she must not lose sight of her goal.

"Warm night, isn't it?" Sarah said cheerfully.

Tabor's lips were almost on Lilah's when his aunt breezed into the parlor. Lilah stepped back quickly, but this time she was able to greet Sarah without a blush.

"Yes, it is," she answered. "I was thinking of taking a walk later. I saw the roses blooming in the garden. I thought they would be especially fragrant this time of day."

"You stay close to the house if you go out alone. It's not likely that skunk Chapman could get on the ranch without being seen, but I don't want to take any chances on him getting his hands on you again." Sarah knew Tabor had some of the hands posting a guard; she wasn't sure if he had told Lilah about the precautions.

"I won't get out of sight of the house." Lilah cringed. She hadn't thought about Chapman all day. It was good that Sarah had reminded her to be careful, but she would just as soon not have recalled that torturous experience.

Sarah saw her flinch. "Consarn it!" she said. "I shouldn't have reminded you of that varmint. Never did know when to keep my mouth shut." She went ahead and poured the wine. "Now, don't you pay me any mind. You're safe enough here at the ranch."

"It's all right, Sarah." Lilah smiled softly. "I hope he's not recovered enough to cause anybody any trouble yet."

Sarah shook her head regretfully. "The least I can do is give you something nice to think about. There's a barn dance in Sandy Flats tomorrow night. Wyrick Young's taking me, and I'd like for you youngsters to come along."

Lilah smiled. "That sounds like fun." She turned to Tabor. "Could we go with them?" Then quickly back to Sarah. "What should I wear?"

Tabor laughed at her impatience. "Wear your prettiest dress and your dancing shoes," he answered for Sarah. "And don't expect this dance to be like the ball at Damon House. It really is a barn dance."

"I'm going to love it," Lilah insisted.

Lilah and Sarah spent the morning baking a cake for the refreshment table at the dance. In early afternoon Sarah took her for a short ride around the ranch. By late afternoon both women were busy getting dresses and hair just the way they wanted. Tabor had been away from the house since dawn, making up all the work he had let slide the day before.

Wondering why almost every garment she had required a maid's assistance, Lilah started for Sarah's room for help with the infinite line of buttons on the back of her bodice. She met Tabor in the hall and was surprised to see him already bathed and dressed. She could swear men had a mysterious way of taking care of their ablutions so that they took no time at all. Tabor couldn't have had more than half an hour for grooming, yet he looked as if he had spent the day at it. Tan cord trousers that fit snug and lean on his legs were tucked into the shiny boots she had seen in the kitchen the day of her arrival at the ranch. Gleaming silver studs and bright turquoise stones decorated his tooled leather belt. His shirt was white linen with a crossover yoke and buttons running down either side. He carried a buckskin jacket with fringed sleeves and a strip of Indian beadwork across the back.

"Wyrick's here. I was about to call Sarah," he said, pausing to give Lilah a glance worthy of her appearance. "You look gorgeous. And you look ready."

Lilah smiled. "Except for these top buttons. I need Sarah to do those for me."

"Allow me," he said gallantly. "I admit to more experience unbuttoning, but I think I can manage those."

Lilah hesitated a moment, then turned her back to him. He must have forgotten about buttoning her dress that disastrous night at his hotel. Quite aware Tabor couldn't see her face, she smiled slyly. Had she known that night what wonders lay in store for her, she wouldn't have been so quick to run away.

With his jacket tossed over his shoulder, Tabor made quick work of fastening the tiny buttons.

"Thank you," she said softly, reminded by his warm touch of the gentle magic those fingers could work on her body.

Tabor stood back and looked at her again, his eyes beaming approval. Blue silk swathed her body, accentuating her soft feminine curves. Her hair hung in a cascade of curls rich in color as a vein of gold. The pearls at her throat were the same ones she had once lost in his hotel room. What a long way the two of them had come since then. She wore Delilah's perfume, the scent that reminded him of Oriental silk and spice and darkened rooms. As he breathed deeply of it, he was suddenly aware of his rapid heartbeat. As it was every time he was close to Lilah, the pull of desire grew stronger. It was by sheer force of will that he stood in the hall and conversed politely instead of luring her to his bed.

"You'll be the talk of the town, Miss Lilah Damon. I'll be lucky not to have to fight a dozen cowboys over you."

She threw her head back and gave an airy laugh. "Between fights, don't forget I'll want to dance."

He shot her a twisted smile. "You're a heartless witch, woman. Tell Sarah to get a move on or none of us will get in any dancing." Before he left, Tabor gave her a quick peck on the cheek.

She and Sarah went down together, Sarah in a plum-colored muslin dress with lace collar and short cuffed sleeves, her black eyes sparkling with a youthful light. Lilah met Wyrick Young and felt shame creep over her when her first thought was that the heavyset man with the intriguing white handlebar mustache was Sarah's lover. Wyrick was utterly charming and had a trace of a southern drawl which he said had followed him all the way from Georgia.

Even the self-assured Sarah pinkened when Wyrick presented her with a nosegay of wildflowers to pin at her waist. Not to be outdone, Tabor presented Lilah with a corsage of white rosebuds trimmed with pink ribbon. She had told Tabor a bald lie when she said white roses were her favorite flower, and yet she found it touchingly sweet that he still remembered the remark. She thought perhaps from now on she would cherish white roses.

Wyrick's buggy held three comfortably. Tabor rode alongside on a saddle horse. Lilah didn't give much notice to the length of the ride in; the conversation was too spirited for that.

On the edge of town, music and light poured from the wide-flung doors of Tompkin's hay barn. Cowboys and ladies in Sunday-best clothes strolled the hay-strewn path leading into the lamp-lit interior. The livery, handy next door, had put up a temporary row of hitching rails. Wyrick drew the buggy up to the barn, where Tabor dismounted and assisted Sarah and Lilah down. While the ladies waited, Sarah tapping her foot to a fiddler's tune, the men moved down the line of horses, buggies, and buckboards.

"All set, ladies," Wyrick's deep bass voice boomed over the fiddle's whine as he and Tabor returned.

The dancing was in progress under the flag-draped lofts. Those who weren't on the dance floor stood around and clapped while they caught their breaths. As soon as Sarah had given her cake to the ladies in charge of refreshments, Lilah found herself in Tabor's hold, skipping down a double line of dancers. The only face she knew was that of Sally Ann Caufield, but it wasn't long before that cool one was replaced by dozens wide with smiles.

When every couple had traveled through the arch, double pairs of dancers broke off and festooned the floor. Lilah lost sight of Tabor but occasionally picked out his laughter in the happy sounds of the dance. The fiddlers never tired and the music went on and on. People around Sandy Flats were a friendly bunch and Lilah discovered most of the cowboys and ranchers dancing the reel already knew her name. Her head spun with trying to keep new names and faces together. She was glad when she twirled into the arms of Wyrick Young.

"Whew!" he said. "Reckon I could talk you off the dance floor and over to the refreshment table for a glass of cool lemonade?"

"With a word," Lilah answered.

Glad for a short rest, she hooked her arm through Wyrick's elbow and accompanied him to a corner of the barn where there seemed to be almost as much activity as on the dance floor. Those who hadn't come to dance, Lilah discovered, came to eat. The choices were good, since every woman around Sandy Flats had spent part of the day baking. Lilah took a glass of lemonade. Wyrick got a slice of Sarah's cake as well.

Once he had introduced her to another dozen people, the two of them found a bench and sat down.

"This your first barn dance, Lilah?" Wyrick asked.

Lilah shook her head. "Papa took me sometimes when I was a little girl, but I never got to dance. I've been to my share of balls in London and San Francisco." She smiled gaily. "But they weren't like this."

Wyrick laughed. "I've been to a few of those San Francisco soirees myself. A man has to stand around like he's had a fencepost run down the back of his coat. No, sir. Those pretty affairs aren't for me." He pointed to the lively dancers on the floor, laughing and yelling to each other in complete abandon. "This is more my style. Or it was." He mopped his brow, then went on. "Ten years ago I could have outlasted the best of them."

The music stopped for a minute, then started up again. A young cowboy walked over and asked Lilah to dance. Wyrick urged her to go on, but Lilah started to refuse, finding it difficult to forget Aunt Emily's remonstrances that a lady never danced with a gentleman who hadn't been properly introduced. But when she saw Tabor and Sally Ann glide by she had a quick change of heart. With a petulant smile on her face, Lilah stood and took the cowboy's arm.

As soon as the dance ended, another cowboy hurried to her side and asked her to dance. The routine continued, and no sooner did the music end than Lilah found herself besieged by requests for the next dance.

Her fourth partner was a rangy boy hardly out of his teens. "I'm Ben and I reckon you're the Miss Damon staying over at the Cooke ranch."

"Yes, I am. And you may call me Lilah."

Ben responded with a boyish smile and a whoop as the fiddler's strings spurred the dancers to pick up the pace. During the last four dances Lilah had seen Tabor spin by once with an elderly lady who was surprisingly light on her feet. The last two, though, he had again held Sally Ann. Getting in step with the music, she told herself it was quite all right for Tabor to be dancing with Sally Ann. This wasn't the sort of formal ball she was accustomed to. The number of times partners danced together meant nothing.

In fact there were no formalities at all. The ladies had no dance cards and everyone from the oldest to the youngest took a turn dancing. A spin around the floor meant no more than a howdy on the street. Reminding herself that everyone was here to have a good time, she tried to concentrate on the music and avoiding Ben's awkward feet. But her eyes kept searching for Tabor's black hair and Sally Ann's crimson dress.

"Lilah's a mighty purty name," Bent told her loudly. "And I reckon you're just about the purtiest girl here." He lowered his voice as he went on. "Ain't really no need in you being shy about it."

"Shy?" Forgetting about Tabor and Sally Ann for a moment, Lilah looked into Ben's smiling face. What an odd thing for a stranger to say. What had prompted it? Inside her head a little bell of warning rang. "Where did you get the idea I'm shy?"

Ben's face puckered up in annoyance at himself. "Dern my skin!" In his agitation he missed a series of steps and Lilah had to be quick to avoid getting her toes crushed. "I wasn't supposed to say nothin' about that. But you can thank your friend Sally Ann for lookin' out for you."

Lilah's temper sped high color to her cheeks, affirming Ben's belief that she suffered from shyness. Lilah swallowed the barbs on her tongue and offered Ben a smile that would have dissolved even a stronger man.

"Sally Ann's the sweetest thing," she said softly.

"Always looking out for her friends. What is it I ought to thank her for tonight?"

Seeing he hadn't caused Lilah to become upset, Ben relaxed and told her what she wanted to know. "Sally Ann got the boys together and told them all to be sure to ask you to dance tonight, seein' as how otherwise Tabor would be stuck with you for every dance. 'Course none of the boys minded askin', you bein' so purty and all." He winked conspiratorially at her. "No need for you to look for a chair again, ma'am. The boys are gonna keep you dancin' all night long."

Poor Ben might not have deserved it, but Lilah stomped his instep anyway. He let our a muffled yelp of pain.

"Oh, Ben! I'm so sorry," Lilah cried. "I don't know how that happened. Does it hurt?"

Ben gritted his teeth, unwilling to admit Lilah's tiny foot had inflicted so much agony. "Just a mite," he said, his voice climbing.

Fortunately the fiddler stopped about that time. Lilah thanked Ben for the dance, then watched without an ounce of sympathy as he limped off the floor. Hiding herself behind a pair of portly matrons, she scanned the room as the jump-alive music started again. Sally Ann Caufield had a few well-chosen words coming her way and Lilah was in a frame of mind not to care who else heard them.

She forced herself to appear calm when Sarah tapped her arm. "Having a good time?"

"This is all so stimulating," Lilah replied, keeping her lips fixed in a smile. "Have you seen Tabor?"

"Not for a while." She glanced around. "He'll turn up."

Hanging on to Sally Ann, Lilah thought, that sneaky little cat. With the next dance well started, she

decided she wouldn't be hounded by any more of the
cowboys Sally Ann had set on her. Slowly she made
her way through the crowd, watching the dancers.
Spotting Tabor and Sally Ann exiting the barn's back
door brought a flash of anger across her face. She
stopped dead in the floor and got bumped by a boy of
about ten brushing by her skirts, his hands and face
sticky with taffy candy. The boy gave her an idea. She
stopped the youngster.

"Do you know Mr. Tabor Stanton?"

The boy turned his candy-coated face up and smiled
at the pretty lady. "Shore do," he said.

"Well, I've been looking all over for him," Lilah
said sweetly. "I think he might be outside. Would you
mind stepping out there and telling him there's a message for him at the refreshment table?" Lilah held out
a coin and the boy eyed it covetously.

"Thank you, miss," he said hollowly. "But my ma
wouldn't let me take no money fer bein' polite."

"You take it anyway and buy yourself some more
candy," Lilah told him. She pressed the coin into a
gummy hand. "Don't forget, it's Mr. Stanton you're
looking for."

The boy hurried off and Lilah hid behind a stack of
wooden boxes near the door. A few minutes later the
boy ran back in, and shortly behind him came Tabor
and Sally Ann.

"I'll wait for you here, Tabor," Sally Ann's honeyed
voice crooned. "Don't forget my lemonade when you
come back."

Tabor gave her a distracted backward glance and a
nod, then cut a path through the crowd to reach the
refreshment table across the barn.

Smiling smugly and fanning herself with a Japanese
silk fan, Sally Ann waited in the open doorway. She

gave a surprised little staccato cry when Lilah appeared and caught her by the elbow.

"Well, Miss Popularity herself." Sally Ann recovered quickly and smiled. "You've become the belle of Sandy Flats tonight," she said innocently. "It must be that lovely dress."

Behind her smile Sally Ann appraised the dress and jewels and to her disappointment tallied up a figure that surpassed the cost of her ensemble.

"Maybe it is," Lilah replied, her voice as falsely sweet. "Or maybe it's just that the men of Sandy Flats are starved for a look at a pretty face."

That was too much for Sally Ann. "Don't be absurd," she snapped. "Why, I arranged . . ." Sally Ann covered her mouth with her hand.

Lilah took the opportunity to grasp her elbow again, and while Sally Ann still suffered from surprise, ushered her out the door and into the shadows of the barn.

"I know what you arranged, you conniving little wench."

Sally Ann jerked her elbow free and gave a snickering laugh. "Serves you right," she said. "Coming down here and interfering in things that are none of your business."

"And what would that be?" Lilah asked icily.

"Tabor Stanton is my beau," Sally Ann insisted hotly. "Why, we're going to be married someday."

"Oh!" Lilah cocked her head to one side. "Then doesn't it seem rather peculiar to you that he's invited me for a visit?" She went on without giving Sally Ann a chance to respond. "And I *don't* have to contrive to have a dance with Tabor."

The truth nettled more than any sharp thing Lilah could have said. Sally Ann's eyes flashed fire and she swung her hand at Lilah's cheek. The sound of the

slap was as loud as a clap of thunder and echoed in the
one Lilah gave her in return. Sally Ann screeched and
dove for Lilah, but Lilah quickly stepped aside and
Sally, losing her balance tumbled forward, spiraling
against a water trough. She caught herself just before
she plunged into the water.

She turned to face Lilah.

"Tabor might enjoy a little tryst with you," she said,
her voice cold and mocking. "But when it's over, he'll
come back to me. We've been lovers since the day I
turned sixteen. He promised to marry me and he will.
You'll see!" She braced herself on the edge of the
water trough and jeered at Lilah. "He only brought
you here to make me jealous."

Sally Ann's words unleashed something harsh in
Lilah. It completely slipped her mind that she wanted
nothing more to do with Tabor after the end of the
week. All she could see was Sally Ann's red dress and
taunting face and the opportunity she had missed.

Muttering a cry of cold fury, Lilah drove herself
into Sally Ann and sent the unfortunate girl toppling
backward into the trough. Soaked from head to foot,
Sally Ann began a sputtering that quickly became a
tearful wail, but in between cries she managed to hurl
a lifetime of oaths at Lilah.

Lilah left Sally Ann to climb out of the trough
alone. Her cheek still red from Sally Ann's slap, she
marched back through the barn, her head held high.
Dancers stopped in mid-step and conversations stopped
in mid-sentence as she breezed by. Once she had
passed, a tittering of whispered talk started behind
her. Lilah ignored the stares, the whispers, everyone.

Baffled because no one at the refreshment table
could explain why he had been summoned to receive a
message, Tabor claimed a glass of lemonade and started
back to Sally Ann. She was being as pesky tonight as

she had been as a pigtailed girl following him around town. He hoped the lemonade would pacify her while he gracefully said what needed saying. He was anxious to get away and find Lilah. The last he had seen of her was when she had spun by in the arms of Ben Wagner, her face so intent on the young cowboy's that she hadn't even noticed him.

Dammit! He hadn't expected to get separated from her so early in the evening. And seeing her locking eyes with Ben had irritated him to the point he had almost walked off from Sally Ann and demanded Lilah restrict her dance partners to him alone.

If he hadn't felt so bad about embarrassing Sally Ann, he would have done it. He'd taken her outside to try to make her understand she ought to set her sights on some other man. But that kid had come along and interrupted, and since Tabor still had Judd Chapman on his mind, he'd rushed inside. While he was tying up his horse, one of the men from the Paradise Saloon had told him a stranger had been in asking about him. He doubted it was Chapman, but the description was close, and as a precaution he had asked that word be sent to him if the man came back.

The kid must have made a mistake, or maybe he was only playing a joke. He supposed Sally Ann was still waiting for him by the back door. Before she made a fool of herself and started any more tongues wagging about the way she had asked him to dance, he had to explain things to her. Her infatuation with him was getting out of hand. She'd be mad, but she'd get over it. Anyhow, she had plenty of suitors mooning over her.

Tabor heard a murmur run through the crowd and wondered at the cause of it. The fiddling stopped and he looked around like everybody else. Where the hell was Lilah? He didn't see her anywhere inside. If she

was out walking with one of those skirt-hungry cowboys, there was going to be hell to pay. Where the
devil was she?

Like the trapdoor on a gallows, Tabor's mouth fell
open as he came face-to-face with Lilah. He almost
spilled Sally Ann's lemonade when he saw her blazing
eyes and fire-red cheek. Nose in the air, she marched
past him without a word.

"Lilah!" Had one of those cowboys gotten fresh?
Tabor handed the lemonade to the nearest person and
caught up with her just as she passed through the main
door. He had blood in his eye for whoever had done
this to her. "Your face," he mumbled. "What happened, sweetheart?"

Lilah whirled around and nearly cut him to the
ground with her enraged look. "Ask that hussy who's
waiting for you out back," she hissed, and turned her
back on him.

Guessing what had happened, Tabor looked around
for Sally Ann. He wondered which of them had gotten
the worse of things, then concluded it would turn out to
be him. Though Lilah resisted his touch, he led her
out of sight of the crowd.

"Don't move from this spot," he warned. "I'll get
Sarah and Wyrick and we'll leave for the ranch."

Stamping her foot as he walked away, Lilah did
precisely the opposite of what he had asked just as
soon as he walked in the door.

Tabor hurried through the buzzing crowd. The fiddlers had started up and a few couples had gone back
to dancing, but they stopped too when Sally Ann, wet
as a drowned cat, stumbled in the back door.

"Just look at me," she moaned, holding the sodden,
dripping crimson skirt away from her legs. She caught
sight of Tabor and lifted reproachful eyes to him.
"Look at what that San Francisco tart did to me."

Tabor edged away, figuring this wasn't the best time to explain things to Sally Ann. He spied Sarah and made a beeline for her, still hearing Sally Ann wailing behind him.

Sally Ann had many friends in Sandy Flats, but there were a few who gloated at seeing her get her comeuppance. She was met with as much laughter as compassion. At least one of the wide-eyed observers had the presence of mind to produce a horse blanket and wrap it around her shaking shoulders. Another found her parents and from them Sally Ann got the consolation she needed.

Sarah, seeing Sally Ann and reading a look from Tabor, grabbed Wyrick by the arm and made for the door.

"You sure stuck a stick in a hornet's nest, boy," Sarah chastised as they escaped the crowd. "I hope Lilah's not as sad-looking as that imp Sally Ann."

Tabor scowled. "Watch your tongue, Sarah. Lilah's fine except for her temper, and I think she blames all of this on me."

"Small wonder," Sarah commented dryly. "You should have made yourself clear to Sally Ann way back instead of stringing her along."

"Don't nag, Sarah. I'm in no mood." Tabor's scowl deepened. "I didn't want to hurt her feelings."

"You don't think they're hurt now?" Sarah asked forcefully. "Being humiliated in front of the whole of Sandy Flats?"

Tabor didn't answer. He halfway felt all of this *was* his fault, and wondered how he was going to deal with two she-cats who would like to claw his eyes out along with each other's. What was worse, he noticed Lilah wasn't waiting where he'd left her.

"Goddammit!" he said, mindless that Sarah didn't cotton to his profanity. "Where the hell is Lilah?"

Sarah let out a heavy sigh, one of those that said it was going to be a long night. "There," she said, pointing to Tabor's mount galloping by almost covered by blue silk skirts. Lilah's long hair streamed out in a banner behind her.

She was riding away from the ranch and out into open country. Tabor shouted after her but she never looked back. He glanced around at Sarah's stern face and moaned. Now he had three females ready to shoot him in the back.

18

Pulling a long leather glove tight over his bandaged hand and wrist, Judd Chapman led his horse down the blackened length of the alley across from Tompkin's barn. A smile as wicked as the split of a serpent's mouth shone from his face. For hours he had watched the festivities in Sandy Flats and now he was to be rewarded for his patience. What he wanted would come to him as if he'd sent a formal invitation.

He watched the rider, a woman, streak by in defiant disregard of the darkness or the few people on the street. Her hair flew out behind her and caught the moonlight. No woman but Lilah Damon had hair like that, like copper beaten into gold. Even if those streaming tresses had been covered he would have known her by the shapely silhouette of her curves and by the angry set of her mouth. How well he remembered the tempting fullness of those lovely lips. And they were but one of her gems.

He thought of sampling them, and though his way was alien to other men, the picture in his mind sent a surprising rush of blood into his manhood. At the unexpected surge and tightening there, Chapman fell against his horse, for a moment unable to mount. Fires of hell! Just the thought of her had made him hard. He couldn't count the years since that had happened.

"Lilah." He rolled the name off his lips as he thought of the lush curves and satin flesh that would soon be his.

It almost seemed a shame to disfigure that lovely body, but the thought of the pleasure it would be to see red blood against that milky skin outweighed the few shreds of his conscience. He licked his lips, thinking of the salty taste of it mingled with her sweetness. He would take it slow with her, only a few nicks at a time. And if she could keep him hard, he would keep her with him a long, long time.

Chapman immediately spat out a curse. Stanton! Stanton would be hot on her trail in a matter of minutes. He didn't doubt that. With his gun hand useless, there wasn't a way he could face Stanton. Cursing, Chapman spurred his horse to a run. The serpent's smile returned to his lips as his twisted mind worked in its devious way.

Why should he face Stanton? The last time they had met, his mistake had been in letting the girl go. If he'd held on to her, Stanton would have yielded to him. The same would work now. Stanton wouldn't risk hurting Lilah. All he had to do was get to her first, and Stanton would be finished. A harsh laugh rumbled out of his throat. Putting a bullet in Stanton would be a big pleasure.

Afterward Damon would give him the claim for the promise of getting his daughter back. Chapman laughed even more scornfully. He had to stop thinking small.

Damon was a rich man. Lilah would be worth more to him than just the claim.

Praising Lady Luck for giving him such an easy chance at getting rich and another chance at being a man, Chapman turned his horse to a high trail above the road. Not far ahead he heard the clatter of another horse's hooves.

Tabor untied a mount from the hitching rail and leapt astride, shouting for Wyrick to let the owner know what had become of the animal. Lilah had a few minutes' start and a faster horse, but less skill as a rider. He counted on her tiring of the strain of hanging on at a gallop. She would slow her horse after a while and that would give him a chance to catch her shortly. Maybe. He thought grimly of how unpredictable Lilah could be when mad. If she cut across country instead of staying on the road, he would have a hellacious time finding her. Looking for tracks in the dark would slow him down plenty. But even Lilah wouldn't be foolish enough to take a risk like that.

Yes she would. Mad as she was, she'd ride over the devil's horsemen to get away from him. He had a good mind to thrash her when he caught her, or at the very least to give her the dressing-down she deserved. Didn't she have a thought for danger or the worry she was causing Sarah? He just hoped Chapman *wasn't* around anywhere. This opportunity was the sort that bastard would wait for to get Lilah in his clutches again.

He ran the gamut of curses. That redheaded vixen was more trouble than a dozen women. Thrashing was too good for her. He could be better served by hog-tying her and locking her in his room. He cursed himself for ever letting her out of sight at the dance. At the ranch his men had kept a watch on her when he wasn't around. Lilah didn't know that even her walks in Sarah's garden were done under the watchful eye of a guard or that one of the reasons he'd stayed around the house while Sarah was midwifing was to avoid leaving her alone.

He didn't want her dwelling on the possibility that Chapman would nab her again. No point in her staying scared all the time. Now he wished he had gone ahead and told her how vile the man was, that he was even more unstable than she realized. Hell! He had been selfish in not wanting to spoil her mood. He had counted on the men at the ranch doing a good job of protecting her. And they had. He was the one who had failed, figuring that she was safe enough in a crowd. He could have kicked his backside for being so careless. If that stranger asking about him had been Chapman, she was risking her life to spite him.

Lilah rode at a full gallop until she felt sorry for Tabor's horse and slowed him to a trot. The wind in her face felt cool and restorative, but even it hadn't the power to ease her fiery temper. Much of her anger was directed at herself. She was horrified by what she had done to Sally Ann Caufield. Of course she never would have dreamed of doing anything so reckless if the girl hadn't kept goading her.

Lovers since her sixteenth birthday, Sally Ann had said. Why, Sally Ann had been just a child and Tabor well into his twenties when . . . That brute! Did he get sadistic pleasure out of ruining virgins? This was definitely the limit. Just as soon as she saw him again she would tell him so in no uncertain terms.

Lilah shivered, becoming aware of the black gloom around her. In the distance a coyote yowled, or was it a wolf? For the first time since riding out of Sandy Flats she considered that she didn't know where she was going or even why she had passed judgment on

Tabor. As experienced as he was at lovemaking, she could hardly have believed him a saint. So why the grief over learning Sally Ann was one of those with whom he had honed his skills? What possible difference could it make to her if he had bedded that overgrown brat? Or promised to marry her? Let them make each other miserable until eternity. She didn't care.

What did upset her was being subjected to Sally Ann's ire. She hadn't bargained for that. Nothing in the agreement between Tabor and herself included being ridiculed by another of his ladyloves. Oh! How could she even include herself in the same thought with Sally Ann? She wasn't staying at the Cooke ranch to become a member of Tabor Stanton's scattered harem. He'd had his fun, taken her virginity, taken her . . . She gasped at what leapt into her mind. Had she been about to say "heart?" Even a hint of it was utterly ridiculous. She wasn't jealous of Sally Ann. She didn't love Tabor. She didn't want him to ask her to stay with him. She would marry Barrett the way she planned. Nothing would stop her.

Bristling with renewed indignation, Lilah reined the horse around sharply, determined to ride back to Sandy Flats and demand Tabor release her from the obligation. In the quick turn the horse stumbled in the loose gravel covering the roadbed, and one leg slid out from under him so that he almost went down. Lilah managed to stay in the saddle by grabbing the horn and hanging on. She immediately slowed the animal to a walk. But it was soon apparent that some injury had been done to the steed's hoof, and Lilah was forced to dismount and attempt a look. Enough moonlight shone down that she could detect a small sharp stone wedged between shoe and hoof.

A sigh of despair escaped her. To make the creature

go on would be cruel, and she had nothing with which to remove the stone. Another coyote yowled at the moon. Lilah felt just as forlorn. Had there been any use to it, she would have cried. Instead she petted the poor horse and murmured soothing words she had once heard Tabor say. She had really used her head, she lamented. And here she sat, miles out of town, with a lame horse and absolutely no idea if there was a ranch house near. Feeling as if the air had turned inhospitably chill, Lilah led the animal off the road and tied him, but stayed near, finding the horse gave her some sense of security.

Presently she heard the sound of another horse. Tabor? Surely he would have come after her. She hurried toward the road to flag him down, but stopped short before reaching it. Suppose it was someone else, someone unfriendly. Lilah turned back and looked about for a place to conceal herself.

"Yo there!" Glee threaded into Chapman's voice as he spotted Lilah's horse off the road. Damned if Lady Luck hadn't winked at him tonight. The horse was lame and Lilah hadn't had time to get more than a few yards on foot. He reined his mount to a stop.

From behind the one boulder large enough to hide her, Lilah crouched in the dust. The sound of that voice frosted her blood and turned her limbs to water. Chapman! Suddenly her quarrel with Tabor seemed minuscule, no more worrisome than the buzz of a bothersome mosquito. Dear Lord, help her. For almost nothing she had thrown herself into the gravest danger. She was alone and unarmed. What hope did she have that that fiend would go away without finding her?

'You hidin' from me?" Chapman taunted, slipping from his saddle. "Ain't no point in it. I been waitin' days for you to be alone again so I could make my move." He laughed. "Been thinkin' about strippin' you naked and doin' whatever strikes my fancy. That sound good to you, Lilah?"

Shaking like a wind-whipped leaf, Lilah clapped both hands over her mouth so she wouldn't cry out in fear and give herself away. That was what he wanted, to frighten her into making a sound that would indicate her location. Praying silently, pleading that by some miracle Chapman would leave or Tabor would come, Lilah shut her eyes, too terrified to face even the darkness.

The scrape of his boots on the ground, the loud jangle of his spurs, sent her heart into a wild thumping. And then there was silence, silence that stretched into minutes. Chapman was too quiet. Lilah held her hand over her heart, certain the beat of it echoed from the rocks. She ought to hear Chapman's spurs or the sound of his horse if he rode away. Weighted with fear, her eyelids refused to rise even for assurance that her peril had ended. After a few more seconds she brought them up by force of will and found the night blacker and more ominous than before. Aching with fear, Lilah peeped around the boulder for a look. Her horse stood where she had left him. She saw neither Chapman nor his mount.

An easier breath flowed into her lungs, but she didn't forget caution. Chapman might have walked off to look elsewhere. That didn't mean he wouldn't be back. Now she bit her tongue to keep from crying aloud. If only he had left his horse in view, she might have a chance of getting to the animal and riding off before he saw her.

With great care she settled back behind the boulder to think over what she should do. Did she dare make a run for Chapman's horse? Yes. Yes, if she could spot the animal before leaving her place of hiding. Inching her way around, Lilah turned on her heel, planning to peer out from the other side of the boulder and see if she could spot Chapman's mount.

In the midst of her slow turn she met a sight that skewered her heart. Gasping, Lilah stared at a pair of feet in dusty socks and knew in that terrible instant that Chapman had foxed her by slipping out of his boots and easing around the boulder to get behind her. His guttural laugh tightened the knot in her stomach. By degrees she looked up into the cold eyes and the barrel of the gun held in Chapman's left hand.

"'We're gonna have us a good time, Lilah." He smiled diabolically and motioned for her to stand.

"Tabor's coming for me," Lilah countered, holding her fear briefly in check.

Chapman nudged her toward his horse with his gun. "If he does, he won't catch me by surprise this time." He howled with laughter. "But maybe he won't follow you at all. Appeared to me you two had a nasty spat."

"You were at the dance?"

"Well, no," he drawled. "I ain't that stupid. But I was close by and saw that unfriendly partin'. You seemed right anxious to get away from Stanton." The awful laughter erupted again. "Reckon you been pinin' after me all this time."

"Certainly not," Lilah spat out in disgust.

"Don't make no difference no way," Chapman went on, unperturbed. "The more you fight, the more I'm gonna like it. Don't reckon you can do more damage to me than my blade can do to you." He laughed louder.

Lilah shuddered. "You won't get what you want from my father if you hurt me."

"Don't reckon I'll tell him what shape you're in until I do." He looked her over as if she were a head of livestock. "How much is a gal like you worth to an old man? Thousands, I'll wager. Looks like you're gonna make me rich and real happy too."

She reached the horse Chapman had left near the road. Chapman ordered her to untie the animal and lead him out in the clear, all the while keeping the gun trained on her. Lilah remembered what he had said about tears and gulped hard to keep any from sliding down her face. She cried within. Oh, Tabor! Tabor! Please, you must have followed me. But what if Chapman was right? What if he hadn't followed? What if he had counted on her cooling down and turning back on her own? If so, he would still be waiting for her in Sandy Flats. She needed a way to stall Chapman, to give Tabor a chance to find them—if he was on the way.

"My horse is lame," she said quietly. "I . . . I'll have to walk along beside you."

"Naw!" Chapman eye her lecherously. "That wouldn't be gentlemanly. You'll have the pleasure of ridin' double with me. But first I'm gonna send that hoss of yours off to make a false trail—just in case Stanton is close behind."

Still holding Lilah in his gun sights, he freed her horse and looped the reins to the saddle horn, then with a heavy limb struck the horse across the flank. Limping badly, the animal bolted across the road and ran off into the night. Lilah's heart disappeared with him. If Tabor followed that trail first, he might be a long time getting to her.

Chapman ordered her to mount the horse first. As he climbed up, Lilah noted the difficulty he had using his right hand. Any pressure on the wound was met with a grimace of pain. She was glad of that. He would need his left hand to guide the horse, and that meant he couldn't use the other one to maul her.

"Where are you taking me?" she asked weakly, the last of her courage shriveling.

"Gittin' anxious for my lovin', ain't you?" He sneered. "You won't have to wait long, darlin'. I found a deserted cabin about two miles off. Got a lamp and some oil and an old cot. All we're gonna need till morning."

Lilah shivered as if she had just been handed a sentence of death. Maybe she had. Chapman needed to keep her alive only until he claimed a ransom from her father. She didn't doubt her father would pay, but the thought of what such a request would do to him frightened her more than Chapman's threats. Poor Papa. He would be worried sick. And his heart. Oh, Lord! His heart. Knowing she had been kidnapped by the likes of Chapman would kill him.

For the first time ever she regretted her scheme of revenge. There might have been other ways to bring those six men to justice. But she had wanted a personal hand in evening the score. Look what it had brought about. She was on the threshold of being responsible for hurting, maybe killing, the very person she had wanted to avenge.

"I want to write a letter to my father," she said. unexpectedly. "I don't want him to know I'm in any danger from you. His health isn't good. A shock could be fatal."

"Won't make no never-mind to me if he drops dead," Chapman reported.

"Well, it should!" Lilah said defiantly. "If he dies there will be no one to pay a ransom. You won't get a penny."

Chapman saw the logic of what she said and agreed she should write a letter to her father. The old man would be quicker to respond to her plea anyway. And a letter was best. Sending such a message in a telegram might stir up suspicion too quickly. A letter was slower, but then he was in no hurry to turn over the girl or make a run with his claim, whatever the outcome might be.

Lilah wished the ride would take forever, but they were at the cabin in an amazingly short time. The ramshackle place had been vacant a long time. Weeds grew in abandon right through the broken boards of the steps. The hide windowpanes were ragged and torn and had long opened the interior to the elements. The door, however, was still stout, and Chapman bolted it behind them, licking his lips as he thought of the treat in store for him.

Chapman ordered Lilah to sit on the hewn log which served as a bench. He was anxious to get mundane things out of the way so that he might satisfy his lust. While Lilah waited, he produced writing materials from his saddle pouch.

With some thought, Lilah penned a letter which explained her plight without letting her father know how despicable Chapman really was. Better he should think she was well-treated than worry himself into a mortal illness. She took her time with the writing, attempting to squeeze every possible moment of delay from the task. After a time Chapman demanded she end the epistle, and when she had signed her name, snatched the paper from her hand. He found her words amusing and took pains to point out how thoroughly she had misled her father.

"You make me sound like a man of the cloth." He laughed raucously. "Reckon you'd be surprised that I took up the Good Book and preachin' once. Never could keep my eyes and hands off them sweet, tender things in the congregation, though. Had to leave my last charge in the dead of night. But it was worthwhile for the time I had with little Polly Jansen."

Lilah knew he wanted her to ask what he'd done to little Polly, but she had no desire to know. Not for a minute since Chapman found her had she been able to free her mind from what he had threatened her with before. All her muscles were knit into tight knots in dread of what lay ahead. For once her ready tongue failed her and she could think of nothing else to lengthen the delay.

"Get up!" Chapman demanded.

Lilah stayed on the bench, but only until Chapman jabbed the pistol in her back. Though it must have been excruciating to do so, he held the gun in his right hand, the hammer back and ready. He ordered her to hold her hands out in front of her, and when she did, he slipped the loop of a rope over them and pulled it painfully tight. With surprising quickness he knotted the rope around her wrists, and before she could give him much of a fight, tossed the end over a beam and hauled her into the air so that her feet barely swept the floor. He stood back and laughed.

"Got me a candy apple hanging up here." Chapman stepped near and lifted her flowing red hair with his gun barrel. He brushed a few strands caressingly against his face. His voice was droll, his eyes dancing with crazy lights. "Ain't nothin' sweeter to bite than a candy apple."

"Cut me down! You're insane!"

But Chapman only half-listened to Lilah as he rubbed his groin against her skirts and took the red bandanna from his neck. "I'd sure like to listen to you scream, Lilah, darlin'. But sound carries a long way 'round here. Don't want nobody comin' to investigate. No sirree. We don't want nobody interruptin' our fun."

"If you kill me you'll get nothing!" Lilah screamed. She could see that her words weren't penetrating his crazed mind, but kept shouting at him anyway. "There's no ransom if I'm dead."

Chapman silenced her by tying the bandanna over her mouth and around her head. It tasted foul and just the odor of it nearly gagged her.

Laughing evilly, Chapman laid his gun on the bench, where it was handy if he needed it in a hurry. His favorite weapon was his knife, a bone-handled bowie, sharper than a barber's razor. He drew it out of the sheath in his boot, testing the blade's edge on his gloved hand, and with a touch, slicing through the layer of leather. This he performed for Lilah's benefit, and it had a sudden and demoralizing effect as her mind registered the threat.

Chapman moved behind her and with several quick flicks of the blade sliced the buttons from her dress. He cut through the lacings at her waist as well, then gave the garment a tug that sent it into a pool of blue silk beneath her feet.

Lilah moaned and tried to stay still, having learned that any movement caused the rope to notch into her wrists. Chapman's maniacal laugh lit stark fear in her wide eyes. She expected to be split from throat to belly at any moment. Was that the uncontrollable thing he had done to little Polly Jansen, some pitiable child who had believed him a good man? She said a silent prayer.

Chapman picked up her dress and rubbed it against his face, sniffed the lingering scent of her perfume in the silken folds. He held the garment there a moment, then tossed it in the air and caught it on the blade of his knife. Moments later the dress lay in tatters around him.

He saw Lilah's troubled breathing and fear-filled eyes and suffered a moment of pity in her behalf. "I ain't gonna kill you, Lilah, darlin'. Don't fret over that. I ain't even gonna hurt you much. If I had two sound hands I wouldn't even have you trussed up." He sighed raggedly. "It ain't hardly sportin' with you tied."

As he spoke, Chapman walked very close, the gleaming blade held in front of him. In spite of his words, Lilah feared this minute was her last. But again Chapman wielded the knife against only her garments as he cut the drawstrings on her petticoats. They fell and were quickly trampled under Chapman's feet. He eyed the long, slender legs extending from her pantalets and the sleek, bare arms extending from her camisole. Again he rubbed the gloved hand against his loins.

It was happening again. His prick was standing on end. Feeling weak, Chapman gasped for breath as the abnormally fast surge of blood in his loins demanded all his strength. Damn, how he had wanted this to happen, and time after time, woman after woman, it had failed to. Finally he had gotten tired of being laughed at by whores and sluts and had found a way to pleasure himself with a woman even if he couldn't use his pecker. 'Course, none of them ever wanted his money again, and he reckoned more than one woman still wore his teeth prints like a tattoo. But this time, this once, he was going to shove it in a woman like a man.

"You got something special about you, Lilah," he groaned, and indicated the bulge in his pants. "Something real special."

All color drained from her face and most of her strength with it. Soon she wouldn't be able to keep her head up. But what would it matter? Chapman's intent was clear. He would rape and torture her and probably keep her just alive enough to take his pleasure over and over. She closed her eyes so tight they hurt.

"Open your eyes!" Chapman growled, feeling his

erection lessen as she rejected him. "Look at what I've got for you."

"No!" Lilah moaned behind her gag.

Her words weren't clear but her meaning was. Chapman cursed her. "Look, I said!"

She felt his blade on her cheek, the tip of it puncturing her skin. Her eyes snapped open. Chapman dropped the blade, slowly drawing a red mark down her face but never actually applying enough pressure to slice the skin. The story was no different when he reached her breasts. He whisked the knife down and cut open the front of her camisole, baring her breasts to the steel blade and the mad stare of his eyes. With the point of his knife he drew patterns on her soft flesh, not cutting but leaving angry red streaks where his blade touched.

Lilah shuddered, but she preferred the knife to the touch of his hand, for his fondling was rougher and he bruised her flesh between his fingers. Chapman stayed his hand to open the slit in his trousers, moaning in anticipation as he reached for the throbbing rod inside, unaware the power she had over him was to be his undoing. The return of his ability to take a woman sapped him of all caution. As he swung his knife at the tie of her pantalets, he forgot that Stanton was searching for the girl. He moaned incoherently as Lilah hung helplessly before him, naked and inviting. Completely out of his head, he dropped his knife and reached out both hands to separate her legs and drive into her.

Lilah disdained the punishing cut of the rope into her wrists and gathered her legs beneath her, surprising Chapman with a wicked kick. The painful blow on his testicles quickly deflated his precious erection and destroyed his resolve about sparing Lilah's life.

"You bitch!" Chapman screamed, and his face jerked spasmodically with the sudden violent start of the tic in his eye. "I'm gonna shave that red hair off your head and carve my name on your scalp!"

Spitting and fuming with rage, Chapman started to his feet. Before he was up and could make good on his threat, Tabor crashed through the cabin door. Chapman growled like a mad dog and made for his gun. Tabor allowed him the time to raise it before pulling the trigger of his Colt. This time his aim was true and the bullet cut a clear path through Chapman's heart.

Tabor rushed over to Lilah and tore the gag from her mouth.

"He hurt me," she said weakly, coughing and gasping for air.

Such an anguish took hold of Tabor that he could only whisper words of comfort. "I'm sorry, love. So sorry." His voice shook. "He'll never touch you again."

Tabor cut Lilah down and carried her outside. She was half-dazed and he was glad for that. Her soft moans racked him with pain and she clung to him so tightly he had to pry her fingers from his arms to remove his shirt and cover her with it. She went limp then, whimpering like a hurt pup as he carefully pulled the sleeves over the welts and bruises on her wrists.

Tabor bundled her in his arms and held her against him until the soul-wrenching sobs stopped. He wished Chapman had another life to take. Somehow it seemed the man had not suffered enough by dying only once to pay for the torture he had inflicted on Lilah, or even for making the ugly marks on her skin.

"No! Don't leave me alone," she cried when, at last, he eased her out of his arms to search the saddle pouch on the horse he had borrowed. "Please," she begged, and looked back at the cabin in horror.

Tabor could have cried out his anguish. She might not know he had killed Chapman. Did she think he was deserting her, that he would leave her with that bastard? She couldn't know he would never have carried out any of the threats he made against her. Never. Not even when he had thought her deserving of some of them would he have harmed a hair on her head.

Lilah covered her face with her hands. She felt cold and afraid without Tabor's arms around her. She could see he was only searching his saddle pouch for something, but there was nothing she needed more than to have him hold her. Chapman was dead. She would never forget the tortured look or the fury on Tabor's face when he had broken open the door. Chapman's fate had been sealed before Tabor pulled the trigger on his gun. She knew deep in the core of her heart that Tabor would have killed Chapman then at any cost to himself.

In the saddle pouch Tabor turned up a flask of whiskey. He poured a few swallows down Lilah's throat, enough, he hoped, to dull the memories and the pain in her heart. He couldn't bring himself to pour any on her bruised and swollen wrists. Sarah had ointments for that, soothing ones that would not add to the pain. The rope burns were bad and would last for a time but wouldn't likely leave scars. The marks made by Chapman's knife would probably be gone by morning.

When she seemed calm enough, Tabor returned to the cabin and got her petticoats. With Lilah clothed in them and in his shirt, he lifted her onto his horse, then climbed up behind her, balancing her on the saddle in front of him.

"I'm taking you home," he whispered softly. "No one will hurt you again, Lilah. Not even me. I promise you that."

Lilah heard his promises but was too weak to give more than a murmur in response. Her throat ached from all the suppressed screams. Her joints ached from the strain of being hung like a slaughtered animal before the butcher. Somewhere in the still-coherent part of her mind was a longing to speak out and tell Tabor he had never really hurt her at all. She closed her eyes and clung to him, so still he thought she was asleep.

With her head nestled against his chest he nuzzled her strawberry curls, whispering words of caring and sadness. "Lilah, my love," he said. "I wish I could take back this day, this week, every moment of your life when there's been hurt." His throat tightened with sorrow. "My sweet Lilah. This wouldn't have happened if I hadn't forced you to come here, if I hadn't put my pride above the only thing that matters. I love you, Lilah. I wish you could hear me. I love you."

As the moon overhead drifted in and out of the high clouds, Lilah drifted in and out of consciousness. Tabor's declaration of love chased Chapman's harsh words out of her head. Tabor loved her. Hadn't he said that? Or had his voice sounded from within her own murky thoughts? Tabor loved her. Or did she only hear what she wanted him to say?

She moaned softly. Her arms locked tighter around his bare back. She wasn't waking up, though he knew she must be sore and miserable. That she slept was a godsend, he knew. Her trembling had stopped. She would never be able to forgive him for putting her through this with Chapman. Better she not wake up until she was back at the Cooke ranch and could look into Sarah's kind face.

As for himself, he regretted the brashness that had driven him to force her to do his bidding. The whole scheme was unworthy of him and had brought her to bitter grief. He had hoped to win her love but could only expect her continued loathing. A man of conscience would have sent her home after Chapman's first attack. But he had not. He had imposed his stringent will and refused to show the mercy he might have given even to a frightened creature of the wild.

As soon as she was recovered enough to travel, he would make the arrangements for her return to Damon House. The Admiral, Rogue, was hers, and the debt, which now seemed such a trivial thing, was settled. She had paid it several times over with the loss of her happiness and the risk of losing her life. He would have to be content to savor the memories of holding her in his embrace. Hopefully the devastating experience with Chapman would not impair her ability to respond to her husband.

He hoped she found happiness with Barrett. The man seemed possessed of a gentle nature and kind spirit and would doubtless never cause Lilah the trouble she had known at his hand. By God, he had given her plenty of that.

Before reaching Sandy Flats, Tabor met Wyrick and Sarah in the buggy. They had pulled up and waited at the spot where Tabor had tied Lilah's horse. While Tabor lifted Lilah into the buggy beside Sarah, Wyrick used the blade of a small knife to work the stone from beneath the horse's shoe. In his mind Tabor damned Chapman again for sending him out on a false trail. If he hadn't followed the lame horse, he would have gotten to Lilah sooner.

Leading the footsore horse and riding close beside the buggy as it rattled down the road, he saw Lilah find a brave smile for Sarah. His heart split in two when Lilah's tears flowed unchecked and she buried her head against his aunt's comforting shoulder.

The blush of another dawn tinted the morning sky above the ranch house. All night Lilah had fought her demons, the one with Chapman's face, those six who stared down at a helpless child, and one other, who in the fighting had become a tall, lean man, the man she loved. But with the start of a new day she was racked with doubts. Tabor had saved her, had staked his life to save her. But did he love her? Was that one good part of what she remembered about last night true or had she simply invented the one thing she needed to save her sanity?

If only she could remember. Had he whispered the words that now lay like strewn petals in her mind? Had he kissed her face, her hair, and held her with more tenderness that he would have any other? Tabor was a fair man—or at least his sense of justice was as fair as her own. She knew that after what she had suffered from Chapman, he would release her from her debt. He would allow her to leave the Cooke ranch. What she wanted with all her heart was for him to ask her to stay. What she feared was that he would not.

Lilah sobbed. Sarah took her hand and assured her she had no more reason to be afraid. Lilah nodded and took the clean handkerchief Sarah offered. She dried her eyes and nose, then asked Sarah for a cup of tea so that she might have a few minutes alone with her thoughts.

"Tabor will want to see you as soon as you feel up to it," Sarah said softly.

Lilah's sobbing started again. "I can't. Not yet, Sarah," she pleaded. "Tell him I'll need a little while."

What if he let her walk away without a word to stop her? What if all she had seen in his face last night, all she had heard in his voice, had been pity because of her mistreatment by Chapman? What if he didn't love her? Oh! She cried all over again. How could he love her after what she had led him to believe? She was ensnared in the web of lies she had spun. He was convinced she was a woman who had enjoyed many men. He believed she had led a wicked, sinful life as Delilah and that she planned to keep her dark secret from a hapless husband.

He couldn't want such a woman. He wouldn't believe the truth about her now. And she couldn't bear to face him and know he would never return her love.

As Lilah dried her eyes again, Sarah left the room. Tabor stood outside the door, where he had kept a vigil through the night.

"It's good she slept, even if it was a fitful rest," Sarah whispered to him. "The memories aren't as strong now."

The worry on Tabor's face lined it beyond his years. Dark shadows hovered beneath his eyes, and even hours after coming on that scene in the deserted cabin, tension pulled at his muscles and nerves.

"Did you give her laudanum?"

Sarah shook her head. "She wouldn't take it. She asked for brandy and drank down enough to stop the shaking."

"Did he . . . ? Is she . . . ?" Words tangled on his tongue. He thought he had gotten there before Chapman raped her. But the way his pants had been wrenched open, the way he'd had her strung up, and the time he'd had while Tabor chased Lilah's riderless horse, he might have defiled her in other base ways.

"Rape her? No," Sarah assured him. "And her wrists are better this morning. I rubbed in some ointment and bandaged them. The marks from his knife are almost gone. There's a small nick on her cheek but it will heal in a few days." Her lips tightened momentarily. "The worst things she's got to get over are having that scum touch her and remembering the repulsive things he said to her."

"Can I see her? Talk to her?"

"Later," Sarah said, leading him away. "She needs

rest now and she's asked for tea this morning. I don't want to take too long getting back."

Tabor followed Sarah down the stairs and into the kitchen. Feeling as useless to her as he did to himself, he stood back and watched her pour boiling water in the teapot, then prepare a tray for Lilah.

"Does she know Chapman's dead?"

Sarah looked up, her face full of pity. "She remembers you shooting him. She remembers everything." She picked up the tray and started to leave the kitchen, but Tabor pinned her down with one more question.

"She doesn't want to see me, does she?"

19

Lilah's strength came back quickly following a long rest, Sarah's treatments, and two hearty meals. Except for a few sore joints and the bruises on her wrists, she really felt quite fit.

Sarah, satisfied that Lilah had eaten enough to build back her strength, stacked up the dishes and set the tray out of the way. During the long morning with Lilah she had concluded that the girl had more troubling her than Chapman's attack. And in the prudent way of one who had loved deeply, Sarah knew the hurt was one for which she could offer no balm.

"Should I send Tabor in to see you now?"

Lilah hesitated but then agreed. She had put off the meeting as long as she could. Sarah, carrying the lunch tray, descended the stairs and found Tabor in the parlor debating his future with a bottle of whiskey. He wouldn't cure his ills with whiskey, but as with Lilah, Sarah kept quiet, sensing there was little she could do to help. From the time she had met Lilah out on the trail, she had thought something peculiar was going on between them. They strutted around each other like a pair of game birds in a courtship ritual, a pair who hadn't yet realized what the outcome of all that useless fighting would be.

Sarah's supposition had been that Lilah and Tabor were in love and didn't know it. After Judd Chapman had shown his ugly head, she figured they had come to the same conclusion. Now she wondered again. She wished she could simply tie the two of them together like a broken boot lace, but knew that whatever was broken between them, they had to mend.

"Lilah says you can come up now."

Tabor's head snapped forward; he hadn't noticed Sarah at the threshold. "How is she?"

"She's fine. The girl's got spunk. I told you that. It would take more than a run-in with a polecat to get her down."

Tabor finished his whiskey, knowing that if Sarah had been counting she would say he'd had one glass too many. He thought it would take a few more to make him happy with what he'd decided to do. Lilah was here only because he had forced her to be here. From the day he'd seen her on the stairs at Damon House she had wanted nothing to do with him. She had tried everything in her power to keep away from him, and failed. Granted, he had known that all along, but in his bullheaded way had refused to yield to her wants and insisted on satisfying his own.

The least he could do now was let her go without any trouble. A man who let the woman he loved be hurt the way Lilah had been hurt didn't deserve to have her. She had a life without him, a good man waiting to become her husband. It was what she wanted, and he never should have stepped in and tried to change it. He would go to her now and tell her she was free to go home and that she never need fear anything from him.

Sarah left him, understanding he had things to sort out with himself. A few minutes later she heard him climbing the stairs. Sarah headed for the kitchen. The last loaf of bread in the house was almost gone and she had always found bread-making an activity good for calming the nerves. Whatever those two had to say to each other needed no interference from her.

"Lilah . . ." Tabor knocked lightly.

"Come in," she said, shutting the door of the empty wardrobe. Her trunk, which had been stored in a corner of the bedroom, sat open. All around it were her personal articles and clothing.

Her heart cried out when she saw him. She wanted to fly to his arms and tell him all the things she felt. But when he stopped and stood stiffly in the doorway, her confidence wavered. She gave a faltering smile and tried to cover her disappointment by busily dropping things in her trunk.

Torn, Tabor searched for a smile. "You must be feeling better to be getting about like that."

She glanced at him without stopping her work. "Sarah says the sooner I get back to normal, the sooner I'll get over what happened."

"Sarah's usually right." He stepped on into the room and closed the door behind him. "I'm sure you're anxious to get home." Sorrow settled like a dead-weight in his chest. She was still pale, and in spite of what Sarah said, he had his doubts she ought to be out of bed.

"I think I ought to." Forgetting she had a nightdress draped over her arm, Lilah stopped packing and stood staring at him a moment, then painfully went on. "My debt to you will have to be settled in another way."

He felt as if he'd been struck with a whip. "Forget about the debt. I never should have held you to it to begin with. You offered me fair payment. A gentleman would have taken that."

If a lady had offered it. She silently finished the statement for him. But when the offer came from a notorious woman, a man didn't feel obligated to do the chivalrous thing.

"I'll still pay you what the horse is worth."

"No," Tabor insisted. "The horse is yours, free and clear. You don't owe me anything." He hesitated a few seconds, then went ahead and mentioned what was bothering him. "There is one thing I'd like to know. Whether or not you tell me is up to you. I won't insist."

"Go on," she said.

"When Delilah spoke to me in that bar in Yuba City, she already knew who I was and had a reason for searching me out. I want to know what that reason was."

"I didn't . . ." She grabbed for a lie, but when his eyes locked with hers, they sent shivers through her and she couldn't go on.

"Tell me the truth, Lilah," Tabor pleaded. "I need to know. When you invited me to spend the evening with you, I took it for granted it was because you wanted a man in your bed. Evidently that was the farthest thing from your mind that night. Tell me why you wanted me alone that evening, and, I guess, why you took those other men to your rooms."

Lilah's pale cheeks flamed red. These were the answers she had hoped he wouldn't demand of her. She could easily make up a story that would satisfy him. But the burden of all the lies she had told pressed on her like the weight of the world. She wanted to tell Tabor the truth. Could she do it without revealing the treachery of his father?

"I've tried to explain," she said as steadily as she

could. "I mistook you for another man, one who had wronged me. I wanted to get even."

Tabor looked at her incredulously. "By having me—him—jailed on concocted charges."

Lilah sighed, seeing he wouldn't be satisfied until he learned more. "Being falsely jailed isn't nearly as serious as what prompted me to seek revenge."

Tabor swiftly crossed the room. "The other men you entertained, were you getting even with them too?"

"Some of them," she answered, closing the trunk lid and seating herself on the ribbed back of it. "Others were more or less decoys. I really do enjoy a game of poker."

"An honest one?" He quirked a brow at her, remembering her skill at cheating.

A slight smile appeared on her lips. "Those aren't nearly as much fun."

"I take it poker is all you played with those other men."

Now Lilah's entire face reddened. "Why, no," she said in haste, suddenly finding herself back on the same old track and dependent on a lie to save her. "Some of them were my lovers."

"I see." Tabor shuffled away a few feet, his back to Lilah. He had asked for the truth and hoped she would give it. But for some reason, she still didn't think she could trust him with it. That fact was one that told him what was in her heart. If Lilah cared about him, she would tell him the truth. Hiding his disappointment, Tabor turned to face her.

"I'm sure you understand," she went on.

Tabor nodded. "So the truth is, you play at being Delilah because it gives you a chance to pick and choose your lovers."

"No!" Appalled at the way it sounded when he said

it, Lilah answered too quickly. "I became Delilah only to get even with the men who wronged me."

"Couldn't the law do that for you?"

"No. There was never any proof of what they had done. I couldn't have proved their crime in a court. But they were guilty. I was there and I know."

Again he raised a dark brow. "I'm not the one to say there aren't times a person has to be judge and jury. Out here that may be the only law there is. I'm not sure I would have let Chapman live if he hadn't gone for his gun. No man has a right to do that to a woman."

"I'll never forget what you did for me," Lilah whispered as her conscience gnawed at her. This man had saved her life. Twice. Maybe he didn't love her but he had saved her from Chapman. In her heart she knew he would have done the same for Sarah or Millie Franklin or any other person who needed him. Knowing that only made deceiving him seem worse.

Tabor shook his head slowly. "What I can't understand about what you're telling me is why Clement Damon wouldn't have found a way to punish men who had wronged his daughter."

Lilah looked him straight in the eye. This time she had to abandon her path of lies. "He would have," she said. "But the men I wanted punished harmed my father, not me." Her voice quivered. "Because my father dared to work Chinese laborers and pay them fairly, those men drove a herd of horses through his mining camp. Many of his men were killed. Papa was trampled. I saw it happen."

Tabor couldn't speak for a few seconds. So that was it. That was what had happened that hurt her so much. "I'm sorry, Lilah. I didn't know. I didn't know you had seen what happened to your father." His heart wept for her. At last he understood. She must have

been a mere child then, and all the years since, she
had been haunted by what she had seen. He thought
of the pain building inside her all that time. Poor,
sweet Lilah.

"There were six of them," Lilah said. "And it was
planned. Maybe they didn't know my father would try
to outrun the horses to save me, but they were glad
about what happened to him. Afterward he was too ill
to do anything about it. He had to send Dinah and me
to Aunt Emily in London. He was afraid for us to stay
in California. You know how mining towns were. They
had their own law and it was mostly that whoever
survived was right. Papa never tried to get even. He
put all of himself into building the Damon enterprises
and believed a higher law would take care of those six
who almost killed him."

"And you decided to be that higher law."

"Yes," Lilah said. "I never forgot what those men
did and what they said or what they took away from
him. I swore they would pay for killing our friends and
for maiming Papa. I became Delilah to do it.

Tabor remembered the ruckus down the hall the
time he had taken the room next to Delilah's in Crescent City. He remembered the newspaper account of
what had happened there. "You were responsible for
Newell going to jail. He was one of them, wasn't he?"

"Newell was one of them," Lilah confirmed. "He
was behind the attack."

"Did you get them all?"

Lilah hesitated. "Most of them. There are two more,
brothers. I'll do one more tour as Delilah and the
Penns will wind up where they belong."

Tabor's brows flickered. He didn't think Lilah realized she had mentioned the name of the brothers. He
tucked the information away. "I guess I can understand your reasons. A woman couldn't very well call

out the men responsible. In your place I might have done the same thing."

"I'm glad you understand," she said softly.

"I understand your reasons. I understand why you needed another identity to carry out your plans. What I don't understand is why you got me confused with one of those six men."

Lilah choked back the lump in her throat. "One of the men was named Stanton. I'd hired a detective to investigate but I didn't give him time to verify that you were the right man. I *thought* I had the right person, I got in a hurry to be done with one more of the six. I'm sorry about the mistake," she said, hoping he wouldn't realize the full scope of it. "There must be many men in California named Stanton."

"Not so many," he said as a sense of dread filled him. Things were coming together in his head that he hadn't connected before. He had been in Yuba City that day by chance. Lilah's detective couldn't have known he would be there at that time. The Stanton Lilah expected to find there was another man. He was a worn-out prospector, an old drunk who lived up in the hills, a man who had abandoned what humanity had to offer, a man whose dying thought was the debt he owed Clement Damon. Tabor Randall Stanton. *His father.*

Torn with conflicting emotions, Tabor could only stare silently at the lovely but sad-faced woman before him. Once again he had discovered another dimension of Lilah Damon. He held one more piece of the puzzle. The picture was quite different from that of a flame-haired temptress in a Yuba City hotel room. That night and that woman seemed a lifetime away.

Lilah. Delilah. His mind sped through his numerous perceptions of her. Onstage she was half-devil, half-angel, striking fire in a man's loins and devotion in his heart. Across the table from her in a poker game he had decided Delilah was a stylish seductress who got a thrill out of beating a man at cards before she bedded him. When he'd realized she never intended sleeping with him, he had figured her for a man hater.

Later, at Damon House, she was someone else entirely, a rich young woman bored with her tame society life. It was that Lilah Damon he had thought needed a lesson about trifling in a world where she didn't belong. Only Lilah wasn't that shallow girl any more than she was the torchy Delilah. She was a little girl who had witnessed a terrible deed done to her father and as a woman had been unable to live with the injustice of what she had seen.

To right that wrong, Lilah had gambled, losing both her pristine reputation and her life of ease. He had to admire that deep courage even if he didn't like her taking such boundless chances. His mind leapt to the brave girl whose spirit never broke under Chapman's torture. She was made of strong stuff, as Sarah said. Now he understood why she was so adamant about keeping her actions secret from her father. With Clement's health as bad as Lilah reported, knowing she had confronted those dangerous men might cause him a heart attack. And yet Tabor understood that for her ever to lay that matter to rest, all six of those men had to pay for their crime against her father.

How could she even stand to look at him? One of those men had been his father, and all this time she hadn't told him.

"Tabor . . ." Worried because he had been silent so long, Lilah called his name softly. He knew. She could look at his face and tell that he knew. "I'm very sorry you had to find out about your father. Perhaps it will help a little if I tell you he wasn't the worst of them.

He wanted to help Papa and me that night. The others wouldn't let him."

The shock of what she was saying hit Tabor like an earthquake. His father, a good man who for a long-unexplained reason had turned his back on everyone and everything he loved. Now he knew that reason. He recalled the things Clement had said about his father and the things Sarah had said about both men. It all added up. His father had participated in running down innocent men because of someone's hatred for another color of skin. Afterward the guilt had torn him apart. Maybe Stan had thought he was unworthy of the ones he loved. Tabor guessed he would never know just what had happened to his father after that night.

He looked at Lilah with baleful eyes. "You knew when I came to Damon House that I was the wrong man. That's why you fainted when you saw me."

"No," Lilah confessed. "When I saw you in the hall with Papa, I still thought you were the right Stanton. Only after I talked to Papa did I learn you were actually . . ."

"His son."

"Yes." Lilah sighed softly. "I was quite upset at what I had done. I planned on finding a way to repay you for your losses—short of returning the Admiral. I was selfish about that. The stallion made Papa happy, and for that reason I wanted to keep him."

"I don't think there's anything selfish about you, Lilah."

"Oh, but there is. I was thinking only of me and my family. I tried to come up with a plan to make you go away. I wouldn't have told you the truth. I would have sent you money and an apology—as Delilah. When Papa offered to show you his stable that night, I panicked. I thought if I threw myself at you and then told you I would be penniless if Papa knew, that you would fly."

Within his misery Tabor found a wry smile. "You can't be foolish enough to think any man would fly if you threw yourself at him. You were so sweet and convincing, I thought I would find angel wings on your back."

"When did you look there?" Lilah queried without thinking.

Tabor's smiled left. She had led him on in the conservatory simply to create a reason to send him away. But in his memory her caresses were more convincing than the slap she had given him.

"One thing still puzzles me," he said. "After you sent me away that night, why did you invite me back the next day?"

Lilah took a long, deep breath. "That picnic was Dinah's idea. She got it in her head to play Cupid. I've no idea why. I knew nothing about that invitation until you arrived at the house."

"So you used the occasion to reaffirm your wishes to have me leave."

"I wanted to prevent you seeing the stallion, but of course Papa thwarted my success at that."

"And then you couldn't get rid of me."

"No," Lilah said, wanting to add that she was glad to have failed. "After that I couldn't see that I had any choice but to do as you asked if I was to prevent Papa from finding out what I had been doing."

"You must hate me for doing that to you."

"No—" Lilah started, but he interrupted.

"After what my father had done to your family, I'm surprised you didn't just shoot me." He shook his head. "I don't know any way to tell you how sorry I am, Lilah. I could hate myself for making it worse for you."

"No," Lilah said. "I don't hate you. I don't blame you for what your father did. From what I've heard you and Sarah say, you suffered as much from him as I did."

But Tabor's mind was no longer on his father or the rights and wrongs of his life. He was thinking of Lilah and how the time they had made love, it had seemed as if they were one. It rankled him to know she had given him her body to protect her secrets. It rankled him more to know he had demanded that price from her. He had taken her virginity and he could see that she still wasn't ready to admit he was the first man to make love to her. He could understand that. She had pride. She preferred he not know he had taken such a precious thing. The least he could do was allow her to keep that secret safe.

"How soon will you be ready to leave the ranch?" he asked abruptly.

"Tomorrow," Lilah answered quietly. "If there's a stage I can catch." Her heart sank to her stomach. He was anxious for her to go. He regretted what he had done, but then, he hadn't asked to be involved. And after she had stolen his horse and had him put in jail, he had every reason to want to settle the score. He wanted her out of his sight. How could he look at her now without feeling worse about his father?

She understood his dilemma. She reminded him of things he preferred to forget. He might be able to reconcile himself to the fact that she had sought revenge against her father's attackers, but in his eyes she was still a loose woman who had taken advantage of being Delilah to sample fruits forbidden to Lilah Damon. Sally Ann loved him, and Lilah didn't doubt that in time Tabor would settle down and marry the girl.

Tabor was right to want her to leave as soon as

possible. The sooner they were out of each other's sight, the sooner they could forget all the dreadful things that had transpired between them. And, she added sadly, the sooner her heart could start to mend.

"There's a morning stage," he told her. "I'll send one of the boys in with you."

"Oh?" She barely heard what he was saying.

Tabor nodded. "One of the boys will ride along as bodyguard. I want to be sure you get back to Damon House safe. I owe you and your father that and more."

"Tabor—" Lilah made one last try to say what was in her heart.

He cut her off. "There's just one more thing I want to ask of you, Lilah."

"Yes?" she asked hopefully.

Tabor went on. "If I had known any of these things, I never would have asked of you what I did. I can't change any of that now. I can't bring back what my father took from Clement. I can't erase all the suffering he caused you. What I can do is even up things with the Penn brothers you mentioned. It won't undo what was done, but maybe it will put to rest all that hurt you've lived with because of what happened to your father."

Lilah stared in amazement. "I can't let you do that. You have no quarrel with the Penn brothers."

"You're wrong. You said the others kept my father from helping when he saw Clement hurt. Maybe if he could have done one decent act then, he wouldn't have stopped being a man. Maybe he could have been the one to see justice brought to those other five men." And maybe I would have had a father and my mother a husband, he said to himself.

Lilah started to reach for his hand, but then drew back. "Even if that's true, I can't let you take on my fight. I'll find a way to get the Penn brothers."

"I don't think you understand me, Lilah." Tabor's voice went harsh. "I'll keep your secret about being Delilah. I'll keep everything you've told me today a secret. But only if you agree to my stipulation."

"Which is?" she asked warily.

"Which is that you never again become Delilah." Tabor's grim face belied the tenderness in his heart. He might never hold Lilah again. He might never get used to the idea that she would wed another man. But neither would he allow her to put herself in danger again. Knowing she was both safe and happy would make it a little easier to live without her.

"That's preposterous," Lilah said after a moment of silent astonishment. "I have to—"

"No!" Tabor insisted. "You don't ever have to be Delilah again. The Penn brothers belong to me. I promise you they will get what's coming to them. You promise me you will never again assume the identity of Delilah. Be Clement's daughter. Be Barrett's wife. Be happy. But don't ever be Delilah."

"But why do you insist . . . ?"

He couldn't tell her the reasons. He couldn't tell her he couldn't bear the thought of other men ogling her, that he couldn't stand the thought of other men sitting in her bedroom even if it was only for a card game. He couldn't tell her the Penn brothers hadn't grown soft and fat like Hoke Newell. He had heard of Jasper and Thurlow Penn. They were still a mean pair and not worth the risk of her lovely neck.

"Just consider it a whim," he growled. "I do insist. You listen to me carefully, Lilah. If Delilah ever takes to the stage again, I will personally ride to San Francisco and reveal her identity to Clement Damon. I'll take out a full-page ad in the *Chronicle* and announce it to the world. And that after I've dragged you off the stage by the hair. Understand?"

"Yes." Her voice sounded shrill. What had brought on the tirade? Why should he care if she become Delilah? She could think of only one reason, and that was that he associated Delilah with his father's downfall. His memories of the elder Stanton were difficult enough without having learned what she had revealed today. If it bothered him that much, she was willing to comply. She would do anything in her power to make him happier. If only she could tell him so. "You'll send me word when you've settled up with the Penn brothers," she said.

Tabor agreed that he would, and asked her to tell him all that she knew about them. She revealed what the detective had told her and said that she would have the man forward a copy of his report. When she finished, Tabor rose to leave.

"I'll be out on the range tomorrow," he said. "Sarah will see that you get to the stage on time. Give your father my regards. Tell him I'm sorry about everything."

"Everything?"

Tabor shook his head in the affirmative. "Yes, and I think now we've said enough about all of it, Lilah. As soon as the Penn brothers are taken care of, I'm going to start forgetting what happened with you and me and how wrong things went. You do the same."

Lilah could only nod, knowing that if she spoke, she would burst into tears.

20

Lilah dressed in a gown of shimmering gold silk and wore an outrageous hat Papa claimed had more pheasant feathers than one of the birds who gave them up. As the weeks following her return from the Cooke ranch dragged by, Lilah filled her days with shopping, social calls, parties, any activity which could serve to keep her mind occupied. Today's outing was to be a carriage ride to Woodward Gardens to witness the flight of a steerable balloon. Normally she would be excited about the advent of a new means of travel, but as she reluctantly admitted, since her return home nothing held her enthusiasm for long.

Not an hour passed that her mind didn't drift back to the Cooke ranch and Sarah's unique parlor or warm, cozy kitchen, or, as was more likely the case, to the oversize bed in Tabor's room. Did Tabor ever think about her fondly? Or was he simple glad to have her out of his hair? It bothered her greatly to think those stormy gray eyes now locked rapturously with Sally Ann's. She supposed Sally Ann was the kind of girl he could love. Certainly he had never made any pretense about what he wanted from her. And though he had made love to her with tenderness and adoration and had said the things lovers say, he had never uttered the words which would have held her heart in tow forever.

Sadly Lilah slid a hatpin into her bonnet so that it would rest securely on her head. Hearing the sound of someone on the walk out front, she hurried to her window and looked out to see one of the servants strolling in with the mail. Lilah started to rush downstairs but held herself in check. What was the use? With daily regularity she had met the post, hoping for a letter from Tabor. Always she was disappointed.

Letters arrived from Dinah and from Aunt Emily and even from Sarah. Sarah discreetly avoided mentioning her nephew, as he no doubt had asked her to do. She had slipped in a mention of Sally Ann Caufield's engagement, which was clue enough to Lilah. In answering Sarah's notes, Lilah used equal discretion, mentioning neither Tabor nor Sally Ann.

Surely, though, Sarah had told him that Lilah was completely recovered, that Ching's treatment with a poultice of herbs had healed her wrists without leaving even a trace of a scar. And Sarah must have reported some of her activities, and certainly she had found a way to mention that Lilah had begun plans for a late-summer wedding to Barrett.

What a laugh Tabor must have had about that, knowing Barrett had been cuckolded before he even became a bridegroom. How despicable he must think her, believing she had indiscriminately bedded so many men.

Oh, what a tangled web we weave, when first we practice to deceive. The old adage ran through her mind, a nagging reminder of the predicament she had put herself in. Nothing in her explanation of why she had become Delilah accounted for the promiscuity he believed her guilty of. And though it wasn't true, Tabor thought otherwise.

Lilah sighed, toying with the thought of canceling the afternoon's engagement. She didn't really feel like going. Perhaps she should check the mail after all. Tabor had promised to let her know about the Penn brothers and had indicated he would see to the matter soon. She regretted agreeing to that. She should never have let him bully her into allowing him to bring them to justice. Only he hadn't given her a choice. Oh, she supposed he had needed to do the deed. It was a kind of penance for him, something he needed to do so that he might clear his mind and wash his hands of the entire Damon family.

Listlessly Lilah descended the stairs, still debating whether or not she would go to the park. She might as well. With Dinah gone, the house was too quiet, and quiet led to too much introspective thought. Papa had informed her he would be busy all day. Trying to shake off a cloud of gloom, she stepped lightly into the hall. She was surprised when her father wheeled into sight and spoke to her.

"Lilah, there's something we must discuss."

"Is it urgent, Papa? I was just going out."

"Call it off," he said brusquely. "And come with me."

Clement was so rarely disagreeable that it stunned Lilah to hear him speak gruffly. She put aside her parasol and followed her father into the library. Ching quietly closed the door behind them and took up his post in front of it.

"What is it, Papa? What's upset you?" Lilah frowned, seeing by the direction of his eyes that the source of irritation was a letter open on his desk. A nervous chill ran down her back. Was her secret out? Had Tabor changed his mind and told Papa about her?

Clement handed her the letter, then cleared his throat loudly. "You had better read this and you had better do it sitting down."

Bewildered, Lilah took the letter and took a seat. Most of her anxiety fled when she saw that it was from Dinah rather than Tabor. She silently read the curly writing while her father nervously drummed his long fingers on the arms of his chair.

My dear Papa,

Barrett would have written to you first, or even Aunt Emily, but I prevailed upon them to leave the matter to me. We had a lovely voyage over and I have written to you about that previously. But there is something I failed to tell in my earlier letters. It is that on that long voyage Barrett and I fell in love. Perhaps it is closer to the truth to say Barrett fell in love with me, for I had loved him a long, long time before we set sail for England.

I am sure you are thinking now that I am immature and that what I speak of is a mere infatuation and on Barrett's part a loyalty I have mistaken for love. But, Papa, that is not the way it is between Barrett and myself. We are truly in love, deeply in love, and have decided to spend all our lives together. Shortly after we arrived here, Barrett and I were secretly wed. We did plan to keep this a secret from everyone until our return to San Francisco, but as Aunt Emily will tell you, she became alarmed that Barrett and I spent so much time with each other.

I am sorry to have upset Aunt Emily; however, it became necessary that she know of the marriage. The news gave her a considerable shock. She is growing accustomed to my new status, though, and has asked Barrett and me to reside at her house.

Of course, by now you are alarmed for Lilah. You are thinking that she has been jilted, that her sister has stolen her fiancé. Please keep in mind, Papa, that Barrett and Lilah were never formally engaged. And since our wedding took place so far from home, I am sure the scandal will be lessened. Papa, you must understand that I would not have hurt Lilah. I love her, Papa, as I do you.

Lilah herself can tell you she does not truly love Barrett. Oh, she would have wed him, I have no doubt. But she would have wed him because he would have made you a good son-in-law and because he could head the Damon enterprises. That is why I was keen to accompany Aunt Emily to London. I knew that once Barrett and I were alone, he would realize he loved me too.

Please do not despair of this news, Papa. Barrett and I are very happy. Lilah will be happier too, for now she is free to give her heart to a man she loves.

I trust you will tell Lilah this news and that you will do it gently. I anxiously await hearing from you, Papa. Perhaps in my next letter I can send word that your first grandchild is on the way.

> *I love you with all my heart,*
> *Dinah*

Two weeks after receiving Dinah's letter, Clement fretted about his daughters. He supposed Dinah would be all right, though he didn't totally approved of her marriage. But the promised letters from Barrett and Emily had followed that startling one from Dinah. Her aunt and her new husband had written assurances that the couple was indeed happy.

He even decided against calling the pair home immediately. They were, after all, under Emily's watchful eye and he had sent Barrett to London to handle a most important business deal. If it worked out as he planned, he would permanently maintain a branch of his business in England. They would get a sharp piece of his mind when they did come home, though. Both of them deserved it.

Lilah was the real source of worry. Although she insisted Dinah was correct about her feelings for Barrett, she had done nothing but mope since the word had come. With any other girl he might have thought embarrassment over being jilted was the problem. But that didn't seem to be the cause of Lilah's distress. She herself had written the announcement for the *Chronicle* and had openly told her friends of the elopement. He wondered if her despondency might instead be attributed to the recent letter she had received from young Stanton.

Lilah hadn't talked much about her trip to the Cooke ranch and he had assumed the traumatic thing that had happened had dashed any chance of Tabor and Lilah getting together. He needed to get a letter off to that young man. Since Chapman had been so damned anxious to get hold of Stan's claim, he'd sent a team of men down to study the land. They had turned up the reason for Chapman's maniacal efforts. That land was devoid of gold, but it was rich enough in borax to make a man enormously wealthy. The very least he could do for Tabor after he had saved Lilah's life was to give him the land. What irony there. Poor Stan had been holding a fortune and didn't know it.

Lilah walked into the library as Clement was thinking about her. "Papa, I'm meeting Loo in town. We may do some shopping."

Lilah's voice lacked the merry ring he enjoyed hearing in it. Clement caught a glimpse of her eyes and saw that they were shadowed underneath. His concern about her well-being increased. She looked as if she had lost weight. The poor girl was worrying herself sick about something. Maybe this shopping trip would boost her spirits. But whether it did or not, tonight he would demand to know what was troubling her.

"Have a good time," he called after her. "Get whatever you want and tell Loo I miss her here at Damon House." He wished Loo hadn't decided on moving into a place on her own, though he understood her reason for seeking a life of her own. He did hope the afternoon with her would be good for Lilah.

Lilah and Loo scurried along the sidewalks, going from one shop to another. Few of them held anything that caught Lilah's eye, but Loo had purchased a new reticule at the last establishment. Already annoyed at the shopkeepers for their cool treatment of Loo, Lilah was ready to call for the carriage and leave for home. Of course none of the shopkeepers would actually refuse to serve Loo, even though she was half-Chinese, not when she was accompanied by Clement Damon's daughter.

"I think I've seen enough today, Loo," Lilah said wearily. She looked down the street for the carriage. In the last two weeks she must have bought a dozen new gowns and bonnets, but no amount of finery, she had discovered, could fill the emptiness in her heart. This outing today had been a mistake. Maybe what she needed was a trip back east, or to London for a visit with Dinah and Barrett. But no, it was too soon for that. Not enough time had passed that the three of them wouldn't feel uneasy together. Sighing so loudly that Loo gave her a worried look, she signaled for the driver to come and pick them up.

"Lilah, this has got to end." Loo had kept quiet

for weeks, but now, seeing someone she loved so unhappy prompted her to speak up.

"What has to end, Loo?" Only half-hearing what Loo said, Lilah watched the carriage wheels spin to a stop in front of her. Out of automatic politeness she turned to look at her friend.

"Your pining away over that cowboy—"

"Shhhh," Lilah silenced Loo, her eyes growing big and bright. "That's Sally Ann Caufield going in that shop."

Loo looked around quickly. "The girl from Sandy Flats—the one the cowboy is supposed to marry?"

"The same one." Lilah turned her back on driver and carriage. She supposed the time had come to let bygones be bygones. Sally Ann had won her man, and Lilah ought to have the courage to acknowledge it. "Come on," she said to Loo, hoping she had masked the hurt in her voice. "I want to congratulate Sally Ann."

Though her voice was calm, Loo saw the look of pain in Lilah's eyes. She caught her friend gently by the arm and held her back. "Do you think you should? I don't imagine the girl likes you even a little."

"Nonsense," Lilah said, easing her arm free. "She can't still be mad at me. She's got what she wants."

Reluctantly Loo followed Lilah into the shop. Sally Ann was looking over a display of negligees when Lilah approached her.

"Hello, Sally Ann." Her voice was artificially light. "Remember me?"

The brown-haired girl whirled around and, surprisingly, wore a big smile. "Why, Lilah Damon. I don't suppose I'll ever forget you."

"I suppose not," Lilah said, deciding she had made a mistake by speaking to Sally Ann. Seeing so much happiness in her face only made Lilah's sorrow seem greater. "I saw you come in and wanted to congratulate you on your engagement."

"That's nice of you." Sally Ann sounded genuinely pleased. "To think it might never have happened if we hadn't had that fight. Oh!" she said. "I'm forgetting myself. I heard what happened when that horrible man kidnapped you. I'm glad he didn't hurt you."

"Thank you, Sally Ann. And I really do hope you and Tabor will be happy."

"Tabor?" Sally Ann gasped. "For goodness' sake! I'm not marrying him. I'm marrying Horace Glenn!"

"But I thought . . ." Lilah trailed off, completely befuddled.

Sally Ann laughed. "I can't imagine why. Tabor Stanton has been just like an irritable old bear ever since you left the ranch, Oh, I admit I chased him around at one time, but I outgrew that girlish crush when I met Horace. I just thought everybody knew about me and Horace, but of course you were gone," she chattered on.

"Knew what?" Lilah asked.

"When I came in the barn that night with my dress and hair all ruined, Horace wrapped a blanket around me and told me how beautiful I looked even dripping wet. It was the sweetest thing anyone ever said to me. I looked up into those big brown eyes and fell head over heels in love. We were engaged a week later. That's what I meant when I said it never would have happened if we hadn't had that fight."

"But you said you and Tabor . . ."

"Made love?" Sally Ann whispered. "I just made that up to make you mad. Tabor never even kissed me, and Lord knows I gave him plenty of opportunities." Her eyes widened as she looked into Lilah's disbelieving face. "Why, for goodness' sake! You don't even know, do you?"

"I don't even know what?"

"Tabor's in love with you. That's what's made him such an old bear. He went off on a trip and when he came back he was so irritable Sarah told him he could stay in the bunkhouse. When that didn't help his disposition, she asked why he didn't go after you."

"What did he say?" Loo asked, unable to stand the suspense.

"He told Sarah to mind her own business, then felt bad about that and apologized and asked if she thought he ever would have let you go if there had been a chance you could love him. Well, it's just too bad you don't," Sally Ann babbled on. "He told Sarah you were marrying another man. I wish you happiness too."

A sudden grin spread over Lilah's face. She had heard all she wanted to hear. "It's been good to see you, Sally Ann." With a wave good-by, Lilah spun on her heel and walked away so fast Sally Ann was left with her mouth gaping open. Loo said a quick good-bye too and rushed off after Lilah.

As Lilah climbed into the carriage without waiting for the driver's assistance, Loo saw a dangerous Delilah sparkle in her friend's eyes.

"Lilah, what are you thinking? What are you going to do? Lilah, answer me."

Lilah sat back in the carriage and smiled, letting Loo's questions roll off her like rain on an oilskin southwester.

At dinner she wore the same smile and looked so distracted that Clement was convinced the worst had happened and she had gone off her head. Finally he could stand it no more.

"Lilah, child, you have to tell me what's troubling you. I've tried to keep quiet because you didn't seem to want to talk about it. But now I'm just too worried.

You've been depressed for weeks, and suddenly tonight even the most mundane thing is amusing."

Poor Papa, she thought. He's been terribly worried about me and I've been so busy basking in my misery I couldn't see it. She smiled at him gently. "I was depressed, Papa, but now—"

"Lilah, did something happen with Chapman that you haven't told anyone about. Did he . . . ?"

Lilah had the good grace to blush, realizing the error of her father's thoughts.

"Good heavens! No! Nothing happened I haven't told you about. At least not with Chapman," she added.

Clement's cheeks puffed out and his face turned red. Ching had to catch him to prevent his pitching out of his chair. "Stanton! And to think I trusted that scoundrel! I'll send the sheriff . . ."

Even Clement's alarm failed to take the smile from Lilah's face. "Papa, Papa," she said softly. "You misunderstand. Tabor never did anything but make me fall in love with him and then let me believe he didn't love me back."

Clement refused to be pacified. "Ching!" he shouted. "Get ready to leave for the Cooke ranch! Immediately!"

"No, Papa," Lilah said calmly. "Ching can help me later, but in another way. Right now I have some things to tell you that I'm sure you'll find shocking. I hope that once I've told you my story, my motives will be evident."

Before she started, Lilah insisted on moving to the library, where she knew her father would be most comfortable. Telling her story would take hours. But a change had come over Lilah since afternoon. She knew the time had come to untangle her web of lies. It had suddenly become clear to her that she wasn't protecting her father by keeping her secrets from him. He could see the strain of them in her face, and not knowing the cause of her anxiety was as hard on him as would be knowing the truth.

She started her tale by recalling her feelings when she had seen him trampled by the horses. Later she told him how she had practiced the card tricks old Sulley had taught as a way of remembering the happy times in the Damon camp. She told him how she had carried her burden of hatred for the six men who killed their friends and maimed him, how the desire for revenge had guided her every move since childhood.

Astonishingly, once Clement got past the shock, he was more amazed than disgusted to learn his daughter was the infamous Delilah. Lilah noted with some small satisfaction that even Ching's expressionless face yielded up a look of surprise at that revelation. Clement took much less well learning his daughter had carried out a program of revenge on his enemies. Lilah suffered through a lengthy and wordy reproach.

"Lilah, I refuse to believe you took such risks or allowed Dinah to."

"Papa, I was quite careful to keep Dinah away from those men. I assure you she never saw any of them or even knew their names." The calm she felt in her heart and soul surprised her. How good it was to have the truth flow from her lips instead of swallowing the bitter bile of her lies.

His eyes scanned her face. "I had no idea *you* remembered the names spoken that night."

"I could never forget them, Papa. As soon as I returned to California I engaged a detective to investigate each of them for me. I was very careful there too. I planned everything to the last detail."

"Except where Tabor was concerned."

She sighed heavily. "He was my only mistake."

Clement was thoughtful a moment before he spoke

again. "So I wasn't imagining that I saw sparks flying between the two of you?"

"No, Papa. Sparks did fly." And flames enough to leap and burn and consume her.

She told him everything, leaving out only the more intimate details of her time with Tabor. A woman, after all, was entitled to a few secrets.

Clement folded his hands in his lap and stared at his daughter a long time. He had admitted to Lilah that he had read about the misfortunes of his old enemies and been heartened by them. That didn't mean, as he explained to her, that he approved of what she had done. He might admire her daring and courage. But he didn't approve.

"I'm not sorry, Papa," she told him. "Not about bringing those men to justice. They deserved it. I am sorry about all the trouble and grief I caused you. But it's all over now. Tabor has dealt with the Penn brothers. He sent me notice of their arrest. Now all six have come to justice."

"And one innocent man."

"Tabor?" Lilah queried. "I wouldn't exactly brand him innocent."

"You said you loved him. What are you going to do about it? I hope no daughter of mine is going to give up the man she loves without a fight. Your mother didn't and neither did your sister." Clement astonished her. She had expected resistance. Tabor wasn't, after all, in the least like Barrett.

Happily and boldly she met his eyes. "I have a plan, Papa. With your permission, I'd like to carry it out."

"My permission!" Clement guffawed. "When have you needed my permission for anything?"

The handbill arrived at the Cooke ranch by messenger. Tabor read it and turned white with rage. She had been in his thoughts too much that day. That happened when he was out riding fences or herding cattle. Hard as he had tried, he hadn't been able to put her out of his mind. Nor could he forget the despicable way he had treated her. Undoubtedly the ordeal had been less painful for her than he thought or she would not have dared to do this.

Tabor read the handbill a second time, still disbelieving what it said.

Delilah, Flame of the West, in a special performance at the Paradise Saloon in Sandy Flats.

What the hell was the meaning of it? He had warned her never to become Delilah again. He'd kept his part of that final bargain. The Penn brothers were behind bars for a long time. Lilah Damon had no reason to assume the guise of Delilah. Except one. She really did enjoy playing the seductress.

Tabor tore up the handbill and decided it was no concern of his if she wanted to become Joan of Arc. But as the day lengthened and the time of her performance drew near, his mood grew darker. By dusk his temper had reached a danger point and all the cowhands were steering clear of him.

His eyes blazed and he dented the bottom of the coffeepot slamming it back on the stove after finding it empty and cold. Where the hell was Sarah? She had left the ranch before noon without a word about where she was going. Did she already know about this? Was that why she had cleared out? Hell! She was probably in town to see the performance. He wouldn't put it past her.

Only there wasn't going to be a performance. By God! He was a man of his word. And he had warned her. A deal was a deal, and it was time Delilah and/or Lilah Damon learned that.

What had happened to that soft soled fiancé of

hers? A scowl that would scatter cattle set on his face. Couldn't Fenton do anything about controlling his intended? Temper worsening, Tabor stormed around the house like the irritable bear Sally Ann had labeled him. An hour later, washed and with his clothes changed, he rode into town still wearing the same black look. He *had* warned her.

The Paradise Saloon had gone all-out for Delilah. A huge banner proclaiming the dubious event hung above the front doors. The streets were filled with more horse and buggies than he recalled ever seeing in Sandy Flats. Inside the Paradise, red bunting draped the paneled walls. Baskets of fragrant flowers lined the makeshift stage. The floor had been swept and sprinkled with fresh sawdust. The room was packed with men sitting shoulder to shoulder. The lamps burned low and nothing above a whisper sounded in Sandy Flats' rowdiest saloon.

Tabor burst through the swinging doors, giving both halves a shove that shook them on their hinges. Hardly a head turned to see the cause of the disturbance. Those that did gave him angry scowls. Tabor could see and hear why. Delilah, all dolled up in pink and silver, strolled the stage and had her audience hypnotized. Her hot, sweet song washed like warm wine over everyone within hearing range. The poignancy in her voice affected him no less than any other man in the room.

Hell! He was a lost man, he said to himself, stopping cold in his tracks at the sight of her. Tabor sighed, and instead of tearing through the crowd and dragging Delilah offstage as he had fully intended to do, he found a stool near the back and sat down to listen and watch.

Her hair glowed a fiery red again, her voice sounded

more provocative than he remembered, particularly in the strains of her last number.

> *She'll tempt you, she'll tease you, she'll raise all your hopes.*
> *Then leave you standing with your arms full of smoke.*
> *So listen to me, stranger, whatever you name,*
> *You can get burned in Delilah's flames.*

Delilah's flames. Tabor felt them scorching his skin. Delilah had him in her spell again. He was weak as a newborn colt and just as powerless to carry out his threat. The wanting built up inside so fast and hard he could scarcely draw a breath. Why the devil did he have to love her? Beads of sweat broke out on his brow as he saw her extract the small silver mirror from her pocket.

> *If you choose to love her, you've no right to complain,*
> *You've had your warning, stranger, of Delilah's flames.*

The turmoil of doubt raged within him. He wasn't sure what he would do if Delilah flashed that mirror on any man other than him. Fortunately he didn't have to find out. The bright beam of light shone the invitation on his face.

Half an hour later Tabor found himself knocking at the door of Delilah's hotel room. In the short wait, his temper had turned on him again. He sauntered in feeling like he had a mouthful of briars. "I suppose you're going to tell me you like being Delilah too much to give it up," he said, tossing his dusty hat to the seat of a chair and glancing around. "Where are the two tin cowboys? And do you mind leaving off smashing the bottle on my head this time?"

"Good evening to you too, Tabor. It's been a long time." Her words poured out like warm honey. "I don't use Todd and Seth anymore. I'm taking a more direct approach to my work now." She smiled invitingly at him. She stretched out a finger and rested it on his chin for a second, then trailed it sensuously down his chest, stopping and tapping her nail on his belt buckle. "You are absolutely right. I do enjoy being Delilah. Oh," she said, raking her finger up his abdomen and chest again and speaking as if an insignificant thought had occurred to her. "I know you warned me not to be Delilah again, but I found," she went on deliberately, slowly, hooking her finger beneath his chin, "I missed the physical part of it too much." She eyed him coyly. "You know what I mean."

"I damned sure don't!" he growled, twisting his head away. The touch of that one finger had started a crazy hunger inside him. "You were a virgin when we made love out on the trail." His dark brows rose swiftly. "Of course I don't know what you've been up to since."

Lilah could have laughed out in joy. So he had known all along she was a virgin. Why hadn't he said so? Well, her curiosity would have to wait to be satisfied. First things first.

"Call me Delilah," she said, half-lowering her lids. "I haven't been up to anything yet. But I do have a few things in mind for tonight."

Her bordello moves tormented him. "Like what?" he asked warily.

"Like another poker game." She brushed by him, rustling the skirts of her pale pink gown.

Tabor turned and followed her with his eyes, still scowling. The poker table was there, the cards laid out, but he had failed to notice anything in the room but her. "I see," he said curtly. "Just what's your game this time, Delilah? Are you after the ranch now?"

"Uh-uh," she replied as she unpinned a cascade of black feathers from her hair. "Papa has a ranch."

"So what, then?" He shrugged, hoping she couldn't tell how every little gesture, every little move drove him closer to the edge. "You still have the stallion."

Lilah just smiled and poured two glasses of brandy. She sat at the table sipping from one, then motioned for him to join her. "I'm going to give you a chance to win the Admiral back. Sit down," she said. "And deal."

He didn't trust her, but he obliged her and sat down across the table and drank the brandy. It burned a streak down his throat but was no hotter than the fire already burning in his blood. Damn the horse! This wasn't about a horse. This was about something he wanted a hell of a lot more.

"Let's up the stakes," he said as he dealt cards.

"To what?"

"To you." God! She was having an effect on him. Just being in the same room with her was driving him mad. He burned like he had a fever and his head felt like a spinning wooden top ready to drop over on its side. Lilah poured him another drink and he swallowed it quickly.

"I'm agreeable," she said coolly. "But this time there will be a matter of a wedding ring."

Tabor's vision blurred so he could hardly see the cards in his hand. Damned little wench. She had put something in the brandy. But whatever it was made him feel so good that any stakes she wanted would be fine with him. He told her so. His mind went blank for a few moments. He had no idea what went on in the game. Her voice brought him back a little.

"Your cards, Tabor. What do you have?"

Tabor brought the cards close to his eyes so he could read the figures and faces. It took him a while to put them together but finally he had it. "Three kings, and you can't beat them." His words slurred and the cards dropped out of his hand.

She smiled wickedly. "Oh, but, Tabor, I can with the aces." Delilah fanned out her cards in front of his face so that he couldn't miss them. "And I've already made the arrangements with the preacher. He should be here shortly."

Tabor faded in and out the next few minutes, barely coming to when the Reverend arrived as scheduled and started the ceremony. Reverend Mead thought he had seen nervous bridegrooms before, even drunk ones, but he had never seen one as befuddled as Tabor Stanton. But then, he supposed marrying a woman like Delilah could make a man unsure of himself, maybe even a little loco.

Tabor shook his head, feeling like a man who had stepped outside of his body and watched his life take place before him. He saw Preacher Mead come in, and Sarah with him. He heard himself agreeing to what the preacher asked. He saw himself slipping a ring on Delilah's finger, then kissing her. And when the preacher was gone, and Sarah was gone, he made love to Delilah with a savoring thoroughness and sweet deliberation he both watched and participated in.

Delilah. Delilah. The delicious onslaught of sensation took him. His body was fire and ice, her hands lighting the flame, her lips cooling the burn. His hands slid with feathery strokes over her skin, from the warm hollow of her throat to the rose crests of her breast. Beneath his palms those tight peaks stiffened with desire and he took them in turn in his mouth, suckling gently, tasting her, drinking in her sweetness.

His fingers slithered down her belly until they probed
hotly between her thighs. But that was not enough and
Delilah squirmed beneath him, impatiently telling him
she had waited as long as she would. Her legs opened
to him, her words were of love and forever as he
positioned himself above her and dived into the fiery
quicksilver pool of Delilah's flames.

Tabor Stanton awoke twelve hours later and his
head cleared in a flash just as Ching had assured Lilah it
would. She held out her left hand and admired the
gold band she wore.

"Goddammit, Delilah! You cheated!" he snarled,
and bolted upright in the bed.

"I know," she answered sweetly, and edged closer
to him. "But we're married just the same."

"Dammit!" he growled, realizing the amazing dream
he'd had was real. "Which one of you did I marry,
that conniving bitch or that sweet little society witch?"

She made a purring sound and kissed him on the
face a dozen times before answering. "That's the best
part, darling. You married us both."

About the Author

Always a romantic, Andrea Parnell enjoys creating characters whose passions for life and for matters of the heart run deep. When she isn't at work on a novel, she can be found taking a quiet walk in the woods, attending her flower gardens, or simply enjoying the serenity of country life with her family. Andrea Parnell, a former home economist, lives near Athens, Georgia.